I0524864

The Light
of the Guild

By Molly McGinty

This is a work of fiction. Names, characters, places, and incidents either are the product of the author's imagination or a used fictitiously. Any resemblance to actual persons, living or dead, events, or locales is entirely coincidental.

Copyright 2024 by Molly McGinty

All rights reserved. No part of this book may be reproduced or used in any manner without written permission of the copyright owner except for the use of quotations in a book review.

First paperback edition April 2024

ISBN: 979-8-9893535-3-8

Cover art images from https://perchance.org/ai-character-generator, created using Canva.com

PROLOGUE

Four trade masters sat together at a circular table with three of them staring at the man who had called them together. His dark hair was mostly hidden by a blue scarf tied tightly around his head and his bright blue eyes looked in turn at his companions.

"Why have you gathered us together?" the other man seated at the table gruffly asked.

Edmund's gaze didn't flinch at the anger directed at him. He looked at the man that he had once called his brother, seated at the table and the two women that flanked him. "I have brought us together in the name of Athelstan and the Light of the Guilds. We must put aside all our personal feelings in the name of the Light."

"This sounds very serious," one of the women said. "If it is a matter of the Light and all the Patrons, why just the four of us? Why did you not invite any of the others?"

"I don't know where anyone else lives anymore," Edmund answered. "I know where Seb lives," he gestured to the man. "And I know where you live, Sidonia," he said to the beautiful woman whose deep blue traveling cloak was still wrapped around her shoulders. "And I know that you know where Kloma lives." He pointed to the other woman with a round, kind face that was framed with auburn hair. "But I don't know where anyone else is anymore."

"I'll ask again," Seb said, leaning forward, "why have you brought us together?"

Edmund glared at Seb for several long seconds. "Because I have seen something most extraordinary; a child with the Light."

The three Patrons gasped in surprise looking at each other in bewilderment before turning their gazes back to Edmund.

"But that's impossible," Sidonia said.

"Are you sure?" the other woman, Kloma asked.

Edmund nodded. "There is no mistaking the Light."

"Where is this child?" Seb asked.

"In the village of Erthenhorn. I was there with my company, just two months back, walking the streets of the village when I came across a mother with three children. The youngest child, well, an infant, because she couldn't have been much older than two or three months, glowed with the golden Light of the Guild."

"Who is this child? An Heir of Athelstan perhaps?" Kloma asked.

"Perhaps," Edmund said. "But clearly, she has some sort of destiny with the trade guilds. A child has never been born with the Light before. In the three hundred years we've been alive and working as trade guild Patrons, there has never been anyone but us who possessed the Light."

"Until now," Sidonia said, her voice full of wonder.

"What is the child's name?" Seb asked.

"Joia," Edmund answered. "Her name is Joia."

CHAPTER ONE

Joia

Joia flung open the second-story window of their home over the bakery. The sounds and smells of morning in the village filled the cottage. "It's a beautiful day," she said, taking in a deep breath.

"Come and get the men's breakfast ready," Joia's mother said from where she was flipping sizzling ham on the pan over the kitchen hearth.

Joia went to where her mother worked and scooped up a spoonful of porridge from the pot, dumping it carefully into a bowl. She filled a second bowl with the porridge and placed it on the tray. Her mother slid a slice of ham into each bowl of the porridge and covered the tray with a brown linen cloth.

"Ask your father if he needs any extra help today," Joia's mother, Liadan said.

"I will," Joia said, picking up the tray. She went down the narrow staircase from their home to the bakery below, counting the steps as she went, hitting the third step with a squeak. She had counted the steps every time she went up or down them since she was a small child. It was helpful for her to know the number when she was carrying a tray of food down and couldn't see her feet on the steps of the dark, narrow staircase. When she hit fifteen, she reached the bottom step and reached her hand out to find the door handle. Opening the door to the bakery brought with it a waft of hot, fragrant air. Joia loved the smell of the bakery. Her brother David was standing at the counter, helping a customer, who happened to be one of her friends, Beatrice.

"Morning Joia," Beatrice said.

"Good morning," Joia replied, setting the tray of food down on a table.

"Bringing breakfast for your brother?" Beatrice looked back to David and batted her eyes at him. Joia was amused that Beatrice was always trying to get David's attention. He was always polite, but as far as Joia knew, he had never reciprocated the admiration that Beatrice had for him.

"And Father," Joia answered.

"That's sweet of you. Will you be coming to the spinner's shop today?" Beatrice asked.

Joia nodded. She loved going to help at the spinner's shop. She enjoyed working the wool, but it was also the best place in the village for gossip and news. "I'll be there as soon as I've finished my morning chores."

"I'll see you then. Bye David," Beatrice said, giving David a flirty smile while paying for her bread.

David let out a loud sigh after the door closed, and then he laughed. "She won't give up."

"Well, you are a handsome available man," Joia said.

"And I am promised to another," David laughed and then turned his attention to the tray that Joia was still holding. "Mmm, do I smell ham?"

"You do," Joia said, taking the linen cloth off the tray and handing her brother one of the bowls. He dug into the food, biting off a large piece of ham. "Where's Father?" Joia asked.

"At the back oven," he said, swallowing and then going for a spoonful of the porridge.

As bakers, her father and brother started their day at the bakery long before the sun rose, usually grabbing a biscuit to eat as they headed down the stairs to start their day. It was one of Joia's jobs to bring their breakfast several hours later after the first of the breads was done baking.

David, and their father, Thomas, were master bakers and known all around as having the best breads in their village. David had apprenticed with his father for half of his life, starting when he was ten and had recently been named master baker by his trade guild. They ran the bakery together, her father specializing in delicate pastries while David made perfect loaves of bread. Joia felt she had to be one of the luckiest girls in the village to have her father's and brother's creations at her table every evening.

The back door opened, and Thomas came in. His face was red from being near the big oven that was behind the bakery.

"Morning, Joia," he said, taking the other bowl from off the tray.

"Good morning, Father," she said. "Is your day going well?"

He nodded and scooped up a spoonful of the porridge. "Well enough."

"Mother wanted me to ask if you need any help today?" she asked.

He shook his head, his mouth full of breakfast, and then he swallowed. "No. Not today, I think," he finally answered.

David scraped at the bowl for the last bite of porridge. "Next time, could you add a bit more?" he asked Joia. "And maybe some butter?" He put the bowl back onto the tray and Joia nodded.

He went to the worktable and removed a cloth that had been covering a lump of dough. He gently poked it with a finger before coating his hands in flour and punching the dough down.

Joia watched with interest. She had grown up watching her father and brother baking and knew how they had to feel the dough to determine if it was ready to be shaped into loaves of bread. She enjoyed watching people working their trades. Each trade was so different from the others, requiring their own skills and tools, but at the same time, each trade required focus, deft hands, and years of experience to work the craft well.

The store's door opened and Derry, the cobbler, walked in.

"Good morning, Derry," David said, coming around from the worktable. "Want your usual today?"

The man nodded and noticed Joia standing nearby. "Good morning, Miss Joia. How are you today?"

"I'm well, thank you," she answered.

"And how is your sister? And mother?" he quickly added.

Joia smiled at Derry. "Ebba is very well. They both are."

"I'm glad to hear it," he smiled. Derry was one of the few single men in the village and an interest to most of the single women in town. He was a trade master with his own shop, young, and good-looking. If Joia had to guess his age, she would put him in his early twenties, which was a perfect age for marrying someone like Joia's sister, who was nearly nineteen years old.

David brought over several items, a round loaf of unleavened bread and two smaller rounds of biscuits. Derry laid out a cloth and David placed the goods onto the cloth and then tied them up. Derry paid and nodded to David and Joia. He turned to Thomas.

"Sir, if I may, may we speak together for a moment?"

Thomas nodded, set his empty bowl down and the men stepped outside.

Joia smiled at David, who winked at her. "I hope this is good news for Ebba," Joia said.

"So do I," David nodded, "but what would you do if he was interested in you?"

Joia looked at him in surprise. "You don't think he is, do you?"

David laughed quietly. "No. I think he's smitten with our sister." He patted Joia on the shoulder, leaving big flour prints on her dress. "Well, I've got to get back to work."

"Watch it," Joia said, trying to dust off the flour from her shoulder.

David just laughed at her. "See you tonight."

Joia picked up the tray and went back upstairs. She wondered if she could think of an excuse to get Ebba down to the bakery before Derry left.

Ebba was sitting by the window, sewing in the light. Joia put the tray down on the table and rushed to kneel at her sister's side.

"Ebba, Ebba, guess who I just spoke with at the bakery," Joia grinned.

"Who?" Ebba laughed.

"Derry, the Cobbler. He came in and bought some bread, then he asked to speak to Father, privately," Joia said, the words spilling out.

Ebba's hazel eyes grew wide. "Really? Do you think he could be asking Father?"

"Maybe. You should go down there," Joia said.

Ebba blushed. "I can't. I don't have any reason to be downstairs."

"We can think of something, or you can be pretending to go out to run an errand for Mother," Joia pulled on her hand.

"But that's silly," Ebba said, reluctantly pulling her hand away.

Joia grasped it harder and pulled at her. "Come on. You can come with me to the spinner's shop." Joia went to grab a basket. "Carry this."

"We don't have any reason to go to the spinner's," Ebba said, but still putting her sewing away.

"Derry doesn't know that," Joia said. "Come on. It takes us right past his shop."

Ebba got up and ran her hands over her hair. "Do I look all right?"

"Beautiful," Joia said.

Ebba was a beauty. She was slightly taller than Joia and graced with lovely curves, long light brown hair, and bright hazel eyes. She also had a cheerful personality, which made her pretty face all the lovelier.

Liadan came into the room from downstairs, carrying the garden basket. It was filled with small, young carrots and a handful of flavorful herbs collected from their garden just behind the bakery. She stopped when she saw the two girls.

"What are you two doing?" she asked.

"We need to make a quick trip down to the spinners," Joia said.

"Why?" Liadan asked. "We don't need anything from there right now."

"Because we want to be downstairs when Derry and Father finish talking," Joia said.

Ebba blushed but nodded.

A quick smile flashed across Liadan's face and then was gone. "All right. You can go but come right back. And Joia, I expect you to wash these dishes when you return."

"I will Mother, I promise," Joia grinned and grabbed Ebba's hand. They hurried downstairs and Joia hoped that they hadn't missed Derry.

They came through the door with a crash, making David jump in surprise. They both looked around. "Did we miss him?" Joia whispered.

"Who?" David asked.

"Derry, of course," Joia said. "Has he left yet?"

David nodded. "Only just. He's probably still not far from the door. If you hurry, you can catch him."

Joia ran to the door but when she turned back to Ebba, she found her sister had not moved. "Come on, Ebba. We can catch him."

"No, this is ridiculous," she said.

"No, it's not," Joia said. "What do you think, David? Should we follow Derry?"

David smiled at them and nodded. "I think he would be very happy to see you, Ebba."

Joia opened the door of the bakery and looked up and down the street. "I see him. He's headed towards his shop. Let's go. It's on the way to the spinners."

"Go on, Ebba," David encouraged.

Ebba nodded once and went to the door. "Quick, before I lose my nerve."

Joia grinned, put her hand in the crook of her sister's elbow, and they started out together. They walked quickly until they saw Derry stop to talk to someone, and then they slowly approached, trying to walk casually past him.

He turned and smiled when he saw them approach. "Miss Ebba," he bowed kindly. "Hello again, Joia."

"Good morning," Ebba said. "We were just on our way to the spinners."

"May I walk with you part of the way?" he asked.

They nodded and he said goodbye to the man he had been speaking with. They walked slowly and for the first few steps, it was silence.

Joia decided she needed to get them talking. "It's a beautiful day, isn't it?"

They agreed it was.

"Has business been well for you?" she asked Derry.

"It has," he answered. "This time of year, business is a bit slower. Not everyone's too concerned about shoes during the summer and that gives me time to clean up my shop, inspect and repair tools, and get the supplies I need because when autumn starts to arrive, that is when everyone wants their shoes repaired or new shoes made for growing children."

"That makes sense," Joia said. "I remember Mother taking us to the cobbler on the last day of summer, every year. Ebba usually got new shoes and I got the ones Ebba grew out of."

Derry laughed. "I understand what it is to be the youngest. I've got four older brothers. You can be sure I never got a stitch of new clothing. Everything I wore had been through four previous owners."

Ebba smiled. "You have four siblings?"

"Five," Derry said. "I have one poor sister, right in the middle of all of us brothers."

They reached Derry's cobbler shop just as he said this. He turned to them. "Would you like me to walk you the rest of the way to the spinners? I don't mind."

"We'd like that," Joia said.

They started walking again and Joia suddenly stopped. "Oh, I remember, I wanted to ask Caris about some herbs. I'll meet you at the spinner's in just a few minutes." She turned and went down a side street before Ebba or Derry could say anything. As soon as she went around the corner, she stopped and counted to three. Grinning with her plan to give

Ebba and Derry a few moments to be alone, she slowly peeked around the corner and saw them still walking slowly together.

She watched as they reached the spinner's shop and Derry gave her a slight bow. He turned and started back up the street. Joia hid in the shadows of the street, pressed against a house until she saw Derry pass by. Counting to three again, she stood up straight and turned the corner, and as casually as she could, she walked to the spinners.

Once inside, she found Ebba was talking to Beatrice, and they were talking about Derry.

"I can't believe Derry walked you over here," Beatrice was giggling.

"It's not like that," Ebba was stuttering. "We were coming here and passed Derry, and he offered to walk with us the rest of the way. That's all. Right, Joia?"

"Of course," Joia smiled.

"I wish he would go on a walk with me," Beatrice sighed.

"You're better off without a man," Letty, the master spinner said. She was a thin, older woman, and Joia couldn't remember if she had ever seen Letty out of her spinner shop. Unmarried, and with no children, she had dedicated her life to her craft. She also felt that everyone else should do the same.

"I can't wait to get married, Beatrice said. "I want to be someone's wife and become a mother."

Letty shook her head. "Your marriage should be to your craft, your life should be dedicated to spinning, and your children should be your beautiful creations of yarn."

Joia had to hide her smile. Letty was dedicated to her craft, but Joia wanted to be a wife and mother too, no matter what the spinner said.

They stayed for a couple of minutes and borrowed some yarn for their walk home. Joia promised to return it when she came back later in the afternoon.

"We could use your help," Letty said. "I've got a lot of wool that I just dyed. It needs to be carded."

"I'll be back," Joia promised. She and Ebba left the shop and Joia started back home.

Ebba reached out and grabbed her by the elbow. "Wait. We can't go back that way."

"Why not?" Joia asked.

"Because Derry will see us," Ebba blushed.

"Isn't that what we want?" Joia smiled. "We ran our errand and now we're going home. Besides, what if he's watching for you to pass by again?"

Ebba's blush deepened, but she agreed. They started to walk back towards the bakery. "Can you believe Derry is the youngest of five brothers?"

"I can't imagine five brothers. What would we do?" Joia laughed. As they approached the cobbler's shop, Joia was not surprised to find Derry standing just outside the door, sweeping the threshold.

"Hello again," Joia said.

"Get what you needed from the spinners?" he asked.

Joia held up the basket with the yarn. "Ebba's a talented knitter."

Derry smiled at Joia's older sister. "I'm not surprised. She seems to be talented at many things."

"Thank you, Derry," Ebba smiled.

There were a few moments of them smiling at each other before Derry gave a little cough. "I hate to keep you from your errands. I hope you ladies have a nice day."

"Thank you," Ebba blushed again.

Joia didn't think she had ever seen Ebba so pink and flushed before. "Good day, Derry," she waved as they started home again.

"Why is it so easy for you to speak with him?" Ebba whispered.

"Because I'm not in love with him," Joia whispered back.

"I'm… I'm not in love with him," Ebba stammered.

Joia gently pushed her elbow into Ebba's side. "Of course, you are."

"But you don't seem to have any trouble talking to Hakon and I know you love him," Ebba whispered back.

This time, it was Joia's turn to blush. "Hakon and I are friends. We've known each other our entire lives. We've grown up together. He was my friend before we became interested in each other."

"So, you admit that you love Hakon?" Ebba grinned.

"Shh, not so loud," Joia looked around. "We've been friends for years."

Ebba laughed. "I know that."

They reached the bakery and after saying hello to their father and brother, they went upstairs to their home. The dishes were where Joia had left them on the table. Her mother gave her a pointed look when they walked in, and Joia immediately took the dishes to the wash basin. She happily worked on the dishes and then the rest of her morning chores, thinking about Derry and Ebba, Hakon, and going to visit the spinner's shop again.

"Mother?" Ebba asked Liadan, "What was it like when you met Father? Did you love him right away?"

Liadan gave a gentle laugh. "I didn't love him right away. Remember, our marriage was arranged by our parents through the village elders. We didn't know each other until just days before our wedding and I was leaving my village for his. But I remember when I met him, I noticed that he was very handsome and strong. He was already a master baker and his first gift to me was a loaf of the most delicious bread I had ever eaten."

Ebba gave out a happy sigh and Joia wondered what Derry would give to Ebba if they were to marry. A pair of shoes?

Liadan smiled. "Your father had a good heart. I could see that right away. He was a little rough around the edges and could be quite stern, but he had a good heart. He has softened over the years into the good man, husband, and father he is today."

"He's still stern," Joia said.

"You, my love, test him the most," Liadan patted Joia on the shoulder. "Your brother was happy to take his place as your father's apprentice when he was ten and they have worked together ever since. Ebba has been happy to learn the homely jobs that a good wife needs to have to run her home."

"Have I not learned those same jobs?" Joia asked, hurt to know that her mother didn't think Joia was capable of being able to run a home or be a good wife.

"You have, my child, and very well" Liadan nodded. "But you have a freer heart, and I've encouraged that. I have always felt that you needed to learn about the trades. Somehow, you are connected to them."

"What do you mean?" Joia asked. "I'm too old to become a tradesman."

"No, no. Not like that," Liadan said, and Joia didn't miss the dark shadow that flickered across her mother's eyes. "Just, I don't know, you are somehow involved with the trades."

"Perhaps when she marries Hakon and becomes a tradesman's wife, she will need to understand something about his trade," Ebba grinned.

Joia turned to her sister. "Ebba!"

Liadan laughed. "What are you so surprised about, Joia? Everyone knows how much you and Hakon like each other."

Joia's face turned hot. "We are friends and have been for as long as we can remember."

Liadan kissed her daughter's head. "I know, Joia. And that is the best foundation for a lasting relationship."

It was midday before Joia finished her chores and was able to leave again for the spinner's shop. She didn't want to pass Derry's shop again in case he saw her and wondered why she was going back to the spinners. She took another way around, passing by the blacksmith's forge. She stopped for several moments to watch the smithy hammering at a red-hot piece of metal before sticking the metal back into the forge. It always amazed her how metal could be changed and shaped by heating it in a very hot fire.

Joia arrived at the spinners and was greeted by Beatrice and Meg, Letty's two apprentices. The women here were fun to be with, and Joia loved the magic of taking raw sheep's wool, washing it, drying it, and carding it until the wool was feather soft before gently rolling the wool into fluffy rolls. Each soft roll was placed in a pile next to the spinning wheel.

Letty sat at the wheel, pushing the peddle with her feet, making the wheel spin with a light whirring sound. She would take the rolls of soft wool and add them to the thread as it was twisted by the wheel. The wool would become thread and be wrapped around the spindle, ready to be knitted or woven. It was quite the process to go from a mass of sheep's wool to a beautiful yarn used for knitting or weaving.

Joia picked up two carding tools and sat next to a pile of wool that had been dyed light green. Taking a section of the wool, she placed it onto the sharp bristles of the card and started to brush the cards together.

"I heard that the entertainers are coming," Beatrice said as they worked. She was the older of the two apprentices and was at a second spinning wheel, spinning two different colors of already spun thread so they became a double strand with the two colors twisted perfectly together. This double thread would be used for heavier cloths, like winter cloaks or skirts, and it gave the cloth a wonderful color that could not be achieved by a single strand.

"I love the entertainers," the younger apprentice, Meg said. She was around twelve years old and working with Joia to card wool. "I love the music and dancing."

"I do too," Beatrice said. "They are so much better than old Noll who sings on the corner next to the tavern with that one-stringed lute of his."

The women laughed. "He can tell a good story though," Joia said.

The entertainers were a trade that Joia had spent little time around. There were some, like Old Noll, who knew how to play an instrument or tell a story but were not guild entertainers. True trade entertainers lived in traveling companies that went from village to village, putting on shows for the local people.

One of the village wives, carrying an infant in one arm with another small child holding onto her apron, came into the shop and was greeted by Letty. "Welcome Bronwyn. How are you today?"

The mother smiled and nodded. "I am well, thank you, and I will be better when this little one starts to sleep through the night. She's keeping all of us awake."

Meg nodded in understanding. "My youngest sibling is still crying much of the night."

Bronwyn sighed and kissed her baby's head. "Well, I need to get a skein to replace my husband's stockings. I don't understand how he wears them out so quickly."

Letty stood up and showed Bronwyn the skeins of strong yarn. The young wife picked one and paid. "Did you hear that the entertainers have been spotted heading this way?"

"I look forward to their visits every year," Meg said. "I love to watch the dancers."

"They aren't to be trusted," Letty said.

"Why not?" Beatrice asked.

"Because they aren't that's why. They don't live in a respectable way, now, do they? They live in wagons, traveling the countryside, and do nothing for their bread except sing. How can one live that way? You can't. They must steal to survive," Letty nodded her head at them, expecting the other women to believe her words.

Bronwyn held her baby closer to her chest. "I heard they steal children."

"Steal children? You're joking," Beatrice laughed. "I've never heard of that, and they've certainly never stolen anyone from Erthenhorn before."

"Just because they haven't, doesn't mean they won't," Letty warned.

Joia had heard this before, but like Beatrice, she had never known of anyone disappearing after the entertainers had come through. Joia had never seen anything threatening about the entertainers, even though she knew many people feared them. They danced, sang, and seemed to be a very happy group of people. They kept to themselves when they weren't performing but considering the way most of the villagers treated them, Joia didn't blame them for staying in their camp just outside the village borders.

No matter the rumors, Joia enjoyed it when the entertainers came. It was certainly a nice change from Noll and his dreadful one-stringed lute.

Joia thought the entertainers were wonderful. Their music was beautiful and exciting and played working instruments. The singing was stirring and the dancing exhilarating. The women moved together in unison, their skirts a flurry of colors while the men jumped high into the air.

But Joia's favorite entertainer was the mysterious storyteller. He was tall and had bright blue eyes that were the color of the sky on a summer day. His dark hair curled around his ears, usually from under a colorful scarf that was tied around his head. He had the most incredible voice. When he told his exciting stories, Joia was certain she could hear the sounds he described and smell the smells he wove into the story. Hearing the storyteller while he worked his craft was mesmerizing. She had never heard him tell the same story twice or sing the same song. Every time he came through, his stories and music were different.

He was also a little frightening to Joia because he seemed to glow with a golden light. No one else among the entertainers glowed, just him. As a child, she asked her mother about the glowing storyteller, but this question made her mother surprisingly upset and Joia was scolded for asking such a ridiculous question. She was told he did not glow and was to never mention that again. It was several years later before Joia saw that particular storyteller again and she saw that he still glowed with a golden light. She knew better than to ask her mother, so she turned to her sister, but Ebba had laughed at her and told her no one was glowing.

Joia never did figure it out, so she quit asking and accepted that this storyteller had a golden light about him. Thinking of him, even now, Joia had many questions, but no one had any answers. Perhaps it was time she approached him and asked him herself. He would either answer and she would have her curiosity satisfied, or he would not answer, and she would not be any worse off than she was right now.

"All the same," Beatrice went on, waking Joia from her thoughts of the storyteller, "I love their shows. Sometimes I wonder what it might be like to travel around the country the way they do. I think that would be most exciting."

Letty grunted. "No need to travel the country. Everything you could ever need is right here in Erthenhorn. Best to stay here and keep out of trouble."

"Have you ever left Erthenhorn?" young Meg asked.

"No," came Letty's firm answer. "And I never will."

"I have," Beatrice said. "Remember the fair to celebrate the birth of the King's son?"

"Our family went to that," Joia said. "It was so much fun. I had never seen so many people before." Joia's father had baked some of his most wonderful breads and fanciest pastries and took them to the fair to sell.

"So did my family," Meg said. "But I was very young. I just remember that it was a really long journey and I had to walk most of the way."

"My family went as well," Bronwyn said. "It was where I met Gunnar."

The fair had been a week-long celebration with a two-day journey, on foot, but it had been worth it. Tradesmen of all kinds had brought their finest wares. Entertainers put on shows, and animals were bought and sold. There had been tournaments of craft and weapons fighting. Many people had gotten married while at the fair. Families separated by miles of travel enjoyed reunions. News, gossip, and stories were shared. It had been the most exciting week of Joia's life.

Her hands automatically worked the wool and the cards while her mind was busy remembering the fair. She remembered that the mysterious, glowing entertainer had been there. Joia spent one afternoon, sneakily trailing the entertainer, hoping to learn more about him, but all he did was wander about telling stories, whether it was to one child or a whole crowd. She finally gave up on him when it started to get dark, and she had to return to her family's camp. Lost in her thoughts about the fair and the mysterious entertainer, Joia was surprised to hear her name being called.

"Joia? Joia, are you all right?" Letty was asking her.

"What? Yes." Joia shook her head, realizing that she had completely lost herself in her memories." I'm sorry, I was daydreaming."

"We could tell," Beatrice laughed.

"It's getting late, dear," the old spinner said. "Hadn't you better get home to your mother?"

"Oh, yes!" Joia jumped up. "Thank you for the lovely afternoon. Goodbye!" she called out as she quickly left. The sun was getting low in the sky, and she hurried out the door. The trip from the spinner's home to her home was short, and she passed through the common square. Several people were standing there, talking. There were always people visiting and conducting business in the square. She saw her good friend Hakon, son of Arik the Thatcher.

"Joia! Hello!" he called out.

She jogged toward him. "Hello, Hakon."

"You're late today," he smiled as she came to a stop in front of him.

"I know. I got caught up in the spinners. We were talking and I just lost track of the hour."

"Any good gossip today?" he asked.

"The entertainers are coming," Joia answered.

He laughed. "That is always a fun time." He looked up into the evening sky. "I've got to get going, but I hope we can visit more tomorrow."

Joia nodded. "So do I. I'll see you tomorrow."

She wished she had noticed the time of day earlier. She would have left the spinner's house earlier and then had time to visit with Hakon before going home. She ran the rest of the way, going into the closed bakery and finding her father and brother at their worktable, getting dough ready for the next day.

"It's nearly dark," her father greeted. He was sweeping the floor of the bakery.

"I know, I'm sorry. I didn't pay attention to the time. I'll go up and help Mother."

Her mother and sister were at the hearth preparing dinner together. They both looked up at Joia and her mother frowned at her.

"I'm sorry I'm late," Joia said breathlessly. "The ladies at the spinners were talking about the entertainers that are coming to the village and I just got caught up in the conversation.

Her mother, Liadan, looked at her youngest daughter in surprise. "The entertainers are coming?"

"Yes," Joia answered, picking up a knife and starting to chop at the roots her mother had harvested from their garden. "At least, that's what Beatrice said, and Bronwyn said she had heard the same thing."

Liadan turned away from Joia and busied herself with stoking the fire.

Ebba placed a hand on her mother's shoulder. "Are you well, Mother?"

Liadan nodded. "I'm fine. Joia, are those roots chopped yet?"

Joia scooped the roots into a bowl and took them to her mother. She didn't miss the troubled look on her mother's face, as Liadan took the bowl and dumped the contents into the simmering pot. Joia looked over to her sister, who just shrugged. What had her mother so upset?

CHAPTER TWO

The Light of the Guild

It would still be a little while before Thomas and David would leave the bakery to come up for dinner, which was simmering lightly in the large pot hanging over the fire in the hearth. Ebba had gone back to her sewing and Joia was sitting near the hearth with her knitting needles, working on repairing her favorite shawl that had gotten caught on a nail a few days back and tore a hole.

Liadan came up to her daughter. "Joia, come down to the garden with me."

Joia nodded and set down her shawl and knitting needles. She stood and looked at Ebba, who shrugged and went back to her sewing. Joia followed her mother down the stairs and out to the garden.

The summer night was warm, and the garden was fragrant. The small stream that ran not far from their home gurgled as it churned in its shallow, rocky bed. Joia took several deep breaths, inhaling the familiar, earthy scents.

They walked to the edge of the garden, near the stream, and sat down together in the grass. Joia was curious about her mother's behavior. Why bring her out into the garden, after dark, to sit in the grass? What could she possibly have to say that could not be said in their home or in front of Ebba?

Liadan looked around, making sure they were alone. Then she took a deep breath and took Joia's hands into hers. She gave them a gentle squeeze and looked into her daughter's face.

"Mother? What's wrong?"

"Joia, my dearest, you've grown up so much. I sometimes forget you're seventeen. I still want to think of you as a little girl." Liadan smiled and put a hand on the side of Joia's face. She sighed, "But you are not a little girl anymore and there is something you need to know. So, let's start at the beginning. Back when you were a very young baby, not more than two months old, the entertainers arrived in town as they did every year. You children were very young, I didn't dare take you into the square with the rest of the village to see the entertainers. I decided to go to the butcher that day instead. You were in a sling and David and Ebba were holding my hands. I was just heading out when a tall man, playing a lute passed by me. I knew right away he was an entertainer and I waited for him to pass by, but he saw you and stopped. He approached me, never taking his eyes off you.

"This child," the entertainer said, "what is the babe's name?"

He looked into Liadan's face, and she was surprised by the intensity of his gaze as if those blue eyes could see into her very soul.

"Joia," Liadan answered.

The man smiled gently. "She's lovely," he said, "as all your children are." He looked at Ebba and David, but his gaze returned to Joia. "But this child is very special. She has the Light. Like the Patrons of the Guild."

"There is no light about her," Liadan said.

The entertainer looked back into her face and studied her for a moment. The intensity of his eyes, the way he spoke, and the words he said all made Liadan nervous. "You do not see it?" he asked.

She stepped back. "I'm sorry, sir, but we really must be going."

"Wait, please," the man said, holding his hand to touch her elbow, "Who is Joia's father? What is his trade?"

"He is Thomas, a master baker."

The man nodded his head. "Excellent. Joia must learn about the trades and their Patrons."

"Excuse me, sir, but I must be off." Liadan stepped to the side, but the stranger stepped with her and stood close to her. He leaned in. "Joia has a special light about her. The Light of the Guild. Take good care of her and raise her well. I will check on her again in a year. Farewell." Then he turned and walked away.

Liadan was quite alarmed and instead of going on to the butchers, she turned around and went home. That night, she told her husband what had happened, but Thomas wasn't concerned.

"He's an entertainer," Thomas said. "They're odd folk. He will be gone tomorrow, and all will be as if he had never arrived."

For the first time since meeting the entertainer, Liadan breathed easier. Thomas was right, of course, and two days later, the entertainers were gone, but Liadan could not forget her encounter with the tall man.

Joia stared at her mother in surprise. "Did that truly happen?"

"It did," Liadan nodded.

Joia looked at herself. There was no light about her. She was just herself. "What is this Light of the Guild?"

"I don't really know," Liadan answered.

"Did the entertainer return the next year, like he promised?" Joia asked.

"He did," Liadan nodded. "A year passed, and the entertainers arrived again in the village. I wondered if the entertainer with the blue eyes would come back to see you. I half-heartedly told myself that I was being ridiculous. The entertainers traveled all over the country, went to many places, and met many people. What was the chance that one man would remember us or even our home? I laughed at myself for being so silly, but I couldn't stop worrying either."

Liadan did not go out of her house that day. She had heard the entertainers in the square. Their music filled the village, but she would not risk the chance of a run-in with any of the entertainers. She hoped that he would not be among the company this year, but that afternoon, as she was cooking their dinner with the three children playing under Liadan's feet, there was a knock at the door. Warily, she opened the door and was shocked to see the same blue-eyed entertainer who had spoken to her so mysteriously the year before.

She stood, dumbfounded, and stared at the man.

"Hello," he said. He looked into the room and saw Joia playing on the floor with Ebba. "I'm glad to see she is healthy and growing."

Liadan tried to close the door on the stranger, but he stuck out his foot. "Wait a moment, please," he said, "Let's get off to a better start." He gave a slight bow. "My name is Edmund, the Entertainer. I don't know if you remember me, but I spoke with you last year about your young daughter."

"I remember," Liadan said.

"Good," said Edmund. "Do you remember anything I told you?"

"I remember every word." The conversation had been branded into Liadan's heart and she had pondered about it a great deal over the year while she had watched Joia play and grow.

"Then you will remember that I said this girl was special and has the Light of the Guild," Edmund said. Liadan nodded. "I came to see if she still has that Light and I'm glad to see that she does," he said.

Liadan knew she should close the door on the entertainer, but she had to know what he had meant and despite her better judgment, she invited him in. She offered him tea and he accepted. He watched Joia at play, smiling as she squealed when David threw a blanket over her head. She pulled it off and held it up to David, who took it again and tossed it onto her head.

"It is a game they enjoy," Liadan explained. She sat across from the man and leaned forward. "Tell me what you mean when you said she has the Light of the Guild."

"The Light of the Guild? What does that even mean?" Joia asked.

Liadan shook her head. "I had never heard of that either, so when I asked him what he meant, he told me you needed to learn about the trades because you had a destiny with the trade guilds."

Joia was confused. "A destiny with the trade guilds? I don't understand. I'm not a tradesman."

"I don't quite understand either," Liadan shook her head. "But this man, Edmund, has returned to the village every few years or so to check on you."

"Why have I never seen him?"

"You probably did and didn't realize it," Liadan answered. "He told me that when the time was right, he would come for you and help you find your connection to the Trade Guild."

"What do you mean, he'll come for me?" Joia was quite alarmed now. "Have you promised me to this man?"

"No, Joia. It's not like that at all. It's more like, he's promised himself to you."

"I'm not marrying this stranger," Joia said, moving back away from her mother.

"It isn't about a marriage, Joia. I believe it will be more like a master to an apprentice. I don't know anything for certain, but I just have this feeling that this year will be the year he reveals who he is to you."

"Wait. You said that this entertainer told you I glow with a Light?" Joia gasped. "Is that what this Edmund said?" Joia asked, her mind grasping at who this could be.

"Yes," Liadan said. "He said you glow with the Light of the Guild, but I have never seen it."

"Wait, this Edmund, he's the storyteller, isn't he?" Joia asked as her mind started to put together the riddles. Things were starting to make sense.

Her mother swallowed hard and nodded her head. "Yes, I believe he is."

"The one who glows," Joia said, her eyes growing wide.

Liadan grasped at her daughter's arms and held her firmly. "He doesn't glow, Joia," Liadan said, remembering how Joia asked about the glowing performer back when she was a small child. "I've seen him perform with his company several times over the years. He doesn't glow. No one does. Not him and not you."

"Maybe you can't see it because you don't have the Light of the Guild. Maybe that's how he knew I have this Light. Just like I see him glowing with a golden light, perhaps he sees that too." Joia was trying to explain this, but more to herself, to make herself understand.

Liadan's grasp on her daughter's arms tightened. "No. It's just the sunshine, nothing more."

"This Edmund, isn't that the name of the entertainer's Patron?" Joia asked, trying to remember what she knew of the Trade Patrons.

Each trade had a Patron, who had been the first to learn the trade and teach it to others. But according to the traditions and lore of the tradesmen, Patrons had been around for hundreds of years. There was no way that a man could live that long.

"I believe Edmund is the name of the Patron to the entertainers," Liadan answered.

"But I thought the Patrons weren't real people. I always assumed they were mystical beings."

"They are mystic beings," Liadan said. "But I suppose they might also be real people. If this Edmund is who he truly says he is, then he is a Patron."

"So, the entertainer that I've seen over all my life, the man who glows, is *the* Patron of his guild? How do we know he is truly Edmund, the Patron of the entertainers? Perhaps he is simply a man named Edmund. It's not that uncommon of a name."

"That could be," Liadan said, "but when he's around you, you feel different. I can't explain it. And his eyes. He looks at you with these eyes that are so intense," Liadan shivered, "it's like he can see through you, right into your soul."

"Why have you never told me about this before?" Joia asked.

"To protect you." Liadan sighed. She took Joia's hands in hers. "Because it didn't make any difference at the time. I've seen you every day since the day you were born and while you are a light of joy in my life, you don't glow with any special, mysterious light."

"Perhaps it is a light that only a Patron can see," Joia's voice choked and in a whisper. "And this Edmund wants to talk to me?"

Liadan nodded, "He does. In years past, he has said it was not time yet, but you are grown now, and he might decide it is time for you to find your place with the trades."

Joia sat quietly for several moments, thinking. This was insane, but somehow, the more she thought of it, the more curious she was.

Suddenly, behind them, the door to the house opened. Joia and Liadan jumped in surprise as the light spilled out of the house and into the darkened garden.

"There you are," Joia's father stood in the doorway. "What are you doing out here, in the dark? Ebba's got dinner ready."

Liadan's voice perked up, "Excellent. We're coming in now." They stood up and started to the door. Liadan leaned close to Joia. "Not a word to your father. We haven't spoken of this to each other in many years."

Joia nodded. Her mother had just thrown such an incredible story into her lap; she needed time to think before she could even hope to talk to someone about this. Not even her sister.

Ebba was waiting at the table. The hot stew had been ladled out into bowls and a loaf of fresh bread sat in the center of the table.

"Thank you, Ebba," Liadan hugged her daughter. "Let's eat."

Joia always knew when her father and brother were home, the house smelled strongly of yeast and flour. It was a comforting, pleasant smell, that, in Joia's mind, meant family and safety.

The family ate, listening to David talk about the day in the bakery and there was some slight teasing of Ebba and Joia about their little walk-through town with Derry.

"Derry came and spoke with me," Thomas said to his family. Joia and Ebba exchanged glances and waited to hear what their father had to say. "He would like to court Ebba."

"And you said, yes, right?" Joia asked.

Thomas frowned at her. "You know better than to interrupt me."

"Sorry, Father," Joia said, looking down at the bowl of half-eaten stew in front of her.

There was an uncomfortable silence for several moments as Thomas ate another bite of stew. Joia didn't dare move.

"I spoke with Derry at length about this and did agree that he may court you, Ebba," Thomas finally said.

Ebba let out a happy sigh. "Thank you, Father."

He smiled kindly at his eldest daughter. "It is a good match."

Joia was very happy for Ebba but didn't speak again during supper. She did not wish for her father's annoyance and anger to fall on Joia again and take away from Ebba's happiness. She wished she could make her father proud like her siblings did, but as her mother had said, Joia had a freer heart and had tried and tested her father's patience on more than one occasion.

When dinner was done, the sisters helped Liadan clean the dishes while David sat down to read from the one book that they owned. With the cleaning done, Joia picked up her knitting and sat back down next to Ebba. Her hands worked of their own accord on the repetitive job, allowing her mind to wander. Her parents began talking about local news.

Ebba, who was always talkative, began talking about Derry, what it would be like to be married to him, and the new dress she was making for herself. Joia just listened. She wasn't in the mood to reply, but Ebba, it seemed, didn't need Joia to reply, just listen. All Joia wanted was to be alone with her thoughts, but that would have to wait until she went to bed.

That night, after Joia lay down and said goodnight to her sister, she started to think about what her mother had said. She wondered about the Patrons, the Guild, and this light her mother spoke of. Joia was certain more than before that the storyteller she had seen over the years did glow. She wondered if she glowed too. But no, that was ridiculous. She would have known if she was glowing, right? Her mind tossed these questions around before she finally fell into an uneasy sleep.

Joia needed information. The conversation with her mother the night before had disturbed her sleep all night long. If Edmund the Entertainer was the Patron of the Entertainer Guild, then could other Patrons be real? Did they all glow?

She took her father and brother their breakfast in the bakery and then quickly completed her morning chores. She was eager to get out. While scrubbing the floor that morning, Joia made a plan. She would go about the village today and ask some of the tradesmen that she knew about their Patrons.

As soon as she was free, she headed out. The midday sun was hot and bore down on her as she walked. She went first to Letty at the spinners.

"Who is your Patron?" she asked after greeting Letty, Beatrice, and Meg. They were still carding their way through a large stack of dyed wool.

"Kloma, the Spinner," Letty answered.

"How do you dedicate your days?" Joia asked.

"We place our hands on the spinning wheel and say, Kloma, we dedicate our day to you. May our fingers be deft as we clean, card, and spin wool."

Beatrice and Meg nodded.

"Sometimes," Beatrice said, "if we have a project that we will be working on all day, we adjust our dedication to include that project like the day we spent dying wool."

Joia nodded as she listened. "Do you think Kloma is a real person? I mean, do you think she is someone who walks the world like we do?"

Letty shook her head. "I don't think so. She would be very, very old if she were alive. Hundreds of years old."

"Then why dedicate your days?" Joia asked.

"Because the Patrons are not mortals, like you and I," Letty said. "They are mystical people who guide us and help us when we work our trades. Just ask Ellota at the weaver's shop. She'll tell you the same thing."

The weaver's shop was Joia's next stop.

While the spinner's shop was a great place to work if you wanted gossip and conversation, the weaver's shop was a great place if you wanted peace and quiet. Not that the weaver's shop was a silent place, in fact, when the weavers were at work, there was quite a bit of noise from the loom. The raising and dropping of the loom's shafts, the shuttle being sent back and forth, and the beater after each drop of a heddle, all made noise, but it was rhythmic and constant. It required concentration to keep the rhythm going.

When Joia would help at the weaver's shop, she would fetch bobbins of thread for the weavers or help to wind the cloth around the beam, giving the weavers more room to work with on the loom. Today when she walked in, she noticed right away the absence of the clacking and whooshing of the looms.

"Ah! Joia, welcome. Would you come in and help Sara for a moment?" the master weaver, Ellota asked as soon as Joia was in the shop.

"Of course," Joia said, going to stand next to Sara.

Ellota was preparing the loom with new threads. She stood on one side of the loom, where currently, hundreds of individual threads were stretched across the back beam of the loom. Sara was standing on the other side of the loom, holding thick bundles of the threads, trying her best to pull them tight while Ellota cranked the handle on the beam.

Sara gave Joia half of the threads and they both took a moment to comb their fingers through them and make sure nothing was tangled.

"Good, this will go faster now," Ellota nodded. "All right, girls, pull."

Sara and Joia pulled back on the bundles, making the hundreds of threads go tight. Ellota turned the crank, which spun the long roller, which turned to pull the threads further back. Ellota took a long piece of thick parchment and stuffed it between the roller and the threads.

"Why do you do that?" Joia asked.

"It keeps the layers of threads separated. When I am done, there will be dozens of layers of threads wound around this roller. I don't want to take a chance that they will get tangled in each other. The parchment separates them," Ellota explained as she gave the roller another crank.

Sara and Joia released their tension and let some of the threads from their bundles loose. Joia peeked down at the back roller and saw what Ellota was doing. "I see," she said, looking at the roller, which already had half a dozen full layers of thread, separated by the paper, on the roller.

Ellota nodded and once again the girls pulled at the threads, giving even tension as Ellota made the next few cranks on the roller.

"May I ask a question?" Joia asked.

"Yes, of course," Ellota answered. She leaned over several threads and untangled them.

"Who is the Patron of the weavers?"

"Her name is Sidonia, the Weaver," Ellota answered.

"My father dedicates his days to his Patron. Do the weavers dedicate their days to Sidonia?" Joia asked.

Ellota looked up at Joia for a moment from her threads. "Yes, every day. All tradesmen dedicate their days to their Patrons."

"How is it done, for the weavers?" Joia asked.

Sara pointed up to a spot on the wall, "We touch the bit of cloth on the wall and say, 'Sidonia, the Weaver, today we dedicate our work to you. May our warps be strong, and our weft be neat. We are your weavers.'"

Ellota nodded and cranked the roller on the loom twice.

Joia looked to the spot where Sara had pointed. She saw a small square of gold-colored cloth nailed to the wall. She had visited the weaver's shop many times and had seen the gold cloth on the wall, but now, she looked at it with a new eye. The cloth wasn't just golden in color, it was glowing. Joia was sure of it. "It glows golden?"

Ellota looked up from her work and looked at the cloth. "No, it doesn't glow, except maybe when the sun shines on it. No, it is a pure white cloth. Quite incredible when one considers how old it might be."

"And how old would that be?" Joia asked, fascinated.

"Well, it was given to me by the weaving master I apprenticed under, and it was given to her by her master. All young apprentices learn the story of Sidonia."

Sara nodded. "In the beginning, Sidonia was the only weaver. She gathered twelve together and taught them how to weave. When they had learned and were ready to go off on their own, Sidonia wove a cloth of pure white, cut it into twelve pieces, and gave one to each of her students. As long as they had their bit of cloth and dedicated their days, her gifts would always shine on the work of her tradesmen."

Joia looked at the cloth again. "So that bit of cloth is a small section of the original cloth, woven by Sidonia?

Ellota nodded. "That is what I was told when it was given to me. Who knows how long that bit of cloth has been passed on. I can only believe it was woven by Sidonia herself because a white cloth would have yellowed some with age, but this is still pure white."

Joia stared at the cloth while pulling at the threads for Ellota to crank the roller again. There was no doubt that the cloth was truly glowing. Just as the entertainer glowed with a gold light, so did this cloth. That meant that Sidonia had to have been a real person, just like the entertainer. And if he was alive, could she be as well?

She and Sara untangled their threads and Joia ran her fingers through them, combing out some parts that had snagged. Then, she had a thought. Sara was Ellota's apprentice, and years ago, Ellota had been an apprentice to another master weaver. Perhaps the title of Patron was passed along in the same manner.

Edmund must be the current person acting as Patron to the Entertainers. The name and title had to be passed along, much like an apprentice being named a master by their guild. This could not be the first Edmund, but a man who had been chosen for his great skills to take on the title of Patron. She nodded to herself. That made sense.

Still, she was curious to know what Ellota thought. "Ellota? Do you think Sidonia is a real person?"

Ellota nodded. "I do. I believe my Patron is a real person, who spends her day at a great loom, weaving the finest cloth."

"But wouldn't she be very old?" Joia asked.

Ellota shook her head. "She is ageless. She has always been the Weaver and she always will be."

It was a while longer before the huge loom was finished. Sara and Joia tied their bundles of threads with a huge knot. Later, Ellota would thread each individual piece of yarn into the heddles that were tied onto the shaft frame. Joa was no longer needed, so she bid the weavers goodbye and headed out again.

That had taken longer than she had hoped, so she walked quickly over to Derry's shop. The door was open, and Joia walked in. The room smelt of leather and oil. She took in a deep breath. It was a very pleasant aroma.

"Miss Joia," Derry said, standing from where he was working.

"Hello Derry," Joia said. "What are you working on?"

"I've been punching holes in this sole," he gestured to an oddly shaped stone with a piece of leather, shaped like the bottom of a shoe, and two tools that she recognized as an awl and a hammer.

"How does that work?" she asked.

He sat down on the stool and brought the stone onto his lap between his legs, which gripped the stone to keep it from moving. With the awl in one hand and the hammer in the other, he placed the sharp awl on the sole and gave it a hard tap with the hammer. A new hole was formed.

"How many holes are in a sole?" she asked.

"It depends on the size of the shoe, but this one will have over one hundred," he answered.

Joia raised her own foot and looked at the shoe. Derry followed her gaze. "Your shoes are not one of mine," he said.

She shook her head. "I've had these for four summers, I believe. I quit growing and Father allowed me to get these for my fourteenth birthday."

Derry looked at it more closely. "They are looking very thin on the bottom. You should have them resoled."

Joia nodded. "It would probably be good to do before winter."

"Let me measure them, then I can have the soles ready for any time you want to have them fitted," Derry stood up, placing the stone aside with the awl and hammer. "If you will take them off, I will make my measurements."

Joia smiled and started to untie the strings of leather that kept the shoe firmly in place on her foot. She slipped the well-worn shoes off and gave them to Derry. He had two pieces of thin leather. He took her shoes into his lap and started to fit the leather around the sole.

"May I ask you about your Patron?" Joia asked.

"Of course. What would you like to know?" Derry asked.

"What is his name? And what can you tell me about him?" she asked as she watched Derry measuring her shoe.

"He is Wealcan, the Cobbler, and long ago, he taught others how to use leather to cut, shape, and sew into shoes. He showed the first cobblers how to use awls, and strong needles with threads of sinew. The work we do changes as we find new tricks that work best for us, but for the most part, we make shoes the same way he showed us."

"So, Wealcan is a real person?" Joia asked.

"I suppose so. Or he was a real person. I suppose now he would be hundreds of years old." Derry said, tracing her shoe with a piece of sharpened coal. "I've never really considered it."

"And you have a dedication that you say each day?" she asked.

He nodded. "I do. It is the same as the one that my teacher taught me and the same one that his master taught him. Perhaps they are the words that Wealcan himself requested that his tradesmen say."

He handed Joia one of her shoes. She slipped it on as he worked on her other shoe.

"Do you have anything that was made by your Patron?" she asked, looking around.

"No," he said. "But I have seen something that was said to have been made by Wealcan. It was in the possession of my teacher. It was a piece of cut leather in the shape of a sole. I cannot say for certain that it was something of Wealcan's own making, but I liked to think it was. Why all these questions about Wealcan? Are you thinking about becoming a cobbler?"

Joia laughed. "No. I was just curious." She was hoping that she would call this cobbler her brother one day. She tried to think of any way she could get some idea about his feelings for Ebba, but Derry did that for her.

"How is your sister this morning?" he asked.

"She is well," Joia smiled. "She is home and working on a dress. She's very clever with her sewing."

He smiled. "You said that yesterday about her knitting."

"She is at that too," Joia said. "She's very clever at all things of the home."

"That does not surprise me. She also seems to have a very good nature," he said.

Joia nodded. "She really does. You'll never meet anyone who is as sweet and kind and steady as Ebba. She's also intelligent and fun to talk with. She will make someone a wonderful wife one day."

Derry turned slightly pink. "I have no doubt of that. Here you are," he handed her the second shoe. "If you come to me in about ten days' time, I can have those soles ready for you."

"I'll be back," Joia smiled. "Thank you for your time, Derry."

"Of course," he said. "Please tell Ebba that I said hello."

"I will," Joia smiled as she got up to leave the shop. She said goodbye and headed towards the common square. It was a little early to meet Hakon, so she went to watch the blacksmith at work. When she got there, it looked like he was closing for the day.

"Hello Joia," he called out when he saw her.

"Good day, Bernard," she waved. "All finished for the day?"

"I am," he said, coming over to her. He was a strong man with dark brown hair pulled back by a leather thong, and his face looked weathered beyond his years thanks to the heat that he stood over all day. "What brings you around today?"

"I've been visiting some of the tradesmen," she said. "If I may ask, who is the Patron of the blacksmiths?"

"He is Ciar, the Blacksmith," Bernard answered. "It is said that anything he crafts never needs to be repaired or sharpened. It stays as perfect as the day he makes it."

"That would be incredible. I think of my friend, Hakon, who must constantly sharpen his tools so he can work his trade," Joia said.

Bernard nodded. "Imagine if he never had to sharpen his knives and sickles again."

Joia whistled in surprise. "He would be most pleased," she laughed. "So do you believe Ciar is a real man?"

"He's a Patron," Bernard said. "I'm not sure what that means, but when I dedicate my days to him, my work goes better."

"My father says the same thing about his dedications," Joia said.

Bernard nodded. "We are lucky to have such good Patrons that help us work. I must be off. Goodnight Joia."

"Goodnight," she said and went back to the commons in time to see Hakon approaching. Her stomach did a little flip and her heart beat faster when she saw him.

"Evening, Joia," he said, coming close to her. He was tall; much taller than her. His blond hair had a straw twig in it. She reached up and pulled the twig out, holding it out for him to see why she had just reached for his hair in public. He laughed and her heart fluttered again.

"Did you get showered on by straw?" she asked.

He laughed. "Sort of. Father was working on the top of a roof, and I was trimming up the thatch around the base."

She felt his hand lightly touch hers. Her fingers wrapped around him and held him for several moments before letting go. Too much physical contact was frowned upon. "Whose shop have you been visiting today?" he asked as he led her over to a stone wall to sit.

"I went to see several today," she answered. "Letty, Ellota, Derry, and Bernard. I had some questions for each of them and I would like to ask you."

"All right," he said. They sat down together on the wall, close enough that their fingers could touch.

"Who's the Patron of the thatchers?"

Hakon looked surprised. "This is what you've been asking everyone about? Their Patrons?"

She nodded. "I've seen my father and brother dedicating their days to Ferran and it got me wondering."

"Well, my Patron is Thek, the Thatcher."

"How do you dedicate your days to him?"

He smiled at her and laid his hands on her arms, just below her shoulders. "Well, we hold out our shearing hook and say, 'Thek, the Thatcher, I dedicate my work to you. The tools you shared with us are strong and sharp. May our work be sturdy and tight.' And then, we touch the hook to our forehead."

Joia watched him with interest. "Do you know if Thek has left anything to show that he is real?"

Hakon was confused. "What do you mean?" he asked.

"Well, at the weavers, she had a bit of cloth that was said to be woven by the hand of their Patron. Has Thek left anything he has created?"

"Nothing that I'm aware of," Hakon said, "But there is a story that says there is a castle devoted to the Patrons of the Trade Guild."

"There's a special castle for the trades?" She had never really thought much about the Patrons before today.

"That's what I've heard, but it's only a story Joia. I wouldn't get my hopes up about being able to visit it." Hakon took Joia's hand in his, his grip stronger than the fleeting touches from a few moments ago. "Joia, what's got you asking all these questions about the Patrons? Why the sudden interest?"

"Oh, I don't know. I just am." Joia had to think quickly. She wasn't ready to tell Hakon anything about what her mother had told her. Until she had talked to this Edmund herself, Joia did not want to discuss what her mother had told her with anyone else. "I mean, I guess I knew that every trade has a Patron, but I've never really thought about it before, and really, it's very interesting. Do you think these Patrons are real people, who walk the land like you and me?"

"I don't know if they walk among us. The Patrons are mystical."

"But are they real?" she earnestly asked.

"In their way, yes," Hakon answered.

Hakon's father, Arik, walked up to them, surprising them from their conversation. Joia quickly let go of Hakon's fingers. "Good evening, Joia," he said.

"Good evening, sir," Joia smiled.

"How are your mother and father?" Arik asked.

"They are well, thank you. And you, sir?"

"Can't complain," he chuckled. "Hakon, we need to be off."

"Coming," Hakon nodded, and his father walked away. He took Joia's hand in his and whispered, "I'll see you tomorrow?"

Joia nodded. "Yes, see you tomorrow."

CHAPTER THREE

The Arrival of the Entertainers

That night, Joia pondered everything she had learned about the Patrons. No one seemed to know if they were real people or not, but it didn't matter to them. The tradesmen loved their Patrons and honored them. They said their dedications, and all felt they were blessed by their Patrons. They all had a similar story of being the first to learn the trade and teach the trade to others.

Joia wondered if all the trades developed at the same time, and if so, how had that happened? How was it that each Patron and each trade formed at the same time? Perhaps they were mystical beings who all sprang up together from the ground during a single night and started to teach the trades.

"Guess who I went to see today?" Joia said as she and Ebba settled into their bed that night.

"I'm sure you saw Hakon," Ebba said.

"Of course, but I also went to see Derry. He wanted me to tell you he said hello," Joia grinned.

Ebba turned to her. "You went to Derry's shop?"

"I did. He's interested in you."

Ebba grabbed at Joia's hand. "What did he say? I want to know."

"Well, he asked how you were, and I told him you were doing very well and at home sewing. I mentioned that you were very fine at sewing, knitting, and cooking and that you would make someone a fine wife one day."

"You didn't!" Ebba hissed in the quiet.

Joia giggled. "I did and you should have seen the way he blushed. He told me that he thinks you must be good-natured, and I told him you were kind and intelligent."

"Joia," Ebba covered her hands with her face. "How do you find it so easy to talk to him? I want to talk, but I get all tongue-tied."

"I told you. It's because I'm not in love with him like you are." Joia pulled Ebba's hands away from her face. "I think Derry's just as tongue-tied to talk about you as you are about him. And you are everything I said you are. You're clever, talented, kind, intelligent, and beautiful."

"You told Derry I'm beautiful?" Ebba asked.

"No, but you are, and he knows it."

For the second night in a row, Joia didn't sleep well. All she dreamt of was glowing cloth, glowing shoes, glowing bread, and glowing straw roofs. When the morning came, Joia's mind was weary. All she wanted to do was work on something familiar and ordinary and not dwell on the Patrons or trades.

She went out into the garden and took a deep breath. The morning sun felt nice on her skin. She sat next to the vegetable patch and started to pull the weeds out from around the growing food. With every weed she pulled from the ground, it was accompanied by a burst of a warm, earthy smell. The nearby stream gurgled and somewhere nearby, a bee buzzed about. It was pleasant work on a very pleasant morning.

But no matter how hard she tried to concentrate on the weeds and the garden, her mind kept wandering back to her recent conversations about the Patrons. It was making her uneasy. And, if Beatrice's calculations were correct, the entertainers would be arriving today. What if Edmund the Entertainer was among them? What would that even mean? She didn't have any mysterious light. There was nothing special about her at all. She was just Joia. Nothing more. She wasn't even trained in a craft so what could Edmund possibly want with her?

The door opened, startling Joia. Ebba stepped out of the house into the morning light.

"Would you like some help?" Ebba asked. She didn't wait for an answer as she sat down next to Joia and began pulling weeds.

"Thanks," Joia said, glad for Ebba's company.

"I've hardly seen you these last few days. Even when you've been home, your mind seems elsewhere. What's wrong?"

"Oh," Joia started but wasn't sure really what she wanted to say. "I don't know."

Ebba huffed, "Don't be silly. I can tell when something's bothering you. What is it?"

Joia sighed. "I don't really know how to explain it. I guess I've been thinking a lot about the future. David's been promised to a girl and we know Derry has plans to court you. I don't know what they have planned for me."

"That's normal," Ebba smiled kindly. "Everyone worries about the future." She sat back, crossed her legs, and then leaned forward. "Anything or anyone in your future that you are specifically thinking about?"

Joia blushed. "I don't know what you're talking about."

Ebba laughed. "Well, I saw Tessie this morning, and she told me that she saw you talking to Hakon in the square yesterday." Ebba had a big smile on her face.

"Yes, we did talk. We usually meet in the square every evening to visit. You know this." Joia said.

"Yes, but Tessie also said you were holding hands and seemed to be talking very seriously." She leaned in closer to Joia and was almost whispering.

Joia blushed again and smiled. "We were talking about the thatcher's guild Patron," Joia answered. It was perfectly true.

"While holding hands?" Ebba seemed quite pleased with herself.

Joia yanked another weed from the garden bed, doing all she could to avoid Ebba's smug smile. "Fine. Yes, we held hands, briefly."

Ebba laughed again. "Would you marry him if Father gave his consent?"

Joia looked up in surprise. "Why? What do you know?"

"Nothing, Joia, nothing. Just curious. Besides, you don't have to answer that question because I already know what you would say. Of course, you'd marry Hakon." Ebba went back to pulling some weeds.

"Shh," Joia hissed. "Not so loud." She looked around to see if there might be anyone close by.

"But you would, wouldn't you?" Ebba asked, with some seriousness in her voice.

"Yes, I would. What do you think about courting Derry?" Joia asked.

Ebba smiled. "I am very happy about it. Do you remember when he arrived in Erthenhorn with his wife?" Ebba asked.

Joia nodded. He had come to Erthenhorn just two years ago with a beautiful wife, heavy with child. They were a happy couple, excited to be settling down in their new home and their new family. The wife, Myla, had been a sweet woman and accepted immediately among the other women in the village. Unfortunately, her baby was born in the middle of winter, and it was a hard birth. She and the baby died of a fever just two days later.

"Mother really liked Myla. Everyone did," Ebba said. "It would be hard to fill her shoes."

"Everyone in Erthenhorn loves you," Joia said. "And really, all you need is Derry's love."

"Do you think he'll be thinking of her when I am with him?" Ebba asked.

Joia shook her head. "No. When Derry sees you, he is thinking of you. He's ready to move on and you are a perfect match for him. Do you want to be married to Derry?"

"Yes," Ebba giggled. "He's a good man and a good-looking man. And being the cobbler's wife would be a very respectable position."

Joia nodded in agreement. "And, the best part is that you will remain in Erthenhorn." Ebba grinned. "I know. We won't have to be apart."

Joia leaned over to give her sister a hug. "This is so exciting! I hope it all works out for you."

"So do I," Ebba agreed.

Joia thought about how wonderful it would be to see Ebba as a married woman, living in her own home on the other side of the village. Ebba would be a great wife for any man, and a good mother too someday. Joia hoped it wouldn't be long before she could become an aunt.

Ebba chatted about marriage and the future possibilities of being a wife as they continued to pick weeds. Joia listened with a glad heart. She forgot her own worries for a while as they planned Ebba's future wedding.

As they were finishing their chore, they heard a sound that was only ever heard once a year in Erthenhorn – the arrival of the entertainers. At no other time in the village would you hear the sounds of flutes and tambourines. From all over the village, people would be running out of their homes and into the streets or peeking out of windows for a view of the entertainers as they danced their way through the village on their way to the square.

Ebba squealed with delight and grabbed Joia by the arm. "The entertainers are here! Quick, let's go."

Joia's heart skipped several beats as excitement and concern filled her. They untied their aprons and dunked their hands into the rainwater barrel just outside their door. With the dirt from the garden washed off their hands, they ran out and followed the procession of entertainers and villagers into the common square.

The square was packed with townspeople, and dancing in the center of the square, were people dressed in brightly colored clothes. The exciting music and energetic dancing drew Joia in. She laughed and clapped her hands and watched the dancers twirl.

Four women in multi-colored skirts danced with colorful scarves in their hands and small tinkling bells tied to their waist. They jingled in rhythm with the music. Joia admired the way they moved in unison to the lively music. A man jumped onto the stage, and everyone gasped as his powerful jump seemed to fly right over the heads of the women on the stage. He landed and spun before jumping into the air again with his legs spread out perfectly parallel to the ground. He went to one of the women dancers and lifted her high into the air, spinning her as he did before catching her again.

Joia was astounded by the acrobatic feats of the dancers. It certainly wasn't anything like when they had festivals in the village. The villagers would dance in their own traditional dances. They had square dances, pair dances, and dances with long lines of people. They were fun ways to dance, but they did not possess the grace or energetic moves of the entertainers.

When the music ended, they finished their dance in a wave of color. Everyone broke into applause. The musicians played a kind of fanfare and suddenly, as if by magic, a tall man appeared in the center of the square. Several ladies cried out in surprise and even Joia was startled.

The man was wearing brown pants and brown boots. His shirt was made of the greenest cloth Joia had ever seen, with a matching green scarf tied to his head. His eyes, bluer than the sky, looked out across the crowd, bringing them to silence. He had a commanding presence.

But the most extraordinary thing about this man was the way he glowed with a soft, golden light. This was Edmund, the Entertainer. A true living Patron stood before Joia, and she was paralyzed by the realization.

For a heartbeat, his eyes caught Joia's and he held her trapped with his gaze. Then, with the sweep of one arm, he started to speak. His voice was deep and rhythmic. "Gather round and you will hear a story fit for all. A story of mystery and a journey. Come and hear destiny's call."

Joia felt a shiver run through her body. She was about to witness a Patron performing his trade.

When the story was done, Joia felt intense relief and yet a longing for the story to go on and on forever. The villagers clapped and cheered for the great Storyteller. Joia looked around at the people cheering for him. They had no idea that a Patron of the Trade Guilds was standing right here among them. To them, he was just an entertainer. Joia looked back at the man and marveled at his light. He bowed and moved off to the side. The musicians began to play again and the dancers danced away from the square. The show was over. The crowd of people began to break up and return to their homes. The musicians moved through the village once again, announcing to all there would be another performance that night.

"That was the most beautiful story I've ever heard," Ebba smiled, dreamily.

Joia could only agree. It had been a fantastic story with adventure and romance. "It truly was. That storyteller has always been one of my favorites."

Ebba nodded and then suddenly grabbed her by the arm. Joia," she whispered. "Look. It's Derry. He's talking to the tailor."

Joia looked and nodded with a grin. "So he is. Do you think he might be asking about wedding clothes or maybe a new cover for a wedding bed?"

Ebba, who had been staring at Derry, turned her head so fast, that Joia wondered that she didn't hurt herself. Ebba's mouth was open and her face beet red. Joia laughed. "Why don't you just go over and say hello?"

Ebba looked completely scandalized. "Only if you come with me."

Joia laughed. "No, you do it. Just go over and say hello. He would probably love the chance to talk to you without me there. Go on, now. I'll see you later." She turned, leaving Ebba, and began to walk away. She felt compelled to find the Patron Edmund and so started in the direction she had last seen him. She searched the crowd for a glowing light.

Just as Joia reached the other side of the square, the parade of entertainers came back across her path. They were still playing their lively music and Joia stopped to watch them and let them pass by. The storyteller was with them, and he and Joia caught each other's eye at the same moment like he had been looking for her as well. He stopped and waited for the rest of his company to move away before stepping up to her.

"Joia?" he asked.

"Yes."

"My name is Edmund, and I am the Patron of the Entertainers," his deep voice rang clear, but quietly.

Joia gave a small curtsey. "I am honored, sir."

"May we talk?"

Joia looked up and was momentarily transfixed by his gaze. "Um, yes. We can go to my home. Mother is there. I understand you have met my mother before."

"I have," Edmund replied. "Lead the way."

She turned and began to walk home. Edmund walked side by side with her and said nothing, but nodded his head kindly at the villagers as they passed them.

"My mother told me about how you met her when I was a baby," Joia started.

"I did," he answered. "She told you what I said?"

Joia nodded. "Will you explain it all to me?"

"Yes," he answered. "At least, as much as I can, for there are some things I don't quite understand myself."

"Will I be permitted to ask you questions?" she asked.

He looked down at her and nodded with a smile. "You will."

When they arrived at the bakery, Joia's father, Thomas was there. He looked up, ready to greet a customer, and then frowned when he saw Edmund.

"What can I do for you, Entertainer?" Thomas asked, his voice was not friendly.

"I've come to speak with your daughter, Joia," Edmund said, seemingly not bothered by Thomas's unfriendly tones.

"What could you possibly have to say to my daughter?" Thomas stepped forward, gripping his hands into fists.

"Father, please, let's go up and talk," Joia quietly said. They went up the stairs, Joia first, followed by Edmund, and Thomas, stomping as he came up last.

Liadan looked up to see the guest who had been invited into her home. She stood and dried her hands on her apron and gave a little curtsey to her guest. "Master Edmund, welcome back to our home."

"Thank you," he answered. "It's nice to be so welcomed."

"You know this man?" Thomas went to his wife, getting very close to her face.

"Yes. I have told you of his visits, remember?" she asked.

Thomas's expression went dark, and he turned back to Edmund, who seemed to be completely unbothered by the conversation. He was only looking at Joia and she, in turn, could only stare at him as well. He was glowing. This was no trick of the sun. Nothing else in this house glowed. The light radiated from him.

"I believe introductions are in order," Edmund said. "I am Edmund, the Entertainer."

"Thomas."

"It's an honor to meet you," Edmund said.

Liadan brought several cups to the table and poured hot tea from a kettle into each cup. Thomas and Liadan sat down at the table, across from Edmund. Joia and Edmund picked up their cups and sipped at the tea, but Thomas remained still, staring at Edmund as if his very glare could make the entertainer disappear.

Thomas was just starting to say something when the door opened and Ebba came in. Her expression went from happy wistfulness to surprise as she took in the scene of her parents sitting across the table from a stranger.

"This is my sister, Ebba," Joia said, making the introductions. "Ebba, this is Edmund, the Entertainer."

"I recognize you," Ebba said. "Joia and I were just in the square. We heard your story."

Edmund politely bowed his head. "I hope you enjoyed it."

"We did. Didn't we Joia?" Ebba said.

Joia nodded. "It was very good."

"Your praise honors me," Edmund gave Joia a gentle smile.

"Enough of this," Thomas said, "what have you come here for?"

"I've come to speak to Joia, and it is to her I will speak with now," Edmund said to a very stunned family. He turned to face Joia. "Do you know who I am?"

"You introduced yourself as Edmund the Patron of the Entertainers. Are you truly a Patron?"

"I am," he nodded. "But do you know what that means? Do you understand who the Patrons are?"

"Patrons were the first to learn the trades and teach them to others," Joia said. "But I thought Patrons were legends. I didn't know they were real."

"We are very real. Each trade guild has a Patron. And you are correct; we were the first to learn the trades, long ago. We taught our trades to others and so the trades have been passed on for three centuries now."

Joia looked at this Patron with wide eyes. Three centuries? Surely, he could not be three hundred years old. He certainly didn't look his age. He looked younger than her father, but not by too many years. Except for his eyes. They were bright and clear, but they seemed too old for his face. "Are you immortal?" she asked.

"Not quite. We Patrons live as long as our trades do."

"May I ask you another question?" she said quietly. He had been kind so far and she hoped he wouldn't be insulted by her lack of knowledge or constant pestering. Liadan had always told Joia she asked too many questions, but Edmund nodded his consent. "Are you really glowing, or is it my eyes?"

Edmund smiled and seemed very pleased by this. "They are both true. I do glow, but only your eyes see it."

"I don't understand," Joia said. She could see her family giving each other confused looks.

"Joia, those of us who are Patrons, glow with a golden light called the Light of the Guild, and everything that we create also has the same Light. However, only those blessed with the Light of the Guild are able to see the Light and this is where you are such a curiosity to me," Edmund said, looking at Joia.

"So, no one else sees the Light?" Joia asked. "What about the other entertainers?"

He shook his head. "The entertainers in my own camp, which whom I travel and perform, don't see the glow."

"But they are your tradesmen," Joia pointed out.

"But they do not possess the Light of the Guild, so they cannot see it. But you do, and this is very strange. You have the Light of the Guild, which means you glow as well, but only Patrons, like me, can see that."

"The Light of the Guild? I don't understand what that means," she told him.

Edmund's voice was quiet, but clear as a bell. "The Light of the Guild is a special power that each Patron holds. and our work contains the Light, but only those who possess the Light of the Guild can see the Light. That is the golden glow that you see."

Joia's head ached as she thought about everything Edmund had thus said. "This is all very interesting, but I still don't understand what it has to do with me. I'm not a tradesman and I don't glow."

"You can't see it on yourself, because you have always seen it on yourself," he answered.

Joia shook her head. "Why would I have this light? Do all people have the Light of the Guild before entering a trade?"

"No, they don't, which is what makes you so interesting." Edmund gave Joia a curious look. "Only those from the original guild have the Light. Only the ones that were taught by Athelstan, the Father of the Trades have this Light. There has never been anyone born with the Light, until you. You are quite unique."

"I just don't understand," Joia said.

"I have counseled with several of my fellow Patrons, and we have come to the conclusion that you have some sort of destiny with the trade guilds. It is time for you to meet with the other Patrons."

Joia was shocked. "My destiny?" She could hardly believe what she was hearing.

"Yes, Joia," Edmund said. "You have a purpose beyond this village. A destiny with the trades. You have been chosen by the Light and so you must go out and fulfill it."

"No!" Thomas cut in. "No, no, no." He stood up, pounding his fist on the table. "Joia will not be leaving home to go on some fool's quest to find some ridiculous light. She has no special light about her."

"Father's right," Joia said, looking sadly at Edmund again, "there's nothing special about me. I'm just Joia. Nothing more."

"No," Edmund's voice resonated in her ears, "you are Joia, born possessor of the Light of the Guild."

"But what does that mean? What am I to do?" Joia implored.

"You must leave here. Come with me and I will take you to meet the other Patrons."

"No!" Thomas shouted again.

Joia ignored her father's protest, keeping her eyes on Edmund. "Leave home? I couldn't do that. I wouldn't know how to start or where to go." She glanced at her parents. Her father was red with anger. Her mother had tears in her eyes.

"She will not leave home!" Thomas yelled.

"The choice is yours," Edmund's eyes never left Joia's face. "If you choose, you can come with me. We can travel to meet the other Patrons or go to Athelstan's castle. I am leaving tomorrow morning, along with the rest of my company of entertainers."

"I can't," Joia's voice cracked. She shook her head. "I can't leave my family."

Edmund laid his hand on Joia's shoulder and spoke quietly, "Joia, I think you must, but the choice is yours. I will not force you to go."

Her eyes filled with hot tears and for a moment, they looked at each other. Joia's breath caught in her chest. She knew what she needed to do, but how could she walk out that door?

"I leave tomorrow at sunrise." Edmund nodded once and turned to leave. "Thank you for the tea," he said to Liadan before walking out the door, closing it behind him.

Tears fell down Joia's face. Her mother came and put her arms around Joia's shoulders.

"Listen to me now, Joia," her father stood before her, his entire body shaking in rage. "You are not to go. I forbid it. You have no light. You have no mystical destiny. You will stay here and live a normal life."

"But I can see his Light," Joia hiccupped.

"No, you can't. There is no light!" Thomas roared at her. "Now, you forget about this ridiculous conversation. Get the idea out of your head. There is no Light and you're not going!" He stormed out, slamming the door behind him.

Joia began to cry. "What am I to do?" She looked at her sister and mother.

"Don't go," Ebba pleaded. "I don't want you to go."

Liadan hugged her daughter. She leaned in and whispered in Joia's ear, "The choice is yours."

CHAPTER FOUR

Joia's Choice

Joia lay in bed, long after Ebba had gone to sleep and thought about everything that had happened and everything that Edmund had told her. She held up her arm in the darkened house and looked at it. She didn't see any kind of light about her, but she could not deny that Edmund did, and he said that she did too. What was she to do? If she left and went with Edmund, she might never see her family again. She might never see Hakon again. She squeezed her eyes tightly closed and felt more hot tears running down her face.

She had made her choice already, back before Edmund had even left her home, but now, she wondered if she was strong enough to do it. She would need to leave while it was still dark. Her father and brother woke early and if they got up first, Joia would never be able to sneak out. She needed to leave now. In the distance, she heard a horn call. It had to be the entertainers, packing up to leave. Joia sat up. It was now or never.

Carefully, she climbed out of bed. She moved quietly, following the plan she had set in her head. First, she needed to pack.

She pulled a large piece of linen cloth out from under her bed and laid it flat on the floor. She placed a grey underdress and her favorite blue tunic, stockings, a long linen head covering, leather ties for her hair, a needle, a bundle of clean rags, and a roll of wool thread; everything she could think of that she might need on a journey. She changed from her night dress into her other daily dress, a white woolen underdress with a red over-tunic. She placed the night dress into her bundle and tied it up.

As she moved away from her bed, she saw a golden light glowing from her sewing basket. Curious, she went to it and pulled out a section of cloth that she had recently purchased. Why did it glow? It had never glowed before. She was sure of that. She would ask Edmund, so she tucked the cloth into her bundle and went to the door that would take her out of her home and down to the bakery. The fire in the hearth was still glowing with orange embers, casting a little bit of light in the room.

Joia looked around the room, taking in every detail she could. She had lived here her entire life and knew the room's every nook and cranny. With a silent goodbye, she opened the door and avoided the third step down, which squeaked loudly when stepped on. Joia wanted to avoid any noise that might wake her father.

Quietly, she tip-toed down the stairs to the bakery. Grabbing a loaf of day-old bread, she unbolted the door and went outside. A summer breeze blew. Her skirts quietly swished in the wind while her hair whipped about her face. The trees moved in the wind as if to wave goodbye. Joia took in a deep breath and pushed away the tears that were building. She wondered if she would ever see her home again.

She took a few steps away when the sound of the door closing behind her startled her and Joia turned to find her mother standing in her nightdress with a shawl pulled tightly around her shoulders.

"You are leaving then?"

Her mother's hair, which was usually pulled up into a bun on the back of her head, was flowing loose around her face. Joia couldn't remember seeing her mother like this. Overcome with emotion, Joia threw her arms around her mother's shoulders. Tears began to flow again from her eyes. "Yes."

They hugged tightly and silently for several moments before the younger woman stepped back. Liadan held Joia's hands in her own. "It's all right. You must do this."

"But Mother, how can I leave you? How can I leave my home?"

"When I married your father, I had to leave my home village of Whitebury and my family. I was your age and had to come to a place I had never been and marry a man I had never met. I was very scared, but I was also very excited. If I had never been brave enough to leave my home, I wouldn't have married your father. I wouldn't have had you children. I have loved living in Erthenhorn. But I never could have had all of this if I hadn't left home."

"I suppose so," Joia said, not having thought of that before.

Liadan cupped Joia's cheeks in her hands. "You are like I was, never quite content to just stay at home. You are ready for this adventure." Liadan hugged Joia again. "You're strong and I have no doubt you will find what you are looking for and perhaps, once you have, you can return to us."

"Oh, Mother," Joia hugged her again, thankful that her mother supported her and encouraged her in this. "What about father? And David and Ebba?"

"I will explain it to them. They'll understand. Oh Joia, I love you so much."

Joia didn't want to let go of her mother. It was too much for her to bear. "I love you, too."

Finally, Liadan let go of her. "Hurry now, your father will be up soon."

Joia hugged her bundle to her chest, took one last look at her mother, then turned around and walked down the street, into the village. She would take the most direct path through the town square, then to the main street that led out of the village. Joia figured the entertainers were probably camped just outside the village boundaries.

Erthenhorn was dark and quiet and almost unrecognizable to the busy, noisy village that it was during the day. She crossed into the square and stopped to look at the wall where she and Hakon sat nearly every day to talk. She would miss Hakon. What would he think of her when this evening, he would wait for her, and she would never show up? Would Ebba go and find him and tell him? She hoped so and she hoped he wouldn't be too angry with her.

Joia nearly turned around. She would go home and forget about all this, but just as she did, she caught a glimpse of a golden light in the trees. The golden Light of the Guild. She knew in her heart that she had to find out what it meant.

With determination, she started walking again, turning to walk down the main road that led out of Erthenhorn. She had just made that turn when she heard someone walking towards her. Joia quickly moved into the dark shadows of a house and flattened herself against the wall. She held her breath as a tall figure walked around the corner and in her direction. She hoped it was Edmund coming to meet her, but instead, she saw that it was

Hakon. She felt her heart jump. What was he doing out in the village this early in the morning?

Hakon walked past her without seeing her, but he was looking back and forth like he was looking for something. Or someone. She waited until he had gone around the next corner before she moved again. Now that she was resigned to go, Joia knew she had to move on and get as far away from the village as possible. If she didn't go now, she never would.

She had almost reached the edge of town when she heard footsteps again. Joia walked faster and the footsteps behind her moved faster as well. She panicked and began to run. The footsteps behind her started to run, too. Joia ran for the woods, ducking behind trees. She could see the campfires of the entertainers' camp and ran for those, but just before she could reach the camp, her follower caught up with her and grabbed her.

She flailed her arms, desperately trying to get loose.

"Joia? Is that you?" A familiar voice spoke.

Joia stopped flailing and looked at the man who had grabbed her. "Hakon!" Joia flung her arms around him and held him tight.

"What are you doing?" he asked.

How could she explain this to him? "I'm leaving. I have to go." She couldn't look him in the face. "Really, I have a very good reason to go."

"Joia, have you lost your mind?"

Joia pulled away from him and started for the camp. Hakon followed, taking her by the hand and pulling. "Stop, Joia, please."

Joia stopped and turned to face him.

"Why are you leaving?"

"I don't know how to explain this, but I have to go. My family knows and supports me," she said. It was partially true. Only her mother knew, but she didn't feel like explaining. She knew that if she tried, she would talk herself out of it. "I'm sorry, Hakon, but I must go."

She walked into the camp, and everyone stopped to look at the intruders. A man stepped up to them and stopped them.

"What are you doing here?" he asked.

"Good question," Hakon said, still pulling at Joia's elbow.

"I'm here to see Edmund. He invited me," Joia said.

The man laughed. "Edmund sent for you? Why?"

"Please, if I can just speak with Edmund, he will explain," she said. She looked around and saw his golden Light. "There he is, please, let me speak with him."

"She is welcomed," Edmund said, approaching them.

"And the boy?" the entertainer asked.

Edmund looked at Hakon for several long moments before nodding. "Him as well."

The entertainer stepped aside with a surprised look, but no one gave them any more trouble. They reached Edmund's wagon and he turned to her.

"Are you ready?" he asked.

Joia held up her bundle and nodded. Edmund whistled like a bird, then he stooped down and rolled up what looked like a flattened tent.

Behind her, Joia heard more movement from the camp. She turned to look and saw the last of the camp's possessions being thrown into wagons. Several men were hitching up horses to the wagons.

"The second to last whistle," Edmund explained. "We roll out very soon." He finished rolling his tent, picked it up, and tossed it into the back of his wagon. He said no more and began untying a smoky grey horse from a tree and hitching it to his wagon.

Joia cradled her bundle and turned to Hakon. He took her by the shoulder and led her a few steps away from where Edmund was working. "Why are you running away with the entertainers? You can't sing or play an instrument."

Joia was a little offended. "I might not play an instrument, but I sing decently enough."

"You don't have to leave home to sing," he said.

"I'm not running away to become an entertainer, I promise," she said.

"I can't let you do this," he said, taking her by the elbow again. His brow was furrowed in confusion and concern as she pulled gently at her elbow and felt her resistance.

"Hakon, I have to. I can't explain why, but I have to go," she felt tears in her eyes again, but she couldn't cry. Not in front of Hakon and Edmund.

A shocked expression passed over Hakon's features. "No, Joia, please tell me it's not true. You're running away with an entertainer? Do you love him? Or did your father promise you to him? You haven't… He didn't…" Hakon took a step back and stared at Edmund.

"No! Of course not," Joia cried out, pulling her elbow from his grasp. She was not leaving to marry Edmund and she was certainly not leaving in shame because she had fallen with child. "It's nothing like that at all. I promise you, it's not. Hakon, I don't have time to explain. I just have to go."

"Then I'm coming with you," Hakon said, his eyes fixed on her.

"You can't."

"And why not?" Hakon demanded. "Because you are truly in love with him?"

"No. That's not it. This has nothing to do with love. I just," she sighed. "I see a special golden light on Edmund, and he can see it too on me. I have to go find out why I can see this light." It was the best she could do.

"Have you taken leave of all your senses, Joia? There's no light. I can't let you go. I don't trust these people," he looked over her shoulder at Edmund and whispered furiously at her, "I'm not leaving you alone with them."

Edmund came around from the other side of his horse and tightened the harnesses. He turned and looked at Hakon. "Who are you and why have you come here with Joia?"

"I'm Hakon."

"Do you have a trade, Hakon?"

"I am a thatcher. I am in the status of a journeyman, working with my father, who is a master in the thatching guild," Hakon answered.

"Do you dedicate your work to Thek?" Edmund asked.

Hakon nodded, "Every day, sir."

Edmund's eyes held Hakon's for a moment. Joia knew what it was like to have Edmund's ancient eyes gazing upon you. It could be quite unnerving. "Thatching is a good trade. Thek is a good man," Edmund said. "You're quite right, you can't let Joia go alone. You will accompany her." It wasn't a request.

"Wait, what?" Hakon asked, but Edmund was climbing onto his wagon. He whistled again and this time, the whistle was met by others whistling back. It was time to go.

Joia didn't know what to do. Edmund looked down at her from the wagon seat, "Quick girl, throw your bundle into the wagon and climb up next to me."

Joia started toward the wagon, but Hakon grabbed her hand. "No, you are staying here, where you belong."

"I can't Hakon. Come with me and I'll try and explain this better, but there isn't time now." Joia pulled her hand away from Hakon's and climbed onto the wagon. She sat next to Edmund and held her bundle tight to her chest.

"Joia, this is madness!" Hakon yelled at her.

"Then come with her," Edmund's calm, deep voice said. "Come with us and you will learn why Joia must go. If you decide to return to Erthenhorn, you will only be a day's walk away, but if you don't come, you will never understand. The choice is yours. Joia has already made hers." Edmund snapped the reins on the back of his horse and the wagon moved forward. He turned the horse towards the road and the other wagons fell in behind him, forming a long, single line of creaking wagons.

Joia closed her eyes. The tears were rolling down her cheeks again. She was leaving home and headed into the unknown. After several moments, she heard someone running alongside the wagons. She looked back and saw Hakon running to her. He caught up with them and hopped onto Edmund's wagon. Hakon sat for a few moments, catching his breath. Joia smiled. She knew that if she had Hakon by her side, she would be able to face anything.

After several moments, Hakon turned to her, "Now, tell me what this is all about."

CHAPTER FIVE

The Journey Begins

"I think we need to start at the beginning," Edmund said, sitting up straight on the wagon bench. "I will tell you a story. Listen carefully." His voice was still quiet, but it was clear, and each word rang in her ears.

"A long time ago, there was a man named Athelstan. He was very wise and knew all the trades. His services were needed by so many that he couldn't do all the work required of him. He grew weary of the endless work and worried that when he died, all the knowledge would die as well. Athelstan knew that he must share his knowledge of the trades. He found men and women who were clever, talented, and willing to learn. He began to teach them. For many years, they worked in secret at Athelstan's family castle as he taught all he knew to those he had chosen as his apprentices. As his life came closer to its end, Athelstan declared them masters of their trades. He promised them each a special, magical gift, unique to each Patron. They were given one year to discover their gift and on a prearranged date, they were to gather together again to present Athelstan with their greatest work.

"During that year, each of them worked to realize their special gifts and on the appointed date, they gathered together. Each master presented their gift to Athelstan. He was pleased with their work and as a final instruction, he told them that the skills they had learned must be passed on to others so that the trades could never die away. However, the special gifts that each had received were to remain in their power only. Any normal man could benefit from these gifts if they were worthy to receive them, but the actual power was to never be passed on. They agreed and a golden light fell upon the circle of trade masters. From that point on, the masters, who became known as the Patrons, glowed and all work created by them glowed, but only those who were in that circle were able to see the Light. The Trade Guilds were formed, and each Patron went out into the world to teach his trade."

"What happened to Athelstan?" Joia asked.

"He died that very night."

Joia gasped, but Edmund continued with his story.

"And so, for three hundred years, this is how it has been. Until seventeen years ago, when I traveled to this village and I saw for the first time, someone new who possessed the Light. Someone who had not been among that original group of trade masters so very long ago. That person, of course, was you, Joia. You were just a tiny baby in your mother's arms, but you glowed with the light of Athelstan. The Light of the Guild."

"So, why do I have this Light of the Guild?"

Edmund turned and studied Joia in the darkness. "I don't know. But, as soon as I saw you, I called together as many of the Patrons as I could find, which sadly, was only four of us. You see, Joia, over the hundreds of years we have journeyed to teach our trade and have lost contact with each other. Many of the Patrons have established permanent homes, never leaving them and working constantly in their trade. Due to the nature of my trade, I travel and have been traveling for hundreds of years. I thought I had seen everything there was to see in this world until I saw you. Those Patrons I could find gathered at Athelstan's castle to discuss you. We do not know your purpose, but I was appointed to check on you regularly, which I have done. Now, I believe the time has come for you to discover your destiny with the Guild."

"But all this is ludicrous," Hakon said. "Joia and I have been friends since we were very young children. I've never seen this Light you speak of."

"As I said, only those who are Patrons have the Light and can see the Light. No one among my tradesmen can see the Light," Edmund explained.

"Do your tradesmen know who you are?" Joia asked.

"Of course," Edmund explained. "I do not hide the fact that I am a Patron. It is not a secret. But it is not something that I tend to share with others outside of my entertainers."

"I never really thought of Patrons as being a person like Hakon and I are people," Joia said.

"We are real. And, we have all the same emotions and needs that everyone else has. I need food and sleep, just as you do. The difference is that I do not age with the passing of time," Edmund said.

They were quiet for a while and Joia considered what it would be like to be a Patron and never grow old, which would be nice, but at the same time, it would be terrible to watch others grow old and die when you stayed young. She couldn't imagine what that would be like.

"Am I going to stop aging?" Joia asked.

"To be honest, I'm not sure," Edmund said. "I was as you see me when Athelstan's Light descended upon me. I had already lived a life and grown to this age. The same is true with the other Patrons. No one has ever been born with the Light, so we don't know. But you have aged thus far, so I can only assume that you will continue to do so."

Joia wasn't sure how she felt about that. It was disappointing to think that she would age and die, but then, could she live a life, where she continued to be seventeen forever and watch Hakon grow old? She did not want that.

They had passed many miles before the sun started to rise and light their way. Edmund extinguished the lantern that hung from the front of his wagon. Joia was cold in the early morning and pulled the long piece of linen cloth from her bundle. It was not glowing anymore. She wrapped it around her shoulders.

"Edmund, when I was leaving this morning and packing my bundle, this piece of cloth was glowing with the Light, but it's not anymore."

He looked at it and took a corner of the cloth in his fingers. He rubbed at it for several moments and let it fall back around her shoulder. "It does not glow now, but I have found, over the years, that the Light will appear in places that it needs to appear. It might have been the Light's way of telling you to bring this cloth."

"Do you really see a light?" Hakon asked.

"I do," she said. "That reminds me of another recent experience. At the Erthenhorn weaver's shop, there is a bit of cloth. It glows."

"Then your weaver has a bit of cloth woven by Sidonia herself," Edmund explained.

"But my father doesn't have an item from his Patron. Does that mean that when they dedicate their day, is it not accepted by Ferran?"

"Of course it is," Edmund said. "The important thing is that they dedicate their work. When they do, their Patron hears." He snapped the reins gently. The horse trotted a few steps before falling back into a rhythmic walk. "For your weaver, to have a bit of her Patron's work is very special indeed."

The sun rose, promising to be a hot day. Several wagons behind, a group of people had begun to sing. They kept up a constant stream of song and music throughout the entire morning. It had been a very pleasant journey, thus far. She wasn't cold anymore, so moved her shawl from her shoulders and draped it over her head instead to keep the sun from burning her head.

Telling Hakon her story and listening to the music from the entertainers had helped Joia feel more excited about the venture and not miss her family quite so much.

At midday, the traveling group stopped in a shaded area near a stream. The drivers watered the horses, and everyone got out to stretch their legs. As soon as the horses had drunk their fill of cool water from the river, the travelers began their journey again. The afternoon journey was quieter and hotter with the summer sun beating down on their heads. Joia pulled out the loaf of bread she had gotten from the bakery that morning and tore off three chunks, offering pieces to Edmund and Hakon, who gratefully accepted.

When they finally stopped again, it was late afternoon. Joia was hungry and her body ached from sitting in the rocking wagon all day. There had been little conversation between Edmund, Hakon, and herself all afternoon. Edmund often hummed quietly and Hakon looked to be in deep thought. The frown on his face never went away. Joia sat between them, unsure what to say or do.

As soon as the wagons stopped, members of the group began hopping out, immediately setting to work on various tasks. The horses were unhitched from the wagons and taken to be watered and fed. A fire seemed to spring up from out of nowhere and several people set up a grill over the fire and pots of water were soon bubbling.

Hakon helped Joia down from the wagon and Edmund instructed them to help gather firewood.

"It's hard to believe that we were in our village this morning," Hakon said, gathering wood into his arms.

"I know. It seems so long ago now. Can I ask you, why were you out so early this morning, Hakon?" She had been wanting to know all day what Hakon had been doing walking through the village before sunrise.

"It was the oddest thing, but I was asleep in my bed, and I heard a voice call to me. I thought it was my father. I sat up and listened. I couldn't hear him well, so I began to follow his voice. It led me out of the house and down the street. I must have been half asleep not to realize how odd it was that I could hear his voice, but it was leading me further away from the house. I was walking and getting closer to the voice when I saw you walking towards the edge of the village." He sighed and ran a hand over his face. "I've been thinking about that voice all afternoon. It obviously wasn't my father. I believe the voice wanted me to find you." Hakon had long since stopped picking up wood.

Joia stood close to him, "I believe the voice wanted you to find me, too, but whose voice was it?"

"I don't know," Hakon answered.

"Perhaps we should tell Edmund. Maybe he would know." Joia laid a hand on Hakon's arm. He nodded and they went back to the camp and dropped their loads of wood into the pile near the fire. Edmund was nowhere to be seen, so Hakon went back out to collect more firewood.

Joia watched a young woman stirring one of the large pots that was bubbling over the fire. "It smells wonderful," she said to the woman.

"It will be ready to eat soon," the woman replied.

"How did you get the fire going so quickly? It seemed that as soon as we arrived, the fire was ablaze," Joia asked.

The woman tossed some green herbs into the pot. "We carry the fire with us. My husband, Wendell, is the keeper of the fire for the camp. He carries hot coals when we travel and never lets them die. That way, when we stop for the night, we can have a good fire in any weather."

"I see," said Joia.

"It's a very important job. Everyone relies on him." The woman poked at the fire and stirred the bubbling liquid in the pot. She looked over at Joia and quickly looked back to the pot. "We've been talking today, some of the others and Wendell and me, and we are wondering, why are you and that man traveling with us?"

Joia wasn't sure how to answer. Did she dare tell the young woman the whole truth?

"I'm Joia and my friend is Hakon. We've come along with Edmund."

If the woman trusted Joia at all, she trusted her less after Joia's unhelpful answer. "Are you an entertainer?"

"No."

"Then what does Edmund need the two of you for?"

Joia opened her mouth to answer but didn't know what to say. How was she to explain this to anyone when she didn't understand it all herself.

"An important job," Edmund's deep voice answered. He walked up behind Joia and laid his hand on her shoulder. "I have invited Joia to travel with me for a while because she has an important job to do. That should be enough for you, Elin."

The young woman lowered her head, "Forgive me, Edmund."

Edmund smiled. He went to the young woman and lifted her chin with his hand. "Of course, Elin. I promise to explain everything tonight." He lifted his voice for everyone to hear,

"Tonight, we will sing, and I will tell a story."

Everyone in the camp cheered at Edmund's proclamation. He went back to his wagon and disappeared behind it. Hakon was still gathering wood. Joia walked up to Elin. The young woman didn't look at Joia as she approached but made herself busier with the food in the pot.

"Can I help you, Elin?" Joia asked.

The young woman shook her head, "No, thank you. There is nothing left to do. It is time to call the camp to eat." The young woman produced a small bell from her apron pocket, and she tapped it three times with her large metal stirring spoon. The bell produced a clear sound and the tones rang through the camp. Moments later, everyone began to gather around the fire. Joia stepped back and watched the group of people.

They stood around the fire, excited, eager, and holding wooden bowls in their hands. She could see they were ready to eat, but they waited. Edmund made his way through the crowd and held out his bowl. Elin filled it with the stew from the pot.

Edmund sipped at the food in his bowl. "It is excellent. Thank you, Elin." He stepped away from the fire and as soon as he did, the rest of the group held out their bowls and Elin began to ladle stew into each one. Joia stepped back, away from the crowd and Hakon joined her after dropping off another armful of firewood. They didn't have bowls and being uninvited guests, she suspected, no one wanted to share their food with two strangers.

After everyone had been served, Joia and Hakon still stood awkwardly away from everyone else. "I guess I'll go get the rest of my bread," she said. "But if that is our only food, it's not going to last us much longer."

"Then let's not waste it," Hakon said. "We had some not long ago. We can save the rest for tomorrow."

Joia sighed. Her stomach growled. "I wish I had brought more."

Hakon nodded. "We can go back and sit near Edmund's wagon." He took her by the elbow and started to back away. Everyone ignored them. They sat down on the ground, close together, and tried not to watch everyone else eating.

Joia lowered her head down to hide the tears that were forming again. What had she been thinking, coming on this trip? She was completely unprepared, and Hakon, even less so, because he had nothing but the clothes on his back.

She felt him stiffen next to her. "Joia," he whispered, and Joia looked up to see Elin, the cook, walking their way, holding two bowls.

She held out the bowls. "I saw that you didn't get any and I wanted to make sure you ate." Elin held out the two bowls, full of steaming stew.

"Are you sure it's allowed?" Joia asked, looking around at everyone else, who was ignoring them.

"I'm sure," she said. "You are Edmund's special guests. I don't think he would want you to go hungry."

They reached out to take the bowls. "Thank you," Joia said. She held the bowl to her lips and took a sip at the hot liquid. "It's wonderful," she looked at Elin, who smiled.

"Will you come and sit with Wendell and me?" Elin asked, looking shy and embarrassed.

Hakon and Joia followed Elin back to the campfire. Elin ladled up a bowl of the stew and sat down next to a man with flaming red hair.

"This is my husband, Wendell."

"It's good to meet you," Joia said. "I'm Joia and this is Hakon."

Wendell looked the visitors up and down for several moments. "Are you entertainers?" he asked.

"No, we're not," Joia answered. "But I know that you are. I remember seeing you perform yesterday."

He nodded, looking a little more pleased. "How long have the two of you been married?"

Joia and Hakon looked at each other in surprise and at the same time said, "No, no, no. We're not married."

"We're friends," Joia added.

Now Elin and Wendell looked at each other in surprise. Wendell cleared his throat. "Elin and I've been married for two years."

"That's wonderful," Joia said. "Have you always been a part of this company?" Wendell nodded, but Elin shook her head.

"I'm from a village far to the south, near the sea. Since marrying Wendell, I've gotten to travel with the company and become their cook."

Elin didn't seem much older than Joia, perhaps Ebba's age. Joia asked, "Are all meals served like this? As a camp?"

"Always dinner," she said, "and in the mornings, we eat whatever is left of the stew before heading out."

To Joia, that sounded like a hungry life. She would miss her porridge and ham in the morning. Joia finished her stew. She thanked Elin for the food. She then gathered Hakon's and Elin's bowls and took them to the river to be washed.

She returned the clean bowls to Elin and then went to find Hakon. He was sitting alone, twirling his knife in his fingers as he inspected the blade. She sat next to him and watched.

"My father gave me this," he said. "When I first started my apprenticeship with him."

"It seems to be a fine blade," Joia told him, not really sure what to say.

Hakon looked at the knife a moment longer, running his fingers along the flat side of the blade, and then he placed it back into its sheath that hung at his belt.

"I didn't come very well prepared for a trip like this," he said, looking out at the camp. "I have nothing except the clothes on my back and this knife."

Joia had not come with much more, but she had been able to pack a few things. "We'll figure something out," she said.

They sat together, watching the company as they went about with various activities. Many were setting up tents and arranging sleeping areas. A few had pulled out instruments and were inspecting them or rubbing them down with an oilcloth. She hadn't seen Edmund since the stew was served and she hoped that he had not abandoned her, but she figured he wouldn't leave without his wagon, so she felt a little safer staying close to it.

"Where are we to sleep?" Hakon asked.

"I don't know. I hadn't really thought of that," Joia admitted. "Perhaps I had better ask Edmund."

Just as she stood to go find him, Edmund came around another wagon and started towards them.

"I trust you ate well," Edmund said.

"We did, thank you," Joia answered.

Edmund reached into the back of his wagon and pulled out a large canvas bundle. He unrolled it and held out a corner to Hakon. "There are hooks all around the wagon," Edmund explained, place that loop into the first hook, then continue around."

Hakon did and Joia watched with interest as the base of the wagon became completely surrounded by the canvas, creating a small room. There was a flap that opened on one side and Edmund picked up a bedroll and tossed it in.

"Where are we to sleep tonight, Edmund?" Joia asked timidly.

"Right here of course."

"But this is your tent," she said.

"Yes, but don't worry, I've got extra bedrolls in the back of the wagon. Grab one and pick out your spot."

"I can't share a tent with you," Joia pointed out.

Edmund looked at her with a hint of a smile. "It's not just me you're sharing the tent with. There's Hakon too. Get your things, unless you'd rather sleep on the ground in the open.

"But I can't," Joia started.

"Did you bring your own tent?" Edmund asked.

"Well, no, I didn't."

"You can sleep outside, under the stars, or in my tent, but I'm afraid those are your only options. You didn't bring a tent, my wagon isn't large enough to sleep in unless I remove all my belongings, and I'd rather not do that, so you either sleep outside or in the tent." Edmund tossed in a second bedroll.

Joia looked to Hakon. He shrugged his shoulders. "I don't think we have much of a choice. If I had known I was coming along on this harebrained trip, I would have been better prepared."

"Harebrained trip?" Joia asked, offended that Hakon would think her destiny with the Guild as harebrained.

"Yes," Hakon turned to Joia, "The purpose of this quest is honorable enough, but the lack of preparation you or I have made for this journey is foolhardy and until we come up with something better, I think we have no choice but to accept Edmund's hospitality."

"A wise choice," Edmund said. "Now get your things and try not to snore."

The sun had set by the time Joia finished wrestling with her mind's debate on propriety versus necessity and finally agreed to put her bedroll into the tent with the others. Once her bedroll was in place, she went back to the campfire and found Hakon sitting on a log near the fire. She sat down next to him but was still upset with him for calling her journey harebrained.

Soon others began to join them around the fire. They talked and played their instruments. Several songs were sung. Edmund walked over and stood before the group. Immediately the noise died away. All eyes were on the tall storyteller.

"I know each of you have wondered about our guests. I will tell you who they are and why they are here. The young lady is Joia, daughter of Thomas the Baker, from the village of Erthenhorn. I first met her seventeen years ago when she was just a small baby. I noticed something different about her. She had an aura that is unique to only the trade Patrons. Now she has come of age for the life she is destined to lead. The young man who travels with Joia is Hakon, a thatcher." Everyone looked at Joia and Hakon. Some timid hands were raised in greeting.

Edmund called out in his clear voice, "Do you know your Guild Patron my good people?"

Everyone cheered and called out Edmund's name. He smiled and held out his hand. It immediately grew quiet.

"You are among the few to have personally met your Patron and work alongside him. Most tradesmen never know their Patrons and are not sure that the Patrons really exist, but they dedicate their work each day in the traditions they were taught and out of respect for their masters. Many Patrons never leave their homes while others, like me, travel the wide world. I have seen many things and met many people over my lifetime, but I never saw anything like I saw seventeen years ago when I met this child."

There was some quiet murmuring and Joia squirmed a bit at the feeling of so many eyes looking at her.

Edmund held out a hand and pointed at Joia. "She has a destiny among the Guild Patrons, and it must begin with a journey. That is why Joia travels with us. I will help her start that journey and her companion will protect her."

Edmund turned to a man sitting behind the group. He nodded his head and immediately the man began to play a lute and sing a song. The song retold the story that Edmund had just told. Joia realized that the man had no time to make up the words he sang, for he had only heard the story himself, but there he was, singing a beautiful song about Joia and her destiny with the Guild Patrons.

Hakon scooted next to her. "I'm sorry about earlier. I'm," he sat for a moment and ran his fingers through his hair, "frustrated at myself, I guess. I wish you had told me you were going to do this."

"When I saw you last, I had no idea myself. The entertainers arrived and Edmund came to speak with me. It was all a surprise," she said.

"He just pops up out of nowhere, tells you that you have some special light, and you believe him and leave home with him?" Hakon asked.

"There's a little more to it than that, but essentially, yes," she said, realizing that maybe Hakon was right. This was a harebrained plan. Edmund was practically a stranger and she had just accepted him and left with him.

Hakon sighed. "This is unbelievable. And you came with nearly nothing and I came with nothing. Now, we must share a tent with each other and someone we hardly know."

"I know," she said. "It is ludicrous, as you said, and yes, maybe harebrained, but what's done is done. You can go back home tomorrow. On foot, it might take you more than a day of travel, but we aren't so far from Erthenhorn that you can't return home."

"You want me to leave?" Hakon asked.

"No," she quickly said. "I don't. To be honest, I'm scared because I have no idea what I'm doing or what to expect. I'm putting all my faith and trust into a near stranger. Having you here is comforting. But if you want to go home, I won't blame you."

Hakon was quiet for a long time and Joia just watched as the camp sang songs together. A few couples performed a dance they were working on. Friends gave them suggestions and they practiced a few steps over and over.

"I never considered how much practice needed to go into those dances," Joia said.

"This is their trade," Hakon shrugged. "To be good at any trade, it requires time and practice."

"Yes, I know, but, oh, I don't know. Entertaining, as a trade, isn't the same as say, a blacksmith or a thatcher," Joia said.

"No, not the same, but they still require practice. If you and I were to attempt to learn a dance or a song, it would take us much, much longer to learn than one of those couples who are dancing now. We could practice a dozen times and not be nearly as good as they are after two practices. They are used to dancing. They know how to move and how to memorize the steps. You and I are not trained to learn like that. But if they and I were given a roof to thatch, I am confident that I could do most of the roof in the time it would take them to do a small section. I'm trained. They are not."

Joia nodded. "That makes sense," she said and was embarrassed because she could not perform any trade.

As the fire died down, families started to head to bed in their wagons or tents. Joia yawned. She had not slept at all the night before and today had been a long, exciting, and scary day. She was very tired, but also very nervous about going to bed.

Hakon came over to her after she had unsuccessfully tried to hide a yawn. "Come on, Joia. Let's go to bed. I don't know where Edmund is and right now, I'm too tired to care."

Joia looked up and saw Edmund right away. He was easy for her to spot with the golden Light shining around him. "He's right over there, talking to that big man."

Hakon looked around. "How did you find him so quickly?"

She yawned again. "It's the Light. In my eyes, he's glowing and it's easy to spot him in the darkness."

Hakon shook his head. "Again, with the light," he sighed. "I'm headed to bed."

"I'm going to use the privy and then I'll be there," Joia said, standing and going to the area that had been designated the lady's area for bodily business. Joia was used to using a chamber pot. This squatting over a hole in the ground was awful.

After finishing there, she headed to the tent. "Hakon?" she asked as she reached the door.

"Come on in, Joia," he said.

She knelt and crawled in. Hakon was lying out in the middle of the three bedrolls. Edmunds was on Hakon's left and Joia's was on his right. She moved to her bedroll, sat down, and removed her shoes. She remembered that Derry was going to resole them and she wondered what he would do when he found out that Ebba's sister had gone missing with the entertainers. Would he still want to court Ebba? The very idea that Ebba might suffer disgrace because of Joia's choice, made Joia feel sick.

What was done, was done and Joia could not change it, and she realized that she would not change it. As scary as this was, to be away from Erthenhorn and staying with strangers in an entertainer's camp, she was also very aware of her feelings of peace at the decision. It didn't make sense.

She pulled the blanket around her and lay down. It was very dark in the tent and only a muted orange glow from the campfire in the center of camp provided her with any light. She felt for the bundle she had brought and made sure it was close to her.

She shifted, trying to get comfortable.

"I don't know how I'll ever get to sleep," Hakon whispered.

"I don't know either," she said, feeling something small and hard under her shoulder. She reached between herself and the ground and found the offending pebble. She missed her bed. She missed the yeasty aroma of her home over the bakery. She missed the gentle breathing of her sister as she slept. She missed the warmth of her home. Doubt crept in where moments before she had been at peace. Had she done the right thing in leaving?

Joia didn't know when she fell asleep, but when she woke, it was to the sound of a horn. She sat up so fast that her head hit the side of the tent.

"Calm Joia," Edmund's deep voice sleepily said. "It is the call to wake up and get ready to move out."

"Why do you leave so early?" Hakon asked.

"There is much to do and many miles to travel," Edmund said, sitting up and rubbing at his eyes. "Pack up your bedrolls and put them into the back of the wagon." He put on his shoes and crawled out from under the wagon. Immediately, the canvas surrounding the tent began to fall away as Edmund unhooked it from the wagon.

Joia sat up with a shiver. The early morning air was chilly. "I can't believe I managed to get some sleep last night," she said.

"It wasn't long, though," Hakon said, rubbing at his own eyes and face.

She slipped on her shoes and then rolled her sleeping blanket into a neat bundle, which she tied closed with a long piece of string.

Joia climbed out of the tent and tossed the roll into the open back of Edmund's wagon before placing her bundle in the wagon behind the bench where they would be sitting later. Then it was back to the women's privy area.

The camp was full of the sounds of activity, but eerily quiet after last night's noise-filled campfire with singing, laughter, and the entire company of entertainers talking to one another. Now, it was just quiet movement as they got ready for the day's journey.

Edmund brought his horse around to the front of the wagon and started to hitch it to the wagon. "Hakon," he began, "have you decided what to do? Are you going to accompany Joia on her journey?"

"I have. I don't like leaving her alone with a bunch of strangers, and only you to share a tent with," Hakon answered.

"Good." Edmund walked away back to his wagon and hopped in.

Joia stared at Hakon for several moments, conflicted because she felt comforted by his staying with her and a little disappointed because of his reason. She had hoped he would want to stay with her because he liked being with her. She had always felt that their visits with each other at the end of the day were much too short. Now, they could be together all day, but Hakon didn't seem very happy about it. Embarrassed that he was staying because he didn't feel he could trust her, she turned back to the wagon, ready to get in.

"It's not that I don't trust you." Hakon followed her. "It's them," he pointed over his shoulder.

"I'm glad you feel you can trust me," she said, trying to take comfort in his concern. She climbed into the wagon, not needing help anymore to get up, and waited next to Edmund. She missed not having any personal space anymore. At home, she had been free to go where she wanted, so long as she was done with her chores. Now she sat all day in between Edmund and Hakon and couldn't go anywhere on her own.

The whistle to signal they were headed out soon sounded. Hakon climbed in beside Joia. She tried to make herself small, not touching either one of them with her shoulders. Edmund didn't seem to care if he was on this journey with Joia or not and Hakon was most assuredly not happy. She wondered if there was anything she could do to make Edmund and Hakon happier about being stuck with her, but the rocking movement of the wagon, lulled Joia into asleep, sitting up, in between Edmund and Hakon.

When she woke, the morning sky was lighter. The sun was nearly ready to peek over the horizon. Not that they would see it for a while. Not on the road through this dense forest.

"Where are the entertainers going next?" Joia asked.

"To Whitebury," Edmund answered. "It is another two days of journey before they reach there."

Joia was excited to see another village. She wondered if it would be anything like Erthenhorn. The company stopped mid-morning to let their horses rest for a bit. Joia hopped off the wagon and walked around stretching her stiff legs. She found Elin passing out some wafers of food to everyone and she gave one to Joia.

"A little morning meal," she explained. "Do you want to ride with Wendell and me for a while?" she asked. "We'd enjoy your company."

Joia nodded. "I'll go tell Edmund where I am, so he doesn't wonder where I've gone when we set out again." Joia wandered back to Edmund's green wagon. He was standing next to his horse, petting its gray neck while it drank from a nearby stream.

"Edmund, Elin invited me to ride with her and Wendell. May I?" she asked.

He nodded. "I'm sure you would enjoy her company more than mine."

"It's not that, Edmund, it's just, different company, you know?" she felt bad that she had insulted him, but he had never seemed happy to have her in his company, so she figured he wouldn't mind her not being around him the rest of the afternoon.

He smiled. "I was not upset with you. Just stating that you will probably enjoy her company. She and Wendell are a joyful pair to be around. You, Hakon, and I have much to talk about, but we will do that tonight when we stop for camp."

Joia joined Elin and Wendell at their wagon for the rest of the afternoon. Elin told stories about life in the entertainer's camp. Elin was kind and chatty and talked almost non-stop while she darned colorful sock after colorful sock. Wendell was a storyteller in his own right, but his stories were humorous. As he told the stories, he had the most wonderful facial expressions, made funny sounds, and would sing silly songs while telling his story. He told one to Joia that he was working on, and she couldn't remember laughing so much.

The company came to a stop in the late afternoon, giving them plenty of light to make camp. Joia asked to watch Wendell start the fire right after they arrived. He pulled from his wagon a pottery container and took it to where several children had dropped off handfuls of kindling for the fire. Wendell carefully arranged the wood and then dumped the containers of the pot. After a few hardy blows, the kindling caught fire and he started to add more wood around it. It wasn't but a few minutes later, that a large fire was ablaze.

Moments later, Elin had the cooking set up and going. She moved quickly around the large pot that hung over the fire. Joia joined Hakon in gathering firewood.

"Edmund wants to talk to us tonight," Hakon said as they headed back to camp.

"That's good. I'm curious to know what he thinks the best plan is for us," she said.

"We should have asked that yesterday," Hakon grumbled, leaning over to pick up a stick as long as his arm.

Joia turned to him. "You can still return to Erthenhorn. It will be a few days of walking, but you can still go. That way you don't have to deal with me or the Light, or anything else."

Hakon let out a sigh. "I don't want to go and leave you alone."

"You don't need to feel obligated to watch over me," she sighed. "It's bad enough that Edmund doesn't seem to care whether I'm here or not, but I don't want you here if you think you have to watch over me all the time. I'll be fine."

He shook his head. "It's not that, Joia," he dropped his armful of firewood to the ground and went to stand in front of her. "I'm not here to watch over you because you are helpless. I can't go home when you are not there. I don't want to be home if you're not there," he said.

Joia stopped and looked up at him. Did he truly feel that way about her? She wasn't sure, but she knew her heart. "I don't want to be away from you either."

Hakon stood before her and gazed into her eyes for several long moments. Then he took her armful of firewood from her, gently touching her hands, as he did and took it back to the campfire. Joia watched him walk away, unsure what had just happened between them.

After the meal was cleaned up, families went back to their own wagons. Songs began and music played from the different areas of camp. Edmund ignored it all and invited Joia and Hakon into their tent. He lit a small candle, sat down on his bedding, and stared at them with his intense eyes.

"There is much for us to discuss," he said.

"Edmund," Hakon began, "before we begin the planning, I wanted to ask you about an experience I had. Early yesterday morning, I was sleeping in my bed at home. A voice that sounded like my father woke me from my sleep. The voice called to me, and I followed it. It led me through the village and that's when I found Joia on her way to you. Who do you think was calling me?" Hakon asked. "There is no way it could have been my father."

Edmund sat back and looked at Hakon for a moment. "I don't know who called to you, but obviously you were meant to find Joia and accompany her on this journey. Something strange is happening in the Guild, I believe."

"So, I have this light, and we've begun our journey, but what are we doing?" Joia asked.

"I've been thinking about that," Edmund said. "Originally, I was planning on taking you to Athelstan's Castle, that is where all of us learned our trades, but the more I think about it, I'm not sure that's the best place."

"Why not?" Hakon asked.

"Because there's nothing there, really," Edmund answered. "It's an empty castle." He seemed to have more to say, but he didn't speak again for several moments. He looked deep in thought, stroking his chin, which was covered in dark stubble. "We will go see Sidonia the Weaver," he finally said. "She isn't far from here. You might remember, Joia, when I told you the history of The Guild, that each Patron has a special gift that can be given to anyone who can prove their worth?" Joia nodded her head. "Sidonia has a most amazing gift called the Life Tapestry. It is a very difficult gift to be worthy of, but I don't think you will have a problem in proving your worth. After all, the Light of the Guild shines in you." Edmund smiled.

"So we are not going to Athelstan's castle?" Joia said.

"No. Not yet anyway," Edmund said, "I believe that eventually, our journey will lead us there, but right now, I don't feel it is the best place to start."

"How do we find her?" Joia asked.

"Sidonia has lived in the same cottage for two hundred years. We will travel with the camp for one more day and then we head west for a day and should arrive by nightfall."

"How many Patrons are there?" Joia asked.

"Around two dozen at the last count, but it has been nearly two hundred years since we were all together. I assume that we all are still alive, but I cannot be sure," Edmund said.

"Did Athelstan teach you everything?" she asked.

Edmund shook his head. "He taught me very little of my trade. I learned it all on my own, but what Athelstan did was give me the resources I needed to create and improve my trade. The experience of each trade was different. Ciar the blacksmith was already doing metal work when he started working with Athelstan, but the trade of a blacksmith did not exist. Athelstan taught Ciar everything he knew, but Ciar already had an innate sense of working the metal. Athelstan taught him, but again, gave Ciar the tools, resources, and opportunities to learn and improve."

"So why is he called the father of all trades if you and Ciar already knew your trade?" Hakon asked.

"There was no trade, at the time. Athelstan taught us and helped us to grow, but I think more importantly, he organized us and named our trades. It is hard for you to understand that back in those days, there were no trades as you know them today."

Joia started to ask another question, but Edmund held up his hand. "No more questions tonight. We will part ways with the company in two mornings, and if all goes well, we will be at Sidonia's home by that second night. You will get your Life Tapestry and we'll decide what to do at that point. Now, we need sleep." Edmund blew out the candle and lay down on his blankets.

Joia was embarrassed about all her questions and ignorance, which came out more and more with each question. "Sorry, Edmund," she whispered in the dark.

"Whatever for?" he asked.

"My mother always told me I asked too many questions and that people get annoyed when they are questioned too much," she said, trying to keep the shame out of her voice.

"Questions are how we learn," he said. "You can ask more questions in the morning."

Joia felt somewhat better, but she needed to remember what her mother had taught her. You wouldn't need to ask question after question if you spent more time being observant. Joia would try harder. She moved to her own bedroll and stretched out. She could hear Hakon doing the same, and from the darkness of their tent, Edmund started to sing, very quietly.

Joia closed her eyes and pulled her blanket up to her chin. She listened to Edmund's deep voice and felt herself relax. Soon the music died away and Joia fell asleep.

CHAPTER SIX

Sidonia the Weaver

By her third day on the road, Joia started to feel a little more comfortable in the group of entertainers. After so many years of hearing stories about how the entertainers weren't to be trusted or that they kidnapped children, Joia found them to be good people. They watched out for each other and shared with each other. Most were from several generations of entertainers and whenever they met up with another camp of entertainers, at least one family in their camp was related to a family in the other camp. They were a close-knit group. There was always music being played, songs being sung, and stories being told. It was a tough life to constantly be on the move and never have a permanent home, but they were a happy people and Joia was very much enjoying her time among them.

That night, the group gathered around the cooking campfire and Edmund announced that he would be parting ways with the group. The camp burst into protests. Joia was very impressed that no one wanted Edmund to leave. It was obvious that he was loved by his tradesmen. He promised them that they would see each other again soon. Music started to play, and the group began singing songs about parting ways and friendship. Edmund sat among them, accepting their farewell, and in turn, he sang to them.

Having resigned to the harebrained adventure, Hakon started to relax and was more his usual, cheerful self. They sat together holding hands while watching the entertainers. They had never had the chance to be alone if you could call yourself alone in the company of entertainers. But no one was paying attention to them. They were able to just sit together, hold hands, and not worry if the village busybody was watching them. Joia liked the feel of Hakon's hand around hers. She might be far from home, and a little homesick, but she was with Hakon, and that made her very happy.

The next morning began as usual, although they got up later than usual. The sun was up and Elin was fixing breakfast for the camp.

"This company usually likes to get going before the sun rises, especially if we are leaving a village, but once in a while, they choose to sleep in," Edmund explained. "They use the time for rest and to make sure their wagons are in good working repair."

Joia found Elin at the main fire, stirring a large cauldron of delicious-smelling food.

"I'm sad that you're leaving today," Elin said as she and Joia sat down together to enjoy one last meal.

"So am I. I have a sister who is just a year older than me," Joia explained. "I miss her, but being with you has been like being with my sister."

Elin grinned. "I'm so glad we've become friends. I hope that when Edmund returns to this company you will come with him. I would love to see you again."

Joia nodded. "With Edmund as a link between us, we'll keep in touch."

There were many goodbyes shouted to Edmund, Joia, and Hakon as they rode past in their line of wagons on their way out. Edmund turned his smoky grey horse down another path, and they began their journey west.

"Edmund? What's your horse's name?" she asked.

Bard," he answered. "A bard is a poet or someone who tells epic stories."

"Seems like an appropriate name for a storyteller's horse. I like it," Joia smiled.

They traveled through miles of trees, meadows, and farmland. Joia had heard of the western mountain range but never thought she would see it. Now she saw them, distant and purple in the morning sun. Edmund told Joia and Hakon stories about the mountains, people he had met, and things he had seen. There were also a few stories about some of the other Patrons.

Joia listened and tried to remember everything Edmund was telling her.

"You have been very kind to us. Are all the Patrons like you?" Joia asked.

Edmund shook his head, "For the most part, or they were when I knew them last. But if you were to meet them, they would all see your Light and would help you." He sighed and looked at Joia, who always sat in the middle of the bench, between Edmund and Hakon. "It is sad that I could not tell more of the Patrons about you. There was a time when we regularly gathered to discuss the affairs of the trades, but as the years passed, fewer came to the gatherings and now we have not held a gathering in centuries."

"Where did you hold these gatherings?" Joia asked.

"At Athelstan's Castle," he answered.

"What about Sidonia, the Weaver? What is she like?" she asked.

Edmund smiled. "Sidonia is beautiful inside and out. She is very kind and will help you. We should reach her cottage around nightfall."

Joia missed having Elin's company that day. Edmund was often humming or singing and Hakon was a quiet companion. The day passed quietly and slowly. Joia was more used to riding in the wagon now, but the hours of sitting still made Joia feel stiff and sore.

Just as the sun started to set, they arrived at a small cottage, surrounded by a large, fragrant garden. Edmund stopped the wagon and hopped off.

"This is the home of Sidonia," Edmund said, tying the horse to a nearby tree.

Joia was nervous as they approached the house by going up a footpath that led through the garden. Joia took a deep breath and remembered her smaller garden back home. She loved the earthy smells and she recognized a few of the scents, like lavender and lemon balm. For half a moment, she was homesick again and wished she was sitting in her garden with her mother and Ebba, but then, Edmund knocked on the door and Joia was reminded that she was about to meet another Patron.

She hoped that this Patron would accept her.

A woman opened the door and light spilled out from the house into the garden.

"Edmund," the woman grinned, "welcome. It's been many years since you came to see me last."

"Sidonia, it's wonderful to see you" Edmund answered. He leaned in and kissed Sidonia on the cheek.

The woman looked at Joia and gasped, "The Light shines around this girl! Is this the girl you spoke of many years ago?"

"She is. Sidonia, this is Joia of Erthenhorn and Hakon the Thatcher of Erthenhorn. Hakon, Joia, this is Sidonia, Patron of the Weavers."

"It's a pleasure to meet you," Joia said, giving a polite curtsey.

"The pleasure is mine. Welcome." Sidonia stood aside and pulled the door open wider, "Please, come in."

The cottage was clean and cozy. The first thing Joia noticed was a large weaving loom in the middle of the room. She had never seen a loom so big before. It took up most of the space in the cottage and it was glowing with the Light. Beautiful blankets were draped around the room over all the furniture and large tapestries hung on all the walls. It seemed like everything was glowing with a soft golden light. Then Joia realized that it was all the blankets that were everywhere. They had been made by Sidonia, so they were glowing. It was almost overwhelming. This Light would take some getting used to.

Sidonia replied. "Please everyone, have a seat."

They sat down around a small table near the hearth and Sidonia pulled out cups and poured tea for them all. Joia watched with fascination the new Patron as she tended to her guests. Sidonia was taller than Joia. Her hair was long, brown, and plaited down her back. Her dress was of a most beautiful fabric. Joia couldn't figure out what color it was. Most of the time it looked blue, but the more Joia looked at the dress, the more she noticed how the colors changed.

Sidonia noticed Joia staring at her dress. "It's a lovely fabric, isn't it? I wove it myself from the dust trails of fairies." Sidonia busied herself at the fireplace.

"Fairy dust? Are there fairies here?" Joia had heard tales of fairies, but no one in the village had ever seen a fairy. Occasionally, one of the old timers in the village had talked about how their grandparents had seen fairies, but fairies had disappeared from that part of their land long, long ago.

"No, there are no more fairies here. It was a long time ago that the fairies flew in my garden, leaving their dust floating in the air and settling on my plants. Every morning, I would go out into my garden and collect the dust. My dear friend Kloma spun the dust into thread for me and I wove this fabric from the thread. It is my favorite cloth I have ever woven. Edmund," she turned to him, "some wine?"

He nodded. "Please."

She offered some to Hakon and Joia. Hakon accepted, and Joia declined, happy with her tea.

Sidonia smiled and sat down on the bench at her loom since there were no more chairs at the table. Joia took a drink from her cup. It was sweeter than any tea Joia had ever tasted before. It was delicious and she sipped the hot liquid again.

"I want to know all about you both," she smiled. "Hakon, you are a thatcher? How do you know Joia?" Sidonia asked.

"Yes, I am. I am nearing the time when the thatching guild can make me a master if they all agree, that is. I was," he paused, "I am looking forward to that next year." He swallowed. "As for Joia, she and I have been friends for many years. I've come along to help her," Hakon answered.

"I'm glad you are here," she said, her voice full of sincerity.

"And tell me about you Joia. Do you have a trade?" the weaver asked.

"No," Joia shook her head, blushing with some embarrassment. "Although I have spent time in my village's spinner and weaver shops. I know how to card and roll wool and I have helped the weaver to dress her loom."

Sidonia was very pleased with this. "Excellent. And how have you been, Edmund? Still traveling, I guess?"

He nodded and set his cup of wine down. "Yes. I recently parted with one of my companies to bring Joia to you."

"I'm so glad you have. I've wondered over the years if I would ever get to meet you," she said to Joia. "Now, Edmund, you must tell me what you can about Joia, the Light, and what help you need from me," Sidonia said.

"You will remember when the few of us met seventeen years ago at Athelstan's Castle to discuss Joia. We didn't know why she had the Light and I was asked to check on her regularly. This I did over the years and so I saw her grow from a baby into this young woman. However, we still don't know why she has the Light. Her family did not tell her of my visits, nor did they tell her about the Light. I was hoping she would have a better understanding of the Patrons."

"My family was trying to protect me," Joia said. "How was it I never saw you when you came to visit?"

"After you reached a certain age, you started to come to my performances. I could spot you in a heartbeat with that Light of yours. I did not approach you because I didn't wish to startle you. I asked your mother to teach you about the trades and the Patrons, though."

"I learned about Ferran from my father, but I know that he doesn't believe Ferran is a real person, like the two of you are real."

"Ferran is real and a very kind person," Sidonia assured her. "Long ago, when we all lived in Athelstan's castle, Ferran would bake bread each day. It was so delicious. I've never found anyone who can bake half as well as he."

"My father is very good," Joia promised. "I don't think they taught me much about the Patrons because they didn't know any others and it never occurred to me to ask the spinner and weaver in Erthenhorn about their Patrons, or Hakon about his," she blushed, "until just a few days ago."

"What changed then?" Hakon asked.

"My mother told me about Edmund's visits. She wanted to warn me since she knew he would most likely seek me out this year."

Edmund took in a deep breath of frustration. "Well, the past is past. It is time now to find out why you have the Light. That is why we have come to you." He looked to the weaver, who nodded in understanding. "Would you tell Joia of your gift?"

Sidonia turned to Joia. "I have a gift, as each Patron does, to give to those who seek it and can prove themselves worthy of the gift. My gift is a woven tapestry. The Life Tapestry is special because woven into the fabric are stories. The stories can tell the past and the future and they can answer questions. It depends on what the person is seeking when they look at the tapestry."

"It can tell me my future?" Joia asked in complete amazement.

"In a way, yes. But what you will see in the tapestry isn't always easy to interpret. There will be symbols and pictures that might not make sense at first, but if you keep it, study it, and follow it, the tapestry will become clear in its meaning."

"How do I prove my worth for your gift?" Joia asked, afraid of the answer. She worried that she wouldn't be worthy of any of the Patron's gifts. Perhaps the Light of the Guild chose her by mistake. She would let Edmund down and Hakon would be mad about being forced to leave his home for no good reason. The last thing in the world that she wanted to do was disappoint Edmund and Hakon.

"You must spin the thread yourself," Sidonia answered. "Did you notice my garden when you arrived?"

"I noticed it, but I couldn't see it well. It was getting dark when we arrived." Joia said.

Sidonia smiled, "My garden is very impressive. It contains many plants. You must take the fibers of the plants and spin them into thread.

However, you can't just pick any plant that you desire. You must pick the right plants and in the proper order. Only in that way will the tapestry make sense when it is woven together."

"But how do I know which plant is right?" Joia asked.

"I cannot tell you. For each individual who tries, it's different. You will have to learn. Some of those who have successfully spun their thread have told me that the plants spoke to them. They heard whispers from the plants or smelled a certain plant. One even said that the sunshine would come from the trees and land on certain plants and those were the ones they picked. You will have to learn your way as you do it."

Joia was quite worried now. Suppose she stood out in the garden and saw nothing? She swallowed hard and pushed her fears aside. "When do I begin?" she asked.

Sidonia smiled. "In the morning. You must be tired after your travels, and you need to be awake and strong to spin your thread. I will prepare a bed for you. Edmund, I assume you prefer to sleep in your wagon?"

"I do, thank you." Edmund stood up.

"What about you, Hakon?" Sidonia asked.

"Don't worry about me," Hakon said. "I've got my bedroll."

Sidonia nodded. "Let me give you some extra blankets for comfort," she said and picked up a handful of the glowing blankets. She placed them in Hakon's arms.

"They are so soft," Hakon said, running his hand over them.

Sidonia let out a soft chuckle. "I hope they help you sleep more comfortably than the hard ground can offer."

"Come on Hakon and help me with the horse and tent," Edmund said. Hakon said good night and followed Edmund out the door.

Joia watched Sidonia as she moved about the small cottage. She was graceful and her dress changed colors as she moved. She felt a stab of homesickness in her stomach. Watching Sidonia taking care of this task or that dish reminded Joia of her mother.

"First time away from home?" she asked.

"Am I that obvious in my homesickness?" Joia asked.

Sidonia gave her a gentle smile. "A little."

Joia stood up and went to Sidonia's wash basin. "Let me help you wash our cups." She took the cleaning rag and started to work. "I miss my mother and sister. I miss my father and brother, too, but my mother and sister more."

Sidonia nodded. "Yes, I understand. Long ago, Kloma, the Patron to the spinners, lived in a cottage on the other side of the garden from me. We spend every day in each other's company. When she moved, I was very lonely."

"Why did she move away?" Joia asked.

Sidonia gave her a kind smile. "She fell in love. Now, the dishes are done, how about we fix up your bed." She walked over to a corner of the room, picked up several blankets, and laid them out on the floor. "I'm afraid all I have is this corner for you. It is nothing more than a stack of blankets on the floor, but they are soft, and you should be comfortable."

"That is very kind, thank you. Sidonia, I see the Light everywhere in this house. I grew up not seeing it at all, except when Edmund would come to my village to perform. In our travels so far, the only other things I've seen with the golden Light are the instruments Edmund plays. But here, your entire house seems to glow. How do I get used to it?"

Sidonia looked around the room. "It does glow, doesn't it?" She stood close to Joia and covered her eyes with her hand. "Close your eyes for a moment and take several deep breaths. I can't imagine how difficult this must be for you. Those of us who have the Light are quite used to it. It is just the way things are and so I don't notice it anymore."

Joia kept her eyes closed, breathing deeply.

"Good. Remember, you have the Light too. It is part of you, and you have some measure of control over it. Don't let it overwhelm you. Let it guide you. Open your eyes now."

Joia slowly opened her eyes and let out her breath. While the Light still shown all around, it wasn't so bright. It was a soft light now that shown gently on the blankets.

"Better?" Sidonia asked.

"Much," Joia said. "It's still there, but it's soft now,"

"Good. You will get used to it and learn to see it without seeing it."

Joia's confusion was quite evident on her face because Sidonia chuckled. "You'll understand one day, but for now, it's time to sleep. You will need to be well rested for tomorrow's task."

Joia turned back to the pallet of soft blankets and laid down. They were wonderfully soft, especially after two nights of sleeping on the ground. and sat down on the blankets.

Joia closed her eyes and thought about the task ahead of her. What if she was not able to spin the thread properly. She really didn't know how to spin. Yes, she had assisted the spinner back in her village, but she had done very little spinning herself. Using a spinning wheel took many hours of practice. Joia wasn't sure what she was going to do. She opened her eyes again and while the cottage was dark, the golden light shown around her. It was like another blanket that surrounded her, and she felt peace.

The next morning, Joia was up with the sun, feeling refreshed. Sidonia greeted her and Joia expressed how comfortably she had slept, which pleased the weaver. They worked together to prepare breakfast. The tasks of cooking and tending the fire were so second nature to her, that she didn't think that Sidonia might not want a stranger in her cooking space.

"Lady Sidonia, may I ask you something?" Joia asked.

"Of course you may."

"Back in my village, there is a weaver. Her name is Ellota. She told me that each day she dedicated her work to you. Do you actually hear the dedications from each weaver, each day?"

Sidonia smiled. "An interesting question. I thought you might ask me about your task for today."

"Well, I'm curious about what I will be doing today and how I will spin my thread when I am not a spinner, but I expect you will give me some instruction before I begin," Joia said.

"Yes, I will instruct you when it's time. Now, back to your question. Do I hear Ellota when she dedicates her day to me?" Sidonia asked. Joia nodded. "To put it simply, yes, I do. But, I don't really hear them. I don't necessarily hear their words or their voices with my ears, but I can feel the dedications. I know when they are said, and I know who says them. I know who Ellota is. She is a fine weaver and very loyal to me. I bless her each day."

"And her apprentice, Sara?"

"I know Sara too," Sidonia said. "She is learning the trade well and will be a great weaver when she reaches her master status."

Joia smiled. She was glad to know that Sidonia was aware of the two weavers in their humble shop back in Erthenhorn. "Do all Patrons know when one of their own dedicates their work?"

"I don't know what it's like for everyone, but, yes, I believe that they do. Now, Joia, let me ask you something. Who are you that the Light of the Guild would choose to shine in you?"

Joia frowned. "I don't really know. I don't have a trade. I am only a tradesman's daughter, and my parents told me that I was to be a tradesman's wife. All my life I have learned to cook, sew, garden, and care for a home. That is all. Now, I learn I have this mysterious light about me, and I don't understand what it is I am supposed to do. That's why Edmund suggested that I come to you. We are hoping that the tapestry you can weave will answer these questions."

"You're a very interesting girl, Joia. I look forward to weaving your tapestry.

"I hope I can be worthy of your gift," Joia said.

Sidonia smiled kindly. "I have no doubt of your worthiness."

There was a knock at the door and Edmund and Hakon walked in. They sat down at the table near the fire. Sidonia laid out plates of food and everyone began to eat. The plans for the day were decided upon. While Joia was spinning her thread, Sidonia would ready her loom and Hakon would go to the nearby village for supplies.

Joia couldn't eat much. She was nervous and her stomach felt funny.

"Eat, Joia. You will need your strength to do the spinning. Once you begin to spin your thread, you cannot stop until the task is completed," Sidonia urged.

Joia nibbled at the bread and meat forcing herself to eat. When the meal was over, Hakon prepared to head to the village. He pulled Joia aside.

"We haven't had much chance to talk recently. I don't understand what it is you're doing today, but I wanted to wish you all the best of luck. I hope that you're able to find the answers you seek. I'll see you this evening when I get back." Hakon bent down and kissed Joia on the cheek, and then he left down the road towards the village.

Joia watched him until he disappeared around the bend in the road. He had never kissed her before. Her cheek burned where his lips had touched her face. She felt warm and confident for the task before her as she walked to Sidonia and stood beside her.

"Are you ready, Joia?" Sidonia asked.

Joia nodded, "Yes I am."

"Very well," Sidonia held out an empty wooden spool. Attached to the spool was a short single piece of white thread. "This is the spool on which you must spin your thread. And this is the starter thread," she twisted the thread in her fingers for a moment. "You will walk through the garden and pick the plants to spin onto the thread. Watch me."

Sidonia went to a flower near the house. She picked the flower, touched it to the starter thread and twisted the flower in her fingers. The flower became a pink thread about the length of her hand and was seamlessly attached to the starter thread. "Do you see?" Sidonia asked.

Joia was amazed how the flower had become thread. She nodded.

"Attach your plant to the thread and gently twist it in your fingers. The plant will become a thread. Wind your spool as you go, adding plant by plant, thread by thread to your spool. When you are done, bring the spool to me and I will weave your tapestry." Sidonia broke off the pink thread she had attached to the starter thread. Now only the pure white starter thread hung from the spool. "Remember, Joia, once you begin, you cannot stop until it is finished."

"How will I know what plant to add and how will I know when to stop?" Joia started to feel nervous again.

"You will know. Don't rush. Wait and watch for the signs and you will be just fine."

Joia took the spool in her hands and looked at the thread hanging from it. Sidonia took Joia's chin into her hand. "May Athelstan and the Light of the Guild bless you," she smiled. "Now go."

Joia turned and looked out into the garden. Sidonia had been right, it was a very impressive garden and much larger than Joia would have imagined for such a small cottage and single caretaker. She looked around but saw nothing unusual about the plants. The sun shone through the trees and a breeze played with loose hairs hanging around her face, tickling her nose.

Joia stepped into the garden away from Sidonia and the cottage. She walked several steps towards a large oak at the edge of the garden. From there, she would be able to look at the entire garden. She stopped and looked around her again. Still nothing. She started to panic. What if Edmund and Sidonia had been wrong about her? Joia felt her breath quickening and she spun around looking in vain for a sign, but she saw nothing.

A small drop of dew from the tree above her fell onto her cheek, right where Hakon had kissed her. It startled her and she stood still. "Deep breaths," Joia said to herself. "Calm down and don't rush." Joia closed her eyes and took three deep breaths.

She felt calmer and opened her eyes. There before her was a yellow daffodil, bathed in a golden glow. She walked to the daffodil, plucked the flower and held it to the white starter thread. A warmth spread through her fingers as she gently twisted the thread. Moments later, a yellow thread hung from the spool. Joia smiled as she wound the yellow thread around the spool. She looked out into the garden again and saw another plant bathed in the golden glow. She went to it, plucked it, and added it to the spool. With another deep breath and a sigh of relief, Joia looked for her next plant. She could do this. The Light would guide her.

CHAPTER SEVEN

Spinning in the Garden

Sidonia watched Joia from the edge of the garden. She had been a little concerned when Joia had stood in the garden for several moments, spinning about in a panic, then watched as Joia stood still with her eyes closed for a few moments. When Joia had walked to the daffodil, picked it up, and spun it gently to the starter thread, Sidonia smiled. Joia was going to be just fine.

With Edmund's help, they moved Sidonia's regular loom to a corner of the cottage and brought out the tapestry loom to the center of the room. Sidonia set to work on preparing the Life Tapestry loom. The loom had been built specifically for weaving the life tapestries and not for regular weaving. It had been made from the elm trees that had grown around Athelstan's castle.

Sidonia did not rush the preparations. She knew it would take time for Joia to spin her thread. Edmund went to his wagon, leaving Sidonia to work.

Several times Sidonia looked out of the window to see how Joia was coming along. In the late afternoon, she walked out of the cottage and into the garden. Joia was bent over some plants in the far corner of the garden. For several moments, Sidonia watched Joia as she walked about the garden, periodically stooping down to pluck another plant and spin it into the ever-growing spool. Sometimes she walked from plant to plant and sometimes she walked around the garden for a while before finding her next plant.

Edmund came from his wagon to where Sidonia stood. Together they watched Joia as she walked through the garden.

"How is she doing?" he asked.

"I believe she is doing very well. You know, I've watched many people try this over the years. Some of the people who have come to me over the years were successful in spinning their thread, but there were many who could not. It is a difficult process, requiring patience, concentration, and a genuine desire for the life tapestry."

"I know Joia has a genuine desire for this."

"Who is she, Edmund?"

"I don't quite know, but she was born with the Light. She has some part in our Guild to play, but I don't know what it is."

Sidonia continued to watch Joia. "Do you think Athelstan sent her?"

"It is possible, I suppose," Edmund said as he watched the young girl. She walked from plant to plant with confidence in her step. Her fingers had become deft at spinning the plant fibers. Joia was walking away from an apple tree when she suddenly stopped and stooped down. They watched as Joia picked up a rock and held it up to her eyes, inspecting it closely. She then held it to the thread hanging from her spool and suddenly, the rock became a thread as she twisted the thread in her fingers.

"Impossible!" Sidonia quietly gasped.

"What?" Edmund asked.

"That is impossible. She spun a rock into thread." Sidonia said.

"Why is that impossible?"

"A rock has no fiber. Plants have fiber that can be spun, but a rock is just a rock. It is impossible to spin a rock into thread."

Edmund smiled. "And yet, she did." He watched Joia pick up another rock and twist it into the thread. The spool in her hand was getting larger. "She certainly is remarkable."

Sidonia turned to Edmund and smiled a sly smile. "I can't wait to weave this, Edmund. Her life tapestry will be, without a doubt, the most interesting of any life tapestry I have ever woven or probably ever will. Come inside, we mustn't disturb her."

Edmund followed Sidonia into the cottage. Sidonia sat down at her regular loom in the corner of the cottage and picked up the bobbin of thread. She began to weave. Her feet moved along the treadles and her hands manipulated the spool of thread back and forth across the beam.

She spoke as she wove.

"Have you seen any others of the Guild recently?" Sidonia asked Edmund.

"No one in a few decades, except for our meeting after I discovered Joia. One of the last people I saw from the Guild was Aren. He had changed, Sidonia. He was not the same man we knew back in Athelstan's castle. He said my trade is not a true one. True trades create physical things that can be used."

"How could he say that about you? He knows what you do. And you do make physical items when you build your instruments."

"He said the smiths are the most important trades." Edmund had brought a large box into Sidonia's house from his wagon. He opened it and gently took out a lap harp. "Aren seemed to think very little of the arts and textiles."

"Every trade is an art. As a silversmith, Aren should know that," Sidonia said. "All the work that tradesmen create is a work of art, from the goblets of a silversmith to the bread of a baker."

Edmund nodded his head sadly. "Yes, I know, and I tried to remind him of that, but the smiths seem to feel that anyone who does not work in metal is of no value."

"Do they wear clothes?" Sidonia smiled. "If they wear clothes, then they should remember the cloth was woven by a weaver like me, and the individual threads in the cloth were spun by a spinner."

"It seems they have forgotten that." Edmund shook his head. He pulled out a cloth and a vial of special oil that he had made. He put some of the oil on the cloth and started to rub at the wooden frame of the harp. "Athelstan would be most upset with them, I think."

Sidonia continued to weave. It was so second nature to her, she did not think about it and talked easily while she worked. "We cannot judge them."

"No? Sidonia, who was the last member of the Guild that you saw?" Edmund was getting upset.

Sidonia paused her weaving. She looked very sad, "I saw Algar and Brynmor about ten years ago. They were also different from our days in Athelstan's castle. Brynmor uses wood from the forests to fuel his furnaces for cooking the pottery and Algar was upset because he uses the same trees for making bows and arrows. They were upset with each other for seeking out the same types of trees. Algar claimed that ash wood was best for his arrows and Brynmor said that the same kind of wood was excellent in his furnaces because they made the pottery strong and beautiful."

"They have forgotten that both of their arts are important. They think only of their trade," Edmund said. "The Guilds are splintering, Sidonia."

She sighed and stopped weaving. She looked over to Edmund at the table. "I know. We fight amongst ourselves when we should be supporting each other." Sidonia began to weave again, and Edmund continued to oil the harp.

"That's a lovely harp," Sidonia said after a while. "Did you make it?"

"Sort of. I designed the frame, but I had a carpenter make it and carve the designs onto it. While I can build with wood, my skill is not that of a master carpenter. He did a wonderful job. I made the strings and the attachments for them."

"Will you play it later?" she asked.

Edmund nodded. "I haven't had a safe place to work on this harp for a long time. It needs to be oiled periodically, and then it must be tuned. While I am traveling, I loosen the tension on the strings to keep them from breaking or damaging the frame."

"That makes sense," Sidonia said. "But I suppose that means a lot of work for you when you want to play the instrument."

"It's not too much work," he said. "Less work than it would take if one of the strings broke."

"What of this young man you brought with you, Hakon?" she asked. He doesn't have the light."

"No, but I've seen his devotion to Joia and his desire to protect her. It also seems that the Light somehow wanted him to come along. It called to him and he knew to follow the call."

"Truly?" Sidonia asked. "He must be essential in helping Joia find her path if the Light called him into action."

Edmund nodded. "He's a decent man. Quiet and thoughtful. I don't mind his company as far as a non-entertainer goes."

Sidonia laughed and they worked on their projects with little more conversation between them. Finally, Sidonia stopped her weaving and stood up. "The day is passing. It will be time to prepare the evening meal soon. Is Joia still working out there?"

"Yes," Edmund answered. He had finished the oiling and was carefully plucking at the strings, tightening them.

"How do you know when to stop?" Sidonia asked.

"When it gets to the correct pitch," Edmund replied. "I hear it. I know when it is right."

She smiled and put a hand on his shoulder. "I'll need my table back soon."

"I'm nearly done, then I'll put it into the box until after we've eaten."

Sidonia went to the window and looked out. Joia was still walking in the garden, adding thread to her spool. She had been at this a very long time. Sidonia walked away from the window and began to stoke the fire. Edmund carefully put the newly tuned harp back into its box, closed the lid, and stored it in a corner of the room. He went to the window and looked out.

"Hakon is returning," Edmund announced. "I'll go out and get him and make sure he doesn't disturb Joia." Edmund left the cottage and quietly walked the path down to his wagon.

Hakon's arms were full, as was the sack slung over his back."

"I got everything you asked for," Hakon slung the sack into the back of Edmund's wagon. He looked over at Joia in the garden, "Is she still working?"

"Yes, and we mustn't disturb her. Come quietly with me back to the cottage. Sidonia is preparing the evening meal." Edmund took some of the load Hakon had been carrying. They walked silently back to the cottage. Hakon stopped to watch Joia. She bent down and plucked a blue flower. She touched the flower to the thread and the flower became a long blue thread. He watched her twist the threads together and then wind the thread around the spool. The spool was quite large now and it looked like she was having a hard time holding it. Hakon went into the cottage.

"She just turned a flower into thread," Hakon said. He was astonished by what he had just seen.

"She is still working then?" Sidonia asked. "This is going to be an interesting tapestry to weave. I don't believe I've ever seen anyone work on their thread for such a long time or produce such a large spool."

"What does it all mean?" Hakon asked.

Sidonia looked into Hakon's eyes. She saw kindness and a genuine concern for Joia. "I don't know Hakon, but we will soon find out."

The cottage door opened and Joia stood on the threshold with a large spool of thread in her arms. "I'm finished," she announced. Sidonia and Hakon were by her side the next moment.

Sidonia relieved Joia of the spool and Hakon put an arm around Joia's shoulders, urging her toward a chair by the fire. "Come sit down, Joia," he said, "you must be tired."

CHAPTER EIGHT

The Life Tapestry

Joia sat down on the stool in front of the fire. She was exhausted and very hungry. How had the day gone by already? To Joia's mind, the day had gone quickly, but her body told her it had been working a long time and was ready for rest.

"Did I do it right?" she asked Sidonia.

"Yes, my dear, you did it just right. I've never seen a spool so full before. How did you know what to add to the thread?"

"The golden Light of the Guild shown on the items for me to spin. It wasn't always plants, though. I spun some rock as well."

Sidonia handed a bowl of hot stew to Joia. "Rocks are impossible things to spin. How did you know you could spin them?"

Joia took several sips of the hot stew and thought back, "Well, like everything else, the golden light settled on the rock. The first time, I held the rock in my hand and thought it very silly to try and spin it into the thread, but I knew that if I ignored the Light, I would lose the power to spin. So, I touched it to the thread, and it worked."

"I have never seen anyone spin earth," Sidonia said. "You are quite remarkable."

Soon everyone was sipping hot stew except for Sidonia. She was doing the final preparation work for the tapestry loom. When she was ready, Sidonia sat on the stool in front of the loom. She looked at the spool that Joia had spun, with its many colors, and she whispered, "Athelstan,

Father of all Trades, I dedicated my work to you in the creation of this Life Tapestry of Joia, who carries the Light of the Guild in her. Bless my hands and my loom that they might perform the talents you have given me."

She pushed the shuttle through the open shaft in the loom's threads and the weaving was begun. Joia watched as Sidonia ran the thread shuttle back and forth across the loom. Slowly, a cloth began to form. It was very colorful, but it looked like nothing more than a piece of cloth.

Edmund brought out the harp again and plucked at it, making sure the strings were tuned to the right pitch, and then he began to play. The music was soft and gentle and after several minutes of just the harp, Edmund started to sing, and Joia knew she had never heard anything more beautiful than the sounds the harp made combined with Edmund's deep voice.

"Will I lady, see thee wed,
Though the stars that shine
May tumble down and splash into the sea,
My love for thee will ever true be.

Will I lady, see thee wed,
When the waters that spring
From the eternal well do finally run dry,
My love for thee will ever true be.

Will I lady, see thee wed,
The oak tree that grows,
And touches the sky might reach the moon,
My love for thee will ever true be."

Joia had never heard such sweeter words sung. They went to her heart and warmed it.

She was so tired. Her body ached and her mind felt weary. She sat close to Hakon and watched Sidonia work while listening to Edmund's song. Her eyes closed and she felt a strong hand around her back.

Sometime later, her eyes opened again, and she found herself lying in the corner on the pile of soft blankets where she had slept the night before. An odd noise came from the center of the room. As Joia's eyes grew accustomed to the dark cottage, she was able to see Sidonia, still sitting at her loom, weaving by the light of the moon that shown through the open window.

Joia laid back down. She was still very tired. Once again, her eyes closed and she let the rhythmic sounds of the loom lull her to sleep.

When Joia next opened her eyes, sunlight was streaming in from the windows. Sidonia was nowhere to be seen in the cottage. Joia sat up and rubbed the sleep from her eyes. She looked to the loom where Sidonia had worked through the night. The loom was empty. Her heart sank. She must have done the spinning wrong, forcing Sidonia to toss it out.

The cottage door opened and Sidonia, Edmund, and Hakon entered.

"Joia, you're awake!" Hakon said. He helped her up off her bed of blankets.

"You must have been very tired. It is mid-morning and we have been eagerly waiting for you to wake," Edmund said.

"Did it work?" Joia asked. "Did the tapestry work?"

Sidonia smiled at her and walked into the small room in the back of the cottage where she slept and returned with a large cloth folded in her arms. "It is the largest life tapestry I have ever woven."

Sidonia handed Joia the cloth. It was soft and warm to the touch. It glowed with a soft golden light, but the Light wasn't so strong that Joia missed how incredibly colorful the tapestry was. But it was nothing more than a jumble of colors.

"It is very beautiful, but I don't understand. I expected the tapestry to have a story woven into it. You know, pictures of me doing something with the Light."

"I didn't mean to mislead you. When I say that stories are woven into the fabric, they aren't the same kind of stories as you might see in a fancy tapestry that is hung in a royal household. Those tapestries can only tell one story. This can tell you so much more."

"How can this tell me anything?" Joia unfolded it more and looked at it, stroking the fabric with her hand.

"Each string is woven into the warp. In this way, the separate threads of the warp become one with the thread on the spindle. All together, they make one piece of fabric. Just as your life is made of many experiences, held together by family and friends, so is your Life Tapestry."

"I think I understand." She looked at Sidonia and asked, "How does it work?"

"You must lay it out flat," Sidonia said. Everyone cleared some space on the cottage floor large enough for the cloth to lie out. Joia looked at the cloth with its bright colors and for a moment she thought she saw a picture form in the cloth, but when she looked harder, the picture was gone.

"You saw something?" Sidonia asked. Joia nodded. "What did you see?"

"Well," Joia looked hard at the cloth again, "nothing except colors. For a moment, I thought I saw something, but then it was gone."

Sidonia was smiling. "Excellent Joia. You must learn to look at it properly and see the pictures within it." Sidonia placed her hands on Joia's shoulders. "Relax your body and your eyes and see the pictures in the cloth."

Joia closed her eyes, took a deep breath, and looked at the cloth again. A form once again took shape. It was a loom. The form changed and Joia saw a wagon. The wagon moved for a moment and stopped at a candle. Then all the pictures went away. Joia closed her eyes again, but when she opened them, she saw nothing in the cloth. She looked up to see Edmund and Hakon staring at her.

"What did you see?" Edmund asked.

"I saw your loom, Sidonia," Joia said. Sidonia's eyes grew large. "Then I saw Edmund's wagon and then a candle."

"Anything else?" Sidonia asked Joia.

"No, nothing else," Joia replied.

"What does it all mean?" Hakon asked.

Edmund's face had a gentle smile, but he waited.

Joia thought for a moment. "Edmund, is there a Patron for candle makers?"

"Very good. Yes, there is. His name is Grian the Chandler."

"That is where we go next. We must find Grian," Joia said.

Edmund nodded and rubbed the stubble on his chin. "It's been a very long time since I have seen the candle maker."

Sidonia produced some food and drink, and everyone sat around her table. "You know, Joia," Sidonia began, "certain plants represent certain things. Like an apple tree is said to bring healing and a sweet pea plant represents friendship. Those who study herbal lore know that every plant represents something. I know a little of that lore, and I know the name of every plant that you spun. I could feel the textures of the plants as I wove, even the scents of some of them. I love it when I weave apple tree fibers. I felt, for the first time, what it was like to weave rock. You also spun fertile soil and a wren feather. I have never woven a feather before, either. The thread you spun was the most interesting thread I have ever touched."

Joia was confused. "If every plant or rock represents something, then what does my life tapestry mean and why did it have a candle? I didn't spin any wax into the thread."

"That is the amazing part of weaving. Everything in a cloth is woven together. Nothing is separate anymore. The individual properties of each plant are joined with all the others. When this happens, anything can result." Sidonia said. "Only you will be able to see the story in the life tapestry and you will have to figure out its meaning."

"Well, it seems that our path has been determined. Where do we find this candle maker then?" Hakon asked.

Edmund looked at Sidonia. She shook her head. "I don't know," Edmund answered. "I haven't seen Grian in more than a hundred years. The last I heard, he had set up shop in the city of Colne, but that city was destroyed in an earthquake sixty years ago. I don't know where to find him now."

Joia looked down at her tapestry again. It took her several moments, but she once again focused her eyes on the cloth. She saw the loom, the wagon, the candle, and a castle with a symbol hanging over it. "A castle!" Joia yelled out. Her shout made everyone jump. "I saw a castle in the tapestry. There was an 'A' over an anvil."

"Athelstan's castle?" Sidonia asked Edmund.

"Sounds like it. We must leave at once for Athelstan Forest." Edmund stood up and went out the door to his wagon. Hakon followed him. Joia looked down at the tapestry again. This time she didn't look at it for meaning but looked at the magnificent colors. She ran her hand over the cloth. It was so very soft. Joia had a hard time believing that the cloth included such materials as rock and tree bark and that she had spun those materials herself. Joia thought back to the previous day and how she had spent the whole of it in Sidonia's garden, spinning a magical thread.

Sidonia was at the table, putting some food into a small piece of cloth.

"The thread that you weave with," Joia said, "not the thread for the life tapestries, but the thread for regular cloth, do you spin it yourself?"

Sidonia turned to Joia and sat down in front of her. She handed Joia a small bundle, "Gingerbread for your trip," Sidonia smiled.

"Thank you," Joia answered, accepting the food. Who knew how long it would take them to get to Athelstan's Forest or the home of Grian the Chandler.

"Sometimes I spin my own thread. I have a spinning wheel and can use it, but I'm not a spinner. Some of the time, I use thread from the local village spinner, but most of my thread comes right from Kloma, Patron of the Spinners."

"Does she live near you? How do you get the thread from her?" Joia asked.

"Did you happen to see the cottage on the other side of the garden?" Sidonia asked. Joia nodded. "A long time ago, that was Kloma's home. After we left Athelstan's castle, we traveled together, teaching our trade. She and I were the only female Patrons, so you can believe that we were the best of friends. We finally settled here, planted our garden, and worked together each day. We were both married and had children. I had a son, and she had a daughter. Our children married each other, making Kloma and I sisters. We were very happy.

My son took the trade of cooper and when he became a journeyman, he left and went far away, taking his wife, Kloma's daughter, with him. About a year later, I received a letter from him. He and his wife had a baby, Wynstan, our grandson, but Kloma's daughter had become very sick. Kloma left to go live with our children and help her daughter with the baby. Another year passed and I got another letter from my son. His wife had died and Kloma had set up a home there and continued to spin and help raise the baby."

"Did you ever get to see your grandson?" Joia asked.

Sidonia smiled and nodded. "A few times during his childhood. He was a sweet boy and I understood why Kloma had chosen to stay close to him." Sidonia shifted in her chair, leaning towards Joia. "Now, Joia, our children did not bear the light, but my son's life was exceptionally long for a mortal, and Kloma and I figured that since I was immortal, perhaps my son received extra years, but he did eventually die, at the age of one hundred eleven. It seems that our grandson is also blessed with a long life and is still alive, although he is quite old now. For a long time, he was the messenger between Kloma and me. He would bring me the thread she spins, and I sent back the cloth I weave from her thread. It has worked well for us, but I miss having her nearby. I'm afraid we haven't seen each other in nearly twenty years."

"That must be hard, but do you get to see your grandson often?" Joia said.

"Not so often anymore. He has grown very old and lives near Kloma but his son, our great-grandson, is named Radstan and he now serves as a messenger between us. I just wish Kloma would come back here, and I know she wishes for me to move out near her. She has invited me several times to make the move, but now can I leave this cottage? How can I leave my garden? Besides, it is much easier for her to move a spinning wheel, than for me to move my looms," Sidonia said.

Joia nodded. "Yes, I imagine so. I notice that your loom glows with the Light. Did you build it?"

"No," she smiled. "Wodwin, the Patron of the Carpenters built all my looms for me. He did the wooden pieces, and Ciar made the metal bits that hold the entire thing together, including the cranking wheels on the beams."

"How did you get it here when you came to this cottage?" Joia asked.

Sidonia smiled. "Back when we lived in Athelstan's castle, Wodwin built me this loom. For many years after I left, I traveled the land, teaching others to weave on several smaller looms that I could transport in a wagon. Wodwin drew up the plans for the looms so local carpenters could build them for my new weavers. But I wearied of the traveling life after half a century on the road and I missed using my great loom." She gestured to the one that sat in the middle of the room again. "I finally decided to settle down in this cottage. My idea was to bring talented women to live here and learn. Wodwin dismantled my loom in the castle and brought it here, where he put it back together."

"It is a beautiful loom. I thought the one that Ellota has in her shop was large, but this is so much more."

Sidonia laughed. "Yes. No one in the world has one quite like this." She rubbed her hands down the side of the frame. "I love my home and I love to weave, but it is very lonely. It has been a long time since I had an apprentice and taught anyone. I just weave now. I am always trying out new techniques and even new kinds of threads. I create new patterns and enjoy the rhythm of it all. I cannot imagine wanting to do anything else."

Joia smiled at her. "Ellota let me try once," she laughed. "It was not as easy as she made it look."

Sidonia laughed. "No, it takes many years to grow as proficient as Ellota is. If you sat at the loom every day, like she does, you would learn the weaver's dance."

The two women stood up and together they folded Joia's tapestry. Sidonia pulled out a cloth remnant from a basket. It was a lovely pale red. She laid it out and folded Joia's Life Tapestry into it.

"Thank you, Sidonia, for everything," Joia said. She hated having to say goodbye to a new friend again.

Sidonia smiled and placed her hand on the side of Joia's face. "It's been an honor meeting you and weaving your life tapestry. I'm sure we will meet again."

"I think so, too," Joia said. She walked out of the cottage and to the wagon. Edmund and Hakon had hitched the horse to the wagon. Edmund took the bundle with Joia's Life Tapestry from her and placed it carefully into the wagon. Hakon helped Joia up into the seat. They said their goodbyes then Edmund snapped the reins of the horse and the wagon lurched forward.

Joia and Hakon waved at Sidonia. She stood at her cottage door, waving back. The wagon turned with the bend in the road and Sidonia and the cottage disappeared.

CHAPTER NINE

Grian the Chandler

"How far is the trip to Athelstan Forest?" Hakon asked after they passed the nearby village.

"Three days if the weather is good and we don't meet with any trouble. It's near the village of Tillmere," Edmund said. He snapped the reins again and the horse picked up a bit of speed.

The three travelers rode quietly in the wagon, each lost in his own thoughts. It wasn't long before Edmund began to sing. Joia loved to listen to Edmund's singing. This particular song was the story about the deeds and valor of a knight called Wilhelm, who faced many terrible foes and starvation to rescue the fair princess Aalys. It was an epic ballad with many stanzas. Afterward, Joia wondered how he remembered them all. He sang until midday when they paused to water the horses and stretch their legs. Joia broke the gingerbread Sidonia had given her into three parts and they ate in the shade of the trees.

The afternoon was warm, and Joia felt tired. She kept nodding off. Finally, after fighting the sleep, Joia felt Hakon's hand touch her head. He gently pulled her head towards his chest and wrapped his arm around her shoulders. Joia leaned into him and fell asleep. The nap didn't last long, and Joia's head jerked up off Hakon's chest. Her sudden movement startled him. Joia looked around. They were still in the wagon; the afternoon sun was high in the sky, and all was as it was when Joia fell asleep.

"Are you all right?" Hakon asked.

"Fine, had a dream, that's all," Joia replied. "The nap was just right, though. I feel rested again. Thank you, Hakon."

They rode on for a while more. Joia thought about her tapestry and the images it showed. She thought about Sidonia, Kloma, and their great-grandson. She wondered about Kloma and what a spinner's magical gift would be. The train of thought led Joia to wonder about the other trades.

What magical gifts did they possess?

When they stopped for the night, Hakon and Edmund set up camp. Joia started the fire and prepared some food. She was still stirring the small kettle when Edmund and Hakon had finished their chores. Hakon had found a long, strong rod of wood. He sat down near the fire, took out his small knife, and began to whittle and work on it. Edmund had a lute in hand. He quietly worked at tuning and polishing it.

"Edmund, may I ask you some questions?" Joia asked.

"Of course." He plucked at one of the strings while turning the tuning knob at the top. The pitch of the note from his plucking at the string changed slightly.

"My mother always told me I ask too many questions," Joia said apologetically.

"Asking questions is the best way to gain knowledge," Edmund answered. "What knowledge do you seek?"

"I was wondering what some of the gifts from the other trade Patrons are?"

"I don't know them all and I don't remember all that I once knew either, but I do remember a few. The Baker's gift is a loaf of bread that never grows old or goes stale and it never runs out. A little bit of the bread goes a long way. It is perfect for travelers." Edmund paused for a moment as he tuned the next string. "The miller can craft a grindstone that will never break, and the blacksmith can forge any tool that will never need repair or sharpening."

"That would be something," Hakon said and held up his knife in the firelight. "My knife is going to need a good sharpening when I can find the right kind of stones," he started to whittle at the wooden rod again. "So, what about the chandler?" Hakon asked.

"You'll find out soon enough. It's best if Grian tells you himself."

They started out on the road to Tillmere the following morning, turning south. The days in the wagon were long and dull. Edmund sang much of the time and Hakon continued whittling at the walking stick, letting the shavings fall into the road.

Joia spent part of the morning sewing a patch over a hole in her dress that she had gotten the previous night while collecting firewood. She had managed to trip over an unseen root, catching her dress on a branch, and tearing a hole in the fabric when she fell. She had not hurt herself but was upset that her dress had torn. Thankfully, it had been an easy repair, but then there was nothing for her to do as they traveled hour after hour and mile after mile.

On the third day after leaving Sidonia's cottage, Edmund said they would reach Tillmere that night and would start asking around to see if anyone knew Grian the Chander.

Joia watched the horse's movements as it walked and found herself counting the swishing of its tail while listening to Edmund humming. Her mind was incredibly bored and her body itching to move, but stuck in between Hakon and Edmund, there was no way she could stretch or move much at all.

Her back was aching, so she twisted herself to her left, toward Edmund, holding the stretch for several seconds before twisting around the right, holding the stretch as long as she could. The wagon started to pass a small sideroad and as Joia looked down at it, she noticed it glowing.

"Stop!" she cried.

Edmund pulled on the reins and brought the wagon to an abrupt halt. Hakon had dropped his knife and was holding his walking stick out like a sword.

"What is it?" Edmund yelled.

"Sorry, Edmund," Joia's face flushed with embarrassment. "I didn't mean to scare you, but the road we just passed," she climbed over Hakon's lap, scooted off the wagon seat, and dropped to the ground. She ran back several feet where she could see the side road again.

Hakon was two steps behind her. He still held the walking stick out in front of him, ready to attack anything. "What is it?"

"The road, Edmund. I think we need to turn down this road," Joia looked up to where Edmund still sat in the wagon seat, holding tight to Bard's reigns.

He pulled back on the reins, backing the horse up until he could see down the road and his face broke out into a smile. "I'm glad you saw it, Joia. I would have gone right past it, and we never would have found Grian."

Joia was grinning as she hopped back into the wagon and sat next to Edmund. Hakon continued to look down the lane. "I don't understand. What did she see? There is no sign to show we turn down this path."

"It's the Light of the Guild, my boy," Edmund said. "It is showing us the way to Grian."

Hakon frowned. He picked up his knife from where it had fallen and put it back into its sheath. He waited until Edmund was able to turn the horse and wagon onto the side lane, then he climbed back into the wagon and stowed the walking stick away.

"I'm sorry I scared you," she said, looking over at Hakon. His face was in a deep frown. Joia wanted to ask him about what had upset him, but he didn't look like he was in the mood for talk, so she let him be.

The road wasn't long, and they soon arrived at a small cottage. Along one side of the cottage were several large kettles hanging from a sturdy frame over a large fire pit. Edmund pulled the wagon to the front of the house and tied the horse to a nearby tree. A strong smell of melted wax filled Joia's nose. It wasn't an unpleasant smell, but it was like burning many candles at once.

Edmund walked up to the wooden door and knocked on it several times. Joia stood behind him and held Hakon's hand in hers. Moments later the door was opened and a small, thin man, stood in front of him.

"Hello, Grian," Edmund greeted the man.

"Edmund! Good to see you, old man," he grabbed Edmund's hand and shook it heartily. "What brings you here? Still traveling the world?"

"Always," Edmund replied.

Grian turned to look at Joia. "Most curious," he softly said and reached out a hand to her. "Welcome. I am Grian, the Chandler. How do you do?"

Joia reached out and took his hand in hers. He lifted her hand to his lips and kissed it. Joia's face flushed as she studied the glowing Patron before her. Grian's eyes were blue, but a pale, cold blue, like ice on a river, very unlike Edmund's bright blue. But there was nothing cold about his face or his manners. His mouth was wide with a smile.

"I'm Joia," she said.

"Hakon," Hakon said, stepping closer to Joia and reaching out his hand to Grian's.

"Who did you gather?"

"Sidonia, Kloma, and Seb. I would have called together more if I had known where they were.

"Excuse me, Edmund?" Joia interrupted, "Who is Seb? I don't think you've mentioned him yet."

Edmund's face grew sad. "Seb is the Map Maker."

"I see," Joia nodded.

Edmund continued with his story, "We decided to wait until Joia was older. We hoped we would come to understand her purpose, but if we did not understand by the time, she was seventeen, we would help her to find her destiny."

"And has she found it?" Grian asked.

"*She* is sitting right here," Joia said, getting quite annoyed at being spoken about, but not spoken to.

"Forgive me, Joia," Grian said, blushing. "Tell me, have you discovered why you possess the Light of the Guild?"

"Well, no, I haven't. That's why we've come to you," Joia said.

"Me?" Grian was surprised. "I seriously doubt I can help you. I didn't know you existed until now."

"Would you tell me about your special gift?"

"My gift?"

"Yes. I know each Patron has a special gift. What is yours?"

Grian touched the candle on the table directly in front of him. He turned it slowly in its holder, looking at his fine workmanship. Joia looked at the candle again and saw the colors and patterns carved into the wax. "My gift is a candle."

CHAPTER TEN

Candles and Thatching

Joia studied the candle on the table. It was a beautiful item, but how could a candle be a special gift?

"What about this candle makes it so much more special than any other candle you make?" Hakon asked.

Grian smiled and his excitement showed in his eyes. "It can hold a flame that never goes out, except by the breath of the one who lit it. It will remain lit and undying in its light, even in the greatest rain or windstorm, nor will it ever get smaller. You can use it for hours and it will never melt." He turned his gaze to Joia. "It will provide light in the darkest places."

Joia thought about the candle that could never go out or melt. She wasn't sure where her quest would take her, but to have a candle that could not go out was a reassuring thought. "What must one do to be worthy of such a candle?" she asked.

"Joia, I see the Light that shines about you. You are worthy of my gift. You don't need to prove that." Grian pushed the candle back into the middle of the table. He stood up and took another candle off the hook it was hanging from. He held it, suspended over the table. "Now, Joia, Hakon, what are candles made of?"

"Tallow and wax," Hakon answered.

"That's right. What is the wick made from?"

"Cord?" Joia asked. She wasn't sure. She was embarrassed to realize that she had never thought about it before, even though she used candles every day.

"Grass?" Hakon asked.

"You are both correct. Candle wicks can be made from either." Grian laid out on the table several things. There were some long strands of straw and grass and there were also several kinds of threads. The threads were all white, but Joia quickly saw the texture of the threads of different materials. "For your candle," Grian continued, "you must choose its core. Pick your wick," he grinned.

Joia looked at the supplies Grian had laid out. They all seemed to be glowing with the Light, which made sense if they had all been made by Grian. None of these stood out more brightly with the Light than the others. Perhaps it didn't matter which one she chose. They were all good. She reached her hand out and touched the various materials. One of the wick materials felt warm under her touch. She picked it up and felt it.

"Linen?" she asked Grian.

"Yes. Three linen strands, twisted together make a wick."

Joia held the linen strands in her hand. She looked at them and ran her fingers along the threads.

"Here is my wick." She said quickly and held it out again to Grian.

"You hold onto it for now," Grian said. He turned his attention to Hakon. "Now Hakon, what about your wick?"

"My wick? No, I don't have the Light or anything special." Hakon took a step back from the table.

"My candles are not for Patrons only. My candles are for anyone who is worthy. You are worthy, thatcher. Not only are you worthy, but you are also Joia's companion and protector. In its own way, this is as much your quest as it is hers."

Hakon stood a little taller. Joia started to realize what this quest she was on might be like for Hakon. Everyone was giving her so much attention. Edmund spoke most often to her. Sidonia had made the Life Tapestry for her. Conversations were about the Patrons, the Light, and Joia. The Patrons they had met were very interested in Joia and paid little heed to Hakon. But Hakon had never complained. He had joined her on this trip and supported her in all she had done. She had never properly thanked him for coming with her.

"Go ahead. Pick out the wick for your candle," Grian encouraged.

Hakon walked back to the table and looked at the materials that were laid out.

Joia understood that this was very special for him, being offered one of the Patron's gifts. She watched him, curious to see how he would choose. He would not have the guidance of the Light as she did. His decisions would be based on something entirely different from hers.

Hakon picked up the dry grass wick from the table. "This one," he said with confidence.

"Very good," Grian said. He removed the remaining wicks from the table. "Bring your wicks and follow me."

He then led them outside to his workspace. Two large cauldrons hung over two fire pits. Grian removed the lids from the cauldrons. He bent down and lit the two fires. Steam began to rise from the clear liquid in the cauldrons.

"This is tallow," Grian pointed to the steaming kettle on his right. "This is beeswax," he pointed to the other. "You must choose how your candle begins and you must be the one to begin it. You will dip the wick into the wax and then hang it here," he indicated a string suspended from two trees. "From there, I will continue to make the candle. Now, make your choice and dip your wick into the wax."

Joia looked at the two vats of wax for several moments before picking the beeswax. She dipped her wick into the wax, up to an inch away from her fingers. She could feel the heat of the wax as her fingers got close to the liquid. She removed the wick from the wax and hung it on the string like Grian showed her.

He nodded his head, and she hoped it was in approval. Joia stood back and watched Hakon make his choice. He stood before the two cauldrons for several moments before going to beeswax. Once Hakon had hung his wick onto the string, Grian stepped forward.

"Very good. I will make your candles now." Grian removed the two wicks from where they had been hung and he put them on a small contraption that held the wicks at their top and allowed Grian to easily dip the candles without getting his hands too close to the hot wax.

"Athelstan, I dedicate my work to you as I create an Everburn candle for Hakon, the Thatcher, and Joia, bearer of the Light. Help my hands to be steady as I dip the candles that they might set properly and burn with your Light. I dedicate my gift to you."

This was the second time Joia had seen a Patron dedicate their work to Athelstan. It was a quiet, reverent moment before beginning their work, bringing their mind, heart, and body to the task at hand.

Grian dipped the two candles into the beeswax, pulled them out, and moved to the tallow. He alternated dipping the candles between the two waxes.

"Joia," Grian said, as he worked, "you chose a linen wick, and you dipped it into beeswax. Why did you choose these things?"

"I don't quite know why. The pure beeswax seemed the best coating for the core." Joia felt very silly. She didn't have a reason why she chose what she did. She made her choice, hoping it was the right one. "In other ways, the Light has guided me, but not this time. Did I do it wrong?" she asked.

Grian stopped and looked at her. "Tell me how the Light has guided you and what happened when you picked your candle."

"Well, when I was doing my spinning for Sidonia for my Life Tapestry, the Light shown on what I needed to spin. I knew exactly what to do, but this time, the Light showed on all the wicks and the wax and tallow. It didn't guide me at all."

"So how did you pick what you did?" he asked.

"I don't know. I just did. The linen felt right in my hands and the beeswax seemed pure and natural."

Grian smiled at her. "Then you chose correctly. The Light might not always guide you, so you need to learn to trust in yourself as much as you have learned to trust in the Light."

Joia let out a long breath that she had been holding. She hadn't done it wrong. Her candle would still work for her. "I have a lot to learn," she quietly spoke.

"Learning is a lifelong process. Even for a three-hundred-year-old Patron, like me." Grian smiled. He dipped the contraption into the wax and then dipped it into the tallow.

Already, Joia could see that the candles were getting bigger.

"And you Hakon," Grian turned to look at the young thatcher. "You were very confident in your choices. Tell me why."

"The wick is grass. It's like straw, which is the basic material for a thatcher. I chose beeswax because it is a good sealer and makes things watertight like thatch should be when it is properly laid." Hakon's explanation was sound and his confidence in his answer reminded Joia that Hakon wasn't just the thatcher's son, but a thatcher himself and truly creditable to his trade. She saw Edmund smiling out of the corner of her eye. He seemed impressed by Hakon's reasoning.

Grian was grinning. "Indeed, you are worthy, Hakon. Your choices are very sound." Grian continued to skillfully dip the wicks into the vats of wax. Joia quietly watched for several moments.

Candle-making was a very long process. Joia began to understand how the candles had to be created, with layers upon layers of wax. It was like weaving, she realized, where the cloth was created one strand at a time. Joia thought about Hakon's thatching. A thatcher constructed a roof, straw by straw, bundle by bundle. Her father, a baker, made bread ingredient by ingredient and pains-taking kneading of the dough. All fine work was done bit by bit. There were no shortcuts in true craftsmanship.

"What happened to your roof?" Hakon asked, pointing to a bare patch in the roof, where the wooden beams could be seen.

"A storm a few months ago," Grian sighed. "A strong wind came and took part of the roof right with it. But the roof was already thinning. It's been here for more than three hundred years and has never been attended to since it was first laid."

"Would you mind if I take a look at it?" Hakon asked. He was already climbing the stone wall near the cottage before Grian could even answer.

"Of course," Grian went on dipping the candles.

Hakon stood on the stone wall and looked over the roof as best as he could from his position. He hoisted himself onto the roof and felt at the reeds of the section of the roof that still seemed to be in good condition. "I am sorry to say this, Grian, but the repairs on this roof weren't done very well."

"That's because this old Patron doesn't know how to thatch well," Grian chuckled.

Hakon looked at Grian in surprise. "You did this?"

"Some of it. When I returned here, about sixty years ago, the cottage was in decent shape, but the roof wasn't. I had seen Thek practice his trade and I figured I remembered enough to make the repairs the roof needed. I only meant it to be a short-term repair, but I haven't seen Thek in decades and I wasn't sure if the Tillmere village thatcher was any good. Besides, it held up for the first few years too, but that was a few decades ago now. Year by year, I've lost more of the roof, but that last storm took more than I can ever hope to repair." Grian shook his head and went on with the candle-making.

Hakon checked a few more areas, then he sat down at the edge of the thatch and slid off, landing on his feet on the ground. "I think I can fix your roof, or at least, mend it until a better job can be done. I wish I had brought my tools."

"I'd be so grateful if you could. The last time it rained, I had quite a bit of water coming into the house," Grian said with a shake of his head.

"Do you have a sharpening stone of any kind?" Hakon asked. He pulled out his knife and looked at it.

"Yes. In the cottage, look in the box next to the hearth. The stones should be in there."

Hakon went into the house. Joia watched Grian as he dipped the candles into the wax again. She wasn't sure what she should be doing, so she stood there and watched Grian work.

"Joia, pull up a chair and sit down," Grian called to her in his good-natured way. He had a happy personality and he seemed to always have a smile on his face. Or perhaps, Joia thought, he was just very happy at having company again in who knows how long. "Edmund, how about a song? I've missed your music these last two hundred years."

Edmund went to his wagon to fetch his lute. There was nowhere to sit, except on the stone wall next to the house, so Joia went there to sit and watch Grian working. Hakon returned from the house, holding a smooth stone the size of his hand. He sat down next to Joia, took out his knife, and began rubbing the stone along the knife's blade with slow, even strokes.

"I like Grian," Joia said, watching the chandler at work. She realized that that probably wasn't the right thing to say to Hakon. "I mean, for a Patron, he's very different from Edmund and Sidonia."

Hakon nodded. "I agree. I can't believe he is making me a candle."

"You deserve his gift," Joia said. "I haven't expressed how thankful I am that you came along with me on this journey, but I want you to know that I am very thankful for you.

Hakon stopped what he was doing and turned to look at her. "Thank you."

"I mean, I know you weren't happy about it," Joia continued, "but I'm so grateful that you came along."

Edmund returned from the wagon and plucked at the strings of the instrument, making fine adjustments to them. When he was satisfied, he began to play. The tune was light-hearted and fun. Edmund's fingers danced along the strings and Joia felt like dancing herself. She swayed gently as he played. Joia didn't think she had seen Edmund have so much fun since she had met him.

When the song ended, Grian let out a happy laugh. "You remembered!" he cried out.

Edmund smiled and nodded. Joia wondered what the significance of the song was to Grian and Edmund, but neither Patron said anything else about it.

Edmund began to play another song. Joia thought about how long-lived the Patrons were. They had three centuries of memories and had lived to see hundreds of generations pass, but they never got older. How can you form friendships when you watch everyone you love age and die? She supposed Edmund's most treasured memories were probably the time he lived in Athelstan's castle with all the other Patrons. Only another Patron could understand what a three-hundred-year-old life meant.

With Edmund singing, Grian dipping the candles back and forth into the two kinds of wax, and Hakon sharpening his knife, Joia felt idle sitting there, doing nothing, and she did not like to be idle. She went to the wagon and opened her bundle. She would work on the shirt she had started for Hakon. As often as she tried to sew while they were riding in the wagon, it wasn't easy. She had not had a good opportunity to do some sewing since starting on this journey, but now was perfect. If she worked hard, she might be able to have it done in a day or two.

She got out the needle and thread. She held up a long length of string. "Could you?" she asked Hakon. He held up his knife and touched it to the thread. The thread snapped in two.

"Thank you," she said, tying a knot into one end of the thread.

"What are you doing?" Hakon asked.

"Sewing," she grinned.

"I know that, but what are you sewing?"

"A shirt for you. You came with nothing, and I wanted to show you my gratitude. Before leaving Erthenhorn, that morning, I saw the golden Light sitting in my sewing basket. When I went there, I saw the length of fabric I had recently purchased. I grabbed it, not knowing why. Then I realized that you needed a second shirt, so I am making one for you.

"That is very generous," he said. "Will it glow with your golden light?" he asked.

She shook her head. "I don't think so. Only things made by the Patrons glow and I'm not a Patron nor do I have a trade. It's just sewing."

He sharpened his knife a few more times with the stone, then put the sharpening stone on the wall next to Joia and sheathed his knife. He walked along the wall until he got to the roof again and he hopped up onto the roof. Joia watched a little as he walked around, feeling at the thatch. She couldn't see what he was doing from where she sat, so she returned to her sewing.

"How long did it take you to make that beautiful candle that sits on your table?" Joia asked Grian.

He laughed. "A long time. The dipping lasted about a week. The candle has thousands of layers of wax and multiple colors. I love the effect of the colors, but to make so many colors take a lot of extra time and resources. I made several candles like that one at the same time since I had so many cauldrons of colored wax going. None of them were as fancy as that one, though."

"How did you make all the designs?"

"After the last coats were put on, I dipped the candle in a very hot, clear wax. While the wax is still warm, I use a knife to carefully cut the candle. Because it is warm, but not hot, the wax is pliable, and I can twist and bend the sections of the candle into the base candle. Cutting into the candle also shows off the multiple layers of colors. It's a long but rewarding process."

"I am learning that all the trades require tremendous patience," Joia said.

"That is why it takes so many years of learning and practice before any tradesman can be considered a master of their trade. It does not come easily. If it did, everyone could be a master of every trade."

"I hadn't thought of that before," Joia said.

Edmund brought over several instruments and sat next to Joia. He put a bit of oil onto a rag and started to rub the wood on a lute.

"Why do you do that?" Joia asked.

"It keeps the wood from drying out and cracking. If the instrument cracks, it will not sound good and will quickly break. The oil protects the wood," he explained.

"I see," she said. "How many instruments can you play?"

He laughed. "Many. But the lute is my favorite. I like the fiddle, but I don't get much chance to play it unless we are stopped for a while at a camp. I can't play it while riding in the wagon and it doesn't travel as easily as my lute does. The same goes for the harp that I played at Sidonia's home."

"I hope to hear you play your fiddle one day," she said.

He nodded. "Perhaps tomorrow. I don't think we will start out until the afternoon. I know Hakon wants to do what he can for the roof."

"Do you have anything you need washed or mended?" she asked. "I can do that tomorrow while Hakon is working."

"I would be grateful if you could," he said. "I am a luthier. I'm not good with needle and thread."

They had another good hour of sunlight in which everyone worked on their various projects before twilight arrived and it was too dark to see anymore.

Hakon quit working and slid off the roof onto the ground with a grunt. "I've got a good start for tonight. I'll finish it tomorrow."

Joia put away the needle and thread back into her bundle. She had also made good progress on Hakon's shirt.

"I'm almost done with this," Grian said, dipping the candles into the wax again. "Joia, Hakon, would you go into the house and re-stoke the fire? When I'm done here, we will eat."

They took their things into Grian's house and Joia set her sewing in a corner while Hakon replaced the sharpening stones in their box.

Joia went to the fire, picked up the iron poker, and prodded at the embers. "We're low on firewood. I saw a pile by the wall."

"I'll get it," Hakon said, and went back out of the cottage, returning just a few moments later.

Joia refilled the kettle and set it over the fire to heat. Hakon brought the firewood and placed it in the hearth. It wasn't a minute later that the fire was blazing, sending light and heat through the cottage.

Joia collected the bowls from where she had put them away earlier in the day and she set the table. For a heartbeat, Joia could picture a life where she and Hakon were married and taking care of a cottage together. He would bring in the firewood and she would cook him dinner. He would tell her about his day while they ate and then they would sit together, working on projects, and talking before going to their bed together.

At that point in her imaginings, Joia blushed. It was not ladylike to think of sharing a bed with Hakon. But she wanted that life so much. She hoped that when this was over and she had done whatever it was she was supposed to do, she might still have that future with Hakon.

He came over to her and took her hand. "It's very kind of you to make me a new shirt," he said.

"I'll need to measure you tonight," she said. "I want to make sure I get the sleeves right. I'm also going to do some washing tomorrow if you have anything you would like me to clean." She was rambling, feeling a strange anticipation in her chest with Hakon standing so close to her.

He shook his head and took another step closer to her. "May I kiss you?" he asked, quietly.

She nodded, wanting nothing more than to know what Hakon's lips would feel like on hers.

He stood a head taller than her, so he was forced to lean down, but when their lips connected, Joia felt her entire body shudder with joy. Nothing had ever felt so lovely and exciting. He pulled his head away but rested his forehead on top of hers.

"Sweet Joia," he whispered and caressed her face in his calloused hands.

"Hakon," she choked out.

They heard a sound from outside; like iron scraping against iron and Joia figured that Grian was putting the lids back on his kettles of wax. They stepped apart but were both smiling at each other.

"Edmund's going to know," she said.

"How? Does your mystical Light tell him that too?"

"No, but if I look as happy as you do at this moment, he's going to know what passed between us."

He smiled and laughed softly. "You're right."

She cleared her throat. "It's good of you to mend Grian's roof," Joia said. She looked up at the ceiling and where she could see patches of sky through it.

"I hope I can do a proper job," Hakon stepped away and sat down at the table. "Without the right materials or my tools, it won't be easy. But I also feel that I can repay Grian for making me a candle. It's very generous of him. And besides, I enjoy working my trade. I haven't had a chance to work in weeks now and I miss it." Hakon had moved back to the other side of the hearth and was shifting the burning logs.

"Are you going to be able to do much to the roof?"

"Not really. I just don't have the proper tools or supplies. To truly repair the roof, it would take many bundles of thatch, but I think I can work with what I've got. It will be a quick patch-up, but it should keep the rain out, anyway."

"I'm sure he will appreciate staying dry on rainy days," Joia said.

Until Grian came back in, there wasn't much Joia could do. She saw a broom in a corner and started to sweep. She needed to be doing something with her hands or else she would find herself moving back in Hakon's arms.

"Are you all right, Joia?" Hakon asked.

She let out a quiet giggle. "You ask me that after you just kissed me?"

He smiled and shrugged. "Do you regret it?"

"Not at all, and if I didn't fear Edmund or Grian walking in on us at any moment, you can be sure I would be kissing you again," she said. "I don't think I'll ever be the same."

He looked proud of himself, went to her, and kissed her again.

"I never imagined it would be so nice," she sighed.

"You are wonderful," he said. He pulled her to sit down at the table and he held her hands in his.

Outside, Grian dipped the candles once more as he watched as Joia and Hakon went into the house. He was done with the candles. They would solidify now. He hung them on the line and started to clean his work area. Hakon came back out of the house, collected some firewood, and went back in.

"Edmund?" Grian called softly.

Edmund had put his lute back into the wagon. He returned and stood near the kettle that held the beeswax. "What is it?"

"This girl, Edmund. Who is she? Could she somehow be a descendant of Athelstan?" Grian asked.

"I don't know," Edmund answered. Sidonia had asked him the same thing. She is a simple villager, the daughter of a baker and has a mother, sister, and brother. Aside from that, there isn't much more to her. She's a mystery."

"Why did you bring her here?"

"She has a destiny. I don't know what it is and unfortunately, she doesn't know either. That's what we are trying to find."

"But why did you bring her to me?" Grian asked.

Edmund looked surprised. "Why not? You are a Patron."

"You said you didn't know where I lived and yet you sought me out. You could have taken her to a half dozen other Patrons, I'm sure. So why bring her to me?" Grian asked.

"I took her to Sidonia first," Edmund started, but Grian's laugh interrupted his answer.

"You always did like the lovely weaver," Grian chuckled.

"Grian, do you want me to answer your question or not?" Edmund frowned.

"All right, all right. Yes, Edmund, I would like you to answer my question," Grian said, scattering the dying embers around his kettles and putting their lids back on with a loud scrape of iron on iron.

"As I was saying," Edmund began again, "I took Joia to Sidonia. You know her gift is the Life Tapestry. I figured she would be our best starting point for this unknown quest. And she is one of the few who I knew where she lived. Joia fulfilled Sidonia's requirements and Sidonia was able to weave a tapestry. One unlike she had ever woven before. Joia's reading of the Life Tapestry is still inexperienced, but it showed her a candle and your cottage by a castle. So, we came here."

"I see," Grian thought for a moment. "Do you have any ideas? Any inkling at all as to her purpose?"

"None. She's intelligent for a girl her age with no experience in life, but she is not trained in a trade. Other than the Light, she does not seem in any way extraordinary. You saw her this afternoon. When you questioned her about her choices in the making of her candle, she was unsure, whereas Hakon knew exactly what he was doing. He is a tradesman."

"The Light in her is extraordinary enough," Grian said, looking back at the house.

"Indeed," Edmund said. "As far as we are aware, no one has ever been born with the Light about them."

"Tell me about Hakon. He seems like a good person. He offered to fix my roof. Or patch it, anyway." Grian said.

Edmund nodded. "He is a good man. His experiences as a thatcher make him more knowledgeable about many things and he's traveled outside his village to work so he is more aware of the world than Joia."

"Are they siblings? Lovers?" Grian asked with a sly grin.

"No," Edmund said, "although it is clear that Hakon loves her a great deal and she seems to return his affections. They are not courting or even promised to each other, so far as I know, but from what I have witnessed between those two, I would not be surprised to learn one day that they had married."

Grian looked at the house for several moments. "It seems to me that the Light would choose someone more like Hakon than Joia."

"You would think so," Edmund said. "But the Light has chosen Joia. There must be a reason so we must trust the Light."

Grian and Edmund went into the house. The fire was blazing, and Joia had set bowls on the table. Grian produced more of the same food he fed them earlier in the day. He laughed as they ate, "I'm not a cook. My meals are simple."

"They are fine. You are kind to share with us," Joia said. She washed the bowls when their meal was done. "Will you let me fix you a morning meal tomorrow?" she asked.

Grian laughed. "If you can find enough to make a meal with, then you are most welcome to cook. I get tired of eating my own cooking."

Grian allowed Joia and Hakon to sleep in his house. He extended the offer to Edmund, who declined to go sleep in his tent. Joia and Hakon laid out their bedrolls and Grian provided them with as many blankets as he could to soften the floor. They were made as comfortable as possible and thanked Grian, who extinguished all the candles before going to his bed.

"Hakon, are you asleep yet?" Joia whispered into the dark.

"Not yet," he said. "Is there something wrong?" he asked.

"Do you think we'll ever be somewhere so dark we won't be able to see and will need to use Grian's candle?" Joia asked. She tried to sound casual about the question, but in truth, she was quite terrified to think that she might ever be somewhere so dark.

"Well, I doubt your Life Tapestry would have told you to come here if you didn't need one of Grian's candles," Hakon chuckled.

Joia had known in her heart that was probably true. Why would the Light have led her here if she didn't need an Everburn candle? The cottage was dark, but some moonlight showed through holes in the roof. She couldn't imagine a place with no light.

"Where is your hand?" he asked.

"Here," she reached out towards Hakon. A moment later, he found her hand and held it tightly in his. She felt comfort in his warm touch.

"You're worried about this, aren't you?" Hakon asked.

"Just a little," she replied. She swallowed hard at the lump that had formed in her throat. "All right, a lot. I don't know what I'm doing. I'm afraid I've read the Life Tapestry wrong, and I made Edmund bring us out here for nothing. I'm afraid of being somewhere so dark that a magical candle is the only source of light I'll have. And what's worse is I'm afraid that I'll be alone."

"If I can help it, you'll never be alone, Joia." Hakon squeezed her hands.

"But what if I am?"

"Then you have your candle," he said.

Joia sniffed back the tears that had formed. "You'll stay with me? No matter what"

"Of course, Joia. I always will."

Joia woke early the following morning. She was pleased to find Grian had a small, but nice supply of salted meats, some vegetables, flour, lard, and a small crock of butter. Edmund brought in the last of the food they had purchased while they were staying with Sidonia, but they had only gotten what they needed for a three-day journey, so there wasn't much left. Joia started making a stew and was adding the potatoes into the pot when Grian came in.

"Mmm, that smells so good. I'm going to go to Tillmere and buy some bread," he said.

Joia nodded. "That will be nice to have. Thank you so much for hosting us with no notice. You have been so generous to feed us and give us soft blankets to sleep on.

"It has been a long time since I had visitors, especially one so lovely as you. I am very happy to have you here." Grian grabbed a worn hat from a peg and headed off to town. Joia soon had a nice stew cooking.

While Grian was gone, Hakon went outside to start working on the roof. He had found several pieces of wood in the wood box that he said would be acceptable substitutes for some of his missing tools.

Hakon climbed up onto the wall and then onto the roof. Carefully navigating his way through the old thatch and wooden beams, he began working at the reeds near the bare spots on the roof. Joia brought out a bowl of biscuit dough and kneaded it while she watched Hakon work. He cut apart some of the bundles of reed that were still in good condition and thinned out some of the larger bundles of reed into smaller bundles and used his newly sharpened knife to cut and trim the reed. Using a piece of flat wood, he beat the bundles of reed into place.

Joia had never watched Hakon work before. He was very efficient and intense in his concentration on the job. He had rolled up his sleeves and she could see the well-defined muscles in his arms as he worked. It was several moments of watching his muscles before she realized what she was doing. She looked away, feeling rather embarrassed, hoping that Edmund hadn't noticed the way she had been staring.

She took her dough back into the cottage and fried the biscuits in a hot pan. She looked up and could see Hakon working.

He laughed when he saw her watching him. "Don't let the thatch fall into the food," he said.

"I'm keeping a close eye on it and you," she returned.

Hakon had the first patch completed by the time Grian came back from the market with a loaf of rye bread. Hakon climbed off the roof and Joia brought out the bowls of stew and a plate of fried biscuits into the morning light. Edmund brought out a few chairs from the house and they either sat in the chairs or on the stone wall while they ate.

"Joia, that was wonderful. Your cooking is so much better than mine," Grian said as he rubbed his stomach.

She laughed and thanked him as she gathered the dishes they had used and took them out to wash. Joia might not know much about the trades, but she knew how to take care of a household and feed hungry men.

She returned the dishes to the house, then she gathered up the clothes that needed washing. She went to the stream with a large bowl and filled it with water. Using some lye soap that Grian had given her, she started to wash the clothes. She scrubbed at the material, singing a song that she and Ebba would sing while washing. She missed her sister during times like this. They had always done the household chores together.

I saw a woman washing,
Her hair was white as snow.
She dropped her dress in the river,
And watched it start to flow.

I saw a woman washing,
She stood to find the dress,
She slipped in the river's mud,
Her clean dress now a mess.

She jumped into the river,
And swam for all her life.
She caught her floating dress,
And lamented about her strife.

I saw her swim to shore,
Dripping, soaked, and wet.
She had managed to accomplish,
Three washings in one get.

"Where did you learn that song?" Edmund came to her at the stream's side.

Joia blushed. "My sister and I made it up. We're not very clever with our words, as you can easily tell, but it helped pass the time. I don't know how many verses we came up with, but at one time, it was a very long song."

He laughed. "It's very clever."

"No, it's not, Edmund. Certainly nothing like your songs."

"It's perfect for the task and even better because you created it yourself with your sister," he said.

She was hit with another wave of homesickness. Her father and brother would have been at the bakery for hours by now and her mother and sister were probably working in the garden.

"I miss them," she said. "But right now, I wouldn't want to be anywhere but here on this journey." She dunked her washing back into the stream. "I just fear I'll disappoint you all," she quietly said.

"There is nothing to fear there. I might not understand your purpose yet, but I feel a kind of anxiety stirring in my soul. It is where I feel my entertainers when they say their dedication to me. Some of them are feeling worried and discouraged. That is very unusual for them. Something's wrong that has never been wrong before and I think that somehow, you are the way to setting things right again."

"Do you think so?"

He nodded. "I do. And whatever it is you need to do, Hakon and I will be by your side."

"Thank you, Edmund. I know I am not skilled in a trade or even have much knowledge, but you've been kind and patient with me, and I appreciate that," she said, feeling better and more worried than before at the same time. How would she find out what was wrong and how would she fix it? It seemed an impossible task.

Then, she remembered kissing Hakon last night. Had that been real or a dream? She could almost feel his lips on hers. She had never experienced anything like it before.

She wanted to kiss him again but knew that the opportunity was nearly nonexistent with Edmund always around, but that's the way it should be. They weren't even promised to each other, nor had ever talked about marriage before. What if he didn't want to be married to her?

Edmund stood up. "We've got a few hours left before we leave. If you get those clothes laid out on Grian's stone wall, they should be mostly dry by the time we need to head out."

"Yes, of course. I'll be done soon," she said, coming out of her thoughts. She blushed when she realized that she had been thinking about kissing Hakon while Edmund had sat with her. She doubled her efforts at scrubbing. She dumped the water from the bowl and took the clean clothes to the stream again. She rinsed them and squeezed them hard, twisting them to get as much of the water out as she could. Then she put all the clothes back into the big bowl and went back to the cottage.

It was midmorning now and the summer sun was already quite hot. Edmund and Grian were standing near the kettles of wax, talking, while Grian dipped a half dozen candles into the wax. Hakon had moved and was working on another section of the roof.

Joia started to lay out the clean clothes on the wall and Grian's things were hung on a rope where he had Joia and Hakon's Everburn candles hanging. When the clothes were laid out to dry, Joia grabbed her sewing, went out to sit on the stone wall, and sat next to the drying clothes. She looked up and spent several minutes watching Hakon. Thatching was hard work. Each reed had to be in place for the bundle to be tight.

Edmund came and sat next to her. "I've always enjoyed watching tradesmen at their work," he said. "Each trade is so different and requires great skill and patience. It takes years and years of practice to be able to do it properly."

"Yes," Joia agreed. "I've spent years watching my father and brother at work in the bakery. Every batch of dough must be just right for the type of bread it is, and they must be kneaded to a specific texture before they can be baked. I've also spent a lot of time with the village spinners and weavers, too. I know how to clean, dye, and card wool. The Erthenhorn spinner is named Letty. She let me try spinning a couple of times. It's much harder than it looks."

Edmund chuckled. "I imagine so."

"I've never seen Hakon work his trade before," Joia admitted. "I had no idea what was involved in thatching a roof." She laughed, "For starters, I'm impressed with his balance on the beams. I'm sure if I tried, I'd fall off."

"Better keep you off the roof, then," Grian said walking up to them. He sat down on the stone wall on Joia's other side. They all watched Hakon at work, who sensed he was being watched.

He peeked over his arm and saw the three faces staring up at him. "You're making me nervous, watching me like that."

"Sorry Hakon," Grian laughed. "Just watching a tradesman work his trade. We three here have great respect for that. However, I'll take this opportunity to finish up the work on your candles and make sure they are ready for when you leave." Grian hopped off the wall and walked to where he had the candles hanging from a line.

"I'll go pack the rest of our things into the wagon," Edmund said. He left Joia sitting on the wall, alone. She found herself staring at Hakon again, no longer watching the process of a roof being thatched, but watching the thatcher. He was very handsome when he worked. She smiled, enjoying her view.

Hakon pulled out his knife and used it to cut away at the thatch, evening it up with the rest of the roof.

"Hakon," she called up to him. "How long does it take to thatch a roof?"

"Depends on the size of the roof," Hakon called back to her.

"Well, how about a roof like Grian's?"

"A couple of weeks to do a proper job. I'm not too happy about my work here. I could do much better if I had some more straw to work with."

"Well, if you get the holes in the roof covered so rain's not dripping down on his head, I'm sure Grian will be happy with your work." Joia smiled.

He used his flat piece of wood and beat the reeds into place. "It will be covered, but barely. This is only a short-term fix for the roof. He needs a thatcher with better tools and supplies to get the repair work that needs doing."

Grian walked back over to the wall and stood next to Joia. "That settles it, then. When you're done with your adventures, come back and I'll make sure you have the materials you need to do a proper job on this roof."

"Sounds like a deal," Hakon said. He climbed down from the roof. "There you go. I've done what I can."

"Thank you, so much," Grian said looking up at the roof. Joia couldn't see any holes in the thatch at all. If this was poor work, in Hakon's eyes, she wondered what a good job looked like. Maybe she would be able to come back and watch Hakon do a proper job of repairing Grian's roof. She smiled, feeling her face getting hot again.

"Your candles are ready," Grian said. He handed Joia her candle and Hakon his. Joia studied her candle. Grian had carved a vine with flowers into Joia's candle. She noticed the wick that poked out at the top of the candle had a soft golden glow.

"It's lovely, thank you," she said.

"This is very generous of you," Hakon agreed.

"I love it when I get to make an Everburn candle for someone. Doing both of your candles has been a joy for me. So, what are your plans? What will you do now?" Grian asked.

They all looked at Joia. "I don't know," she said. "I suppose I had better look at my Life Tapestry and see if there is any direction on what to do next."

She took her new candle and placed it in her bundle of personal belongings. From the red bundle, she pulled out the beautiful length of cloth Sidonia had woven for her. Grian cleared off his worktable and Joia spread the cloth onto it. She looked at it, at first only seeing the swirling colors, then the colors began taking shape. She saw a scroll. The scroll opened and showed a blue river, a green forest, and pointed peaks all bunched up together. A dotted line moved along the scroll from image to image. Then the colors went back to their usual place in the cloth. Joia blinked her eyes a few times and looked up at the three men.

Hakon asked. "What did you see?"

Joia thought for a moment, "Well, at first there was a scroll. It was rolled up. Then, it unrolled, and I could see drawings on it. There were small, well, I don't know how to explain them, peaks?" Joia held her hands together. Her fingers were pressed together, but her palms were separated. "It is like a pointed peak." Edmund nodded his head in understanding. "There was a blue curvy line, like a river, and a small drawing of a forest. A cluster of trees. All these things were connected by a dotted line."

"Interesting," Edmund said. "Grian? Hakon? Any ideas?"

"Those peaks, clustered together, could they be a drawing of a mountain range?" Grian asked.

"It's a map," Hakon replied. "This scroll is a map."

"A map! That's it!" Joia said.

"Do you think she needs to go to see Seb?" Grian asked.

"You mentioned Seb recently, but who is he again?" Hakon asked.

"Seb is the Patron of Map Makers," Grian explained. "Did you know that his special gift is that he can create a map?"

"I figured as much," Hakon said.

Grian laughed. "Yes, Hakon. But his maps move."

"What do you mean?" Joia asked.

"Seb creates a map that moves with the user," Grian answered.

"How is that helpful? Why would you want a map that moves? You'd never find anything that way," Hakon said.

"Well, I suppose it depends on what the user wants to find. I don't claim to understand it," Grian said. He laughed again. "Edmund, you are unusually quiet. Don't you have anything to say about Seb and his maps?"

Edmund looked at Grian with a scowl. "I'm not terribly excited about the idea of going to see Seb."

"Why not? You two were the very best of friends," Grian said.

Edmund sighed. "We had a falling out about one hundred fifty years ago." He looked at Joia, who was folding her tapestry back up.

"You and Seb?" Grian asked in surprise. "You were like brothers."

"And brothers fight," Edmund growled. "We've been lucky, Joia. So far, the Patrons you have met have been kind and helpful. Seb might not be quite so friendly." Joia and Hakon looked at each other with worried expressions. "Seb is aware of you, Joia. He was in that first gathering I had after I saw you for the first time."

"You invited Seb to your little meeting and not me?" Grian put on an offended look.

"I told you Grian, I didn't know where you were, but I knew where Seb was," Edmund said. Grian smiled at having gotten Edmund worked up. "He has lived in Yondalla most of the last three hundred years."

"Then that's where we should go next," Joia said.

Edmund took a deep breath and let it out slowly, then he nodded. "We go to Yondalla."

It didn't take them long to get ready. Edmund had already packed the wagon and only needed to hitch up Bard. He did this quickly, giving his horse a carrot as he did. When he was done, he climbed into his usual seat and took Bard's reins.

"Joia, it was a real pleasure to meet you," Grian said. He took Joia's hand in his and kissed it.

Joia blushed. "And you. Thank you for the candle. It's wonderful. I hope we meet again, soon."

"Yes, I hope so," Grian helped Joia climb into the wagon's seat. He then shook hands with Hakon. "Best of luck, Hakon, and thanks for working on the roof. Don't forget, you promised to come back and repair the rest of it."

"I won't forget. Thank you, Grian," Hakon said. He climbed into the wagon and sat next to Joia.

"Well, Storyteller, you know where I live now. Don't be several centuries before you visit again."

"Don't worry. We'll see each other again soon, I'm sure." Edmund snapped the reins and his horse started walking. "Goodbye!" Everyone called goodbye to each other and soon Grian's house was out of sight.

"Before we head out to Seb's we are going to the village to get some food for the journey. I have a few coins left and I'll let you two do the shopping," Edmund said.

Joia felt quite guilty every time Edmund had taken them into a village for food. She had brought no money and thus far, all their food had been provided by Edmund, Sidonia, Grian, and the band of entertainers they had briefly traveled with. She had not helped to contribute to their food at all.

"Edmund, you have been so kind to help me on this journey. You have made it easy for me, taking me to the Patrons in your wagon and providing our food. Is there anything I can do, to help or repay you?"

Edmund smiled. "No, Joia. You have been a wonderful help in preparing food and washing our clothes, so I feel that we have a fair trade-off. Besides, this journey is fascinating and curious. I'm honored to be a part of it."

They pulled up to the edge of the village. Edmund found a place to park his wagon and tied up his horse. From a pouch, he produced several coins and pressed them into Joia's hands.

"Find us some meats, breads, and whatever else you think we might need. We have a long journey to get to Seb's and he isn't as likely to share so freely when we do get to him."

Joia took the coins from Edmund. She and Hakon started into the village and immediately, it felt like she was home. She loved the village life. People walking about all the time. There was always someone to talk to and things to do. The markets were busy, and children were running around, playing games while their parents worked or shopped. It was all wonderfully familiar to Joia.

Hakon quickly found the main center where the market. He and Joia walked from cart to cart to see what was available. Someone was playing music and singing a song. On the other side of the marketplace was a man juggling four round balls. Joia and Hakon stopped to watch him.

"I wonder if any of Edmund's people juggle like this?" Joia asked.

Hakon shrugged. "Ask him. You know how much he loves to talk about his people."

After purchasing some salted meats, they went to the bakery. The smell of warm bread filled their noses and Joia felt tears spring to her eyes. The bakery smelled like home.

"Are you all right, m'dear?" the lady in the shop said after seeing Joia.

"I'm fine," Joia sniffed. She collected some bread and three meat pasties and was out of there as quickly as she could. She left the shop and went back to the market. Every night before falling asleep she thought of her family and missed them. But walking into that bakery and smelling those familiar smells made her realize just how much she missed her family.

Hakon was right behind her, holding the small basket of their food. Joia turned and placed the pastries and bread into the basket.

"Joia?" he asked, moving close and pulling her to him in a hug. Joia leaned into his chest. She dabbed her eyes with her sleeve.

"Forgive me, Hakon. It was silly of me to act that way," she sniffed.

"It wasn't silly at all. You miss your family."

"Yes," Joia answered.

"I know. I miss my father, too, but it's all right, Joia. We'll see them all again, one day, and until then, you and I are together."

Joia smiled. "Yes, we're together. Thank you for coming with me. You left your father and your home to go with me into the unknown. You've been so patient while the Patrons discussed me and the Light. I don't know what I would do without you."

Hakon squeezed her a little tighter. "I'm happy to be here, with you." He held her for a moment longer before letting go.

Joia dabbed her eyes once again, stood up straighter, and looked Hakon in the face. "So, where now?"

"Well, we have our meats, our bread, and another coin," Hakon answered. "What do you think? Do we need anything else?"

"Let's go to that seller over there," Joia pointed at a cart several feet away. "We can get some vegetables."

Joia and Hakon went to the cart and Joia picked out some cabbage, potatoes, carrots, and a small sack of peas. The noise level in the market had gotten quieter. She and Hakon went to the center of the marketplace and found Edmund there. He was telling one of his stories to an entranced audience. They stood together and watched Edmund work his trade. When his story was done, he broke out into a lively song and sang as people tossed coins at his hat. Joia and Hakon made their way back to the wagon.

Joia began to pack the food away and Hakon went back to the village well to refill their water pouches. It was only a few minutes later that Edmund returned. He carefully put his lute into its box in the wagon.

"I enjoyed your story, Edmund," Joia said.

"Thank you," he answered. "Where's Hakon?"

"Here I am," Hakon jogged up to the wagon, holding the full dripping water pouches. He put them into the wagon and joined Edmund and Joia in the seat.

"I assume you got the things I sent you for?" Edmund asked.

"Yes, Edmund," Joia said. After several minutes on the road, Joia asked Edmund, "Where do you learn all of your stories?"

"From all over. As I travel, I hear others tell stories and I learn some from them. Some stories are from actual events that I hear about or see myself. Many of my stories are ones I made up. As I travel during the day in the wagon, I am often thinking up new stories. It is my favorite way to pass the time."

"Have you been thinking up any new stories lately?" Joia asked.

"Of course," he smiled. "I'm working on an especially exciting one right now." Edmund turned Bard onto the road, and they started to head out of town.

"Will we get to hear your story?" she asked.

"When it is ready," Edmund said, smiling at her. They went down the road, the wagon creaking softly as they went.

"Do any of your people juggle?" she asked after several minutes. "We saw someone in the market who was juggling four balls," Joia told him.

Edmund nodded. "Many of the entertainers do. It's a fun thing to learn and it's especially popular with the children."

"Can you juggle?" Hakon asked.

Edmund smiled. "I can, but I only can do three balls at a time, although I've got quite a few tricks I can do. I have several tradesmen who are quite skilled in juggling and I can think of at least two who can juggle as many as seven balls at a time, but that is very tricky."

"Seven?" Joia gasped.

"They are quite impressive," Edmund nodded.

"Does it bother you when your tradesmen are better at some things than you?" Hakon asked.

"No. In this trade, there are so many things that can be done to entertain. I cannot do them all. I am not a particularly good dancer, and my juggling skills are limited. As a Patron, it is my job to watch over them, guide them, and bless them. Some of my tradesmen come up with incredibly clever things. Things that I never dreamed of, and I am proud of them."

"Will you show us your juggling one day?" Joia asked.

Edmund nodded. "One day."

CHAPTER ELEVEN

Troubles on the Road

The road they were traveling on had a good deal of wild berries. They were plump and ripe with summer. Joia often walked alongside the wagon to pick the berries. They provided a nice addition to their daily meals.

But the days were long on the road and Joia had a hard time with hours upon hours of not being able to do much of anything. She finished Hakon's shirt and was pleased to find she had sewed the size just right. She noticed one of Hakon's stockings had a hole in it, so she spent part of the morning darning it. It wasn't an easy task to do riding in the wagon. When Edmund saw her handiwork, he asked if she would be willing to do some mending on his clothes. Joia was more than happy to help. It gave her something to do and she felt that in her own way, she could show Edmund her thanks.

They were on their third day after leaving Grian's and had stopped Bard at a stream, giving him the chance to drink and rest, before starting out again. The afternoon was quiet, Edmund was humming, Hakon was working on his latest whittling project, a large stirring spoon for Joia to use when she cooked, and Joia was darning a sock.

Suddenly, a man jumped out of the woods, yelling, and running toward them. The yells and sudden appearance of the man scared Edmund's horse, who reared back, knocking Hakon off the seat to the ground. Joia fell forward and almost fell through the gap between the horse and wagon while Edmund pulled on the horse's reins, trying to regain control.

The attacker jumped onto the wagon, right next to Joia, and started to pull at her. She cried out and kicked while Edmund's arm went around her shoulders. Hakon was up in an instant and pulled the attacker off the wagon. They both fell to the ground and scrambled back onto their feet just as quickly. Hakon threw the first punch, and the attacker was knocked over.

Joia pulled herself back into the seat and tried to find something she could use as a weapon against the man, but Edmund was already pulling out a quarterstaff from off the side of the wagon and came around with it just as Hakon got punched in the stomach. Edmund swung out his staff at the man, knocking him back.

Hakon stood up and pulled the attacker up by his shirt holding him tightly by the collar.

"I have to get away!" The man yelled, struggling against Hakon's firm grip. "They'll get me!"

"After you grabbed at the lady like that, you deserve to be captured," Edmund said, his deep voice rumbled with fierceness.

"No, no! Please!" the man yelled. "I'm an honest man who was done wrong."

"You attacked us," Hakon said, giving the man a shake.

"Who are you trying to get away from?" Edmund asked.

"The collectors. Help me," the man looked back into the forest where he had just run from. He turned back to look at Hakon, "Please," he begged.

"Climb on top of the wagon and lay flat. Don't make a sound," Edmund said.

The man's eyes widened. "Oh, thank you. Bless you, sir, bless you."

Hakon released the man and watched as he climbed onto the top of the wagon.

Edmund climbed back onto the wagon seat. "Quickly, Hakon, get in."

Hakon was back in the seat in a moment, glaring at Edmund. "What are you doing?"

"Silence," Edmund whispered. He snapped the reins and the horse started down the road again. It wasn't more than a minute later when three men on horses came out of the forest behind the wagon. Joia sat shaking in her seat. The men rode up to the wagon and Edmund pulled Bard to a halt.

"You there!" one of the men shouted. "Have you seen a villain run past here?"

The second man pointed at Hakon. "I see you have. Your friend is bleeding."

Joia looked at Hakon, his nose was indeed bleeding. She hadn't noticed earlier. Hakon was frowning and doing his best to wipe the blood off his face.

"Yes, we did," Edmund said excitedly. "He ran out at us and tried to attack our wagon, but my brother here fought him off. He ran off into the woods, across the road back there."

The men looked back down the road. "How do I know you are telling the truth?" the first man asked.

"Don't you see that my brother is bleeding?" Edmund asked.

"Where are you off to, entertainer?" the man sneered at Edmund, saying the word 'entertainer' like it was a filthy word.

"Wherever the road takes me," Edmund answered breezily.

"Come on," the third horseman called to his two companions, "We are going to lose him if we stay here talking to these people." With that, he headed back down the road and led his horse into the forest.

"Watch yourself, entertainer. Don't go making trouble in these lands. Our master would be very unhappy and then we would have to hunt you down." The two men laughed cruelly.

"I thank you for the warning," Edmund nodded his head at them. "But have no fears, good sirs, I would do nothing to cross you or your master. Pass our compliments on the condition of the roads through his land. They are much better than others I have traveled on."

With that, the two men joined their fellow and headed back down the road. Edmund watched the two other men ride down the road and disappear into the woods, "Let's go, Bard." He snapped the horse's reins again. "Lay low sir."

Joia's head and heart were pounding. She had never encountered bandits or thieves before. She pulled out one of the water pouches from the back of the wagon and handed it to Hakon. He poured some of the water into his hands and tried to wash off the blood from his face. Joia reached into the back of the wagon and pulled out a canvas bag that she knew Edmund carried strips of cloth, usually to clean and polish his instruments. She handed one to Hakon, who pressed it to his nose.

"I've never," she started, but Edmund stopped her.

"Say nothing right now," he said. "We will be fine."

She pressed her hand to her chest, where her heart was still pounding. Hakon reached out his free hand and clasped hers. Joia sat very still, terrified that the men would return. In her mind, she could only think of Hakon fighting off their attacker and the feel of the man's hands on her waist as he pulled at her. She reasoned that most likely he had not wanted to hurt them, but just steal the wagon and run off, but she couldn't help the shudder that ran through her body.

Edmund started to hum a tune, giving Joia something else to think about besides the man's hands at her waist. It was several miles down the road before Edmund spoke again. "Continue to lay low but tell me what that was all about."

"Thank you for saving me," the man quietly said, his voice coming to them from above their heads. "The landlord said I didn't pay my dues, even though I had. He sent his men to my home. They said I had until sundown to pay, but I had already paid, and I didn't have any more money. They wouldn't believe me, so I ran off. I hoped I would have until sundown before they realized I was gone. I would have had a good head start too, but someone must have told them I ran."

"And just where did you think you could run to?" Edmund asked.

"I don't know," the man sighed. "I just wanted to get as far away from them as I could."

"Stay where you are until we make camp tonight. You can leave our company in the dark and make your way through the forest to wherever you wish to go."

"Thank you," the man said.

"You said something about the roads," Joia said. "Those men's master owns these roads?"

"The king owns all the roads," Edmund told her. "But there are men in the country with high ranks and are appointed governors over parts of the land, including the roads. Some of these men take good care of the land that has been given to them. Others, not so much. There are some roads I've traveled on that are almost impossible for a wagon to navigate. The road between Tillmere and Yondalla is a very well-cared-for road. This suggests that the master of the lands is very wealthy and probably very prideful. He keeps his lands well to impress the king and in turn, hopes to get more land and more rank. Would you say so, sir?" Edmund called up to the fugitive.

"I don't wish to speak ill of my master, it could get me into big trouble," the man said.

"I think you are beyond big trouble," Hakon said, rubbing his tender nose. "You are a wanted criminal."

"I'm just a simple man who only wanted to live out his life in peace. So, to answer your questions, yes, the master of these lands is ambitious and driven. He takes great pride in all he owns, including us peasants who are under his domain, and that is not a compliment on his part."

"Enough talk for now," Edmund said. He handed the reins to Hakon and pulled out a flute from behind the wagon's seat and began to play a tune. Joia had not seen Edmund play the flute before. She wondered how many instruments Edmund could play and if he was hiding anymore in the wagon.

The music, while lovely, felt very out of place. They had been attacked and now they were hiding the fugitive on top of the wagon. It didn't seem right to have music, but Edmund played on, and Joia noticed it released a lot of the tension she was feeling.

They didn't pass more than six people on the road as they traveled the rest of the afternoon, and no one seemed to be any kind of threat, nodding in silent greeting as they passed. When the sun began to go down, Edmund turned his wagon to a clearing off the side of the road. The forest was quickly growing dark and would shelter them from eyes on the road.

"Stay where you are, sir," Edmund spoke quietly. "The time for your departure is soon."

With Edmund's approval, Hakon lit a small fire using their flint fire stones. Joia reheated the pot of soup she had made for their morning meal, and Edmund unhitched Bard from the wagon, tying him up close by.

The man still lay on the top of the wagon and didn't make a sound. If anyone spotted their camp, they would not know the man was up there. But for Joia, just knowing the man was there made her very nervous and she was startled at each sound that came from the forest.

When the soup was hot, Edmund called to the man, "Come down and eat with us, then you must go."

With a grunt, the man climbed down. He stretched and popped his back. In the firelight, Joia could see that his face still had traces of blood on it and his sleeves were covered in it.

Edmund passed him the water pouch and the man poured the water onto his face to wash the blood off. When he was done with his cleanup, Joia handed him a bowl of hot soup.

"Thank you, miss," he said, eagerly taking the bowl and drinking from it. "I'm sorry I grabbed you. I wasn't trying to hurt you, I," he stopped and sighed. "I'm sorry."

Joia nodded her head and then moved to sit close to Hakon. They all ate in silence and after they were finished, Joia noticed there was still a little bit of soup left in the pot. She refilled the man's bowl.

"Here," she said, handing the bowl back to him. "Finish it."

"I have a daughter about your age," he said, his voice full of sorrow. "She is married and moved away. I don't guess I'll ever see her again."

"Enough," Edmund said sternly.

The man nodded and finished his stew.

Edmund stood next to the man, and he pointed off to his right. "That way is west. There is a road not far from here. If you follow the road, the village of Piperhedge is a two- or three-day journey on foot. I suggest you head there and try and start a new life for yourself. If you go south, you'll end up in Yondalla, where the king lives."

"You've been more than kind. I am sorry I attacked you today, but I cannot thank you enough for your help. Had it not been for you, those men would have had me for sure and I wouldn't still be alive right now."

"Go now," Edmund said. His voice was kind, but stern.

The man bowed his head, turned, and headed towards the stream. They heard him splash through the water and after several more moments, they could no longer hear his movements through the forest. Edmund and Hakon looked at each other and sighed in relief. It was dangerous and illegal to hide a fugitive.

"Joia, leave the washing tonight. I don't want you to leave camp." Edmund said.

"Yes, Edmund," she replied.

She suddenly felt tired. The tense atmosphere of the day had exhausted her. She helped Edmund put the tent up around the wagon and then put the bedrolls under the tent as Edmund handed them to her. She laid out all the bedrolls and climbed back out from under the wagon.

Edmund and Hakon were talking near the fire for a long while after the man had left.

"Do you think he was telling the truth?" Hakon asked.

Edmund was quiet for a few moments and looked off in the direction the man had left. "He had seemed earnest enough in his story. I suspect he was nothing more than a peasant and victim of the landlord, but one cannot be too careful."

"We should take turns keeping watch," Hakon said.

Edmund nodded. "I will take the first watch." He went to the wagon and pulled out his quarterstaff. "Get some sleep," he said, "but if I say run, you run, and make sure Joia is safe."

Joia went first into the tent and then Hakon followed. They both lay down on their bedrolls and Joia pulled her blanket to her chin. She rolled to her side and found Hakon staring at her. He held out his hand and she took it.

A noise woke Joia from a fitful sleep. She had been dreaming about the attacker and the three men who were chasing him, but in her dream, they were chasing her. She rolled over and tried to get comfortable, noticing the campfire outside the tent was blazing bright. She could see a figure on the other side of the tent. She sat up quickly, staring at the silhouette. Had the man returned to rob them? She looked to where Hakon had been sleeping and found Edmund in his place, sound asleep.

She crawled to the tent flap and slowly lifted it up. Hakon was there, sitting very still and holding his staff. She crawled out of the tent and went to sit next to him.

"Hakon," she whispered, "How's it going?" She sat down next to him and stretched her feet out to be warmed by the fire.

"It's been quiet," he whispered back, "just keeping watch." Hakon yawned.

"Have you been out here long?" Joia asked.

"A few hours, I think. It's hard to keep track of time in the forest when you can't see the moon passing." Hakon looked up to the sky and its inky blackness.

"Would you like me to stay up and keep guard? You can go back to bed," Joia offered.

"No," Hakon replied, "but thank you."

"Then I will keep you company for a while."

"You don't need to. You can go back to sleep."

She scooted closer to Hakon. "Let me sit up with you for a while."

"If you wish," he said.

She reached over and held his hand. She loved how strong his hands were, but he was so gentle with her. She felt his thumb rub over the top of hers. She let out a happy sigh, leaned her head against his shoulder, and watched the crackling fire.

They sat together in silence and Joia quickly realized that keeping watch was a very dull task. She wondered how Hakon had done it for so long.

"How's your nose?" she asked, breaking the silence.

"Sore, but it will be all right."

"Did you get hurt anywhere else?"

"Banged my shoulder into the ground when he first attacked, and I was knocked out of the wagon." Hakon reached up and rubbed at his left shoulder, right where her head had been resting.

"I'm so sorry," she quickly moved away. "Why didn't you tell me I was hurting you?"

"Because you weren't hurting me. I liked having you there," he smiled. "And you've got nothing to be sorry about. You didn't push me out of the wagon."

"I doubt I could, even if I wanted to," she said, thinking of his muscular back. She had seen it recently when he took off his shirt to wash up. Joia smiled at the thought.

He chuckled and gave her hand a squeeze.

"You've been quiet these last few days. Well, more than usual anyway," she smiled at him. "Got something on your mind?"

Hakon sighed. "We've been traveling, what two or three weeks now? When we left, I thought only of you. I didn't want you to go, but you were determined to leave, so I left too. I came to protect you, but I also came because I couldn't stand the idea of every day in Erthenhorn without you."

"I can understand what you mean. Those times when you traveled with your father, I missed you a lot."

He squeezed her hand again and she thought he might be blushing, but it was hard to tell in the firelight.

"It's just, I didn't think about what my leaving, our leaving, would do to Father. He would have woken up that morning and found I was gone. No explanation, no warning. I left all my tools and extra clothes behind.

My father woke up to an empty house. No one in Erthenhorn saw me leave. No one knew what had happened or where I had gone. You said your family knew you were leaving, right?"

"My mother did," Joia admitted.

"I didn't think what it would mean to our families to find we both left home on the same night. What must everyone in the village think of us?"

Joia had thought of this, many times, but she was afraid of the answers, so she had kept pushing the ideas away. "I don't know," she whispered, "and I don't think I want to know."

"I'm not worried or concerned for us or myself. I know we're just fine, but I am worried for my father. I just left him. We were going to start a new job that next morning. But I left Father to do it alone. What if the owners of the house we were going to do told Father he didn't want him because his son ran off with the baker's daughter? He could lose work because I left without telling anyone."

Joia could feel Hakon trembling. "I didn't even think of how this would affect our fathers' businesses. My father knew I was probably going to leave. He didn't want me to go, and he told me not to go, but my mother told me I needed to choose for myself, and I chose to come. But I was able to say goodbye to her. She would have to tell my family the next morning, but at least she knew." She turned her body to face Hakon's and looked into his face. "You sacrificed so much to be with me."

"And I'd do it all over again, but I would tell my father before leaving and I would have brought my tools." Hakon sighed and once again they sat in silence.

Joia kept her hand in his until he stopped shaking. She should have encouraged Hakon to go home when he had the chance, but she couldn't imagine doing this without him.

"It was good to work my trade again while we were at Grian's," he whispered after several long minutes. "I miss working and I'm afraid of losing my skill."

The fire popped, sending a large spark up into the darkness.

"Did you know," Joia said teasingly, "that among the Trade Patrons, I'm rather special?"

She grinned at the shocked expression on Hakon's face. She went on, "I might be able to ask Thek, on your behalf, to make sure you lose none of your skill while you journey with me on this quest."

Hakon smiled. "Oh, and you are close personal friends with Thek now, are you?"

"Of course," Joia smiled. "We were planning on dining together tomorrow." Joia started to giggle but quickly covered her mouth with her hand. She didn't want to wake Edmund.

"Why don't you go back to bed, oh special Patron lady," Hakon bowed.

Joia almost burst into a fit of laughter. She held her hands over her mouth.

"It will be morning soon. Get some sleep while you can." He held her hand and this time, Joia moved her mouth to his. He was surprised but kissed her back.

"I hope you didn't mind," she whispered.

"Not at all," he said, giving her hand a final squeeze and letting go.

Joia crawled back into the tent. The conversation with Hakon played out again in her mind. He was worried about his father and his trade skills.

She wished she had one of those trained birds that could carry messages. She had heard about them in a story. Perhaps it was one of Edmund's stories. If she had a messenger bird, she would send a note to her father and to Hakon's father. They both deserved an explanation.

Her lips tingled and she pressed her fingers to her lips, thinking happily about Hakon's lips on hers. She sighed quietly and closed her eyes, trying to recall every detail of that kiss. Kissing Hakon was amazing.

When Joia awoke the following morning, she found Hakon groggy, but awake and cleaning up the camp. The fire was out.

"No cooking this morning, Joia," he said.

"That's all right. We'll eat the bread we have." Joia went for the bundle of bread in the back of the wagon. She saw last night's bowls in the wagon. They were clean. "Did you wash the bowls, Hakon?"

"Yes, I did it this morning when the sky first turned grey with light," Hakon said.

"That was very nice of you," Joia said. She handed Hakon a chunk of the bread. "You look exhausted. You should have let me take a turn keeping watch."

"No, Joia, it's all right. I'm sure I'll sleep on the journey today. I'll be fine." Hakon yawned again and finished his bread.

Edmund came out of the tent, holding his bundle. He tossed it into the back of the wagon. Joia gave him some of the bread, which he took and ate. It only took them a few minutes to break camp and load the wagon. They were ready for the road again.

It didn't take Hakon very long before Joia felt him start to nod off. She pulled his head to her shoulder. He rested his head on her and fell asleep. Joia held as still as she could while Edmund hummed quietly to himself.

"I'm glad there was no trouble last night," she said quietly.

"So am I," Edmund said. "I hope the man is able to start anew."

The morning grew hot as they traveled and Joia wished she still had a head covering, but she had used that cloth for Hakon's shirt. Hakon slept on and Joia's body was starting to feel stiff. Gently, she stretched one leg out in front of her, then the other. Edmund continued to hum.

Suddenly a herd of deer jumped in front of the wagon and disappeared into the woods on the other side of the road. The horse whinnied loudly and quickly backed up. The sudden movement startled everyone. Joia gasped, grabbed Hakon's arm, and pulled him to her to prevent him from falling off the wagon again.

"What was that?" Hakon panicked, looking around for another attacker to come at him.

"Deer," Edmund answered. He snapped the horse's reins, and they moved forward again. "Something's startled them. They were running." He peered into the woods looking for whatever it was that had scared the deer.

"Is the road usually this dangerous in this area?" Hakon asked.

"Not in my experience, but as we get closer to the city, there are more people on the road. They are a bigger danger to us than animals. We don't stop until night," Edmund said. "There is an inn not far from here. Let's hope it isn't full. It's not safe on the road right now." Edmund snapped the reins again, urging the horse on.

Joia felt an uneasy knot form in her stomach. Hakon pulled out the staff he had been carving since they had begun their journey, but he didn't get out his knife. He held the staff in his hand, poised and ready for an attack. Joia didn't know what was going on, but Edmund and Hakon were nervous, so she was too.

"How much longer until we get to Seb's home?" Joia asked.

"If we don't meet with more problems, we'll be there tomorrow afternoon," Edmund answered. They rode on in silence. When they came to a stream that crossed the road, Edmund stopped to let the horse drink. Joia turned around and leaned into the wagon. She pulled out the bundle that held their food and divided the meat pies she had purchased several days before. They each had a small portion and ate in silence.

Edmund snapped the reigns when Bard had his fill of water and they moved along. It wasn't but a few minutes back on the road when they heard voices and horses approaching. Hakon gripped his staff and Edmund tightened his grip on the horse's reins.

"Try not to look so menacing," Edmund advised Hakon. "If we look friendly, we will not be harassed. Still, be ready."

Joia took a deep breath. She was grateful to be with two such strong men, but she didn't want either of them to get hurt. Hakon's nose was sporting a blue bruise today.

"I will do the speaking," Edmund whispered. From around the bend in the road, two men on horses came into view. They were dressed simply, wearing villagers' clothes and there were large sacks tied to the back of the saddles. The men eyed the occupants of the wagon and everyone in the wagon stared at the approaching horses.

When they were about twenty paces apart, the two horsemen stopped.

"Good day, friend," one of the men called out.

"Good day," Edmund said back. He slowed the wagon and stopped in front of the men. "It is a hot day on the road." Edmund spoke casually. "There is a stream not far behind for your horses."

"We know this road well," one of the men said. "We are merchants and travel to the nearby villages often."

Hakon's grip on his staff did not lessen, but Joia felt him relax slightly.

"I see," said Edmund. "We have been on the road for a long time and have not heard any local news. Is there anything going on we should know of? Any festivals to visit or trouble to watch out for?"

"No festivals that I know of," the second man said. He looked at his companion who shook his head.

"As for trouble, we have heard there is an escaped convict on the road," the other man said.

"A terrifying thought," Edmund shuddered. "We'll be vigilant as we continue."

"Are you an entertainer?" the first man asked.

"I am," Edmund said. "A singer, by trade."

"Then I would be careful if I were you," the man went on. "The Trade Minister is making work very difficult for some of the trades."

"Surely not a singing entertainer," Edmund said.

"Aye, that includes entertainers," the man said. "Are you going into the city?"

"Yes, we were," Edmund said. "My niece here is engaged to a carpenter. We are taking her to him for the wedding."

Joia blinked as her mind worked out what Edmund had just said. A story. He was telling these men a story so they would find the three of them less suspicious. She tried to act in a normal way, as if she was looking forward to her false wedding.

"Well, if I were you, I'd leave the wagon behind. Don't take it into the city and don't perform when you are in its walls."

"I will take your advice, but why?" Edmund asked. "Does it have something to do with this Trade Minister you spoke of?"

"That's right," the second man said. "Have you heard that all of the art trades have been moved out of the castle's boundaries?"

"No," Edmund gasped. "What do you mean by the art trades?"

"All the tradesmen who work in the arts. Textilers and artists. You know, spinners, weavers, dyers, painters, and masons."

"And they have been kicked out of the castle?" Hakon asked.

One of the horsemen chuckled, "Well, what do you know? He does talk. I thought perhaps your friend here was simple."

"I am not!" Hakon yelled.

"Easy chap," the horseman laughed. "I meant nothing by it."

"Forgive my nephew," Edmund said, giving Hakon a frustrated glance, before turning back to the merchants. "Please, tell me, are the smithies still in the castle boundaries?"

"Yes, they are. I think the carpenters might be too, so your niece should be safe if she is marrying a carpenter. Word has it that it was the smithies who went before the Trade Minister and asked that all the other trades be removed."

Edmund stroked his chin. "This is most interesting."

"Is it?" the first horseman asked.

"Well, yes, I think so," Edmund said, noticing the two men eying him suspiciously. He straightened up. "Well, I will take your advice about leaving my wagon outside the city walls before delivering my niece to her intended. It sounds as if she will be safe there with the carpenter."

"I expect so," one of the men said.

"Then we will continue along our way. Do you know if there is an inn or shelter we can reach before dark? I have a friend in Yondalla, but we will not make it to his house today."

"Yes," the first man answered. "An inn and smithy, called the Raven's Claw, is not far away. You can get there before night. The innkeeper's name is Roger Smyth. He's an honest man."

"I thank you," Edmund said. "We wish you well on your journey."

"Same to you, friend." The two horsemen started down the road towards the stream. Edmund snapped the reins on his horse and the wagon rolled forward.

Hakon lowered his staff. "Do you think those men were telling the truth?" he quietly asked.

Edmund shook his head slowly. "I don't know. This is very disturbing. Why would the trade minister, of all people, want half of the trades kicked out of the castle?"

Hakon nodded. "Income-wise, that is a very bad move. I mean, I imagine all those people paid rent to be in those buildings. And now, the citizens within the castle walls must travel down into the city to buy goods."

Edmund nodded. "The trade minister is supposed to help the trades. Why is no one questioning him? And why would the smithies be instigating such a thing?"

Joia scooted herself on the seat a tiny bit closer to Hakon. "So, I'm your niece now, am I?" she asked.

"Well, I wasn't about to explain our situation, making you my niece makes our party sound respectable," Edmund replied.

"What do you mean, respectable?" asked Joia.

"It is dangerous for a woman to be on the road, unprotected or with men who are not her family," Edmund said.

"You mean scandalous," Hakon hissed. "We haven't been in public since starting on this journey, except for buying provisions in Tillmere. We could get into trouble."

"I didn't even think of that," Joia squeaked.

Edmund nodded. "Hakon and I could get into trouble for having you with us since we are not family. I also wanted to get more information about what was going on at the castle. Telling them you were promised to someone there seemed to be the least suspicious way to get information out of them."

"How did you come up with that story so quickly?" Joia asked.

Edmund chuckled, "I'm a storyteller, Joia. It's my specialty to come up with believable stories."

CHAPTER TWELVE

The Raven's Claw Inn

The wagon bumped quietly down the road for another hour before they saw a few local houses. Joia's legs ached with stiffness when they finally pulled up to an old building. Several chimneys were smoking, and a group of men were gathered near the door, holding large mugs of ale in their hands, laughing heartily. Edmund hopped out of the wagon and instructed Joia and Hakon to wait there. He went to the door and knocked. A large woman opened the door and spoke to Edmund in a quiet voice. Joia couldn't hear what they were saying, but after several moments Edmund returned to the wagon.

"I spoke with the proprietor's wife. She said there is room for us. I have told her that you are my niece and nephew. Joia, why don't you go on in? Hakon and I will get the wagon locked and Bard into his stall."

Joia hopped out of the wagon and walked toward the front door, eyeing the men warily.

"What a pretty one," one of the men said, his speech slurred with ale.

Joia stopped in fear, unable to move forward.

"It's all right, sweetheart," another said. "We'll take good care of you."

"Come and sit with us," the third man said.

Joia backed up a step as one of the men stepped forward. Where was Edmund? Where was Hakon? She didn't know what to do. When one of the men held out his arms to her, she jumped back in surprise and was about to turn and run to the stables, but the door swung open, and a large woman came out. She turned to the men. "You leave her alone," she waved a finger at the men before turning to smile at Joia. "Come on in, dearie. You must be worn out after your travels. I've got a nice room for you and your uncle."

Joia quickly moved to the woman, grateful for the protection.

"Don't you worry about them men," the woman said as she led Joia up some stairs. "They're all talk. But if they bother you, you let me know. I'll give them what for." She opened one of the doors in the dark hall. "Here we are. This is your room."

Joia stepped into the room. It was small but clean. Two beds had been squeezed into the room, which had a window overlooking the stable.

"Thank you, this will be most comfortable," Joia said.

"Once you've got settled in, come on down and have some food. If you need anything you let old Betty know about it," she said, tapping herself on the chest. Betty turned around and left, closing the door behind her. Joia walked over to the window and saw Hakon and Edmund leaving the stable. They would be upstairs soon.

She sat down on one of the beds, still shaking from her brief encounter with the drunk men, and let out a long sigh. What a day.

She put her head into her hands. "Oh Joia," she spoke quietly to herself. "What are you doing here? What were you thinking?" She rubbed her tired eyes. Images of her mother and father came to mind. She doubted very much they would be happy with her right now.

She was enjoying her journey or at least she had been until the recent scares. Edmund and Hakon were good company and the trip had been enjoyable and interesting. She was learning much about the other trades and their Patrons. She had been honored to meet three Patrons now and would be meeting a fourth tomorrow, but she was also feeling very humiliated right now. She was traveling with two men who were not her family. It hadn't bothered her until now.

She looked up as the door clicked and Edmund and Hakon walked in.

"Are you all right, Joia?" Edmund asked.

Joia quickly stood up. "I am. It's been a long couple of days, full of uncertainty. A little food and rest will do me good, I have no doubt." She didn't want him to know what had happened at the door.

Edmund shut the door and looked hard at Joia, before softening his stance. "Yes, a little food and rest will do us all a power of good. However, we need to be clear on our stories before going down and joining with the other guests. Traveling on the road as we have been doing is always dangerous, but so is stopping in places like this. You never know who you might run into."

Joia's body gave an involuntary shudder. All this fear and danger was because of her.

Edmund thoughtfully rubbed his chin for several moments. "The goings on at the castle with the trade minister has me feeling uneasy. Especially if they have turned their backs on all the artistic and textile trades. If those men were telling the truth, my wagon marks me as an entertainer. I will not be welcomed."

"What about Seb? Does he live in the castle boundaries?" Joia asked.

Edmund shook his head. "No, his residence is in Yondalla's walls, but not the castles."

"I don't understand, Edmund," Joia said. "There are two walls?"

"Yes. Think of a circle," he put one finger on the bed and traced a circle, leaving a shallow impression on the blanket. "The castle sits in the middle of the circle. This is the castle wall. Now, imagine another set of walls that surround castle walls." He drew a larger circle on the blanket. "This is the city wall. Inside the little circle is the castle and some trade businesses. The rest of the city is between the castle and the city wall. Do you see?"

Joia nodded, feeling foolish about the things she didn't know. "I do. So, Seb is in that area, between the castle and the city wall?" She pointed to the circles that Edmund had made on the bedspread.

Edmund nodded. "He is. However, his family has owned their home since Seb's grandfather. His home is very close to the inner wall and not far from one of the gates."

"But," Hakon added, "If we understand things right, we should be fine in the city because the Trade Minister has only kicked the trades out of the inner circle, but not the outer. You could still have your wagon in the city."

"I don't have another choice. This wagon is everything I possess. I can't just leave it unattended outside of the city."

"Are there stables in the city we can hide the wagon in?"

"Yes, but it is still dangerous for us." Edmund rubbed his hand over his head and removed the colorful head scarf. His curly hair was flat against his head. He ran his hand through it absentmindedly until it was a fluffy mess of dark curls. "We will deal with that tomorrow. Now, we focus on tonight. I have told the proprietor that you are my niece and nephew, and we are going to Yondalla to visit my brother. Tonight, we stick together. If anyone asks us questions about who we are and where we are going, let me do the talking. It will be easier to keep our story straight if I'm the only one telling it. Agreed?"

"Am I no longer engaged to a carpenter?" Joia asked.

"Only if we need you to be. Just don't answer questions about who we are or our plans," Edmund said.

They agreed and left the room together walking down the creaky stairs and into the common room. It was crowded and smelled strongly of ale, making Joia's eyes water. Edmund pulled a bench to a table near the wall that was close to the kitchen. Betty arrived with three mugs of ale and put them in front of Edmund, Hakon, and Joia. Joia looked to Edmund for help. She didn't drink ale. Her mother had never allowed her that at all.

"Thank you, my good lady," Edmund smiled at Betty. "This is a most welcoming inn. Could we have some meat and a mug of buttermilk for my niece?"

"Of course," Betty said, turning and walking into the kitchen.

"Thank you, Edmund," Joia whispered gratefully.

Edmund smiled and sipped at his ale. Joia looked around and watched the people in the inn. Most looked like peasants and farmers. Two well-dressed soldiers stood in one corner of the room with a young woman, all of them laughing loudly. Joia watched three men playing a game with a button and some cups. There was laughter and an exchange of coins among them.

Betty returned quickly with a platter of thinly shredded ham, three chunks of hard bread, several olives, and a mug of buttermilk. Joia picked up her bread and tried to pull a section off to eat, but it was very hard and stale. She dipped it into her buttermilk, hoping to soften it up. She noticed Edmund and Hakon doing the same thing with their bread and ale. They all looked at each other and laughed.

From another corner of the room, a man started to play a lively tune on a rough wooden flute. Cheers rose from the inn's guests, encouraging the musician to play on. Joia enjoyed the music. After several songs, Edmund called out to the musician, "Hello, good man! Do you know 'I Have a Young Sister?'"

"Aye good sir," the musician merrily answered. "I'll play it if you will sing, for that song needs its words!"

"Then play my friend and I shall sing," Edmund stood and went to the musician, who put the flute back to his lips and he began to play. Edmund sang the lyrics, "I have a young sister, far beyond the see."

The crowd of people in the inn began to clap their hands in beat with the song. They repeated the chorus several times, each time getting a little faster until the flute player and Edmund could no longer perform because they all were laughing so hard.

Edmund stood and clapped the musician's back. "Not bad, good friend," he laughed. "Let's give these poor devils something they can dance to."

These words brought up another cheer from the group. After a few quiet words together, the flutist began to play again, and Edmund sang. For the first time since meeting him, which, Joia realized, was only a few weeks ago, she saw Edmund looking positively jovial. He sang lively songs and laughed heartily. She liked his smile and wished he smiled more.

The crowd grew more and more energetic with the aid of the music and ale. Some dancing broke out in the middle of the floor and one of the soldiers pulled the woman out for a spin. A fiddler joined them and played several quadrilles. Groups of people danced together. Joia and Hakon clapped their hands and laughed as they watched the others join in the singing and dancing.

The music went late into the night and was finally broken up when the inn's owner warned them all of curfew. Too much noise at such a late hour could bring the local authorities around. So, the crowded common room slowly began to empty as guests and locals headed to their various sleeping places for the night.

Edmund returned to their table, grinning. "Well, that was a good evening."

Joia smiled at him. "You were wonderful. It's so much fun to hear you singing."

"You hear me singing all the time," he chuckled.

"Not like that," Joia grinned.

"Let's get up to the room," Hakon said, standing and holding his hand out to Joia. She took it, stood, and followed Edmund up the dark staircase.

Once in their room, Edmund closed the heavy wooden door and slid the lock into place. The noises in the rest of the inn were silenced by the heavy door, and Joia felt a sigh of relief escaped her. They had made it through the evening without any trouble. The room was in near complete darkness, lit only by the small lantern that Edmund held. Joia could hardly see as she felt her way over to one of the beds.

"Edmund, how about I go down and sleep in the wagon?" Hakon said. It's large enough for just me and I'll be able to keep an eye on our belongings."

Edmund nodded. "You are comfortable with that arrangement?" he asked.

Hakon nodded.

Edmund turned to Joia. "Are you comfortable with Hakon not being in the room?"

Joia nodded as well. "I know that I am safe with either of you," she said. "I trust you both."

Edmund pulled out a key from his pocket and gave it to Hakon. "Sleep well. If there is trouble and you need me, don't hesitate to return to the room."

Hakon nodded and bid them goodnight. Edmund reopened the door, and then quickly closed it again, dropping the locking beam down over their door.

"I am honored by your trust in me," he said to Joia.

She nodded, unsure what to say. Despite their short acquaintance, she trusted him with her life.

Edmund went to the window and looked out. For several moments, he was perfectly still as he watched. Then, he let out a quiet breath and relaxed. "He made it to the stables and was admitted inside. I feel better knowing our belongings are being looked after by Hakon."

Joia turned down the blanket on one of the beds and slipped in. It wasn't the most comfortable mattress she had ever felt, but it was better than the ground. Edmund turned off the lantern, plunging the room into darkness.

She could hear his bed creak as he climbed in and lay down. She did trust Edmund. She had to. She was far from home with no way back without Edmund's help, but she knew that as long as she was in Edmund's care, she was safe from everything. Exhausted, she rolled over and looked at Edmund's glowing form on the bed. The golden light was a comfort and it meant safety.

When Joia woke up, the room was grey with early morning light. Outside the window, Joia could hear men talking and a donkey braying. Edmund was standing at the window, looking outside towards the blacksmiths. "Did you sleep well?" he asked.

"Yes, fine, thank you. Is all well outside?" she asked as she climbed out of bed and joined Edmund at the window. She looked down and saw Hakon outside, talking to one of the men. A blacksmith was looking at Edmund's horses' hooves.

"Yes, I believe so," Edmund answered, not taking his eyes off his horse or Hakon.

"Edmund?"

"Yes, my dear?"

Joia didn't know how to say what was on her mind, but something had been troubling her since the previous night. "When I left home and joined you on this journey, quest, or whatever it's called, I did so rather blindly and naively. I joined you without really knowing anything about you. I didn't realize how my traveling with you could be thought of as inappropriate. And then Hakon joined us, which added a whole new level of, well, awkwardness."

Joia noticed a small smile on Edmund's face, though his eyes never left the people on the other side of the window.

"If I may be permitted to ask you a question," he said, and she nodded. "Are you and Hakon promised to each other?"

"Well, no, we're not. I always hoped Father would consider Hakon as a prospective husband, but nothing as far as I'm aware has ever been said or done about it. I have an older brother and sister. My parents must concern themselves with my siblings before they can worry about me."

"I see," Edmund said.

"Hakon and I have been friends since we were young children, but I had always hoped that," she stopped and watched as Hakon held the horse by the reigns while the blacksmith measured a horseshoe against Bard's hoof. "Well, we've never really talked about it. I'm not even sure if Hakon would want to marry me."

Edmund said nothing, so Joia went back to the original question that she had been trying to form. "I know nothing can be done about us traveling together and we've been on the road together for weeks now, but that doesn't put to rest the fact that I'm traveling with two men to whom I am not related."

"And your question is?" Edmund said.

Joia huffed. Could he not see her point? "Did I do the right thing? What am I to do? Should I be in disgrace for," Joia's face turned red. She was embarrassed by what she had to say and more embarrassed because she had to say it to Edmund. He was a Patron. He was practically immortal. He was a man! She held her hands up to her face and felt the heat in her cheeks.

For the first time that morning, Edmund looked at her. His blue eyes twinkled. "Should you be in disgrace for running away with two men? Is that what you were going to ask?"

Joia nodded; the word 'disgrace' echoing in her ears. She felt two hot tears run down her cheeks.

"Joia. Don't cry. You are not in disgrace. You have an important mission. You are on a quest. You were sent on this quest by the power of Athelstan and the Light of the Guild. This is no ordinary journey. It is a journey you have embarked on with the knowledge, consent, and support of your family and all the Guild Patrons. Hakon, the man you love, is here with us. He will make very sure nothing happens to you. You have nothing to be ashamed of." Edmund took Joia by the shoulders and squeezed them. "All will be well, Joia. I promise."

Joia sniffed and wiped her tears away on her hand. She looked up at Edmund and saw him smiling at her. His eyes twinkled and she relaxed.

"Now, the purpose of our quest is all fine and good, but you're right, it doesn't hide the fact that our small company is in an awkward social situation. Others might not understand our relationships, even though it is none of their business. So, we stick to our story. You and Hakon are my niece and nephew. Sticking to that story will keep unwanted questions or attention away from us."

He looked back at the window. "Ah, Hakon is signaling to me that all is ready. I will settle our bill and we will be off. Go and join Hakon in the wagon."

Joia put on her shoes, picked up her bundle, and followed Edmund out of the room. He went to the common room to find the proprietor and Joia went out the door. She feared that the group of men would still be seated around the door to bother her, but there was no one. Just Hakon, sitting on the seat of the wagon, waiting for her.

He held out a hand and helped her up.

"Did you sleep well?" he asked.

"Yes, it was fine. How was your night?"

"Uneventful. Edmund's wagon is kind of growing on me," he said with a wink.

"Perhaps you can become a traveling thatcher," she said. "You travel from town to town, work for a while, and then leave for the next town."

"Not a bad idea," Hakon grinned. "But only if you come along with me."

She flushed hot and she was sure her face was red, but smiled and nodded. "I'd like that a lot."

"Honestly, I don't understand our journey's purpose, but it's nice to be together with you."

Joia blushed again and took Hakon's hand in hers. "I don't quite understand our journey's purpose either, but I like being with you, too."

Edmund walked out of the inn with a small bundle. They quickly let go of each other's hands.

"Food for the journey," Edmund said as he climbed into the wagon, passing the food to Joia. Hakon snapped the reins and the horse set off.

"When we get to Yondalla," Edmund said, "I'm going to have to do some performing. That was the last of our money."

"I'm sorry, Edmund," Joia began.

"Nothing to be sorry about. It's the way I earn my living and thankfully, I can earn my living anywhere I go. Plus, I also enjoy it. We'll be in Yondalla by this afternoon. We can get some real food to eat there."

CHAPTER THIRTEEN

𝔖𝔢𝔟 𝔱𝔥𝔢 𝔐𝔞𝔭 𝔐𝔞𝔨𝔢𝔯

Edmund opened the bundle and passed out the chunks of bread and pieces of hard cheese. They ate in silence as the wagon bounced down the road.

"Food like that makes me homesick," Hakon said, clearing his throat after eating his last bite of food. "That is probably the hardest bread I've ever eaten. Nothing at all like Joia's father. Thomas makes the best bread in the entire kingdom. When we return home, Edmund, you must try some. None finer anywhere, I'm sure."

Edmund laughed. "I look forward to it. That Betty, at the inn," Edmund chuckled, "a good soul and a heart of gold, but you're right, that is some of the toughest bread I've ever tried to eat."

It was another hot day and Joia tried to cool down by fanning herself with her hands before Edmund got out one of his colorful scarves from the back of his wagon and handed it to her. She tied it around her head, with thanks.

After several hours, they stopped at a stream and let the horse drink its fill. Joia and Hakon stretched their legs while the wagon was stopped. Joia found a large leaf on the side of the road and used it to fan her face. It felt nice, so she brought it with her onto the wagon.

"Tell me about Seb and his gift, please," Joia said to Edmund.

Edmund thought for a moment. "Seb is, as you know, a map maker. His guild is small. There are very few map makers compared to say, smithies or entertainers." He sighed. "I suppose I should start at the beginning. Long ago, when we were students of Athelstan, studying our trades and living in his castle, Seb and I were friends. More like brothers. He's an extremely talented artist with an amazing eye for detail. Before being chosen to be a map maker by Athelstan, Seb was a painter. His works were quite remarkable."

Joia noticed Edmund had gone into his storytelling manner. His voice would get deeper and the fluctuations in his voice changed. It was rather hypnotic. She loved it when Edmund told stories nearly as much as she loved Edmund's singing.

"It wasn't long after we became Patrons that Seb was sent for by the king. The king recognized the importance of a good map maker. Seb lived in the castle and created all the maps used by the king. He held this position for more than a century."

"You've mentioned several times that you have lived for centuries," Hakon interrupted. "How can that be?"

"The Patrons are, to some degree, immortal. We believe we can die but none of us has died yet. I believe we live as long as our trades survive. I don't know how long that will be. Perhaps forever."

"Do you want to die?" Hakon asked.

Edmund was quiet for a moment. "I will admit that living for so long is not always easy. I have seen many good friends grow old and die. But I love my trade and I love my tradesmen. I want to always be there for them. So, no, I don't want to die."

Joia couldn't imagine living for so long. It would mean living to see her entire family and everyone she knew age and pass away. She wasn't sure she wanted that. "So, what about Seb?" Joia asked.

"Seb's services as map maker and painter to the king were highly valued for many years, but then a king came to the throne who felt that Seb's maps were no longer necessary. Instead of having Seb keep the maps of the kingdom updated, he demanded Seb draw up false maps to trick the neighboring kingdoms and others who might want to attack. Seb was angered by this and refused. The king sent his men to have Seb killed, but he was able to escape and hid at Athelstan's castle until that king had died. As you can imagine, Seb was angry about losing his status as the royal map maker. The new king did not know of Seb or his talents, and he was forgotten."

"How terrible for him," Joia said.

Edmund nodded. "I'm afraid he became quite bitter. He is not a bad man, but he is not the same as he was when I knew him so long ago."

"What about his gift?" Joia asked.

"It is as Grian said. Seb's gift is a most extraordinary map. It shows the owner of the map wherever she or he is. If you receive one of Seb's maps, you will be the center of that map, no matter where you are."

"You can never get lost with a map like that," Hakon said.

"Precisely," Edmund replied.

Joia noticed the trees were thinning and more homes and shops lined the road. They were getting close to the city of Yondalla.

"Another half an hour, I'd say," Edmund snapped the reins on his horse.

It wasn't long before they could see the tall fortress walls that surrounded the castle and the main city of Yondalla.

Joia had never seen such a structure as the castle. "It's huge," she gasped. "And the king lives there?"

"And his family and dozens of servants, ministers, and special tradesmen," Edmund said.

An entire small village lay on the outside of the city's wall. Edmund looked at all the buildings as they passed. "I remember when none of this existed. There is a river, just back there on the other side of those buildings. I used to go there to collect reeds for pan pipes."

"What are pan pipes?" Joia asked.

"A fun type of flute. I'll show you one day," he said. They rode under the gate and into the city.

Joia had never seen anything like it. She watched with wide eyes as they drove down road after road. It was much bigger than Joia's home village and much more crowded. There were shops of all kinds, people walking through all the streets, singers and beggars on street corners, and children running freely. Carts filled with food and wares of all kinds were being pushed along by old men and women, calling out their goods for sale. There were smells pleasant and not-so-pleasant with each door they passed. Joia had never seen so many people packed into such a small space before.

Edmund could hardly drive his wagon through. "Must be market day," he muttered. "I should get out and perform, earn a few coins."

He found a stable with space enough for his horse and wagon. He gave the landlord his last coin and promised to return the following day with the rest of the payment for keeping his wagon there. Edmund unpacked a few bundles from the wagon. He carried his lute and the largest bundle. Joia and Hakon carried several small bundles of items they didn't want to be left behind, and then Edmund closed and locked the wagon.

"Stay close and keep a hold of your bundles," Edmund said as they headed out. "Seb's home is not too far from here, but you still need to keep a close eye on your belongings."

They followed Edmund through the streets until he stopped in front of one line of buildings on a crowded street. Signs hung from the doors, showing what establishments were there. A small weather-battered sign with a scroll in the middle hung from the door in front of them.

Edmund took a deep breath and went to the door. As they reached the door and Edmund held his hand on the lever, he turned to Hakon and Joia. "Best behavior and careful with what you say."

Hakon and Joia nodded their heads. Edmund turned the lever and opened the door. They walked in. A bell tinkled when the door shut again.

"One moment," a man's voice called out to them from another room.

They stood and waited. The room was lit only by the sun coming through a small window. A tall shelf filled with yellow scrolls stood along the back wall, next to a door. A dark desk covered in candle stubs sat near the window. An open scroll was pinned to the desk at its corners to prevent it from rolling up. The only other thing in the room was a beautiful painting of a castle with men and women standing in various positions at the base of the castle wall. Joia wanted to get a better look at the painting, but at that moment, a man came through the door and looked at them.

"What can I do for you?" he started but stopped short on the last word as he recognized Edmund. "Edmund," he said, his voice deep and gravelly.

"Hello, Seb."

Seb looked at Joia, "Well, well, it's the guild anomaly."

Joia took a small step forward, "How do you do? I'm Joia."

"Oh yes, I know who you are. Edmund told us about you long ago. So, you are of age now, are you?"

"I suppose I am," Joia answered, and was upset with herself and how small her voice sounded.

"And you, boy, who are you?" Seb turned his attention to Hakon. "You have none of the Light."

"I am Hakon, a thatcher, and companion to Joia." Hakon stood at his full height and spoke with confidence.

Joia admired Hakon's ability to not be intimidated by this Patron. Maybe it was Edmund's warnings about Seb or the stern way he was looking at them all, but she was feeling very nervous about Seb.

Seb raised an eyebrow. "A thatcher? I wonder what Thek thinks of you?"

Edmund turned in surprise, "I am sure Thek is proud of Hakon. He is a good man."

Seb chuckled. Joia watched this new Patron with interest. He was shorter than Edmund and Hakon. His brown hair hung to his shoulders. The clothing he wore was a fine material, but it was old and frayed. He had small, dark eyes and did not smile.

He was not openly kind like Edmund, Grian, and Sidonia had been when she first met them, but Joia could easily tell he was a Patron. The Light glowed around him, and he carried an air of mystery about him. The Patrons were ancient and young. They commanded respect and were perfect in working their trades, each with a powerful gift to bestow. No amount of bitterness on Seb's part could hide that he was a man of special powers.

"Why have you come here?" he asked.

"I have come to ask you about your gift," Joia replied.

Seb let out a harsh laugh, "Of course you have. What makes you think that you are worthy of one of my maps?"

"Oh, for Athelstan's sakes, Seb," Edmund's voice rose in anger, "she has the Light of the Guild. That makes her more than worthy for one of your maps."

"Silence, storyteller!" Seb spat at Edmund. "I want to hear from her."

Edmund turned red with anger. "Hakon," he said, almost in a shout, "Stay with Joia. I'll be back later." Edmund turned around and left Seb's shop. The bell tinkled violently as he slammed the door shut behind him.

Seb sneered at the door before turning his attention back to Joia. "Now, answer me, girl, what makes you worthy of my gift?"

Joia was trembling as she looked at Seb. Their gazes locked and she saw a flash of sorrow in his eyes before they returned to their steely, dark stare. She held this contact with him for only a moment and then dropped her gaze.

"I don't know that I am worthy of your gift," she said, thinking hard about his question, and was disappointed in herself when she could not come up with any good reason. "I've been told by Edmund, Sidonia, Grian, and you that I have the Light of the Guild. Other than that, there is nothing special about me. I have no trade and I know little of the world outside of my village. I am not worthy of any of the gifts I have received." She pulled her bundle that contained her Life Tapestry and Everburn candle close to her chest. "I am simply Joia. But for whatever reason, I have this Light. I have a purpose, a task, a destiny to fulfill, but I don't know what that is yet. I want to find my purpose and I think one of your maps will be key to guiding me to find and fulfill my destiny."

She could not look into Seb's face again and she was embarrassed that Hakon was here, hearing her pathetic confession. She knew she was nothing special. Hakon was a great tradesman. Her brother was a tradesman. Either of them would have been better suited to the Light than her.

Seb smiled. "I ask this question of everyone who seeks my gift." His voice was calm and almost friendly. "Most people answered with arrogance, telling me how they are worthy because they are so very great. But you and sincere and you show humility. You claim to be nothing more than you are. Sincerity is rare and I value it."

Joia's face was red from humiliation when she looked up into his face and saw it had softened from earlier. "I am nothing more than as you see me."

Seb went to his desk and unpinned the current parchment. He carefully rolled it up and pulled out a new scroll. "The truth is, you are much more important than anyone I have ever made a map for."

Joia watched him in surprise. Despite what Edmund said, even after having watched them together and seeing their dislike for each other, she could see that Seb was a good man, just like Edmund.

"Yes, Joia, I will make a Life Map for you."

"What will you need from me to make it mine?" Joia asked.

"And how do you know you will need to do anything?" Seb asked. Most people he made the Life Map for were surprised to find they had to actively contribute for the map to be made. Once again, Joia showed herself to be willing and humble.

"Well, in order for Sidonia to weave my tapestry, I had to spin the thread myself. And when Grian made me my candle, I had to choose the wick and core wax. I expect you need me to do something or give something for the map to make it my own."

"You are right, of course. The map will represent you so, you must provide the map's heart. I need something of yours to add to the ink; something of value to you."

Joia thought for several moments. "I have very little," she admitted. "I did not leave home with much more than you see." She looked at Hakon, who shrugged his shoulders. "I cannot give up my Life Tapestry or my candle," she said and patted her overtunic for anything she might have put in there.

She felt Seb's eyes watching her, which made her feel all the more nervous. "I have nothing," and then she stopped. At her neck, she felt a warmth. Reaching her hand to her neck, she felt a necklace. She had completely forgotten she was even wearing it.

Joia pulled the necklace from under her dress so that it hung where it could be seen. "My mother made this for me when I turned sixteen." She reached behind her head and untied the threads. She held the necklace in her hand and looked at it for a moment. It was simply made, four glass beads threaded into three thin cords, braided together. A small blue stone hung from the middle. "I don't guess it is of any value if I tried to sell it, but Mother made it for me. She bored the hole through the stone herself and then woven the strings into the braid." The necklace was glowing with the Light. She didn't want to part with it, but she trusted the light. Joia held the necklace out to Seb. "It is all I have."

"Joia," Hakon said, taking a step towards her.

"It's all right, Hakon," she said. "Mother would want me to do this."

Seb took the necklace from her. "Well done, Joia. I will now create your Life Map." Seb went through the door and into the other room and Joia followed to watch. This room was obviously where Seb lived. It had a bed, a table with a single chair, and an iron pan next to the hearth. The only thing that looked to be of any value was another painting, hanging from a long wire attached to the ceiling. This painting was of a beautiful waterfall, surrounded by a thick forest, painted in autumn colors. It was spectacular, but she didn't have much of an opportunity to study it.

Seb placed the necklace into a bowl. "First, I must make the ink. Once I begin your map, I cannot stop, so don't bother me."

Joia nodded. "I understand."

He took two glass bottles from a shelf onto the single table in the room. He sprinkled a little pink powder into the bowl with the necklace.

Next, he took the larger bottle and poured an inky black liquid into the bowl. Pink vapors rose with a hissing noise from the bowl. Seb took a quill feather and used it to stir the contents of the bowl. When he was satisfied, he took an empty ink jar and a funnel and carefully poured the ink into the jar. There was no trace of the necklace. It had become part of the ink.

CHAPTER FOURTEEN

𝕰𝖉𝖒𝖚𝖓𝖉'𝖘 𝕻𝖆𝖘𝖙

Edmund wore his lute over his back and walked out into the crowded streets to find a corner where two busy roads crossed. He would try and earn some coins with his music, so he could pay the stable master for keeping his horse and wagon.

He found an open space, pulled his lute from over his shoulder, and began to play a tune. He was angry with Seb and even his music couldn't help calm him. What right did Seb think he had in questioning Joia like that? She had the Light.

People stopped to listen to him, so he transitioned from the song he was playing into the next song without ever stopping. He started to sing, which had people tossing a coin or two into his hat. He continued, playing several more songs, which included a request from a lady who was carrying a baby, a basket, and was heavy with another child. She smiled and swayed to the song, singing the words that went along. She had a lovely if untrained voice. When the song ended, he thanked her and purchased one of the pies that she was selling.

It was a pleasant way to spend an hour, but he was finding it hard to concentrate. He was simply too worked up over Seb's behavior. Finally, Edmund bowed to everyone who had stopped and thanked them. He picked up his hat with the few coins he had earned and stuffed the money into his pocket. He swung his lute back over his shoulder and headed towards the stables.

Edmund unlocked the wagon and put his lute back in before he closed and locked it again. He took a horse brush from off the wall and went to Bard, who was happily munching at the feed in his stall. Edmund began to brush Bard's black-gray coat.

He was still angry. Seb had been so rude and arrogant. Typical. When had Seb not ever been rude? His mind flashed to a memory, and he could think of a time when Seb had not been so gruff, just before their fight and fallout. His mind was so caught up thinking of Seb's behavior, that he didn't notice Hakon walk into the stable.

"What's going on, Edmund?" Hakon asked, leaning against the stall's door frame.

Edmund jumped at Hakon's voice. "Goodness, Hakon. Don't sneak up on me like that."

"I hardly snuck up on you," Hakon said. "I've been standing here for several minutes."

"Good for you," Edmund said and continued brushing.

Hakon approached Bard's head and stroked at his neck. "You worked up about Seb?"

Edmund sighed. "I shouldn't let him get to me like that, but he does." He fell silent for several moments before turning to face Hakon. "Wait. Why are you here? I told you to stay with Joia."

"Joia's fine," Hakon said, going to sit on a hay bale in the corner of the stall. "Seb is making her map and I've learned that outsiders are not welcomed while the Patrons are working their guild magic," Hakon said.

"The Patron's gifts are not mere tricks, Hakon," Edmund frowned.

"I know, Edmund, I know." Hakon watched Edmund as he moved to the other side of the horse and began to brush it again. "So, tell me what happened."

Edmund looked up to Hakon in surprise. "What do you mean by that?"

"You know exactly what I mean. What happened between you and Seb?"

"I told you, his employment with the king came to a bad end. It made him angry," Edmund answered. He didn't look at Hakon.

"That answer sounds rather rehearsed and only explains Seb's anger towards the world, but it does not explain his anger at you or yours with him."

"It's nothing," Edmund said.

"I don't believe you. You said that at one time, you were like brothers." He watched Edmund brush the horse. Edmund was clearly uncomfortable.

Edmund's rank as a Patron and his very presence commanded respect. He got it from everyone he encountered, including himself, Joia, and other Patrons, but Hakon had spent the last few weeks constantly in Edmund's company. He knew that while Edmund was hundreds of years old and possessed special powers, he was still a man.

A man with flaws. A man with a three-hundred-year-old past.

"Who was she?" Hakon asked.

Edmund's head popped up and he dropped the brush he was holding. His eyes bore into Hakon's for the briefest moment, but he quickly recovered and picked up the brush. "I don't know what you mean."

Hakon laughed, "Oh come now, Edmund. I know you think I'm a simpleton, and you're the master storyteller, not me, but I know enough about stories to know that there are very few reasons why two men who are like brothers would turn against each other and fight. Politics, or spiritual beliefs, but I'm guessing most often, it is the love for a woman that can make brother fight brother."

"I don't think you are a simpleton," Edmund said. He ran one hand over Bard's coat. "And your observations prove that."

Hakon leaned back against the wall of the stall with his arms crossed over his chest, looking very pleased with himself.

Edmund took a deep breath. "You're right. There was a woman. A beautiful woman. She was not only beautiful but talented. She had a voice like a nightingale and could cook so well that the king's personal chef would be jealous. Anya, that was her name, was kind and lovely and I loved her, but Seb loved her too. I don't know which of us saw her first. We were both Patrons by now and both living in Yondalla at the time. And we both fell in love with her."

Edmund replaced the horse brush in its place along the stable wall. "It all seems so silly now. You would think that in a city the size of Yondalla we would find and fall in love with two different women, but no, we both loved Anya and we both wanted to marry her."

Edmund sat next to Hakon on the hay bale and buried his face in his hands for several moments. "Seb and I got caught up in trying to outdo the other and show Anya who was the better man. Finally, Anya had had enough. She promised she would make her decision and would give us her answer on the night of the next full moon. We were not to see her or even try to see her during this time. It meant over two weeks of waiting, but Seb and I agreed.

"We didn't speak for those two weeks. He was mad at me for being the cause of this whole mess and I felt that it was Seb who should never have gotten involved. The next two weeks were torture. I could hardly work on the instruments I was making at the time, and I felt no joy in performing. On the night of the full moon, Seb and I met and waited at the spot Anya had previously designated. We waited, but she never came. We both became angry with her for not keeping our engagement, so we decided to go to her home and find out why she had never come. When we arrived at her home, we found her mother, crying at the door. Anya and her father had been taken ill and had both died two days previously."

Hakon nodded. He had been right. It was for the love of a woman and both sides had lost.

"Neither of us knew what to do. We blamed each other for Anya's death. Perhaps if we had been ordinary men, we might have dueled each other to the death right then and there, but our callings as Guild Patrons prevented us from seriously harming the other. We had a terrible fight and I left Yondalla. That was over a hundred and fifty years ago and I have never returned until now. Seb and I had no contact until about twenty years ago when our paths crossed again. The old anger was re-kindled."

Hakon patiently watched and listened to this story of Edmund's personal past. For all his storytelling, the old Patron hardly spoke of anything personal.

"Then, seventeen years ago, after I saw Joia for the first time, I gathered as many Patrons as I could find, which included Seb. I considered not telling him, but I knew this business with Joia was bigger than our century-old fight. We both agreed to set aside the past for the good of the Guild. And we have, but it still is not easy to be near him."

"After so many years, why not say sorry?" Hakon asked.

"I want to. I've missed Seb. I didn't want to go on being angry at him, but first, I had to forgive myself for the part I had played in our fight, and in my heart, I also forgave Seb. After all, I knew how he felt towards Anya because I also loved her. And I knew exactly how he felt towards me because I had felt the same way towards him. I forgave him. All there was left was to ask Seb for his forgiveness. But, every time I go near him, he says something that just throws me off and I find myself angry at him all over again."

Hakon nodded his head. "I understand."

"Do you?" asked Edmund in mock concern. "You know what it is to compete for the love of a woman?"

"Yes," Hakon answered. "I know what it means. It's the way I feel right now."

"Ridiculous," Edmund said.

"Ridiculous? No. It's not."

Edmund smiled a half smile, "Hakon, in case you didn't know, you have Joia's love."

Hakon felt his cheeks get hot. He loved Joia and wouldn't have come on this journey with her if he hadn't, but they had never really talked about it. He was glad to hear, although embarrassed to hear it from Edmund.

"I know I have her love, or at least, I've hoped for a long time that I had her love, but right now, I'm competing for Joia against you."

"That's absurd, man," Edmund stepped back away from Hakon. "There is no love between us. I care for her as a trade master to his apprentice."

"I know, but even so, right now I feel the need to compete for Joia against you. And Seb, and Grian and Sidonia. I'm afraid of losing her and her love to this Light of hers. I'm afraid that the Light and the Guild will become so important to her that she won't want anything to do with me ever again. I mean, I can't compete with the Light of the Guild or the entire population of Patrons."

"Ah, I see what you mean," Edmund nodded thoughtfully. "I'm sorry."

Hakon's shoulders sagged slightly. "I want Joia to be successful. She has a providence with the Trade Guild, and I belong to a trade guild. Ultimately, whatever this destiny of Joia's is, it could affect me. But I feel so lost right now. I'm not in my part of the kingdom and I'm far from home, but that isn't why I'm feeling so lost."

"You're a thatcher and should be practicing your craft," Edmund said. Regret filled his voice.

"Yes, but instead I've spent most of the last month in a wagon, listening to you and Joia go on and on about the Light. A light that I don't get to see, but it's all anyone talks about. It seems to be key to everything going on. Everyone else we've met and see this Light, but I cannot."

Hakon stood up and walked to the stable doors, looking out at the busy street. After several moments, he turned back to face Edmund. "Did you know that Joia wears a necklace made by her mother?"

Edmund nodded, "I have seen the necklace."

"She gave it to Seb, who used it to make the ink for this map of his," Hakon explained.

"Did she?" Edmund asked.

"I know how much that necklace meant to her, but she said the Light, this mystical illumination that only I cannot see, told her to use the necklace."

Now, it was Hakon's turn to pace the stable, getting more and more worked up as he spoke. Edmund watched and let him talk out all the frustrations that seemed to have been building for quite some time.

"You're right, Hakon," Edmund said when Hakon's rant ended. "Most of the conversations have been about Joia, the Light, Patrons, Patron's gifts, and the Trade Guild. You have been extraordinarily patient about it all. I forget that you couldn't see the Light as Joia and I do."

Hakon leaned heavily against the door frame again. "I have been of no use on this journey."

"That's not true," Edmund quietly said. "You are a hard worker and generous man. You're fiercely protective of Joia, for which I am grateful. There are times you have been able to see answers that I have overlooked."

Hakon blinked his eyes several times. "I'm sorry for losing my patience in front of you. You're a Patron and I should not be disrespectful."

"Your apology is accepted. And you were not disrespectful. You were upfront and honest with me, which I appreciate. You are no simpleton. I am keenly aware of your intelligence and talent as a thatcher. I meant what I said to Seb about you, I'm sure Thek is proud of you."

Hakon turned in surprise to Edmund. "Do you think so?"

"I do. And I appreciate you taking the time to listen to me. I've never told anyone else about Anya. It's a relief to finally say that out loud."

"There's still time to make amends with Seb," Hakon said. "Do you want to go the rest of your long life without your brother?"

"No, I don't. You're right," Edmund said. "Should we head back?"

Hakon nodded. "Oh, but Edmund, please don't tell Joia I said all of that about her, her destiny, and the Light. I want her to succeed. I truly do."

Edmund smiled. "I know, my friend. I know."

Before reaching Seb's house, Edmund gave Hakon a coin and sent him to the local baker. Edmund found a food merchant with shepherd's pies. He bought four to take back. Hakon soon joined him with a loaf of bread and a jug of buttermilk that the baker wanted to get rid of. Together they returned to Seb's home.

When Edmund opened the door, he found the room was almost in complete darkness. The sun had set and what little light there was came from six candles on and around Seb's desk. He was hunched over and concentrating on his work and did not pay any attention to Edmund and Hakon as they walked in.

Joia came from the other room and waved to them to join her inside.

CHAPTER FIFTEEN

𝔗𝔥𝔢 𝔏𝔦𝔣𝔢 𝔐𝔞𝔭

Once Seb had the ink for Joia's life map, he had set to work immediately. He did not speak as he worked, but carefully dipped his quill and started to draw. For a long while she had sat on a stool behind where Seb sat and watched him work. He drew lines around the paper with inscriptions in runes she didn't understand. His work was meticulous, and she quickly grew bored watching Seb working on the map. Without Edmund and Hakon to keep her company, the time passed very slowly.

She spent a long time admiring the castle mural that hung on the wall. She had never seen anything like it before. It was beautiful. When looked at from afar or simply glanced at, the beauty of the painting was plain and obvious, but when Joia took several steps closer to the painting and started to look at each figure in the picture, she realized how incredibly detailed it was.

The painting was of a grand castle. Some of the castle windows had people in them, doing various activities, like waving to a friend on the ground. In another window, a maid was beating a rug. There was ivy climbing the castle wall on one side and there was a slimy green water line around the base of the castle, like the moat that surrounded it had been higher at some point.

The people around the castle, in its windows and on its walls, were dressed in detailed costumes that ranged from dirty peasants to royals with blue, purple, and red clothes. She could even tell the texture of some of the clothes, like silk, velvet, or wool. The plants and animals in the scene were no less detailed. The hair of the horses shined in the sunshine and the fur of a running dog was blowing in the wind. Various species of trees made up the forest and one woman was swinging on a swing in a tall oak's branches. A little girl was dancing with ribbons that rippled in the wind. Each face in the painting had distinct emotions.

The more Joia looked at the painting, the more she realized there was so much to discover within it and the magnificent painting held Joia's attention for a very long time before she realized it didn't glow with the Light. Surely Seb did not display such a huge painting if it wasn't his own work, but why didn't it glow? She would have to ask Edmund or Seb later.

She finally tore her gaze from the painting and looked around for something to fix for supper, but she found nothing. If Seb had any food, it was put away in some place that only he knew about.

The sun was starting to set, and the room quickly grew dark. Joia went to the back room where Seb had made her ink. An almost dead fire smoldered in the fireplace. Joia worked at it and brought some life back into it. She saw several candles sitting on Seb's worktable. She picked one up and lit it in the fire.

She walked back out to Seb, who was now sitting in almost total darkness. She knew not to speak to him, but he needed to see, so Joia lit the candles, giving him some light in which to do his work. She went back to Seb's room and studied the other painting hanging on the wall. It was smaller than the huge castle painting, but no less magnificent. The waterfall looked so life-like, it was as if she could hear the rushing of the water.

As she was admiring the painting, Edmund and Hakon returned. Seb was still working. She waved to them to join her in the back room and was delighted to see Edmund with his shepherd pies and Hakon with some bread.

"How is it going?" Edmund asked.

Joia looked over her shoulder back to Seb. "He has been working without stopping since just after you left, not even to light a candle when it grew dark. I watched him for a while. It's such a meticulous process, just like dipping candles or weaving cloth. He asked me not to interrupt him."

Edmund nodded. "Like Sidonia and Grian, once you begin a gift, you don't stop until the work is done."

"Did Seb do the painting of the castle?" she asked as they ate.

"He did. Did you look at it?" Edmund smiled.

"Yes. It's incredible. I've never seen anything like it before. To be honest, I've seen but a few paintings in my life, but none of them were as beautiful as that," Joia said.

"Seb is a very talented artist," Edmund ripped off a bit of the bread and dipped it into the juices of his pie.

"But the painting doesn't glow with the Light. How is it that it was painted by Seb and doesn't glow?" Joia asked.

Hakon looked back over his shoulder at the painting, stared at it for several moments, then turned back to his food. Edmund watched Hakon, understanding now how much they talked about the Light and Hakon was the only one not to see it.

"Because he painted it before he became a Patron," Edmund answered. "Our Light didn't come to us until we were made Patrons. But I was living here when he painted that. It was a long process, starting with the selection of the wood, the sketching, and the mixing of dyes for the correct color. He made all the brushes that he used of many different sizes, not to mention the time it took to paint. It was incredible to watch."

"You've known each other a very long time," Hakon said, and Edmund silently nodded.

"Thank you for supper," Joia said to Edmund after they had eaten. She went to the door to check on Seb. Several of his candles had gone out. She brought out some new, fresh candles, lit them, and replaced the old ones. He continued to draw, his quill quietly scratching. Joia saw that the jar of ink he was using was very nearly empty.

Joia went back to the other room. "Did you check on the wagon? Is all well?" she asked.

"I did and all is well," Edmund answered.

"Edmund, where are we to sleep tonight? Here? The wagon? An inn?" Joia asked.

"Well," Edmund began, but he didn't get to say anything more.

Seb stood in the doorway, holding a piece of paper. "You can stay here," Seb said. "You can have your old room back, Edmund."

Once again, Joia was reminded of the long history that the Patrons had together.

Edmund nodded his head at Seb, "That's very kind of you to offer."

Hakon stood up. "I'll go get the bed rolls. I'll be back soon." He looked at Edmund with a knowing look, accepted the wagon's key, and left Seb's shop.

Seb came to Joia and held out a scroll. "Your Life Map, Joia," he said.

Joia took the scroll and carefully opened it. A curious symbol in the middle of the map glowed with golden light. Around the symbol were lines depicting buildings and streets. Names appeared alongside the streets, Flint and Hollow Way. "These are the streets along your shop here?" she asked.

"They are."

"And this symbol in the middle is me?" she asked.

"It is," Seb nodded. "Do you know that symbol, Joia?"

Joia looked at the symbol again. It was a fancy 'A' over an anvil. It looked familiar. She remembered seeing it in her tapestry. It had been hovering over a castle, but she didn't know what it meant.

Edmund looked over her shoulder at the map. "An interesting choice for her, Seb," he said looking at the map maker.

Seb made no reply to Edmund's comment. "That, my girl," Seb pointed to the center of the map, "is the symbol for tradesman. Any respectable tradesman can have this on their door, though there are very few who do these days."

"The 'A' stands for Athelstan, father of all the trades, and the anvil is, well, an anvil," Edmund explained.

Joia looked at it again. She had seen it somewhere else. "Edmund," she suddenly realized, "this is carved onto the side of your wagon!"

Edmund nodded. "Yes, and if you look outside on Seb's door, you will find the same symbol carved into it."

Joia looked at it again. "You said anyone who is a tradesman can use this symbol?" she asked. Seb and Edmund nodded their heads. "My father is a baker and I have been friends with most of the tradeswomen in my village. I have never seen it in my village."

Edmund sighed and sat back down in the chair he had been occupying. "Sadly, many don't remember Athelstan anymore, so the meaning of the symbol is forgotten."

Seb had been poking at the fireplace and he turned back to Joia. "Aren't you going to try it out?" He waved the poker in her direction.

"May I?" Joia excitedly asked.

Seb nodded. "I would be insulted if you did not."

Joia had no wish to insult the Patron who had just spent hours making her gift. She hopped up from her seat and looked at the map. The 'A' was in the center of the room. The borders of Seb's house surrounded her and Flint Street was just outside the door.

She walked into the next room and out the door of Seb's shop. She looked at the map again. The 'A' was still in the center, but the rest of the map had changed slightly. She was standing on Flint Street and the street labeled "Hollow Way" was off to the side of the map almost missing completely. Another street had appeared at the top of the map. "This is incredible!" she called out. She looked up from the map and saw Hakon walking down the street with their bed rolls in his arms. "Hakon, come and see!" She held the paper out to show him. "It's my map."

Hakon arrived and looked at the paper. "It's very impressive and I see that Seb used the trades symbol for you."

"You know that symbol?" Joia asked.

"Yes, of course. It's carved into my thatcher's sickle," Hakon answered.

Once again Joia was reminded of how Hakon was so much more knowledgeable about the Trade Guild than she. It didn't make sense that she had the Light and not Hakon.

"Back inside, you two," Seb called out to them from the back room.

Joia went back in and held the door open for Hakon. Then she bolted it shut and Hakon dropped the bed rolls onto the floor. They went back into the room with Seb and Edmund. Joia laid her map out on the table and looked at it.

"Your work is as excellent as ever," Edmund said to Seb.

Seb gave Edmund a suspicious look. "Thank you," he said with a strained politeness.

"What about you? Still telling stories and singing songs?"

Edmund bristled slightly, but he wasn't going to get worked up over it. "Yes, I do. Being on this journey with Joia and Hakon has given me many new story ideas." Joia looked at Edmund and Hakon raised an eyebrow at him. "Not about you, specifically," he hurriedly said, "but traveling on a quest rather than my normal travels with other entertainers has helped to re-spark the old imagination. It's a change of scenery for me."

Joia laughed. "For a man who is always on the road, a change of scenery seems an odd thing to say."

Edmund nodded, "Only speaking in a metaphorical sense."

Joia turned back to Seb. "Are you ever required to travel when you make maps?"

"It depends on the map and who commissioned it," Seb answered, but offered nothing more to her question.

Joia had hoped to engage Seb in some conversation, but he seemed reluctant to talk much and Joia decided not to push him. She couldn't tell how he felt about her.

He had been mostly polite enough to her. He made her map and was allowing them to stay in his home, but he offered nothing more than a roof over their heads. He seemed to be completely indifferent towards her and Hakon. She realized she might never get on good terms with Seb, but she was determined never to be on bad terms with him.

"Let me have your map, Joia," Seb said, holding out his hand to her.

She thought he was taking it back, which broke her heart, but if the Patron demanded his gift be returned, she wasn't in any position to argue. She held the map up and he took it. But rather than tearing it up, Seb carefully rolled the map and tied a red ribbon around it. He gave it back to her.

"Thank you," she stammered. "There is another pie here," Joia pointed at the fourth Shepherd's Pie. "It is for you."

Seb nodded and turned his back to them. He went to his bed that was sitting in the corner and Edmund took the hint.

"I'm tired," Edmund said, standing and yawning. Joia and Hakon scrambled to their feet too. "Thank you for allowing us to stay here with you." Edmund went back to the front room where Hakon had dropped off their bedrolls.

Joia and Hakon followed, each thanking Seb and bidding him goodnight. He returned a single good night and shut the door that separated the two rooms.

"Nice," Edmund said under his breath. A few candles still burned at Seb's worktable, which gave them enough light to get their bedrolls ready. When everyone was ready, Edmund blew out the candles.

Joia pulled her blanket up around her. She thought about the map Seb had made for her. It was a special gift, indeed, but Joia was unsure what she would need it for. She thought about the other two gifts she had received from the Patrons.

Sidonia's Life Tapestry was an incredible gift. As she was learning to use it, she could easily see how useful it was. It could tell her what she needed to do and where she needed to go. Grian's candle was also a special gift. A light that would never go out. Certainly, that could be very useful, if she ever found herself somewhere dark. And now she had Seb's map.

Joia wondered how many of the Patron's gifts she would have to collect before she was ready to move on in her quest. She wondered if she needed to get one from each of the Patrons. How many were there and how long would that take?

So far, Edmund had been more than kind and helpful, using his own time and wagon to take her all over the countryside to collect these gifts, but he would have to return to his normal life eventually. He was an entertainer and while he would sing a song or tell a story to earn a few coins, it wasn't really performing. She was sure he couldn't go long without feeling the need to return to true performing.

What would she do then, she wondered? What would Hakon do? Would he stay with her, or would he want to return home and become a master thatcher?

Joia's thoughts floated around in her mind, and she worried she might never get to sleep when she noticed Edmund humming very quietly on the other side of the room.

"Edmund?" she whispered.

The humming stopped. "Yes Joia?" he whispered back.

"What is your gift?"

"Ah, I wondered if you would ever think to ask that," he said.

Joia propped herself on her elbow. The room was pitch black and Joia was thankful for that. She was sure her face was red with embarrassment. "I'm ashamed that I didn't think of it sooner."

"I can give one of two gifts. One gift is an instrument made by me. It will never break or ever need to be tuned. I can make lutes, fiddles, harps, flutes, panpipes, and a few others," he said.

"There is a man in my town named Noll," Joia said, thinking about the old man who sat in front of the local tavern. "He has a lute with one string. It's dreadful to listen to, but he plays it all day long. He's not a bad singer, but he's terrible with his lute. Just imagine if he had a lute that never went out of tune."

"I've seen the man," Edmund said, and she could hear amusement in his voice.

"I had to work on the tavern roof once," Hakon's voice spoke quietly in the darkness. "It was sunup to sundown of listening to Noll. Dreadful."

Joia giggled and she thought she heard a muffled snort from Edmund. "You mentioned you had one of two gifts. What is your other gift?" she asked.

My gift is a story or a song, depending on what the person wants. It is a special story or song that I make up especially for that person. That is not extraordinary in itself. You know I am always making up stories."

"Yes, and they are all wonderful," Joia said.

"What makes this story so special is that the person who receives the story will never forget it. They will be able to recall the story word for word anytime they think of it."

"How lovely."

"Yes, but this gift is more than a lovely, perfectly recalled story. It has the power to bring peace and calm to the person anytime they recall it. Think about that, Joia. Have you ever been scared or nervous and sung a song to yourself to help you calm down?"

"Yes."

"And does it always work?"

"Only if I can remember the words. Sometimes it's hard to think clearly when I'm scared."

"Exactly," Edmund said. "When we are scared or nervous, it is hard to calm down, but if you have my gift, you will not have that problem again."

Joia could hear the smile in his voice. "Oh, that is a lovely gift, Edmund. What does someone have to do to be worthy of your gift?"

"When someone asks for my gift, I ask them to talk to me for a while. I like to know a little about the person before I create their song or story," he explained.

"It is something you do often?" she asked.

He was quiet for several moments. "No, it's not. No one has asked in a very, very long time. Not even my tradesmen."

"Do you think the other Patrons are often asked for their gifts?" she asked him.

"You would have to ask them that question, but my guess is no. Grian and Sidonia live alone and probably only see other people when they go to their nearest village for food and supplies. Most people don't know where they are or even who they are."

"One day, would you be willing to give me your gift?" she quietly asked.

"I would be honored. For Hakon as well, if he wishes," Edmund said. "Tonight, is not the time, though."

"No, of course not," Joia quickly said. "Another day, when we are not bumping down the road in your wagon or sitting in the common room of a smelly inn."

She heard him chuckle. It was a deep rumble. "Yes. For me to give you my gift, we would need to be somewhere where there are few distractions. I want to be able to concentrate and you will want to listen."

Joia rolled to her back. "Thank you for telling me about your gift."

"What are you going to do next?" Edmund asked.

Joia turned her head back in Edmund's direction. "I'm not sure," she said. "I guess I'll pull out my Life Tapestry in the morning and see if it has any instructions for me."

There was a long pause and Joia started to wonder if Edmund had gone to sleep, but she heard him shift about on his bed roll.

"That's a good plan," he said. "Good night, Joia."

"Good night, Edmund."

CHAPTER SIXTEEN

Joia Flees

Joia pulled out her Life Tapestry and laid it on Seb's table. The morning sun shone through the small windows and made the room seem almost cheerful. Hakon had gone back to the stable to check on their horse and wagon and return their bed rolls.

Edmund watched as Joia smoothed out the tapestry and ran her hand over its swirl of colors. Unless Joia's Life Tapestry told her otherwise, Edmund had no intention of staying with Seb longer than necessary.

Seb and Edmund stood by, watching Joia as she stood alongside the table and peered at her tapestry. The shimmers of color played along the fabric before shapes began to form. Joia watched the shapes as they shifted and changed. When she had previously done this, the tapestry had only shown her one or two images, but this time it showed her many. She watched it until the colors swirled and fell back into the tapestry.

She was confused. She had seen so many things. An anvil, wagon, and spinning wheel, all sitting side by side, when a dark cloud appeared and covered the wagon and spinning wheel.

"Joia?" Edmund began, "What did you see?"

She rubbed her eyes. "I'm not entirely sure," Joia answered, "but—" She was about to tell Edmund about the many images she had seen, but Seb interrupted her.

"Oh great!" Seb threw his hands into the air. "Life Tapestry, ha! Great gift Sidonia!" Seb stood up and paced the room.

"That tapestry is a perfect item. Sidonia's skill on the loom is flawless!" Edmund cried out.

"Oh right," Seb feigned an apology. "It's not the Patron's gift at all, it is the owner!" He pointed at Joia.

Edmund's fists hit the table causing Joia to jump. "How dare you say that, Seb! Joia has the Light!"

"Oh, I can see that, all right, but it means nothing if she doesn't know what to do with it." Seb was standing on the other side of the table glaring at Edmund.

Joia sat stunned by the two Patron's outbursts. She felt a tear prickle in her eye as she took in a shuddering breath. "He's right Edmund," Joia said quietly.

Edmund's face changed from outraged to devastated. Seb looked smug.

"I don't know what I'm doing, and I don't know what it is I'm supposed to be doing. Why do I have this light? Was it by some divine decision or a fluke? I don't know why I was chosen by Athelstan, or the Light, or whatever force is at work." She looked at Seb and suddenly felt angry that he questioned her worthiness at all. "All I know is that I was chosen, and I will do what I can to find and fulfill my destiny. Whatever it may be, I will do it!"

Her voice rose in volume until she was shouting at Seb. She stood there, shaking as she held his gaze.

Then she remembered who these two men were as Seb and Edmund stared at her in shock. Horrified by what she had just done, she grabbed her tapestry, ran to the other room, grabbed her bundle, and ran out the door.

"Joia, wait!" Edmund called her, but she was already gone. He spun to face the map maker. "Seb, what have you done?" Edmund shouted.

"Me? What about her? Why does she has the Light? The Light that we only gained after fifteen years of practice and through the sacrifice of Athelstan. But this girl with no skills or talents, from some little unknown village is born with the Light, knows nothing about it, and we are supposed to just honor her and kiss her feet?"

Edmund's mouth hung open for several moments. "I cannot believe you just said that. She deserves respect as a woman, no matter if she has the Light or not. Your behavior towards her is completely unacceptable."

He ran to the door and threw it open, but he couldn't see her, and he turned back to Seb. "You had no right to yell at that child. The next time you see Joia you had better apologize to her." He slammed the door shut. Frantically he looked up and down the street, but he couldn't see which way Joia had gone.

Joia pulled the door shut and took off running in the direction of the stables. Hot tears fell down her cheeks. Seb confirmed what she had been fearing since the beginning. She was no one. The Light had chosen wrongly. She couldn't do whatever it was she was supposed to do, and Edmund wasted all that time on helping her. Sidonia and Grian wasted their precious talents on her. Seb had wasted his time with her. And worst of all was disappointing Hakon, but Seb was right. The Light meant nothing if she didn't know what to do with it.

Joia stopped running just before reaching the stable. She couldn't go in and face Hakon and she didn't want Edmund to find her. She couldn't bear to face their disappointment in her. She turned and ran down a small side street, thankful that there weren't as many people there. She slowed down to walk and took in several deep breaths.

Joia's mind didn't stop with the questions and the doubt. She had told Seb, just before she left that she had a purpose and she was going to find it and fulfill it, but now… She let out a long, shaky sigh. No, he was right. She didn't know what she was doing. She was the wrong person for the job. Hakon would be better. Anyone else would be better.

She turned onto another large street and looked around at the unfamiliar buildings.

"What am I doing here?" she wondered out loud. Yondalla wasn't where she belonged. She belonged in Erthenhorn. She should be home, helping her mother prepare supper for her family and helping Ebba plan for her wedding. "I need to go home."

That was it. She would go home. The Guild and trades had survived for centuries without her help. They would last for centuries more. She had no business being here. It was time to go home.

But home was a long way off. She could walk there, but that would take a very long time and probably be very unsafe. There was no way she could take Edmund's wagon. He had been too good to her. She wouldn't take anything of his. She would have to buy passage on a carriage to take her home, but she had no money. Joia stopped and looked at the row of buildings right in front of her. The street had come to an end. She could turn right or left, but Joia looked up at the building in front of her. A sign with a spinning wheel hung over the door. Joia stretched her hand out, opened the door, and walked in.

Edmund moved as quickly as the crowd allowed him towards the stables. Surely, she would have headed straight for the stables. She knew Hakon was there and would go right to him. Edmund was shaking with anger as he marched down the street. He had been ready to forgive Seb and ask for his forgiveness, but now… He was furious with Seb all over again. Seb had no right to treat any lady like that, especially not Joia.

He walked into the stable and found Hakon talking with the owner.

"Hello, Edmund," Hakon said.

"Joia? Where is Joia?" Edmund asked, looking around the room.

"I thought she was with you at Seb's shop," Hakon answered.

"She was," Edmund looked around the stable. "She didn't come here?"

"No. Why would she?" Hakon's voice was filled with sudden concern. "Where is she? What happened?"

"Seb yelled at her. She ran out of his shop. I thought I was only a few steps behind her, but I," he ran his hands over his face. "I can't find her. I figured she would come straight here to you."

"No, she hasn't been here, unless she came in another way." Hakon ran into the stable where Edmund's horse and wagon were kept. He looked in the wagon and under the wagon, but Joia was not there. He ran out into the street to join Edmund.

"Joia!" Edmund called out to the busy streets.

"She wasn't in there," Hakon told him.

"I don't see her anywhere. No trace of her Light. I don't know where she is."

"Did she leave her map at Seb's house? If it is there, we can find her," Hakon said.

"Hakon, you have more sense than all of us together. You're right. Come on, back to Seb's." They ran back down the street to Seb's home. Edmund threw open the door, making Seb jump. "Joia's map. Is it here?"

"I don't know. She might have left it. She might have taken it," Seb answered.

Edmund went to Seb's table and started throwing things aside, looking for the scroll.

"Hey!" Seb cried out. "What are you doing?"

"Joia's missing and we must find her!" Hakon said, going into the other room and searching the floor.

"What? She only just left here. Surely, she went to the stables," Seb said.

Edmund grabbed Seb by the shirt. "She's gone and it's your fault."

"Get off me," Seb threw Edmund's arms off of him. "You blame me? You've always blamed me."

"You're right I blame you!" Edmund stared at Seb.

"It was your fault," Seb poked Edmund in the chest. "You brought her here. If you had just backed away when you had the chance, none of it would have happened."

"You should have been the one to back away!" Edmund shoved Seb's finger away. They both lunged at each other at the same moment and were about to throw a punch at each other when Hakon yelled at them.

"Enough!" Hakon stepped in between the two men. "Look at you. You are arguing like children. You are Patrons for goodness' sake! Joia is missing and we've got to find her. She is more important right now than any personal grudges you hold."

Edmund looked properly chastened. Seb glared at Hakon for a moment before dropping his gaze to the floor. Hakon shook with anger. "There is no excuse for this behavior."

"You're right, Hakon," Edmund said. "Our priority is Joia's safety. A truce Seb? We forget the past for now and work together to find Joia." Edmund held out his hand.

Seb was still and quiet for several long moments before accepting Edmund's hand. "Truce."

Edmund nodded his head, and they dropped hands. "Hakon, did you find her map?"

"No," he said. "Her bundle isn't here. The one where she kept her gifts from the Patrons. She must have grabbed it when she ran."

"We've got to find her," Edmund said. He closed his eyes for several moments, a plan forming in his mind. "All right, Hakon, you go back towards the stables and the surrounding area. I'm going to head towards the castle. Seb, you," Edmund looked at Seb and stopped. "You go your way. We meet back here when the village bell rings ten. Right?"

"Right," Hakon took off.

Edmund and Seb stared at each other for several moments before Edmund turned around and left the shop. Seb walked out behind Edmund.

He could see Hakon rounding the corner to his left and Edmund going straight towards the castle.

"Edmund!" Seb called out. Edmund turned around to face Seb. "The castle is a dangerous place these days. Be careful!"

Edmund raised a hand in understanding and then he turned back around and left.

It was darker in the spinner's shop than outside, and it took Joia's eyes a few moments to adjust.

"Hello dear, are you all right?" a kind voice spoke to her.

Joia saw four women sitting together, carding wool when Joia walked in. Two other ladies were at the large spinning wheels further back in the room. One of the spinners came to Joia and took her by the hand.

"You look like you've been running, dear. Your face is all flushed. Come in, have a drink, and sit down." A wooden ladle filled with water was passed to Joia. She took a drink and allowed herself to be seated among the women. "There now," the spinner said. "Will you be all right?"

Joia nodded. "I will now, thank you." She sat down on a stool by the washing tub. "Please, I am not from around here. I need to buy my passage back home. I've worked in a spinnery before. I can card wool, stir the dye, or do any task you ask. I just need to earn some money so I can go home."

"I'm sorry dear, I don't have any money you can earn. What little I make these days goes to food and paying the taxes."

Joia's heart sank.

"But don't you worry, dear. Things will all work out, I'm sure of it. Stay here for a while and we'll see if we can't think of something." The spinner went back to her spinning wheel.

"What happened, dear?" one of the carding women asked. "Your husband being unkind to you?"

"What? No, it's nothing like that," Joia shook her head. She almost told them about Hakon, Edmund, and Seb, but decided against that. There was no way to explain what she was doing, and it was probably safer not to say anything at all. "If you don't mind, I'd rather not talk about it."

"Of course, dearie," the spinner said. She went back to her large spinning wheel and picked up the end of her last bit of spinning. She stood by the great wheel and picked up a fine section of carded wool. In one hand, she took the end of the last bit of thread she had spun and put the carded wool to it. Using her other hand, she started to turn the wheel and kept it spinning with her fingers while her other hand spun the wool. Joia had never seen such a large wheel before. Letty, back in Erthenhorn's shop, had a similar style, but not quite so large.

Joia looked over at the other woman who was spinning using a distaff and spindle. Joia had learned to spin using a distaff and spindle, but she had never been able to master the process. Her sister, Ebba, was much better, but neither of them was as good as this spinner before Joia. Her fingers were very deft as they pulled at the wool from the distaff and kept the spindle spinning around before quickly winding it up on the spindle.

It was several moments of watching the woman using her spindle before she realized that the spindle was glowing with a soft golden color of the Light. This was very curious.

"My name is Joia."

The women said a collective hello. The spinner who stood by the big wheel nodded. "It's nice to meet you, dear. My name is Hannah. This is Bess," she pointed at the other spinner. "And these ladies are Miriam, Bettle, Gwen, and Frida." The ladies said hello again. Joia smiled at them.

"Excuse me, Bess?" Joia went to the spinner with the glowing spindle. "I have spent many hours sitting with the spinner in my home village and I have also done a bit of spinning, but never have I seen a spindle that was so beautifully balanced."

"Oh! I forgot!" Bess shouted. "It was him who gave it to me. I don't want it! I don't want to see it ever again!" She stood up and to Joia's surprise, started to remove the thread from the spindle onto a wheeled contraption where they kept the newly spun thread. "I never want to use this spindle ever again."

"Why?" Joia asked. "It is a perfect spindle. Why would you want to get rid of it?"

"Because it was him who gave it to me," Bess said, shaking the spindle in Joia's face. "Made it himself, he did, right in his own shop. Before he betrayed me!" She dropped the spindle into a basket and started to dig in another basket. She pulled out an old spindle. Old, but well used. She pulled some wool off the distaff and carefully twisted it until she had her leader thread going, which she looped around the base of the spindle and then started to spin again.

"Who made it?" Joia asked.

"Oh, here we go again," one of the women cried out.

"Who betrayed you, Bess?" Joia's hand curled around the spindle.

Bess sat back down on her stool. Her shoulders slumped. "It was Wodwin, a local carpenter. See, I used to be in the castle. Had a nice shop in the marketplace, I did. For years I spun me wool there, making the finest thread. I had heard there was a carpenter who could make anything out of wood, and it would never, ever break. I went to him and asked him about it and how much it would cost. He said he could do it, without me paying any money, but I had to prove me worth."

"You're worth?" Joia asked. "How do you do that?"

"He asked if I dedicated my work to the Patron spinner, Kloma. I assured him I did. He asked me to spin him some double-spun thread, the color of oak wood. I did it. It took a lot of wool before I could get the right colors of dye, but finally, I got it. I spun it and presented me finest work to him. He thanked me and promised to bring me my spindle the following week. And so he did! A week later, just as I finished dedicating me day to Kloma, he came. Brought me the prettiest, finest spindle I had ever seen. It spun so perfectly."

"So then, why not use it?" Joia asked.

"Because it was him that betrayed me," Bess yelled. "He betrayed all of us. Me, the weaver, the clothier, the cobbler, the artists, the luthiers, and all the entertainers!" Bess was yelling with anger.

"There, there, Bess. Calm yourself down," Hannah soothed. "You see dear," she turned to Joia, "all the art and textile trades were sent away from the castle. The only ones that remain are the smithies, the carpenters, and I believe the bakers."

"But why would the smithies and carpenters want you out of the castle? Doesn't the king and his people need clothes?" Joia didn't understand.

"That's what we said," Bess went on, in a much calmer voice. "But a decree came out from the king through his trade minister, Scrios. He said all of us had to go. Ciar the Blacksmith and Wodwin came to my shop and told me to leave. I had half a day to move me belongings. Thank goodness for Hannah, here. Gave me a place to stay, she did."

"You are very lucky to have such a friend." She looked at the other women. "It seems you have many friends here," Joia said.

The women all nodded at each other. One of them had quit carding wool and had her distaff and spindle out. She was working with some wool that had been dyed a lovely orange. "Bess had an apprentice," she said. Joia thought she remembered the woman was named Bettle. "But her father is a smithy, and he didn't want her to continue her apprenticeship with Bess.

The poor girl was heartbroken. She was still in her first year and was very promising, from what I saw, but her father said no."

"I just can't believe that," Joia said.

"It were a sad thing," Bess sighed. "Agnes, that's her name, tried to sneak out and come with me. We almost made it out of the castle walls together, but her father caught her. He hit her good and dragged her back to his home. She was crying out. I was crying, but there was nothing I could do. Those two, Ciar and Wodwin continued to escort me out."

Joia sat, stunned by the news. "But the trades, I thought, well, I thought they worked together."

"They used to. It's how it should be, but it's not anymore." Hannah started spinning once again.

Bess adjusted her distaff at her hip and started working again. After several moments of silence, the carding women began chatting with each other, at first quietly, but soon the spinners shop was full of gossip and laughter. Joia listened and relaxed. It was comforting to be among the women again. Her whole life had been spent with her mother and sister and the women of the village. For a while, Joia could pretend she was back home. Back where she belonged, until the door to the shop opened and Seb walked in. Joia scooted back towards the shadows of the room.

"Hello Seb!" Hannah called out.

The other women greeted him, too.

One of them, Gwen, stood up and went to him with swaying hips. "What brings you here today?" Gwen asked, teasingly. "Come to visit us?"

"I've come to collect Joia," he stepped in further towards Joia. She couldn't hide in the shadows from Seb. Her own Light gave her away. He looked over at her and held out a hand.

"Come along. Hakon is worried sick."

"She was most upset when she got here, Seb. Was it this Hakon person who made her so upset?" Hannah asked.

"No, it wasn't," Seb said looking to Joia before looking back to the other ladies in the room. "But I do know who it was, and I promise you ladies, that the matter will be dealt with. Come now, Joia."

"I'll go with you, Seb," Gwen winked.

He shook his head. "A kind offer, but I am here for Joia," he said. Gwen looked noticeably deflated.

Joia was about to say no when a thought came to her. Seb had worked in the castle long ago. He would know where this Ciar or Wodwin was. He could take her there. Joia stood up.

She held her bundle close to her. "I guess I had better go," she said. "Thank you, Hannah and Bess, for letting me rest here."

"Come back anytime, dear," Hannah said.

Seb opened the door for Joia. "Goodbye, ladies," he said, and the women called out their goodbyes to him as he closed the door. They moved into the street when he stopped and turned to her.

"Joia, what were you thinking," he started but looked her in the face and stopped. Joia glared at him. "I apologize, Joia. I'm sorry for what I said about you. It was wrong of me. You have the Light and I should trust that." He sighed and rubbed his neck.

"What did I do that upsets you so much?" she quietly asked. "I didn't mean to be so ignorant."

"You haven't done anything," he said. "I am," he sighed again. "I don't quite know what to say and I doubt you would understand. I'm sorry, Joia."

Joia looked at him and saw the hurt and loneliness in his face. She sighed. "I forgive you, Seb."

"It is more than I deserve. Now, we must get back. Hakon looked ready to punch anyone that came near him and I'm sure Edmund is having kittens by now." He took her by the hand and led her down the street.

"How did you find me?"

Seb chuckled. "I've lived in this neighborhood most of my life. I know everyone and I know that everyone on these streets knows everyone else's business. Ask the right nosy busybody and there is nothing you can't find out. A couple of women on the street saw you and it wasn't long before the story of an upset girl not from this neighborhood going into the spinners shop, was floating among the locals."

"Ah. I see," she said and followed him for several steps before stopping. "Seb, I want you to take me to the castle."

"No way." Seb stopped and turned to Joia.

"Please, Seb."

"Are you insane? Do you even have any idea of what is happening in the castle right now?" he asked.

"Is Wodwin the Patron for the Carpenters?" she asked and he nodded. "And Ciar is the Patron of Blacksmiths, right?" she asked.

"Yes. Did Edmund tell you about them?"

Joia shook her head. "The spinner named Bess had a spindle that glowed with the Light. I asked her about it, and she told me it was made by the carpenter Wodwin. He could make her a spindle that never broke and was perfectly balanced. That sounds to me like a gift from a Patron."

"You're right, it is his gift," Seb said.

"Then I need to see him or Ciar."

"Joia, listen to me. It's not safe in the castle walls. They've kicked all the trades out."

"Except the smithies and the carpenters, yes, I know" Joia cut in. "Don't look too surprised Seb. Like you said, this neighborhood is full of busybodies and the best place for gossip is in a spinner's shop."

"Clever." Seb smiled. "But why do you want to see them?"

"I want to get their side of the story. Why would they do this? Was it their idea, or the trade minister, Scrios? Who does this man think he is?"

"Scrios? He is the trade minister. Are you sure that's what Bess said?"

"You've lived here for centuries," Joia said. "How could you not know who the trade minister is?"

"I don't like the people at the castle. And I avoid it and them as much as possible," Seb answered.

"But you know who Scrios is?" Joia asked.

"I know of him or at least I used to know of someone with that name. No. It couldn't be the same man." Seb looked off into the distance, lost in thought.

"What man?" Joia asked. "Who is he?"

They started walking again, but Joia noticed Seb was walking in a different direction, not back to his shop. He was taking her toward the castle wall.

"No, I'm sure it cannot be the same man, but we need to find out. Come on, Joia." Seb walked more quickly. He rounded a few corners before leading Joia to a street with a high wall and a large gate at the end. "This is the quickest way to Ciar's smithy. Through the gate and first street on your left. Follow it and you'll find Ciar."

"You're not coming with me?" Joia asked, suddenly afraid.

"Edmund might be happy to galivant all over the place seeking out Patrons with you, but I told you, I don't go to the castle." He walked her a few paces closer. "There might be a guard at the gate." He looked around and picked up a discarded basket from a pile of tossed waste. He pushed the basket into Joia's hands. "Take this."

"What do you expect me to do with this old thing?" she asked.

He pulled off his over-tunic and placed it in the basket to cover the holes in the wicker. "If the guard or anyone else asks, you are on your way to pick up some tools at the blacksmith for your Uncle Edmund." He looked down the road. "They shouldn't question that."

"You're almost as good at coming up with stories as Edmund is," Joia smiled.

Seb stopped and looked at her. His eyes softened and a small smile escaped his lips. "Hardly. All right, if you're going to do this, you should go immediately." He was sending her in alone.

"Why can't you come with me?"

"I've lived in this city for too long. Too many people know me. I don't know how the trade minister feels about map makers, they might kick me out or arrest me. It's best if I keep away from the castle."

"Oh, I see." Joia looked towards the gate.

She swallowed hard. "Here," she held out her precious bundle to Seb. "Hold onto it for me or give it to Hakon. Please keep it safe."

Seb took the bundle from Joia. "May Athelstan go with you," he whispered.

CHAPTER SEVENTEEN

The Three Patrons

Joia turned around and gripped her basket. She walked up the street toward the gate and saw a group of people headed the same way. Joia quickened her step and joined them as they walked in. The guard at the gate looked over them all but did not stop them. Joia let out the breath she had been holding. She couldn't understand why she was feeling so scared. She was going into the market like any normal person might. She would be talking with a guild Patron. It wasn't like this was the first time she had even spoken to a Patron before.

But this time, she was on her own. Edmund wasn't going to be here to do all the talking. It was up to her this time.

A month ago, she never gave a thought to the trade Patrons, nor did she think the Patrons were even real people. But now, she had met four Patrons and collected their special gifts from three of them. She had the Light. She didn't know why, but she had it. They had to respect her for that, didn't they?

But the conversation with the spinners had worried her. Their story matched the story of the two merchants they had met on the road yesterday. Something was wrong. Why would the Patrons fight among themselves, like Edmund and Seb? Why would Patrons turn their backs on other trades and kick them out of their homes?

Perhaps that was her destiny; to fix the Guilds and bring them back together again. The trouble was, she had no idea how one would even go about doing that.

She reached the first set of streets and turned to the left. In the distance, she could see a sign hung along the wall of the building indicating the way to the blacksmith's shop. She followed the sign and came to a long street of smithy workshops.

The open workspaces were filled with roaring fires with men hitting red-hot metal over anvils. There was a line of horses waiting to be fitted with iron horseshoes. She had never seen so many blacksmith shops in one place before. And she had never seen so many blacksmiths before. Many turned to look at her as she walked past them.

Joia assumed that Ciar would be glowing with the Light, but as she walked, she didn't see him anywhere. No one was glowing.

"Aren't you a pretty, thing," one of the blacksmiths walked up to her.

She took a step back. "I'm looking for a family friend."

"Maybe I can help you," he came closer.

Suddenly, Joia was aware of the situation she had put herself into. If anything happened to her, who was going to know?

The bells, high on the castle wall, struck ten and their sound reverberated through the open market.

She took a few steps back. "No, that's all right. He's not here today, I'll come back another time."

The blacksmith lunged forward and grabbed her. "I don't think so. Why don't you come with me now and we'll have some fun."

Joia let out a yell when she was grabbed and pulled into the man's strong arms. "No, please!" A couple of men around him laughed. No one was going to help her. "I'm looking for Ciar!" she cried out.

The grip around her slackened. "Ciar?"

"Lir, let the girl go!" a booming voice called out.

The man shoved her out of his arms, knocking her to the ground. She landed with a hard thud on the stone street and her basket fell beside her.

A large, glowing hand appeared. She took it and was helped to her feet. Another man picked up her basket and handed it to her. She mumbled thanks to them.

"What have I told you, Lir, about treating women?" the voice boomed.

Joia looked at the man who had helped her and saw the most muscular-looking person she had ever met. If he hadn't been glowing with the golden Light of the Guild, she might have been more afraid of the big man, but she felt safe with the Patron.

"She didn't tell me she was looking for you, or I would have helped," Lir said.

"It doesn't matter. You cannot grab any woman you see. You will go home for the rest of the day and spend your time in the company of your wife," Ciar said.

Lir paled, but Joia felt no sympathy for him. He turned around and started to walk away, to the laughter and jeers of his fellow blacksmiths.

"Come with me," Ciar turned and walked away. Joia jumped to follow him. Ciar pointed to a man, "You, go fetch Aren."

The man ran off.

Ciar led Joia into one of the shops and closed the door. The noise of the smithy quieted noticeably. "Welcome, Bearer of the Light."

Ciar was a big man with coal-black hair that had been pulled away from his face. His top was bare and sweaty, but his chest was covered by a leather apron. A mallet hung at his side the way a soldier wears a sword. He glowed with the soft golden Light.

Joia took a deep breath and tried to calm her nerves that had jumped at seeing the big man. There was nothing to be afraid of, she reminded herself. He was a Patron, true enough, but she had the Light, the same as him. That gave her every reason to be able to speak with him. She stood her full height, knowing that showing Ciar her fear and doubt would not help her get the information from him that she desired.

"I am Joia, of Erthenhorn and daughter of Thomas the Baker."

He crossed his arms across his chest. "You are not a Patron."

"No. I'm not."

"But you have the Light of the Guild. No one but Patrons has the Light."

"That's right.

"How did you find me?" he asked.

Joia didn't hesitate. "I was guided here by the Light." It was more or less true. "Ciar, I've come to ask you something. I heard some rumors that bad feelings are being stirred up among the trades, turning them against each other."

He leaned down to be closer to her height. "Where do you hear these rumors?"

"In my travels, I have met many tradesmen. They have told me that only smithies and a few other trades remain in the castle boundaries."

"That's right," he stood back up to his full height. "We do not need the other trades here. The king does not need anything more than smithies and food suppliers." He stopped and looked her up and down for a few moments, before relaxing his shoulders and giving her a forced smile. "It is hot in here and if you are not accustomed to it, it can be uncomfortable. Would you care for some water?"

She was indeed very thirsty and warm. "Thank you." Since Ciar was avoiding the subject, Joia decided to take the conversation in another way. "Please, Ciar, tell me about your gift."

"For someone who seems to know many things about the Patrons, how is it you do not know about my gift?" He handed her a wooden cup.

She took it gratefully and sipped, thinking of how she would best go about this. "Well, I have heard you can make anything from metal, but isn't that what most blacksmiths do?"

He eyed her suspiciously. "My gift is more valuable than just any common object made by any common blacksmith. I can craft anything made of metal and it will never break, never dull, and never need repair. Whether it is a horseshoe, a tool, a weapon, or a lock, it will never break and always be perfect."

"That is indeed a remarkable gift." Joia thought of a soldier with an ever-sharp blade or Hakon with a sickle that would never need repair, or a sewing needle that could go through any material and never splinter. A tool that could be passed on from generation to generation and be forever as it was the day it was forged.

The door to Ciar's shop opened. Another man, strong and muscular like Ciar walked through, glowing with the Light. He stared at Joia. He also wore a leather apron, but the tools at his belt weren't quite the same.

"I can't believe it," the man said.

"Welcome friend," Ciar walked to the man and slapped him on the back. "Aren, this is Joia. Joia, this is Aren, Patron of the Silversmiths."

Hakon went back to the stables after leaving Seb's house. Joia was nowhere to be seen. He couldn't believe she was gone. How could he let his beloved Joia out of his sight? He had promised her just a week ago at Grian's that he would never let her be alone. He had failed her. Perhaps, she was better left with Edmund. He would guide and protect her better than Hakon could. He let out a long breath as he looked around. She was nowhere to be seen.

Hakon searched up and down the streets without seeing anyone familiar. When the bells struck the hour, he ran back to Seb's. Surely Edmund or Seb had found her by now but there was no one at Seb's shop. Hakon paced the room and decided to wait there in case she returned.

Edmund walked up the street towards the castle, removing the green scarf from off his head and tucking it into his tunic. He needed to look less like an entertainer and more like a villager. He passed two men performing a few songs on the street corner. They played well. He knew they were not trade guild entertainers, but he always appreciated good music. As he got closer to the gate, he passed a caravan of entertainers that he recognized. They were leaving the castle and going back into the city's streets. He waved to them and went to their head wagon.

"Hello Jack," he greeted the group's leader. "It's been a few years since I saw your company last. How are you?"

"Edmund," Jack sneered. "How could you?"

"What? I don't understand." Edmund said.

"You no longer bless us when we dedicate our performing to you."

"That's not so. I heard your dedication today, as I do every day."

Jack huffed. "But you no longer bless us. We are not allowed into the castle walls. We are being told to leave, that we are no longer welcome here. We have performed here twice a year for generations."

"That, Jack, is none of my doing. In fact, I am on my way to finding out what is going on, but I fear it is a power beyond mine that is making these things happen. Go out to the square by the western wall and perform there. You will find better success. Do not give up on me."

Jack nodded his head at Edmund but said nothing as he continued to lead his company away from the gate. Edmund turned back to the castle. What was going on?

He passed through the gate, unchallenged by the guard, and looked around. Immediately he realized there were many shops and homes empty and boarded up. There was not a musician to be seen anywhere. On a day as fine as this, one would normally find a musician on every corner, but today, there was no one. Even the streets were relatively empty with only a few people passing through.

Edmund stopped in front of a shop and looked at its closed windows. It had been a spinner's shop. Two doors down was a boarded weaver's shop.

He remembered what the two horsemen had said to him. All the textile and art trades were gone from the castle, sent away by the trade minister.

He hadn't wanted to believe it when he had heard it from the merchants, but the proof was right in front of him. There were no entertainers, no spinners, and no weavers anywhere to be found in the castle walls.

The smell of fresh bread pulled his mind away from his thoughts. Edmund looked around and saw a baker's shop across the street. The baker was placing several loaves of bread into a hot oven.

"Good day, sir," the baker greeted as Edmund walked in. "What can I get you today? A dozen rolls? They are particularly good today."

"No, thank you, although they do smell delicious. I was on my way to the weavers to purchase new fabric for a shirt, but she was not there." Edmund's stories came easily to him.

"Shh," the baker leaned over his worktable to Edmund. "Not so loud. Where have you been for the last few months? Of course, the weaver is gone. Trade Minister Scrios read the decree from the king. All art and textile trades had to leave the castle boundaries."

"Scrios? No, I didn't know," Edmund said in shock. He had known a man by the name of Scrios long ago, but it couldn't be the same person, could it? "I have been out of town visiting family and only just got back."

"Well, now you know, so don't mention it again," the baker whispered. He stood up and in a louder voice said, "Now, how about a hot loaf of bread?"

"No but thank you." Edmund left the shop. He took off running for the part of the castle where he thought he could remember where the smithies were located. If a royal decree had been made, and if Scrios was indeed behind it, then the smithies were in as much trouble as the rest of the trades were.

CHAPTER EIGHTEEN

Scrios the Uncreator

Joia looked at the two Patrons who stood shoulder to shoulder before her. The muscles in their backs, chests, and arms had been made hard over the centuries of swinging hammers as they forged hot semi-solid metals into tools and weapons. She was small next to the two smiths and their gaze only made her feel smaller.

"Most curious," Aren said. "What is your trade?"

"I don't have one. I am a daughter of a baker," Joia answered.

"Then why do you have the Light? I don't see anything that is particularly special about you." Aren rubbed his chin.

"I, um," Joia said, trying to think of what to say. "I have come here to find out if the rumors I have heard are true. They say that some of the trades have been sent away from the castle."

"You're a nosy little thing, aren't you?" Aren asked.

"The Trade Minister sent them away," Ciar said.

"Why were they sent away?" Joia asked. "What do you fear?"

"Fear?" Aren laughed. "Oh no, dear. We do not fear the other trades. We are far more important than they are. They are silly trades that play with yarn and sing silly songs. They are not worthy of being in the castle, like us."

"Smithies and carpenters are the most important trades," Ciar joined in. "Without us, there would be no tools. No hammers, no sickles, no nails, no horseshoes. There would be no weapons or armor. The would be no candle sticks. No ornaments of beautiful metal to adorn the king's castle."

The door opened a third time and another man, glowing with the Light walked in. "Don't forget about carpenters, my friend. Without carpenters, there would be no tables to eat upon, no chairs to sit in, or beds to sleep on."

"Ah Wodwin, when did you get back?" Ciar asked.

"Not more than an hour ago, Ciar. I was looking in on my men when I heard a rumor that you and Aren had gathered to talk to a strange girl." He looked at Joia. "Never in all my long days did I think I would meet a child with the Light."

The new man was not as tall or broad as the two smithies. He had light brown hair and a gentle face. He smelled strongly of freshly cut wood and oil. It reminded her of Edmund's oil he used on his instruments.

"Has Scrios been informed of this girl's arrival?" Wodwin asked.

"Not yet," Ciar answered. He turned and opened the door and called out into the workshop, "Cola!"

Joia nervously twisted her hands as a young boy appeared in the doorway. Now she was in the presence of three Patrons. Ciar spoke quietly to the boy who nodded his head and ran off. Ciar, Aren, and Wodwin looked at Joia again. She was feeling very nervous and wished that Edmund, Hakon, or even Seb was with her.

"I am Joia," she curtsied.

"I'm Wodwin, Patron to the Carpenters," Wodwin introduced himself. "I can't say I've ever met anyone as young as you with the Light."

"I'm honored to meet the three of you," she said. "Please, if I may, who is this Scrios?"

"How can you not know who Scrios is?" Aren laughed.

"I'm from a village far away from here. I only recently began to travel, trying to meet the many Trade Patrons."

"Who have you met?" Aren asked.

"Oh, um, well, I've met Sidonia and Grian," she said. She knew in her heart it would not be wise to mention Edmund or Seb.

"And how did you know we were here in Yondalla?" Wodwin asked.

"Grian told me the last he heard of Ciar, you were living here in Yondalla. I asked around when I arrived and found out that your shop was here in the castle. So, how was it decided who could stay in the castle and who had to leave?" Joia asked.

"Trades related to textiles and arts were sent away," Ciar said, "that includes spinners, weavers, tailors, cobblers, painters, and entertainers."

"But why?" Joia asked. "Surely you must have disagreed with this."

"No, we support it," Wodwin said. "Those trades are not nearly as important as ours. We make the furniture for the castle, the swords and armor for the soldiers, and shoes for the royals' horses. Why would we need the others?"

"Well," Joia stammered, "clothing, for one thing. I can't imagine the king wishes to go without clothes."

"The king has his personal servants who take care of all of that for him," Aren answered as if this was the plainest truth in the world.

"Perhaps the king does," Joia said, "but what about the rest of the people who live in the castle? What about you? Don't you need clothes too?" Joia could not believe what she was hearing. These were Patrons. They should know better than to think any trade is less valuable than another.

"When anyone needs clothes or cloth, they can just go out and buy them. But how often do you need to buy cloth to make your clothes, Joia? Once a year? Twice at the most? Am I right?"

Joia could only nod. It was true.

"But how often do horseshoes need to be fitted? How often do tools and swords need to be sharpened?" Ciar asked. Joia started to answer, but all she could do was open her mouth before Ciar answered his own question. "Daily. Everyday tools are brought in to be sharpened. The tradesmen who use these tools come to me at least once a week. The swords of the king's guard must always be sharp. And when a tool or sword becomes too unusable or broken, we make new ones. A day doesn't go by that we aren't swamped with work to do. Our trades are very important."

The three Patrons looked very smug.

Joia knew that Ciar spoke the truth. Hakon had told her he often took his thatching tools to the blacksmith for sharpening. The blacksmith in Erthenhorn was always busy. But then, Joia looked at the other two Patrons, she didn't think their trades experienced quite the same level of need as the blacksmith did. Aren was a silversmith. Her mother owned one thing made of silver. Erthenhorn didn't even have a silversmith. She looked at the carpenter. Her family had used the same table, chairs, and beds for Joia's entire life. It was true that she only purchased cloth from the weaver a few times a year, but that was so much more often than they had ever purchased anything from a silversmith or carpenter.

Joia was taking a breath to point this out to the Patrons, when the door to the shop opened a fourth time, and a well-dressed man walked in.

"Trade Minister," Ciar bowed slightly. "Welcome to my shop. May I introduce you to a most special young lady. This is Joia, a baker's daughter."

"It is a pleasure to meet you, young lady," Scrios took Joia's hand in his own and kissed it. She grimaced. When Grian had kissed her hand, it had made her blush, but when Scrios kissed her hand, it felt wrong. Then she realized it was his skin that felt wrong. There was an unnatural coldness about it.

But for a man with so much power over the trades, he was not anything like Joia had imagined. Scrios was a small man. His thinning hair was grey, and his eyes were small, dark, and old. He was finely dressed, which was ironic since he had been the person to evict from the castle all those who had made his rich clothes.

Joia also thought she noticed something odd about him when he walked. It was like the air around him darkened. She blinked at looked at him again, but he was standing still and there was nothing unusual about him. She supposed the heat of Ciar's shop was making her feel light-headed. The four men stood before her. She stepped back in fear and backed into the wall. There was no way out of the shop, they blocked the doorway. Beads of sweat trickled down her back.

"Hello," Joia said back.

"I understand you have some interest in the trades," Scrios said. Joia nodded. "Well, I am the man to talk to about such things. After all, I am the Trade Minister." He chuckled at his joke before turning a cold gaze to Joia. "What is it you want to know?"

She swallowed hard. "I want to know why you have banished some of the trades from the castle."

"That question is easily answered. They are not necessary and take up too much space in the castle streets."

"That's your reasoning? They take up space?" she asked, shocked by the stupidity.

"Yes," Scrios's answer was smug. "Art and textiles are frivolous and silly. They provide nothing of necessity."

"I rather think that clothes are a necessity, and you are wearing a fine outfit. Wasn't it made by the hands of spinners, weavers, and tailors?" Despite her fear, she couldn't help but point out the obvious.

Scrios laughed. "Yes, I wondered if you would bring that up. My clothes were made by those trades, it is true, but clothes do not need to be woven thread. I wear this because the king insists that I look the part of trade minister. I am, however, working to convince the king that clothes can be made without the textile trades."

"But I," Joia began before Scrios held up his hand to stop her. She saw the shimmery darkness again, and then it was gone.

"I know what you will say. How can we have clothes without textiles? Did you know, Joia, that people wore clothes long before the trades were established?"

"I suppose," Joia said. She had never really thought about that before.

"People wore clothes made of animal skins, sewn together. Anyone could make these clothes. They did not need spinners and weavers to do the work for them." He moved again and Joia noticed the air about him seemed to change. It wavered and felt cold.

"I suppose that is so," Joia began, "but now that we have those trades, it seems silly to return to those ways."

"Nothing I do is silly!" Scrios roared at her. He looked at her with fire in his eyes and then calmed himself down. "I don't expect a child like you to understand but this is for the best."

"Well then," Joia stammered trying to regain her courage after Scrios's outburst, "What about the artists and entertainers?"

"After what I've told you, I would think that is quite obvious. Art is frivolous and unnecessary." Scrios sneered at her and moved again. Joia watched the air shiver. She only saw it when he moved. It was very strange. Of course, he was the only one in the room moving. The three Patrons were standing very still. The heat in the shop was becoming oppressive.

"Art might be frivolous, but it is beautiful. It makes the ordinary become extraordinary. It makes us happy," Joia said.

Scrios laughed, "Such words. You are a silly child with a head full of romantic ideas. Art is excessive. Why make something practical into a piece of art? Things should be simple, practical, and functional."

The two smithies and the carpenter behind Scrios nodded their heads in agreement. Joia couldn't believe that they felt this way about art. "But what about Aren, the Silversmith?" Joia looked at Aren and noticed the way he clenched his fists. "Surely the things he creates fall into that category. There are few things made from silver that cannot be made by a blacksmith, but things are made with silver by the silversmith because silver is beautiful."

Aren looked angry. "You think my work can be replaced with iron or other common metals? You show great disrespect to the Patron of Silversmiths!"

"You think my work is common, do you?" Ciar growled at Aren.

Joia tried to step back again but only knocked herself against the wall. The last thing she wanted to do was cause dissent among the Patrons, but she needed to point out Scrios's hypocrisy to them.

She took a step forward. She needed to find a way out. "And the work, created by blacksmiths and carpenters is often finely decorated. My mother has a candle holder made of wrought iron that is beautiful in its design. It has curves and twists that make it as much of a piece of art as it is a functional object to hold candles. Carpentry too. Don't carpenters often carve shapes, patterns, and designs into the furniture they build?"

"This is true," Wodwin said.

"Ah yes, gentlemen," Scrios turned to face them, "I've been meaning to have a word with you about that. Less art. I want your work to be strictly functional."

"What? What makes you think you can tell me that?" Ciar growled.

"I am the Trade Minister!" Scrios sneered back.

Joia thought this man to be quite foolish, antagonizing the three men who were so much larger than he.

"And I am Patron of Blacksmiths! You do not tell me how to work my trade!"

"I could care less about you being a Patron. You throw that in my face like it was something special when it isn't," Scrios turned on Ciar. "If you wish to retain your smithy in the castle and your position as blacksmith to the king, you will do as I tell you. Many fine blacksmiths would love to take your place here in the castle and who would obey my orders; for my orders are the king's orders. And that goes for the two of you as well," he said, turning to Aren and Wodwin.

Joia watched the three Patrons' faces as they contorted from anger to surprise. The heat was getting worse, and Joia was feeling dizzy. The Light from the three Patrons seemed dimmer to Joia's eyes while the darkness around the trade minister grew. She rubbed her eyes, wiping the sweat from her face. It was so hot.

Scrios turned back on her. "You! How dare you come here and cause trouble." He took a step forward. "Just because you have the Light doesn't mean you can challenge me." He took another step forward and Joia tried to move to the side. She needed to get to the door. "I am Scrios," he called out. "I am the Trade Minister."

The darkness that shimmered about him pulsed with a cold that Joia could feel. She was pressed against the wall with nowhere to go and no way out. The room began to spin. Joia reached out with both hands to the wall behind her, trying to brace herself. She pressed herself harder into the wall, doing anything to get away from him and his darkness. A hand grabbed her by the neck, knocking her head against the wall. The fingers around her neck burned with cold, and she let out a scream.

She grabbed at the hands around her, trying to pry the fingers off her neck, but the hands tightened, and she couldn't breathe.

Suddenly, the shop door burst open and a wave of fresh air hit Joia's face. Her head cleared and she saw Edmund in the door's frame.

She tried to cry out to him, but the hand on her neck remained and squeezed a little tighter.

"Joia!" Edmund ran to her, pushing Scrios away, and pulling her into his arms.

"Well, well, Edmund the Entertainer," Scrios sneered. "You and your kind are banned from the castle, yet you dare to come here? Grab him!"

The anger Ciar seemed to have only moments ago for Scrios was turned to Edmund. He and Wodwin grabbed Edmund by the arms.

"Edmund, no!" Joia grabbed for him, but she was pulled away by Aren.

"Take him to the castle!" Scrios ordered.

"Scrios, you can't do this," Edmund called out, but he was being dragged out into the street by the two strong Patrons. Joia ran after him, but Aren caught her.

"Let go of her!" Edmund shouted.

Scrios turned to Joia. "I see your Light, girl. I don't know who you are, but you question my authority and my decisions. You try to be clever, but you are not. You have tried to turn the smithies against me and, worst of all, you are sympathetic to the entertainer. You have one chance to leave this castle right now and never return or be taken prisoner like your entertaining friend here."

Joia didn't want to be taken prisoner, but she wasn't about to leave Edmund to these men. She moved towards him.

"No, Joia!" Edmund cried out to her. "Go, get out of here! Go to the bard! Go to the Light!" Edmund called out.

Scrios hit Edmund across the face. "Silence!" he shouted at Edmund before turning back to Joia, "Get her!"

"Run Joia!" Edmund cried out again before receiving another hit from Scrios. She saw his head drop and Ciar lost his grip on Edmund for a moment before hauling him up again.

Joia turned and ran. There was no way she could help Edmund if she let herself be captured. She needed help. She ran as fast as she could back towards the gate. She could hear men shouting as she ran, but she wasn't sure if they were chasing her or not. She didn't dare look back to find out.

As she passed through the gate, she could see Seb at the end of the street, right where she had left him. She saw him turn around and go back behind the building where he had been standing. Had he just abandoned her? Joia reached the end of the street and turned where she had seen Seb go. He was there and grabbed her by the arm as she made the turn. He pulled her between the buildings and down a narrow alley before pushing her into the cover of an open stable.

Seb grabbed her by the shoulders. "What happened?" he yelled.

"They've got Edmund!" Joia cried, trying to catch her breath. "Scrios," Joia was breathing hard, "he took Edmund." She gulped in the air. "They tried to arrest me too, but Edmund said to run."

"What happened to your neck?" Seb pointed.

She reached her hands to her neck and felt the soreness. "Scrios."

"Come on," Seb took her by the arm and pulled her between several homes.

"No, wait," Joia pulled at Seb's grip, "we have to go back. Edmund needs us."

"Come on," he pulled harder. "You're leaving."

"Seb no," Joia cried. "We need to go back for Edmund. We can't let Scrios take him."

Seb ducked into the shadows of two buildings and stopped. He turned to face her, holding her arms tightly in his hands so she couldn't flee. "Listen, Joia," he whispered, "Edmund told you to run, right?" Joia nodded. "Then I'm going to make sure you do. Nothing can be done for him now. Scrios has got him in the castle, so he is beyond our aid. Back to my house, now."

"I can't leave him," she cried. Tears fell fast down her face. "I thought you'd help me," she said, looking over her shoulder back to the castle as Seb pulled her further away from the street.

He led her down several more streets, between buildings and once through a pig's sty. Joia didn't recognize they had arrived at Seb's home until he pushed her inside the door.

"Joia!" Hakon called out. Joia ran to him, and he pulled her tightly against his chest. "Are you all right? What happened?"

"We have to go back," she sobbed.

Seb bolted the door and went to the back room. He pulled out a bit of cloth, laid it on the table, and started to put food on it. "You're going to leave now."

"What's going on?" Hakon asked, following Seb through the door.

"They arrested Edmund," Joia looked up into Hakon's eyes. "He didn't even do anything wrong, and they arrested him."

"Tell me what happened," Seb said, still piling food onto the cloth. "I need to know everything that happened." He looked up at Joia, who was still standing in the middle of the room, trying to catch her breath. "Tell me."

Joia took several gasping breaths as she thought. Everything had gone wrong right from the start.

"A blacksmith saw me. He grabbed me and said he would take me home to have fun. Ciar showed up and told the man to let me go."

Hakon and Seb growled at this.

Joia took another breath. She could feel herself shaking in Hakon's arms. "Ciar took me to a workshop that was filled with tools. It was very hot. We talked for several minutes. Then Aren joined us and later Wodwin."

"All three of them were there?" Seb asked in surprise. "I didn't even know that Aren was in Yondalla."

"Who are Ciar, Aren and Wodwin?" Hakon asked.

Joia was about to explain, but Seb interrupted her, "Never mind him, tell me what happened next."

"We were all talking about why they had supported the eviction of the other trades from the castle when the trade minister, Scrios, arrived. Who is this Scrios?" she asked. "He seemed to have a history with Ciar, and he knew Edmund on sight."

"Finish your story first," Seb said, tying the bundle of food.

"Well, I noticed something odd about Scrios, but I think it may have just been the heat." She rubbed at her eyes for a moment. "Scrios started to tell me how the textiles and arts were banned because of their frivolousness. He said art was not necessary. Then, he told Ciar, Aren, and Wodwin to stop the designs and art they put into their work. This made them angry. Ciar said that Scrios had no right to tell him what to do with his trade because he was Patron of the Blacksmiths. But then Scrios argued that he was the trade minister and they had to do what he said, or he would kick them all out of the castle."

"By Athelstan," Seb said, turning and running his hands through his hair, the way Edmund did when he was frustrated. "What next?"

"Scrios turned on me. He was yelling at me, getting closer and closer and I was backed up against the wall with the three Patrons blocking the door. Darkness surrounded him and there was an unnatural coldness that came off of his body. He grabbed me by the neck, and it felt like I was being burned, but a cold burning. That is when Edmund arrived. When he opened the door, I felt as if I awoke from a nightmare. He ran in and pushed Scrios off me, and that was when Scrios ordered Ciar and Wodwin to grab Edmund. They pulled him out into the street. I tried to get to him, but Aren held me back. Edmund told me to run. Go to the bard, he said. Go to the light. Scrios hit Edmund. I think he was knocked out and I ran."

Seb muttered something.

"I shouldn't have run away like a coward," Joia said, tears springing to her eyes again.

"You did the right thing," Seb said. "No sense in having both of you arrested." He went to a trunk along the wall, opened it, and pulled out two cloaks. He came to Joia and put one of them around her shoulders. "Long ago, this belonged to Anya, a woman I loved very much." He fastened the clasp around Joia's neck and pulled the hood over her head. "Wear it when you are on the road. Keep your Light hidden."

"It's beautiful," Joia felt it's soft green fabric.

"Of course it is. It was made by Sidonia, but before she became a Patron, so it does not have the Light." Seb pulled the second cloak over himself and pulled up the hood. He handed the bundle of food to Hakon and returned her bundle with her precious gifts from the Patrons to her.

"People in this neighborhood know me," Seb said with his hand on the door. "If any guards are looking for us, I don't want to be easily recognized. Now, come on."

Seb unbolted the door, carefully opened it and looked out.

"Where are we going?" Hakon asked.

"To the stables of course. To the bard," Seb answered.

"Of course! The bard is Edmund's horse," Joia said.

"Edmund was always silly about the names of his horses," Seb said. He slipped out the door with Hakon and Joia following. They moved quickly through the crowds of the street until they reached the stables where Edmund's horse and wagon were kept. Hakon let them in.

When Seb was sure no one in the stable could hear him, he leaned in close to Joia. "You must take the horse and get as far away from Yondalla as you can."

"But what about Edmund? We can't just leave him there," Joia wept.

Seb sighed. His voice was soft when he spoke. "Edmund is the prisoner of Scrios. Nothing can be done for him."

"You could go, Seb," Joia started.

"No," Seb furiously whispered. "I do not go into the castle."

"Why, because some old, long-dead king kicked you out?" Hakon asked. "You're a coward, Seb."

"I am not a coward!" Seb roared. Then he looked around and grew quiet again. "You don't know what you are talking about. Now, leave, quickly."

"Climb onto Bard," Hakon told Joia. With his and Seb's help, she got onto the horse's back. Hakon handed her the bundle of food. Then he went to the wagon, unlocked it, and pulled out two bedrolls and his wooden staff, then he relocked the wagon. He held onto one bedroll while Joia took the other.

Hakon gave Seb the key, then took Bard by his lead. Seb pocketed the key and led them out to the main road.

"Once you get out of the city, get on the horse and ride away as quickly as possible. This horse looks young and strong. He should be able to hold the both of you for a while."

"Where do we go?" Joia asked.

"Edmund told you to go to the Light. I believe he meant Athelstan's Castle. Go there," Seb said.

"But I don't know where that is or how to get there."

Seb shook his head in a frustrated, yet amused way. "Silly girl. Use a map." He slapped Bard on the rump and the horse started to walk away. "May Athelstan go with you," he said as they walked away.

Joia turned to see Seb. He nodded his head, turned, and walked away.

CHAPTER NINETEEN

Escaping Dondalla

Joia pulled her cloak hood further over her face and watched the city slowly pass while Hakon walked the horse down the road. Neither of them said anything. Once they passed the city walls, Hakon continued to walk them until they were out of sight of the gate. Then, he climbed onto Bard's back, behind Joia. He wrapped his right arm around Joia and took the reins. In his left hand, he carried his staff.

Hakon clicked his tongue. "Come on, Bard, let's go." He gave the horse a little kick and it started off in a slow trot. Hakon kicked him again and the horse took off in a gallop. Joia had never ridden a horse before, and she nearly dropped everything she was holding in her surprise. She was grateful that Hakon was behind her and had one arm around her. She wasn't sure if she could have kept her balance without him. They rode on until there were no more homes along the road, and they were alone.

Hakon brought the horse to a stop, and he hopped off. Taking the horse's lead again, he pulled Bard off the road and deep into the woods.

"Where are we going?" Joia asked.

"We are going to talk," Hakon said irritably. He came to a small clearing and helped Joia off the horse's back.

"Are you cross with me about something?" Joia asked as she walked a few steps on wobbly legs after the hard ride on horseback.

"Yes, I am." Hakon dropped the lead and let Bard nibble at the green grass. "Joia, what is going on? Edmund told me that Seb had made you angry and that you had taken off running. The three of us go in searching for you and what happens? Two hours later you come running back with Seb with bruises on your neck and tell me that Edmund's been arrested. You want to fill me in on what happened while I waited in a panic for you?"

She dropped all the bundles she held to the ground. "I'm sorry, Hakon," she said. "Yes, Seb hurt my feelings and I had every intention of leaving Yondalla and finding some way to get back to Erthenhorn, but as I wandered the streets, I found myself at the local spinner's shop. I sat with them for a while, and they told me that the trade minister, Scrios, had kicked all the textile trades out of the castle. That was when Seb found me."

"I hope he apologized to you?" Hakon said.

Joia nodded. "He did. So, I asked him to take me to the castle, because I discovered the Patrons Wodwin and Ciar, were there."

"What are they the Patrons of?" Hakon asked.

"Ciar is the blacksmith and Wodwin is the carpenter. Anyway, Seb took me to the gate, told me how to find Ciar and I went in."

"Alone?" Hakon asked.

"Yes. Seb wouldn't go near the castle. I found the blacksmiths and you heard the rest of my story when I told it to Seb."

"Who was the other Patron you mentioned?"

Joia dropped the bundles she was holding and sank down onto a soft patch of ground. She was still shaking from her ordeal and the following horse ride. "Aren, the Patron Silversmith."

"So, you met three more Patrons?" he asked, and Joia nodded. Hakon chuckled, but there was no mirth in the sound. "You know, Joia, most people aren't even sure if the Patrons are real or if they are mystical beings from a legend. But you, how many Patrons have you met now?"

Joia did a quick count. "Seven."

"You are probably the only person to have met so many of the Guild Patrons in a very long time."

Joia really hadn't thought about it. "Perhaps so."

"And who is this other man, Scrios?"

"He is the trade minister to the king, but I got the sense that he is more than just that. When he moved, the air around him became blurry and it seemed to block out any light around him. He was fuzzy and it was very cold." Joia tried to remember and understand what it was she had seen. "It was so strange and scary. I also got the sense that they had known each other for a long time, and Scrios knew Edmund the moment he saw him."

"And he was able to make the other Patrons attack and restrain Edmund?" Hakon asked.

She nodded. "And that was troubling because Edmund is one of their own. I don't understand why they would obey Scrios when it is obvious that he is trying to control them. They are Patrons and three hundred years old. Why would they take orders from Scrios?" Joia started to chew on her lower lip in thought.

Hakon came and sat down on the ground next to Joia. "It seems to me that this Scrios is more than just a king-appointed trade minister. The way you describe him, it's almost like he is a dark Patron. Do you think that maybe he was a Patron once turned against them?"

"That makes a lot of sense. The Patrons have a light about them, but Scrios has darkness around him. But if one of the Patrons had turned against his own, wouldn't Edmund have told us about him?" Joia asked.

"Not if it happened after the Patrons all separated and went their own ways. He might not have known," Hakon said. Joia nodded her head. Hakon reached out a hand to take hers. "Are you all right?" he asked.

"I don't know, to be honest. Oh Hakon, it was terrible when they took Edmund. They hit him and he was taken prisoner for no other reason than that he was an entertainer. And Seb, oh I'm so mad at him right now. He won't help Edmund."

Hakon pulled her into a hug, "But he did save your life."

"I know, but at the expense of Edmund's life."

"Edmund told you to run. He didn't want you arrested or facing the same fate as him. Yours might have been worse." He moved so he sat directly across from her. His finger came up and caressed her face. "You keep talking about this destiny of yours. Edmund would want you to continue and find it."

Joia took in a deep, harsh breath. "But he's more important than I am. He has so many entertainers who depend on him as their Patron. I'm a nobody. I'm not more important than a Patron."

"You are to me," Hakon said.

Joia's face flushed and she wanted to be in Hakon's arms again. There was only the two of them now. It would be so easy to give in and kiss him again.

She leaned forward to Hakon, and his lips briefly touched hers, but Bard whinnied and nudged at Joia's back.

She turned around in surprise and chuckled at the horse. "Poor Bard. He is probably wondering where Edmund is." She patted the horse's nose.

"Where's your map, Joia?" Hakon's own voice was shaking slightly. "We can't stay here, so close to Yondalla, but I don't think we should get back on the main road just yet. Scrios might send out soldiers to look for you."

She reached for her bundle, opened it, and removed the map that Seb had made for her. She laid it flat on the ground. Her symbol of the 'A' and anvil pulsed lightly in the middle of the paper. All around her were tree symbols and the thick line that represented a road was off to her right.

"It is an incredible map," Hakon said.

"I wish I had asked Seb more about it. How did he draw the entire world in this map? He couldn't have, could he?"

Hakon shrugged. "The Patrons have their strange magic. He probably wouldn't tell you even if you asked him."

"I'm sure you're right." Joia looked at the map for a moment longer and started to notice a golden glow appearing at the top of the page. "Ah ha!" She cried out and pointed to the glow. "We go this way."

"How do you know?" Hakon asked, looking hard at the map.

"It's my map," Joia answered. "I see it's Light."

"Of course," Hakon let go of his side of the scroll and stood up. "The mystical Light." His tone dripped with bitterness.

"What do you mean by that?" Joia turned, defensively.

"Nothing," Hakon mumbled.

"No, that was not nothing. Tell me what you mean by that."

"Look, we need to get moving. We've only got a couple of hours before the sun starts to go down and I want to get as far away from Yondalla as possible," Hakon said. He took the two bedrolls, unrolled them both, placed them on top of each other, and rerolled them into one. He tied them together with some cord and slung it over his back. "Come on. We can ride Bard for a little while."

Joia needed to stand on a log to get onto Bard's back and then Hakon climbed on behind her. Joia looked at her map once more and they pointed the horse in the right direction. It was slow going as Bard had to walk around the trees and shrubs, having no clear path to follow.

Hakon's arm was around her, but only to hold onto the reins. She could tell he was upset with her and it was bothering her.

"Hakon, what's wrong? Can you tell me?" Joia asked after a long while.

"No," Hakon curtly said.

His anger at her was hard for her to take. They had never fought before. She hated that she had disappointed him.

They rode on in silence. Joia checked the map often to make sure they were still going in the right direction. It was hard to tell how much time passed and the slow journey was made worse by Hakon's cold silence towards her.

"Let me get off the horse," she finally said when she couldn't take the silence anymore. His disappointment was too much to endure. She needed to get out of his arms and move on her own.

"No," he said.

"I'm getting off the horse," she said, moving his hand away, throwing her leg over Bard's neck, and sliding off the horse to the ground below. Her feet hit the ground unevenly and she fell.

"Joia," he cried out and was off the horse a moment later, helping her up. "Did you hurt yourself?" he asked.

"No." She answered although she felt that one leg was sore from her fall and her hip hurt from when she was pushed to the stone street in front of the blacksmith's shop, but she wasn't going to let Hakon know about that. There was nothing he could do.

She checked her map, adjusted her direction, and started to walk. Her leg gave her a little pain, but after a few moments, it worked itself out and she didn't hurt with every step. She could hear Hakon and Bard walking behind her.

She was upset with Hakon and felt he was being very unfair about the situation. She didn't like being mad at him, and she certainly didn't like him being angry with her. She loved him.

The realization of that feeling hit her unexpectedly and she nearly stopped in her tracks. She had known Hakon for so long and had always hoped to marry him, but she had never really thought about loving him. Of course, she loved him.

For a moment, Joia nearly turned around. She wanted to throw herself into his arms, but she doubted he would want that, so she kept on. During this journey with him, she had gotten to know him outside of their usual short, restricted visits. They had experienced fear and peril together. She had gotten to see him work his trade when he patched Grian's roof. They had kissed. She hadn't realized just how much her feelings towards him had changed.

She loved him and she did not want him to be angry with her.

Her mind wandered to her sister. Ebba was probably going to marry Derry. Maybe they had already. Joia wondered if Ebba had ever spent any time in Derry's company. Had they ever really talked? Did she love Derry, or did she just love the idea of being married? Was she getting married without love?

Joia wondered if she would ever see her sister again to ask her these questions.

Joia checked her map again. It showed the inn alongside the road where they had stayed going into Yondalla. It was hard to believe they had just been there yesterday morning. So much had happened since then.

Hakon looked over her shoulder at the map. "It's getting late," Hakon said. "We'll stop at that stream for the night." He pointed at the small wavy line that crossed the path in the direction they were headed.

When they reached the stream, Hakon took Bard to the water. The horse eagerly took a long drink.

Joia's legs felt sore after the long walk. She wasn't used to riding a horse or walking so far after all those weeks riding in Edmund's wagon. She sank to the ground and leaned over her outstretched legs, stretching them and her back. With a last look at her map, she rolled up her map and retied it with the red ribbon that Seb had used on the map.

Hakon untied the bed rolls from the horse and dropped them onto the ground next to Joia, then he tied Bard to a tree near the stream where he could have plenty of grass and water. Joia opened the bedrolls and laid them out before she opened the bundle of food. Her stomach cramped with hunger. Breakfast had been such a long time ago and she had walked and run so much today.

Seb had given them a good amount of food for their journey, but not knowing how long it would take them to get to Athelstan's castle, she was careful in rationing the food. She gave a portion of it to Hakon and took a smaller portion for herself. He sat on his bedroll next to her and they ate in silence.

The night grew dark around them. Hakon didn't offer to get a fire going and Joia didn't ask. Finally, she couldn't stand the silence any longer. "Hakon, what's wrong? What have I done to upset you?"

Hakon sighed. "It's not you Joia."

That surprised her. "You just spent the last couple of hours fuming at me. Obviously, I've done something that's made you angry with me."

"I'm upset because I can't see this Light. I don't understand what is going on and I can't help you."

"But you have helped me," she leaned towards him. "So much. I can't tell you how much it means to me having you here." She could barely see him in the darkness of the forest. She reached into her bundle and pulled out her candle from Grian. She clicked two flints together. Nothing happened.

"Help me," she said to Hakon.

"Joia, no fires," he said.

"One candle and only for a few moments," she said.

Hakon took the flints and struck them. The linen wick caught flame and Joia held it so she could see Hakon. He was frowning at her. He also looked very worn out. His new shirt was dirty, and his face looked long and sad.

"Hakon, I can't imagine how frustrated you are right now. I keep forgetting you can't see the Light." She sighed. "I've always been able to see it, but no one else could. When I asked my mother and sister about it, they told me I was imagining it. No one believed me because no one else could see it. But now, I'm around others who see it, like I do, and it's nice to finally have that validation, even if I have no idea why I have this ability."

Hakon let out a long sigh. "I see your point. You never mentioned to me that you could see the Light."

"My mother and sister told me never to mention it to others. They feared I might be seen as crazy or a witch of some sort. And the last thing I wanted was for you to think badly of me."

Hakon nodded and looked away from her.

"Really Hakon, you've been so good and patient with me and all this nonsense with the Patrons and Light. I don't know how or why you've put up with it for so long."

"It's not been all bad," he sighed.

"If you weren't here, I'd be on my own right now. Completely alone and I couldn't bear that. I don't want you to be angry with me."

"I'm not," Hakon said quietly. "Put out the light now. We need sleep."

Joia blew out her candle and laid it next to her. It was so dark now she couldn't see him without the candle. She heard him lie down on his bed roll, so she did the same and held out her hand towards him, in the darkness. "Hakon?"

"Hmm?"

"Your hand?"

She felt his warm hand clasp hers in the dark. She relaxed at his touch. "Night, Hakon," she said.

"Night, Joia."

They were up early the next morning. After a bite to eat, Hakon retied the bed rolls to Bard and let the horse have one more drink before they moved on. Joia's legs and hips were sore and he neck burned. She caught Hakon looking at her neck and she gently touched her neck with her fingers.

"Does it look bad?" she asked.

"It looks red, like a burn. Seeing what he did to you makes me angry. I can't believe he tried to choke you and the Patrons did nothing to help."

"I was scared," she admitted.

"Does it hurt?" he asked.

She nodded. "Yes, but it's not terribly painful. I'll be fine."

They decided to keep to the forest for a while with Joia keeping a close eye on her map to make sure they were going in the right direction.

"I've been thinking," Hakon said. "Don't you find it strange that this Scrios guy turns up, gets the king and smithies to agree to the banishment of some of the other trades, and can tell the Patrons how to work their trades and no one else questions him?"

"Yes," Joia agreed. "You would think it very hard for these Patrons to turn their backs on three hundred years of friendship and tradition."

They walked on a few moments more and Joia thought hard about what she knew about the trades in Erthenhorn. "My father gets his flour for all the bread he bakes from the miller. The miller's grindstone is said to be four generations old and made by a master stonemason."

"Weavers use the thread from the spinners," Hakon went on, "tailors use the cloth from the weavers. Thatchers use the straw that is left over after a miller takes the grain."

"All the trades depend on each other. Blacksmiths, coopers, potters, cobblers, all of them are connected to each other in some way or another," Joia said. "There is no reason for them to fight or feel they need to be divided."

"Perhaps that is your purpose. To bring the trades back together."

"I've thought of that, but how is that accomplished? I can't mediate between their arguments. I'm hoping that Athelstan's castle will hold the answers."

Hakon nodded, "I hope so, too."

The map started to take them deeper into the forest. Joia knew the map would take her right to wherever she needed to go, but she wasn't keen on getting so far away from the road, either.

They talked as they picked their way through the dense woods. They discussed Scrios for great lengths of time and started to wonder whether perhaps he had cast a spell over the smiths. Joia really doubted the Patrons would attack each other the way they had gone after Edmund, but Hakon reminded her that Edmund and Seb had not been the greatest of friends for nearly two centuries.

"Do you know why, Hakon? Why are Seb and Edmund enemies?"

Hakon had forgotten Joia hadn't been with him when Edmund told him the story of Anya. "I wouldn't say they are enemies. They are two old friends who allowed a huge wedge to grow between them."

"Sounds like you know more about them than you are letting on," Joia said.

"Edmund and talked one afternoon. He told me more of his story. A hundred fifty years ago, or so, they had both loved the same woman, Anya."

"Anya? This is her cloak!" Joia said, remembering what Seb had said when he gave her the cloak. "So what happened? This cannot be good if it caused them not to speak to one another for the last century."

"They both courted her, fought over her, and in the end, they demanded she make a choice between them. She promised them an answer, but on the appointed date for the answer, she failed to meet them. They later discovered she had died of an illness not two days before."

"And they blamed each other," Joia said, feeling her eyes sting with tears. "Oh, I see," she said sadly. Hakon nodded. "But after all this time, why not forgive each other?" Joia asked.

"I asked Edmund the same thing. He said he was ready to forgive Seb, but every time he saw Seb, the map maker would find some way to anger him."

Joia sighed. "We saw that, didn't we? Seb would do things to anger or provoke Edmund. How terrible to carry a grudge for such a long time, especially when they had been so close before. I don't' guess there is any hope that Seb will rescue Edmund. Not if he is still so angry with Edmund."

"Probably not," Hakon quietly said. "It's too bad. I liked them both. Edmund has been good to us. He treats me well, even though I do not have the Light nor am I one of his tradesmen. And believe it or not, I respected Seb. He was gruff, but he's a good man."

Joia nodded. "I thought so too, but now, I'm not sure."

One thing Joia had learned about Patrons was that they were like normal people in all ways except when it came to their trades and their immortality. They had the same feelings of joy, sadness, jealousy, and loss as anyone else.

"Do you think they can kill Edmund?" Joia asked.

"I don't know," Hakon answered, "but I would think that yes, he can be killed by someone else's hand."

"What would happen to his trade if he died?" Joia asked, but Hakon kept silent. They both seemed to know that if Edmund died, so might the trade.

Joia hated to think of Edmund, captured. He had done nothing wrong except rescue her from the hands of a man who was trying to kill her. And Edmund needed to be free. Free to travel, to sing, and to tell his stories. Joia didn't know what would happen when she reached Athelstan's castle, but she hoped whatever it was she had to do would set things right in the Guild and free Edmund from Scrios's imprisonment.

CHAPTER TWENTY

Rescuing Edmund

Edmund sat on the cold stone floor, his back leaning against the hard wall. His hands were on both sides of his pounding head as he pressed his palms against his temples. He wasn't sure how long he had been there. A tiny window in his cell had shown at least one night had passed, but he had been unconscious for part of the time, so he wasn't sure if it had been only one night or not.

After being dragged to the castle by Ciar and Wodwin, he was passed off to the castle guards, who had been much rougher on him than his fellow Patrons had been. He had been beaten and when they had finally shoved him into his cell, causing him to fall, his leg caught on something sharp and tore a good-sized gash on his left leg. He had removed his over-tunic and wrapped it as tight as he could around his leg, trying to stem the bleeding. He didn't even want to think about what would happen if his leg got infected in this filthy cell.

He groaned when his injured leg spasmed from being in one cramped position for so long. His leg hurt, his head hurt, and his entire body ached. His stomach growled with hunger and his mouth was dry with thirst. But what hurt most of all was the betrayal by his fellow Patrons.

They had held him back, allowed him to be punched several times by Scrios, and had taken him to the castle. They had turned him in. Ciar, Aren, and Wodwin had been his friends for centuries. Sure, he hadn't seen them in close to two hundred years, but he had never quarreled with any of them. There had been no good reason for their betrayal of him except for Scrios's influence.

If he knew anything at that moment with his head pounding, Edmund knew this Scrios was *the* Scrios. The one who had caused Edmund so much trouble all those years ago. The one Athelstan had hidden them from in his castle, Scrios the Uncreator.

Edmund had noticed how the aura around the Uncreator was dark. The Patrons had Light about them, but Scrios had a darkness that seemed to take away the light. Didn't Ciar remember the destruction Scrios had caused them so long ago or had too much time passed? Scrios was going to tear the trades apart and he was going to do it from the inside out by forcing them to fight amongst themselves.

Edmund felt weak. He slumped down to the hard floor. Pain shot through his body. He hoped he would pass out again because at least the pain would go away for a little while. The light outside was starting to turn purple with twilight and he shivered with the damp cold.

He closed his eyes, hiding the purple light. His hands came up to his face and he felt the cuts on his head. There was one over his eye and his lip had split from one punch he had taken. Thankfully both cuts had quit bleeding a while ago, but the dried blood made his face itch.

He lay there, listening to the dripping water, his head pounding with each drip. When he next opened his eyes, the cell was black with night. He heard footsteps in the hall outside of his door. *Please keep walking,* he whispered to himself, but the footsteps stopped just outside his door. He heard the lock mechanism of his door click and a loud screech as his door was opened. He groaned in pain as his head pounded harder. Someone walked into his cell. Edmund looked at the intruder, trying to see him in the dark through his swollen eyes.

"Edmund?" the man whispered in surprise. He was by Edmund's side in two steps. "What have they done to you? Come on, can you stand up?"

The voice was familiar. Edmund rubbed his eyes. He felt strong hands grab him by his shoulders and pull him into a sitting position. "Seb, is that you?"

"Yes. Come on, get up Ed, we're getting out of here." He grabbed Edmund by the arms and pulled him up, but Edmund's leg couldn't bear his weight. Seb caught Edmund as he fell over. "What happened?"

"Cut my leg," Edmund gasped in pain.

"Lean on me. We've got to get you out of here before we are both found." Seb pulled Edmund's arm around his neck. They hobbled to the door. Seb looked around and, not seeing anyone else, pulled Edmund out of the cell and down the hall.

Edmund gained a little strength with each step as he realized he was being rescued. He grit his teeth and bore the pain as they walked through the halls.

"Seb, how?" Edmund began.

"Shh," Seb hissed, "Later."

Edmund became aware that Seb seemed to know where he was going. There were a few close run-ins with castle guards, but Seb managed to avoid them or hide from them until they passed.

Seb had Edmund's wagon waiting just outside one of the gates, hidden in the shadows between two buildings. It took longer than he would have liked, with Edmund's hurt leg and the couple of detours through the castle they had been forced to make, but he finally got them to the gate.

"Climb up," Seb said as he pushed Edmund into the seat of his wagon. He had borrowed a horse from the stable where Edmund's wagon had been. But the horse he had borrowed was done so without the owner's permission. Another reason why they needed to get out of Yondalla as quickly as possible.

Edmund sat precariously in his seat, swaying dangerously to the edge. "Don't fall out," Seb said as he snapped the reins and the wagon set off. Edmund groaned and grabbed his head.

"I didn't count on you being hurt so badly. We've got to get that leg seen too before we can leave. We'll go to Blue's Apothecary. He'll be discreet." Seb turned a corner and had to reach out to grab Edmund, who lost his balance and nearly fell from the wagon. "Come on, Edmund, stay with me. We'll get help."

Seb took the wagon down several streets. One good thing about living for three centuries in one location was you knew where everything was and every road to get there. Seb knew who was in league with the people at the castle and he knew which people to trust not to say anything to the castle lot. Old Blue hated what went on at the castle almost as much as Seb did and Seb knew he could count on Blue's help. He pulled the wagon around the back of the apothecary's home. Edmund sat on the wagon while Seb hopped out and knocked on the door. Several moments later a man opened the door.

"Seb," he said, "What brings you here at this hour?"

"I need your help." Seb pointed at the wagon. He went to Edmund's side and took out a handkerchief. "Bite on this Ed," he said and stuck it into Edmund's mouth. With Blue's help, they got Edmund out of the wagon and into the apothecary.

Edmund cried out in pain as he was moved, but the handkerchief muffled his cries and gave him something to bite down on. The moment Seb and Blue got Edmund down from the wagon and into Blue's shop, Edmund passed out, collapsing in Seb's arms. Seb lowered him to the floor and took out the handkerchief.

"Probably just as well," Seb said. "Listen Blue, he's got a gash in his leg. Think you can fix him up?"

"Let's see," Blue said. He and Seb lifted Edmund onto a table. Blue set to work unwrapping Edmund's tunic from his leg.

Old Blue got his name from his skin color. Thirty years at the apothecary had exposed him to all sorts of powders and fumes. It had turned his skin blue long ago. Blue was a gruff man and had no love for the people in charge at the castle. Seb trusted Blue to never tell anyone they had been there.

"Ooh, that's bad." Blue started collecting various objects from around the room. "It's for the best that he's passed out. This isn't going to be pleasant. Here," he handed Seb a rag and bucket of water, "wash his leg."

Seb started to wash the blood from Edmund's leg. It was a wicked cut, longer and deeper than Seb had realized. But it wasn't just this cut that Edmund had gotten from his short time as a prisoner. It was clear to see he had been beaten.

Seb wished he had been able to get there earlier, but he had to wait until nightfall. He couldn't help but think about Joia. If she could see Edmund now, she would weep. It had been very clear that she thought the world of Edmund, perhaps even loved him, except that she loved Hakon more. He had seen that, too. He didn't want to admit to himself how much that hurt his own heart. Seb had long given up on any woman loving him, although he supposed if he gave Gwen, from the spinner's shop a chance, he might get a decade or two of love.

Edmund let out a low groan but didn't wake. Seb couldn't believe the condition Edmund was in and this was the result of a single day. If Seb ever got his hands on Ciar, Aren, and Wodwin, then Scrios would be the least of their troubles.

Seb continued to wash Edmund's leg and he couldn't help but remember many years ago when they had been friends, and when Edmund had first appeared in Seb's life. Seb had not been looking for a friend at the time. His mother had recently died, and his brother joined the king's guard. Seb was alone and glad to be, or so he thought. He painted and drew all day long.

Then Edmund had shown up, half dead on his doorstep. That had been a whole other tragic story, but Seb took Edmund in and found a friend he didn't know he was looking for. They had seen each other through so much but a century and a half ago, they had allowed one person to come between them.

One woman. A beautiful woman that Seb wanted very much to make his wife, but even if he had, Anya would have only been in his life for a few decades. Edmund would be around for centuries to come.

He had lost a lot of time being angry at Edmund, and to tell the truth, he didn't want to be mad at Edmund anymore. But after so many years, it was hard to forgive himself for the part he had played.

Edmund's leg twitched as Seb washed and Blue appeared by his side again.

"So, who is this guy?" Blue asked.

"Old friend," Seb answered. "I just busted him out of the castle."

"The castle? Well, well, Seb. What were you doing in the castle?" Blue asked with a mirthless chuckle as he brought several tiny tools over to Edmund's side.

Seb finished washing what he could of Edmund's leg, but it started bleeding again. "I was there getting him out of the dungeons. Believe me Blue, I wouldn't have gone if I didn't have to."

Blue took a bottle of wine and poured it over Edmund's leg. Edmund let out a cry and his entire leg spasmed, but he didn't wake. Blue threaded a needle with an almost clear thread. He gently pushed the needle into Edmund's leg. Edmund jerked. "Hold his arms down, would you?"

Seb did as he was told. This was painful to watch. Seb hated to think about how much pain Edmund had to be in to cry out even when unconscious. He closed his eyes and tried not to watch.

Blue went back to work on Edmund's leg, sewing it up as carefully as he could. "Who did he upset?" Blue asked.

"Have you heard of Scrios?" Seb asked.

"The trade minister? Yeah, I know who he is. I even saw the man once. He made my skin crawl. Bad man if you ask me." Blue continued working. His stitches into Edmund's leg were small and neat. "I've heard what he did to the spinners and the rest of them. Why no one challenges him is beyond me."

"Yeah, well, apparently that is who he offended." Seb watched as Blue worked.

Edmund's body jerked and twitched a few times, but he remained unconscious. Blue finished his work and slathered the gash with a smelly ointment. He wrapped Edmund's leg in a clean cloth.

"I'll do his head too while he's passed out." Blue washed the blood from Edmund's face. "The cut's not too deep," he said. He sewed a few stitches into the cut over Edmund's eye and then wrapped his head in another cloth. "Now, try to keep his wounds clean. Put some of this on it anytime you wash his leg. If you've got any wine, pour that on first, then this." He handed Seb a small tin of ointment. "When he wakes up, he'll be in pain and there's a good chance he'll have a fever. But, if the fever gets too bad, it means there's an infection, which we don't want. Make him some tea with this." Blue gave Seb a small brown bag.

"It's not going to turn him blue, is it?" Seb smiled.

"Never in thirty years have I turned anyone blue, except for myself."

"Thanks, old friend," Seb said. "I've got to get this guy out of town, but I'll pay you the rest when I get back." He dropped two coins onto Blue's table.

Blue picked up the coins. "This is enough. Good luck."

With Blue's help, they got Edmund into the back of his wagon. Seb climbed into the wagon seat, snapped the reins, and they took off into the night. Once they were out of the city, Seb urged the horse faster.

Seb kept a vigilant watch as they traveled down the road. At this time of night, the only people on the roads tended to be robbers. He prayed to Athelstan that they would be left alone.

The hours in the wagon gave Seb more time to think than he wanted. There was nothing to do except think. He couldn't help but remember his years of friendship with Seb and the other Patrons, especially before they became Patrons.

Because of the quiet concentration Seb needed to make his maps, he didn't interact with the other Patrons quite so much, but the meals and evenings together were always full of good company.

Seb never admitted this, but those years in Athelstan's castle had been his happiest years. He had been free to explore painting and map-making without worrying about anything else. Shelter, clothing, and food had been provided for them all. He enjoyed the company of the other craftsmen.

Edmund remained his best friend during all those years and for many decades after. How had they allowed one person to come between their bond as brothers? Seb sighed as the wagon bumped along the road.

When he thought back to those months that he and Edmund had competed for Anya's attention, it made Seb mad. Yes, he had been so angry with Edmund for pursuing the woman that Seb loved. But in the end, he was angrier with himself. Losing Anya's love and Edmund's friendship in one day had hurt. His heart had broken that day into a hundred pieces and taken his mind to very dark places.

Now, when he thought back, Seb realized he could have reached out to his other Patrons for help, but he feared that Edmund had gone to them all and declared that Seb was a cold-hearted villain, so rather than face their scorn, he scorned them first. It had taken many decades for Seb to come back to a place where he could live and work without constantly thinking about his anger with Anya and Edmund.

He even thought for many decades that he was happy without any other contact with the Patrons. No one sought him out, so he assumed that no one cared. And he, in turn, never sought the company of his fellow Patrons. Then, seventeen years ago, when Edmund gathered Sidonia, Kloma, and himself, to tell them about Joia, Seb remembered what true friendship had been like. Kloma had even tried to renew contact with him, but he had ignored her letters. Now he felt horrible about how he had treated her. If he was lucky enough to see her again, he would apologize. Perhaps, when this insanity with Edmund, Joia, and Scrios was over, he could write to her or go and see her.

Seb realized just how much he had missed his friends, especially Edmund. It wasn't going to be easy to repair a friendship broken so long ago and he was going to have to swallow a lot of pride, but it kind of made him feel better to realize that Edmund would too. He just hoped, now, that Edmund would survive his wounds.

When he thought about Edmund's mangled leg and beaten body, he knew three Patrons who would be very sorry they ever sided with Scrios.

It was several hours on the dark road before Edmund woke up.

"Where am I?" Edmund said from the back of the wagon. He sounded disoriented.

"Relax, Edmund. You are in your own wagon," Seb answered.

"What happened, I, ow!" Edmund cried.

"Be still, Ed," Seb said. "Your leg was in bad shape. I took you to a friend who's patched you up, but you just need to lie still."

"Where are we going?" he groaned, sounding like he was trying to move again.

Seb looked over his shoulder. "Be still, Ed. We're going to Athelstan's Castle. Isn't that where you told Joia to go?"

"Joia?" Edmund asked in confusion. "Yes," he slowly said as his mind started to work again. "That's right."

"Then that's where we're going," Seb told him.

"Is Joia here?" Edmund asked.

"No. She and Hakon left two days ago."

"Two days? She's been gone for two days?"

"Yes."

Edmund was quiet for several minutes. Seb hoped he had gone back to sleep. "How did I get out of the castle?"

"Now's not the time for stories, Storyteller."

"But how?"

Seb sighed. "I got you out. I'll tell you the entire harrowing tale later. Right now, you need to rest, and I need to get us as far away from Yondalla as possible."

"Seb?"

"What now?"

"Thank you."

When Edmund next awoke, it took him several moments to realize that he was in his wagon. He vaguely remembered the night before. Seb had rescued him, and he said something about a friend helping them. Edmund rubbed his eyes, trying to remember more. Morning light shone through the openings of the wagon, and he noticed they weren't moving. He could hear a gurgling brook and someone moving, just outside the wagon.

He sat up, feeling momentarily dizzy. He was sore, except for his leg, which was blindingly painful. He looked down at his torn pants and bandaged leg. The bandage was red with blood.

"Seb?" he quietly called out.

"I'm here, Edmund." Seb's face appeared at the opening of the wagon. He looked at Edmund's leg. "Ooh, that leg's not looking too good. Come on, let's get you out and we'll see what we can do for you."

Edmund scooted to the edge of the wagon, but he needed Seb's help to get down. Pain shot through his leg, and he felt dizzy again. Seb's strong grip kept him from falling as he led him to the fire and helped him to sit down on a log. Edmund grabbed his head and took a few deep breaths as the pain subsided slightly.

"Thanks," he finally said.

Seb had kept an eye on Edmund to make sure he wasn't going to fall off the log and hurt himself further. When he was satisfied that Edmund wasn't going to pass out again, he set about getting him some food and his tea.

"Here," he handed Edmund a mug of hot tea. "Tea with something special from the apothecary."

Edmund eyed it dubiously and sniffed it.

"I don't know what it is, but I trust Old Blue. Drink it," Seb said.

Edmund sipped the tea. It didn't taste great, but it was drinkable. "I would have preferred chamomile or mint."

Seb grunted, "Sorry, just out of that. Now, drink up and you can have some food."

Edmund drank his tea as he watched Seb working around the fire. It was odd being with Seb again. They had been such good friends so long ago but had let themselves turn against each other for the love of a woman. Love could do that. Such a powerful thing. Even if she had not died when she did, Anya was mortal and would have died within a few decades, but he and Seb would be around for centuries longer. He realized he had missed an entire century and a half of friendship with Seb.

He drank the last of his tea down. "Ug," he shuttered. "It wasn't bad to start with, but each swallow tasted worse and worse." Seb handed Edmund a biscuit and he took it with thanks. "Now, how about that story you promised me last night? What happened after I was arrested?"

"Not sure if I can tell a story as well as you do," Seb muttered, but Edmund heard the amusement in his voice.

Edmund shrugged his shoulders, "Yes, well, we can't all be me."

Seb sighed and thought for a moment, "Well, Joia came running from the castle gate and told me that you had been arrested. I took her back to my shop. Hakon was there, waiting. I packed them some food, put them on your horse, and sent them away," Seb told him.

Edmund chuckled, "Your storytelling does need some work. Maybe later I should teach you a few tricks of the trade."

"No thanks. You hear it my way or not at all."

Edmund couldn't help but smile. Being with him now felt like old times. He had missed their friendship. "Very well, Seb. Tell it your way."

Seb nodded. "After they left, I went back to my shop. I thought about what Joia told me about Scrios. Do you think he is the same Scrios from long ago? The Uncreator?"

"Yes, I'm certain he is," Edmund answered.

"That's what I was afraid of," Seb nodded, "I think he is too." He paused and his hands twisted together in his lap. Edmund could see he had something to say, so he was quiet and waited. "Since you, Joia and Hakon turned up a few days ago, I've been doing a lot of thinking, and well, I'm sorry about everything. You know, with Anya."

"I'm sorry too," Edmund said.

The two men looked at each other for a moment, each accepting the other's apology. It was something that should have happened long ago, but better late than never.

Seb cleared his throat. "Anyway, I knew I couldn't leave you to Scrios. I didn't know what he would do to you, but he isn't called the Uncreator for nothing. I spent that night making my plans and then I had to wait until last night before I could put my plans into action. I talked to a few acquaintances at the local pub and bribed them into helping me by distracting the guards. I had your wagon at the ready near the gate with the least number of guards."

"Wait, my wagon? But you sent Joia off with my horse, so who is pulling my wagon?" Edmund interrupted. He looked around the wagon to see a strange horse standing there.

"Um, I might have borrowed a horse," Seb answered.

"Borrowed?" Edmund gave a sly smile.

Seb returned it, but only for an instant. "Yes, borrowed. Now if you want to hear the story, don't interrupt me again," Seb said.

"Sorry, go ahead. You had my wagon at the gate," Edmund encouraged Seb.

"Right, your wagon. I had some of the lads from the pub ask the guards about you. The guards told them you were being kept in the dungeons. I snuck into the castle and using a little Patron magic," Seb smiled slyly, "I distracted the dungeon guards." He handed Edmund some more food and then took a bite of his biscuit. He chewed for several moments and swallowed. "I found your cell and got you out. You were in a state, boy. Halfway unconscious, almost completely delusional, and that leg of yours."

They both turned their gaze to look at the bloody bandage.

Seb frowned. He was not looking forward to helping Edmund clean that. "Well, I got you out and we made our way back through the castle. There were a few guards we had to dodge but thanks to you and your wobbly state, anyone who saw us probably thought we were drunk. Amazingly, everyone left us alone."

"How did you know your way through the castle?" Edmund asked.

"You forget, Edmund, I lived there for many, many years. It may have been a century and a half ago, but my mind is a map. I know all the halls and passageways through there, probably better than the king himself."

"What did you mean when you said you used a little Patron magic?" Edmund asked.

Seb smiled. "The guards at the castle might be big and brutal, but they're not very smart or well-paid. I tossed a few coins at them, and they followed my coin trail until they found a most extraordinary map. A map that showed them a secret way to the king's treasury. They followed it and my path to you was clear."

"So, you showed those brutes how to get to the king's gold?" Edmund asked. He knew Seb hated the king, but he didn't think Seb would aid anyone in robbing the king.

"Of course not. If they followed the map properly, and there's no guarantee because they weren't very smart, then they ended up at a door that took them to the boat loading dock on the other side of the castle, next to the river."

Edmund let out a great laugh.

Seb couldn't hide his satisfaction. "I got you to the wagon, took you to Old Blue, and he fixed up your leg. Speaking of your leg, it looks like those bandages need changing."

"Yeah. You know? I don't hurt so much right now. Must have been whatever was in that tea," Edmund said.

Seb poured some hot water into a bowl. "Then we had better take care of this before the tea wears off."

Edmund started to unwrap his leg. "Ow, ow, ow," Edmund said as he pulled the last of the cloth away from his leg. He took several sharp breaths as he examined his leg. "What a mess."

"Let's hope you don't lose it," Seb said and brought fresh strips of cloth and the bowl of hot water to Edmund so he could wash.

Edmund gritted his teeth and carefully started to wash his leg. The pain was excruciating, but he knew that if any kind of infection set it, he would lose his leg or his life.

Once the leg was washed Seb came over with a bottle of wine. "Here, take a drink," he said, handing it to Edmund.

Edmund took it and drank down several swallows before handing it back to Seb.

"Sorry about this," Seb said and then he poured some of the wine over the gash. Edmund cried out and gripped his legs, holding them tight as the alcohol burned. Once Edmund didn't feel quite so dizzy with pain, he took the tin of ointment that Blue had given them and slathered it on. Seb re-wrapped the wound, grimacing the entire time.

"I think it's going to heal nicely," Edmund painfully said between gritted teeth. He took a few deep breaths and waited for his head to clear. "What about my head?"

"Your head has been way beyond help for centuries," Seb said.

Edmund smiled. "Better looking than your head, though," he said.

Seb removed the bandage from Edmund's head and looked at the stitches over his eye. "Blue's good. It's swollen, but it's not bleeding, and I think it will heal quickly. You want the bandage back on?"

"Not now," Edmund answered. He tenderly touched his head and winced. "So, where are we now?" he asked, looking around the area for the first time.

"An old mill, about a day and a half's journey from Tillmere. We should be able to reach Athelstan's Castle in two days, as long as we don't have any problems."

Seb cleared up the camp and re-hitched the horse to the wagon.

"Get some rest, Seb," Edmund said as he painfully climbed up into the wagon's seat with a lot of help from Seb.

"What about you?" Seb asked. "What if you pass out again?"

"I'll be fine. I got plenty of sleep, thanks to you, and whatever was in that tea took away the worst of the pain, along with the wine. I'll be fine for a while. I know this road," Edmund said. "I won't get us lost."

"See that you don't," Seb said as he climbed into the back of the wagon. Edmund snapped the reins and the borrowed horse started down the road.

CHAPTER TWENTY-ONE

Athelstan's Castle

"We're approaching a village," Joia told Hakon as it came into view on her map. "It's Tillmere."

"We've been there before," Hakon told her. He pulled Bard along on his lead. It had been slow-moving through the woods for the last four days and they were all dragging their feet.

"We have? When?" asked Joia.

"It was after visiting Grian's. We went to the village to get some food for the journey."

"Oh yes, I remember now." Joia looked at the map. The Light that showed them which direction to go was moving out of the woods. "So, we probably passed Grian's house?" she asked.

"I guess so," Hakon said. "I wonder why your magic map didn't take us to him."

Joia sighed. "I don't know, but the map is leading us back to the road." It bothered her that Hakon was still acting bitter about the map and the Light. There was nothing she could do about it. It wasn't like she was trying to exclude him.

They turned slightly and walked on. Once they reached the road, Hakon made sure it was clear before they left the safety of the forest. If anyone saw them leaving the woods, it could lead to awkward questions. They both got back on Bard and rode him for a while. As they approached the village, they came to a fork in the road. Joia looked at the map. "We take the road that doesn't lead into the village," she told him.

He nodded and they turned away from the village down the road. The days of walking and picking their way through the woods had been hard. Joia's legs were sore all the time and her hip still felt bruised from her fall. At least the bruising on her neck had mostly disappeared. And to top it all off, she was very hungry. She had done what she could to ration their food, but it had been a good four days without a proper meal. Each step was harder to take. She felt empty inside and so tired.

"Hakon, I need to sit down," she finally said, sinking down to the ground, right where she had stopped.

He turned around and came back to her. "Joia, are you all right?"

"Tired," she said. "And I feel weak."

"Are you ill?" He knelt beside her and put a hand on her face, pushing her hair away from her forehead.

"No. I can't explain it. I feel it, inside, something is weakening."

"Well, you're a lot thinner than you were when we started this. I know how hungry I am, but you look like you're starving," he said.

She nodded. "I am hungry, but this doesn't feel like hunger. It's here," she pointed at her chest. "Inside. I can't explain it."

"Perhaps it is your Light," Hakon suggested.

"I suppose. Ever since I encountered Scrios and his darkness, I've felt this way. Do you think he could take away my Light?"

"Joia, I don't understand this Light business. It could be just as you say. But since discovering you have this magical Light about you, you have always been in the company of a Patron; someone else with the Light. And now you have been away from Edmund and all the other Patrons for several days. Perhaps you are missing them."

"I do miss Edmund." She buried her face in her hands and rubbed her eyes. "It's my fault he was arrested. When I close my eyes, I see it, repeatedly." Joia's insides twisted every time she thought of the way Scrios had hit Edmund.

"Listen Joia, you can't blame yourself for that. Edmund shouldn't have been bothered. If he hadn't encountered this Scrios person, he would have been able to get in and out without trouble."

"Yes, but if I hadn't gone," Joia started.

"Joia, don't. Stop blaming yourself. It doesn't help Edmund."

"I know," she sighed. "I did nothing wrong by talking to the three Patrons and Edmund did nothing wrong by coming into the castle. He saved my life, Hakon. If he hadn't arrived when he did, I don't think the other Patrons would have stopped Scrios."

"If I ever get my hands on them," Hakon growled. "How about we turn back, go to Tillmere, and get food? We're both starving."

Joia shook her head. "My map is leading me to the castle. And, we don't have any money."

He sighed. "If you're determined to go there straight away, then let's get going. Hop up on Bard," Hakon reached out a hand to Joia. "I don't think we're all that far away from the castle now. We'll get there and you can rest."

She reached out, took his hand, and got back onto her sore feet. With his help, she got onto Bard and started their journey again.

She started to wonder if when Edmund was arrested, it split the trades. The Patrons were turning against each other and weakening the guild. It made sense to her, but her head was feeling fuzzy. She was tired, hungry, and thinking too hard made her head hurt.

Still, Joia couldn't help but think that perhaps this was her purpose. She needed to find a way to bring the Patrons back together and unite them.

Just as the sun began to set, they saw a small stone castle ahead of them.

"Hakon, look. There's a castle." Joia cried out. Hakon climbed onto Bard behind Joia, took the reins, and kicked. The animal started to gallop, and Joia leaned back against Hakon for support. She didn't like riding the horse, except when it was walking, and even then, only for short periods.

The castle was very different from the one in Yondalla. That had been a big castle for a king. This was much smaller. It had no gates, just an arched gateway into a small courtyard. The trees grew all around the castle and some of the trees were growing inside of the courtyard. It was clear that it had been abandoned for many, many years, but it still looked to be in good condition.

As they approached the gate, Joia saw a large "A" over an anvil carved into the stone. There was no doubt that this was Athlestan's castle; the very place where Ciar, Sidonia, Grian, Edmund, and all the other Patrons had learned and perfected their trades. Joia's skin tingled as they rode under the gate.

Hakon hopped off the horse and then helped Joia down. He tied the horse to a tree in the courtyard where grass had grown over the stone floor long ago. "Come on, it's almost dark and we need to find a place to sleep." They walked through what would have been the main door, except the doors were missing, and right into a great hall. It was too dark inside the castle to properly see the room. The fading light that came in through the gate showed only that there was a great hearth and little else.

"I don't know quite what I was expecting, but I was kind of expecting more than an empty, abandoned castle." He sighed and dropped their bundles on the ground next to the hearth. "I guess we can camp in here for the night," he said.

"I had hoped we could explore the castle, but I'm too tired," she sighed. She pulled out their bundle with the food. There wasn't much left.

"Eat it, Joia," Hakon said.

She shook her head. "You need to eat too."

"I'll go into Tillmere tomorrow and—" Hakon started, but Joia shook her head.

"We don't have any money and no way to get some if we go back to Tillmere," she said and held out half of the last of the food to Hakon.

"I'll find a way. I promise, Joia." He took his portion of the food and sat next to Joia.

They ate their few bites in silence as the light outside the castle grew darker and darker. Joia shivered.

"I can get a fire going," Hakon said, but Joia shook her head.

"Don't worry about it. I just want to go to sleep."

Hakon laid out their bedrolls, but there wasn't much to cushion them from the stone floor. Joia didn't care. She lay down and closed her eyes. A moment later, Hakon's hand grasped hers. She sighed happily and fell asleep.

She woke in the night, her entire body sore from the hard stone. A fire burned in the hearth and Joia realized that Hakon must have started one after she went to sleep. She stretched and rubbed her hips, trying to relieve some of the pain that the stone floor had caused.

For the first time, she took notice of the room around her. It was hard to tell in the dark, but it seemed that this was a very large room. It was still the middle of the night and Joia was tired, but the idea of lying down on the stone again made her body ache. Perhaps a walk around the room would help her work out the knots in her muscles.

She opened her bundle and pulled out the Everburn candle that Grian had made for her. She held the wick up to the glowing embers in the hearth and the little candle came to life. She stood, held out her candle in front of her face, and tried to assess what was immediately surrounding her. All she saw was a huge empty room.

She walked into the center of the room and saw something curious on the wall where the night wasn't quite so dark. As she got closer, she saw it was a huge multi-colored picture, but not a painting, like Seb had in his home. She approached it and touched the lower part of the picture. Her finger met with a hard surface and when she tapped on it, it felt like glass.

She realized that this was a picture made from colorful glass and the reason it was lighter than the rest of the room's walls was because the light of the outside moon showed through. It was a huge window. Joia had heard about windows like this, but she didn't remember what it was called. Colorful glass window or something like that.

She couldn't wait to see this window once the sun came up.

Joia walked the perimeter of the room. It was empty of all furniture and only had what looked like fox dens in the corners. There didn't seem to be any animals in the little dens, but she didn't want to find out right now, so quickly moved away from them.

She was wide awake now and wanted to explore more of the castle, but questioned if that was a safe thing to do in the dead of night. She turned to go back to her bedroll when from one of the open doors, she saw a golden glow of Light and knew she needed to follow it.

It led her into several empty rooms and down a corridor until she came to a staircase set deep into the wall. The stairwell was dark, but she could see the golden light at the bottom. Holding her candle in front of her, she carefully made her way down. The air grew colder with each step.

She shivered when she reached the bottom and took a moment to look around her. The corridor in front of her was pitch black, except for the golden light that was waiting for her at the other end. The Light of the Guild, which she had come to trust completely was guiding her. She had Grian's candle, which would never go out and only seemed to grow brighter as the passageway went deeper into the heart of the castle.

Halfway down the hall, she arrived at a doorway with no door. She leaned into the room and looked around. It was a small room, windowless, cold, and empty. Another doorway was nearby. She looked in and found it was the same as the other one. Joia wondered if these rooms had been prisoner cells and if Athelstan had ever kept anyone here. Two more similar rooms were along the corridor before it finally ended with one more doorway at the very end of the hall. But while the other doorways along the hall had been doorless, this one had a real door in its frame that had been untouched by the ages.

The golden Light seemed to be coming from the door itself and Joia took a moment to admire the intricately carved shapes in the wood and saw at the center was the symbol for Athelstan. Joia's heart began to race as she pushed on the door. It soundlessly swung open, and Joia stepped inside.

The room was much larger than the others she had seen since coming downstairs. The first thing she noticed was that the entire room was bathed in the golden Light. As she looked more closely, she realized the room was full of items and it was from these that the Light was shining.

Joia walked further in and found in the center of the floor there was a circular pool of water. Something about the pool made her step around it. It seemed very curious to her that there would be a pool of water inside of a castle like this, but then she supposed castles could have leaks or it could be rainwater that had gathered in one spot. She bent down and touched the water with her fingers, expecting it to be cold, but it was surprisingly warm.

Suddenly, a light from within the pool started to glow. Joia jumped back and watched the entire pool glow with a light so bright, it was blinding after being in total darkness. From the light, the figure of a man took shape. He hovered over the pool with a kind, smiling face, and eyes that twinkled. He looked right at Joia and smiled.

"Welcome daughter of the Light. I am Athelstan." His voice was deep and gentle, much like Edmund's voice, and for a moment, she felt a pang of sadness. She missed Edmund.

"I'm Joia," she answered, giving a slight curtsy.

"Welcome, Joia," he said, smiling at her. "I'm so glad you found your way here to the castle. I knew you were here the moment you stepped into the hall."

"You did?" she asked in surprise.

"You are the first person with the Light to step into this castle in a long time. I know when one of my children of Light comes here. Well, what do you think of my home?" he asked.

"I can't say I've seen much of it yet, sir, it has been rather dark."

Athelstan smiled. "You will have time to see it in the morning."

"Are you a ghost, sir?"

"Do I look like a ghost?"

"Well, sir, I don't know. I've never seen a ghost, but I thought they would be grey and cold, and you are made from light. So no, I don't guess you're a ghost."

Athelstan laughed. It was a jolly laugh and made Joia feel very happy inside. "Very good little daughter. No, I am not a ghost. I am a memory; an echo. You see Joia, when I gave my children their immortality so they could go out and teach their trades, a sacrifice had to be made. I gave my life to them, but a part of me has remained here. The castle needed protecting too."

"I see, I think," Joia said uncertainly.

"It's all right, Joia," Athelstan chuckled, "you don't have to understand. You have been on a long journey to reach my castle, haven't you?"

"Yes, I have."

"Tell me about it," Athelstan looked at her.

"Well," Joia started and thought for several moments about where the beginning of this journey had been. "A month ago, my life was normal, and then one day, it was not. Edmund came to our village with a group of entertainers. He told me I had the Light. I didn't understand, but I knew I needed to go with him, to discover what this Light was and why I have it. My dear friend Hakon came along. He is a thatcher."

Athelstan nodded his head, encouraging Joia to continue with her story.

"We traveled to see Sidonia. She made me a Life Tapestry. Then we went to Grian, and he made me a candle. This one, in fact," she held up her candle to Athelstan. He smiled. "Then we went to Yondalla and there I met Seb, Ciar, Aren, and Wodwin. Seb made me a Life Map. I used it to come here to find you, well, to find this castle. Edmund got arrested in Yondalla and Seb helped Hakon, and I escape."

"What did Edmund do to get arrested?" Athelstan asked. "He is not the type to do anything that would cause such a consequence."

"He didn't do anything wrong. There's this man in Yondalla, the trade minister, named Scrios, and he decreed there would be no more textile or art trades allowed in the castle, including entertainers. And Edmund went into the city walls to protect me."

"Scrios?" Athelstan looked surprised. "No wonder my sleep of late has been disturbed. If Scrios has any power that involves the trades, then we are in trouble."

"Please, sir, who is Scrios? Seb was very strange and nervous when I told him about Scrios," Joia said.

"Listen carefully, my child. This is your history. Over three hundred years ago, the trades didn't exist as they do now. Our way of life was very different. The clothes and shoes were sewn from animal skins. Homes were built with no rhyme or reason to their construction. They were made of straw and mud, or wood nailed together. Some were holes in the ground while others were caves in the rocks. Some were lucky enough to have well-built homes or a castle, like me. A well-built home meant the family had money and status."

"Our light was fire and was not easily transportable. When I was a young man, I met another man who had taken a piece of straw and would light it in the fire. He could walk around with that bit of straw on fire, but it burnt away too quickly to be of any use. It got me thinking, was there a way to slow down the flame? I tried all sorts of things and finally found that by coating the straw with beeswax, the straw could be lit and last for a long time."

"So, candle making was your first trade?" Joia asked.

"In a way, yes," Athelstan answered. "I worked for years on all sorts of things, finding ways to make things better in function and better aesthetically. I learned masonry, and metal working, and experimented with textiles. All the things that became the trades, I worked on. People wanted me to do all sorts of things for them, and I taught a few things to people, but the work was too much for me to do all on my own.

I came back to my family's home, this castle, and brought with me men and women who showed great intelligence, talent, and a willingness to dedicate themselves to learning. Many of them already had some experience in what would become their trades. Your friend, Edmund, for example, had already learned how to make several instruments and played them very well by the time I met him. Seb was a well-known artist in his city who had a gift for drawing accurate maps. Sidonia and Kloma were friends and had been working together, exploring ways to make textiles. Grian had no experience with candle making, but I saw a good-hearted, intelligent man and I taught him the first trade I learned. Here at the castle, they all had the freedom to explore, learn, make mistakes, and improve.

They learned early on that they needed each other to make their trades better. I remember when Sidonia had new ideas on how to improve her loom, she worked with Wodwin for years, building loom after loom until they came up with what Sidonia deemed to be the perfect loom. Thek, the thatcher, worked with Ciar to create the perfect shaped tools for thatching. Ferran, the baker, worked on all his breads, coming up with techniques to produce different flavors and textures of bread. His breads were works of art. He worked closely with Grindan the Miller to create the perfect texture of flour for baking bread. All of us in the castle enjoyed the fruits of Ferran's labors as we got to eat all his new creations. Every night, Edmund would entertain us with his stories and music. He built all manners of instruments. Many did not work, but many did, and he learned to play them all. He would tell the most fantastic stories with his deeply hypnotic voice."

Joia laughed, "He still does that."

"I'm glad to hear it," Athelstan smiled. "With each new loom that Wodwin built for Sidonia, he became a better carpenter and Sidonia became a better weaver. With each new shear hook that Ciar made for Thek, the better his craft as a blacksmith became and the better Thek became at thatching. Grian made candles with all sorts of materials. We used his creations at night and would tell him if the candles were a success or not. The tailor and cobbler kept us clothed. Every robe and shoe we wore helped them to become better at their trade. We learned, we grew, we improved our trades. We lived together in this castle happily for nearly twenty years as the trades worked their way into being." Athelstan looked at Joia with a new intensity. "Now Joia, what have you learned from my story and your travels?"

Joia thought for a moment. "I've learned such a great deal about so many things, but what I'm learning more and more is that the trades need each other. The trades depend upon each other. And all trades are needed to have a functioning village or city."

"Very good, Joia. This is what is most important. There can be no division among them. No one trade is more important than the other."

"But who is Scrios?" Joia asked. "How does he fit into all of this?"

"There was a man who sadly, lacked talent in many things. He would see something and try to replicate it but with very poor results. Centuries ago, in the northern forests, five villages would gather for a summer fair. Among other things, people would trade and sell wares. One year, I was there selling candles. One young man was very interested in the candles and asked how I made them. I explained to him, and he was very excited by them.

"The following year, I went back to the fair. It was the year that I met Edmund and Seb. Edmund was selling instruments that he had crafted himself. They were of very fine work, even then. The young man was back and selling candles. But they were very poor quality and poorly made. People who bought them and used them were upset because they smoked badly, didn't last long, and smelled bad. My candles sold well, while his were mocked. Edmund's wares were very popular, and I saw the young man talking to Edmund.

"The next year, I returned to the fair, pleased to see that Edmund was back. In his part of the camp, he played his lute and sang and promised that he would have lutes to sell the following day. That night, his entire crate of instruments was destroyed. But the young man was there, selling his own lutes. They were terrible, poorly made, broke easily, and there was no good sound that came from them. He was mocked and Edmund lost a lot of money that year because he had nothing to sell.

"By this time, I had started to gather those talented individuals and invited them to my castle where they were free to craft to their heart's content. Grian and Wodwin were two of the first. My castle is far away from the northern forest villages, where this young man, who was called Scrios, lived. Over the years, I returned to the fair, with many of my students, including Edmund, Seb, and Ciar. Always Scrios was there, working to destroy the hard work of others. He didn't even bother to bring things to sell anymore. He just came to hurt and destroy and became known as the Uncreator. He was banished from the fair, but by this time, we were tired of the fight. We worked hard, here in the castle, for many years before Scrios discovered us.

"He was actively working to destroy anything we did and the people we taught. It was when I made my final act to protect the trades, the castle, and my children, who had worked so hard. I gave them their Patronage, Scrios was banished from the land, and I passed away into this memory as you see me now."

"It sounds like Scrios was a bitter person who couldn't have things his way," Joia said. "It's rather sad."

Athelstan nodded. "Yes, and he could have learned a trade if he had tried. If he had been willing to learn and practice the techniques, he would have become a tradesman, but instead, he chose shortcuts and used inferior supplies. He chose to destroy what others did, rather than learn from them. It was his own doing that turned him into the Uncreator."

"I have seen over and over that there are no shortcuts in good work," Joia said.

"That's right. Good work requires patience and a willingness to work hard. Imagine what would happen to a house roof if Hakon was not patient or willing to work hard."

"It would fall apart, or not last long," Joia answered.

Athelstan nodded. "Scrios the Uncreator has left us alone for many centuries. I had hoped that he had faded away, and I guess he did for a while. It has been a very long time since any of us had to think about Scrios."

"How is it he is still alive after all this time? He is not a Patron. He was not granted immortality with the other Patrons, was he?" Joia asked.

"It was not intentional if that is what happened," Athelstan shook his head sadly. "It is a troubling question, Joia. Most troubling and I don't know the answer. However, it seems, from what you tell me, that he has returned and is trying to destroy the trades. If he succeeds, it will be the end of the trades."

"We can't let that happen," Joia said. "The trades create such beautiful, useful things. I don't want to imagine a life without them."

"Exactly Joia. The trades create food, clothes, tools, homes, and happiness. Scrios wants to uncreate and destroy. He must be stopped, and you must find the way to stop him."

"Why me?" Joia asked.

"Because Joia, you have the Light."

"But so does Edmund and Seb and Sidonia," Joia pointed out. "Why not them?"

"Because the Patrons are bound to one trade. But you, you are not. You represent them all."

"So, I somehow must find a way to defeat Scrios and bring the Guild back together?" Joia asked. It seemed to be an impossible task.

"Yes, that is right, my child."

"How in the world do I do that?" Joia asked. "Me, of all people. I can't do that."

"Joia!" a voice in the far-off distance cried. "Joia!"

"That's Hakon. He sounds worried." Joia looked towards the door that led back out to the hall with the stairs.

Athelstan's form started to blur. "I will go now, child. Think about what you have learned."

"But I have so many questions," Joia cried.

"Another time." Athelstan's image fell back into the pool. The room was dark again, except for Joia's candle.

"Joia!" Hakon's call came. He sounded frantic.

"I'm here, Hakon!" She left the room, closed the door, and ran down the hall to the stairs. Hakon reached the bottom of the stairs before Joia. He grabbed her and pulled her into a hug.

"Joia, are you all right?"

"Yes. Yes, I'm fine, Hakon. I'm sorry to worry you."

He held her close for several moments more. "Why did you go off on your own? When I woke up and saw you weren't there, I was in a panic. I thought a wild animal had gotten you or perhaps Scrios found us."

"I'm sorry, the stone floor is so hard, and it was hurting my body. I couldn't sleep so I went to explore."

He took her by the hand the led her back up the stairs. It was still dark. They went to the main hall. The fire was nothing more than glowing embers now. They sat down on their bed rolls and held hands.

"Joia, please don't leave like that again without telling me."

"I'll try."

"You'll try?" he asked.

"Hakon, this is Athelstan's castle and if I'm going to figure out what it is I'm supposed to be doing, it's going to be here. Already tonight I have learned so much, but there is still much for me to learn and understand."

Hakon sighed and nodded his head. "I expect you to explain that to me in the morning, but for now, we must get some sleep."

CHAPTER TWENTY-TWO

A Joyful Reunion

The morning dawned bright, sunny, and warm. Joia and Hakon decided to explore the castle together. They walked together through the rooms on the ground floor. It was empty stone room after empty stone room. There was nothing there to show there had once been inhabitants. Little remained and nothing glowed golden with the Light. Joia was quite disappointed.

"Look, this is where the cooking was done, but I've never seen an entire room devoted to cooking," Joia said, walking into the room that felt the most familiar to her. There was a hearth, an open oven, and iron spits. There were hooks on the walls where herbs or freshly killed fowl would have been hung. A heavy cauldron hung from a thick iron chain hanging on an iron bar inside the hearth. Other iron bars stuck out of the walls at various heights and Joia assumed there had probably been wooden shelves at one time. She walked around, looking at all the familiar parts of the kitchen.

"This is huge."

"I wonder if Athelstan had cooks or a serving staff," Hakon said, looking around.

Joia was curious now too. "I suppose that Ferran baked here."

Hakon nodded. "Very probably."

There were several doorways, without their doors. Joia and Hakon peeked into each one. They were small rooms, but nothing to show what they must have held.

"I suppose these could be pantries," Joia guessed. "They were all probably full of food at one time." She went into one and found several piles of metal rings. "What do you suppose those are?" she asked.

"Those were probably butts of ale at one time," Hakon said, picking one up. "The wood of the barrel has long since rotted away, but the rings remained."

Joia nodded. Her stomach cramped at the idea of these rooms being full of food and ale.

She was so hungry.

"I hear water," Hakon said. "Do you?"

Joia nodded. Another door led them to an outside courtyard. This space was enclosed by the high walls of the keep, but a stream ran alongside the wall. Part of the stream had been redirected by stones to form a pool. Joia went to the pool and cupped her hands into the water, bringing up the cold water to drink. It helped her stomach to settle a bit.

Hakon knelt beside her and drank from the stream as well. He finally sat up and wiped his lips with his shirt. He looked around the courtyard.

Joia rubbed her aching stomach. "I have to admit, but I am disappointed by the lack of anything here," Joia said.

"I don't understand why Edmund told you to come here, when it is nothing but an empty castle," Hakon said, dipping his hands into the stream's water again and then washing his face.

Back in the kitchen, Joia noticed several iron pots. A thought occurred to her. "Hakon, how long do you think the castle has been empty?"

"Well," Hakon thought for several moments. "If I understand Edmund's stories correctly, it's been a century or two."

"So, a very long time then." She took a closer look at the iron pots. They were not cracked or rusted. Except for a bit of dirt on them, they looked as good as new. Take a look at these."

He walked over and inspected the pot and pan that sat side by side on the floor. "They are in perfect condition. Not at all like they have been sitting here for several centuries."

"Ciar must have made them, while he was learning his trade," Joia said.

"If his works survived the centuries without a crack, why didn't the wooden furniture?"

"I don't know," Joia said, running her hand over the cauldron. Perhaps because the wood would rot away no matter what whereas the iron would not rot away. At any rate, we can use these."

"For what? We've got nothing to eat or drink," Hakon said.

"I know, but having a cauldron of hot water is comforting," Joia answered.

Hakon chuckled and nodded. He helped Joia to stand again. "Should we go upstairs?" he asked.

She shook her head. "No. There's no point. It's all going to be empty."

"I want to take a look anyway," he said. "Will you be all right by yourself here?" he asked. She nodded her head, but Hakon took her by the hand and pulled her to him. "You won't go running off again, will you?"

"If I do leave, it will be to go back to the kitchen or the stream," she said.

"Good. I don't want to have to come find you again," he said. He kissed her forehead and left.

Joia went out to the front of the castle and found Bard wandering about, nibbling at what he could find. She led the horse right through the castle to the back courtyard. Bard seemed very happy to be at the stream and had a long drink before he wandered around again, finding more plants here to eat.

Joia went back to the main hall and walked over to the large color glass window. She sat on the floor where she could see the entire window. In the center was the symbol for Athelstan. All around his symbol were other symbols. She recognized the scroll that had been at Seb's door. And there was the harp that Edmund had on his wagon. Perhaps each symbol represented a trade. She tried to figure all of them out but was eventually distracted as she came to look at the rest of the window. A blue sky, a castle, and the sun shining down on them all.

Joia couldn't imagine the time it would take to put something like this together. Each piece of colorful glass would have to be made and precisely cut to fit into the frame. All the trades required time, patience, and years of practice.

Her thoughts returned to the night before and her visit with the golden Athelstan. Had that all been a dream? That room with all the items that glowed golden and the pool of water where Athelstan had appeared. It must have been a dream, induced by her hunger. But a dream or not, it gave her a lot to think about. She closed her eyes and tried to focus.

If the Patrons were fighting amongst themselves, how was Joia supposed to fix that? How could she convince Ciar that all the trades were of equal value? Would Edmund ever forgive Wodwin and Ciar for hurting him? Could she forgive those Patrons for what they had done to her and

Edmund? Scrios had been ready to choke her, but none of them had moved forward to help her.

"It's an odd place, isn't it?" Hakon said.

Joia's head jerked up. "What?" she asked.

He chuckled and sat down beside her. "Sorry. I didn't mean to wake you."

"It's all right," she said. "I didn't mean to nod off. The window is beautiful, isn't it?"

Hakon nodded. "Spectacular. How did the creator do all of that? What is the frame made of?"

"I don't know," she said. "But imagine the work that would have taken. Designing such complicated pictures, making the colored glass, cutting it, making the frame, and bending it? So much work, but the result is one of the most beautiful things I've ever seen."

Hakon took her hand in his. "It is another one of the odd things that I've noticed about this castle," he said.

"Odd in what way?"

"The castle. It's been abandoned for hundreds of years yet look at the masonry." Hakon pointed around the walls.

Joia looked. It was nothing but stone walls. "It's a stone wall. I don't understand."

"It looks as if someone lived here yesterday. None of the walls have crumbled. No plants have grown into the stonework. And this remarkable glass window. It has not been cracked or broken. In all these years there is no damage. Any building that has been abandoned this long should be in ruins, but this castle is not. The furniture inside has rotted away, but the castle itself is untouched by the years."

Joia had not considered that, but Hakon was right.

"Another odd thing about this castle is its layout. The inside walls are curved like there is a circle in the center of the castle, but there are no doors that lead inside the circle. At least none that I've found yet. I wonder what is in the center of the castle?"

"How do you notice these things?" Joia chuckled.

"It's my job as a thatcher," Hakon said in all seriousness. "Before I can lay a roof, I look at the shape of the building and I must decide how it is best covered."

"You are a true tradesman," Joia said in awe. She leaned against him and rested her head on his shoulder. "I don't understand why I've been given this Light of the Guilds. You are the tradesman, not me."

"Perhaps it needed to be someone who is not bound to a trade," Hakon said.

Joia's head snapped up. Athelstan had said the same thing last night. At least, she thought he did. She felt so weary and hungry that she wasn't sure what was real some of the time. "I'm getting sore from this stone floor. Let's go check on Bard. I moved him to the back courtyard so he could get a drink."

Hakon stood and helped Joia to stand. "Good idea."

They walked outside into the sunshine that filtered through the tree canopy. The air smelled fresh, and Joia took a deep breath. Bard came up to them, whinnied gently, and nudged her with his nose.

"I'll bet you are missing Edmund," she patted the horse's velvety nose. "So do I."

What had become of Edmund in these last five days? Was he still imprisoned? Was he even still alive?

"We'll take care of him," Hakon promised, also patting the horse's neck. "We just need to find food for us first."

They started to walk along the keep's wall by the stream. A little further down, she discovered a wild garden that had grown along and around the walls.

"I can't believe it," she said and climbed into the garden.

"What?" Hakon asked, coming to where she was kneeling.

"Herbs. This must have been an herb garden at one point," she said, happily collecting the leaves and flowers of the various plants.

"That was three hundred years ago. How can you be sure those are edible?" he asked, looking at them.

Joia laughed. "I'm not smart about a lot of things, but I do know about gardens and herbs. This is chamomile. This is mint, smell." She handed him a leaf that she had just torn away. Its fragrance was powerful. "Here is basil." She pulled off another leaf and handed it to him to smell. "What do you think?"

He nodded. "They smell nice."

She pulled off a few more leaves and noticed another plant with small red flowers. She smiled and dug at the plant until she could get at the roots. After some more digging around, she found a section of a rotting log that had fallen over the wall from the forest on the other side. She picked up the log and found that it easily broke apart when she pulled it.

Using a stone, she scraped at the inside of the log and cleaned it of its debris until she was down to the wood that had not yet rotted away. It formed a small bowl and Joia was very pleased with her industry.

She carried her new bowl and the herbs back into the hall.

"Grab one of those small pots, will you?" she asked.

Hakon did and followed Joia into the hall. Next, she sent him with one of their water skins to refill it at the stream. While he was gone, she transferred some of the hot water from the cauldron in the hearth into the new pot. When Hakon returned with the water, she poured some into the second pot to cool the water, just a little.

"May I borrow your knife?" she asked.

He took it out of the sheath and handed it to her. She started cutting at the root of the last plant she found and dropped it into the pot.

"What is that?" Hakon asked.

"Soap root. I'm going to wash some of our clothes," she said. She used a stick to pound the root in the hot water. When it had dissolved somewhat, she nodded her head in satisfaction. "All right, hand me your shirt."

"You don't have to do this, you know," he said as he took his shirt off and handed it to Joia. Joia took it and put it into the hot water. She added a little more of the cold water so she could put her hands into the pot without burning them. She reached in and started to scrub.

"If you want to give me your pants, I'll wash them as well," she said, kneeling over the pot and scrubbing at the shirt. "Just wrap one of the blankets around you. I'll not look."

"And what if someone comes?" he asked.

She sighed. "I can't imagine who would come here, but it's up to you." She scrubbed at the shirt, holding it up once in a while to inspect it before dunking it back in.

"While I appreciate the offer, I'm going to decline at this time," he said.

She nodded and continued to scrub, singing her washing song. "I saw a woman washing, her hair was white as snow."

Hakon laughed. "I heard you singing that at Grian's house."

"Ebba and I made it up over years and years of washing." Joia missed her sister, but she wasn't feeling quite so homesick anymore, for which she was thankful. All this time away had helped her to adjust, but if she had the chance, she would go home and give her mother and sister a big hug.

When she was done, she wrung the shirt out, squeezing as much water from it as she could. She took the shirt out into the sunshine and laid it out across a low section of the stone wall.

She removed her overdress and put it into the water, adding more hot water and more soap root. She sat there, washing, and singing, just like she had done with her mother and Ebba. It was nice to be doing something normal again.

Letting her mind wander, she thought about the things that Athelstan had told her the night before, but by the time she was done with her washing, she still wasn't sure what she was supposed to be doing for the trades. How did she get rid of the trade minister because no matter what was going on in the trades, he was provoking most of the bad feelings.

Athelstan had called Scrios the Uncreator and destroyer of the trades. How did one small person go about getting rid of someone so determined to destroy the trades? It was a three-hundred-year-old grudge that Scrios was nursing.

Hakon stayed close by. He had a small pile of sticks and reeds. He pulled the reeds into strips and started to tie the bundles together into a frame. She wasn't sure what he was doing, but he seemed to have a goal in mind, so she let him do his project while she continued to wash. Her stomach cramped in hunger. Last night's meager dinner was so long ago.

"Hakon, what do we do about food? We're going to starve soon if we don't get something."

"I know," he sighed. "I'm trying to build a trap. I'm hoping I can catch a hare or fowl, but I have no bait." He sighed and set the trap down on his lap. "I've been thinking about going into Tillmere and seeing if I can find some work for the day. I can make a little money and we can at least buy some food."

"I have all the herbs to make tea, but we have no cups or bowls either."

Hakon ran his hands through his hair. "Joia, maybe we need to give this up and go home. We came to Athelstan's castle, searching for answers, but there is nothing here. Without Edmund or any of the others, we have no idea what we are supposed to be doing."

"I need to find a way to bring the trades back together," Joia sighed. "But all the ideas in the world aren't going to help anyone if we die of starvation."

"We can sell our candles or your cloak. We can get enough money to buy some food, get directions to Erthenhorn, and go home. Later, when we can be more prepared, we can come back, but we can't stay here like this."

"You're right," she nodded her head. She was a failure. She had feared it all along and all the Patrons had known it. All of them had questioned her Light and why she had been chosen. She had asked herself the same question daily since starting on this journey. Hakon or her brother would have been better. Anyone else would have been better. She had failed, Edmund had been arrested and was probably dead, and it was all her fault.

Edmund wasn't coming for her. No one else but Seb knew she and Hakon were here and there was no way he was coming for her. He hated her.

It seemed silly to wash her clothes now. She stopped, wrung out her dress, and laid it out next to Hakon's shirt. She turned the shirt over so it could dry out on the other side.

"Need me to dump this water for you?" Hakon asked.

She nodded, keeping her eyes down. "If you don't mind." The last thing she wanted to see was his disappointment in her.

Hakon appeared next to her, and he picked up the pot. Joia's mouth fell open as she saw his chest for the first time. His arms bulged with muscle as he carried the pot out. For several moments, Joia couldn't remember what she was doing.

She quickly tried to find something else to do, so he wouldn't see her staring at him at his return. She gathered her things and went back into the castle's main hall. Walking over to the huge colored-glass window, she looked up and studied the many symbols that represented all the trades. Here, in the window, they were united in a great circle around Athelstan.

Hakon came back in and set the pot down next to the hearth. "So, before we leave, are you going to explain to me what you were talking about last night when you said you had learned so much? What were you doing down that hall?" he asked.

Joia's face was heated. She sat down facing the fire and thought about what she had seen, and the things Athelstan had said. If she left now, she would be letting Athelstan down. But then, maybe she already had.

"Joia?" Hakon said, pulling Joia from her thoughts. "You're keeping a secret from me, and I don't like that. What did you find last night?"

"I don't mean to keep secrets from you," she answered. "We've been busy this morning, exploring the castle and such. Other things have occupied us, and it's been kind of nice, just you and me, and no Patrons or anything else. It's kind of like making a home together."

He nodded. "Except we don't have any furniture or food." He moved to sit next to her and took her hand in his. For several moments, he caressed her hand. She relaxed into his touch. "You know," he started after several moments, "we've never really talked about that, but, if we had the chance, would you want that?"

She looked over to him. He looked nervous, and that surprised her. "To make a home with you? To be your wife?"

He nodded again. "Yes."

She smiled, loving this handsome man even more. "I've known I wanted to be your wife for many years," she answered, feeling her face flush.

Edmund leaned his head down to kiss her and for several minutes, the rest of their troubles disappeared. When they separated, Edmund rested his forehead on hers.

"But now you have all of this," he waved his hand at the castle. "I'll understand if you don't want a common thatcher for a husband, anymore."

Joia moved to kneel next to him. "You are not common. You're wonderful and I would be proud to be your wife. But as for all of this," she copied the gesture he had made, and waved her hand in the direction of the colorful window, "I just don't understand. I shouldn't be the one with this Light. It should be you because you're a real tradesman. When we were at Grian's house, I got to watch you work your trade for the first time and I was just in awe of you. You've spent years working and learning and you are so close to receiving your master's status. You have skill and knowledge that I will never have."

"You are a master of practical skills, though," he said. "You saw the overgrown garden out there and recognized the various herbs. And I know if we had food, you would be cooking the most delicious meals. You make a shirt from a piece of cloth. You know how to care and comfort people," Hakon said.

Joia blushed and they both leaned into each other at the same time. Their lips met and Joia's entire body felt like it had caught fire. She put her hands on his shoulders, and he pulled at her hips. She had never been pressed so hard against him and without his shirt on, she was able to touch more skin.

Hakon deepened the kiss and Joia thought she would faint with the intensity of the feeling. He finally broke the kiss and smiled at her.

"I would never kiss anyone like that if I didn't want to be his wife," Joia breathed.

They kissed again, wrapping their arms around each other. It was incredible and Joia never wanted it to end.

But they shouldn't be doing this. They weren't married. She wasn't his wife yet. She broke off the kiss and stepped back.

"Have I upset you?"

"Not at all," she smiled. "But we shouldn't be doing this. We're not married. We aren't even promised to each other."

Hakon sighed and lowered his gaze from hers. "You're right." He took her hands into his. He squeezed them and looked directly into her face. "Will you marry me?" he asked.

She let out a giddy laugh. "Yes, Hakon. I would love that very much. I think Joia, wife of Hakon the Thatcher, has a wonderful sound to it."

He grinned and pulled her into his arms. "One day, we will be building our home together and it will be such a joy to live with you."

She leaned into his bare chest and sighed with happiness. "I can't wait."

"Now that we have that decided," he smiled, "how about you tell me about what you found last night."

"Let's get our clothes and see if they are dry," she said.

They went back out to the courtyard and picked up their clothes from the wall. Hakon's shirt was dry, but Joia's heavier overdress was still a little damp. She put it on anyway knowing that if she was going to see Athelstan again, she needed to be completely dressed.

Joia led them back into the castle and they stopped to pick up their Everburn candles. With both of them holding their lit candles, they headed down the hall until they reached the stairs that would take them down to Athelstan's room.

She eagerly walked down the hall, past all the empty rooms that she thought might have been dungeons.

"What's in all of these?" Hakon asked, looking at all the rooms they were passing.

"Nothing. They are empty rooms, like we saw in the rest of the castle, except for this one." Joia pushed the door open with the large intricate "A" in the center.

Hakon followed her in and let out a low whistle. "Ah, so that is what is on the inside of the circle," Hakon said looking up. "Incredible."

"What?" Joia asked.

"Remember when I said that the upper floors were interesting because they curved like they surrounded a circle, but I couldn't find an entrance?" he asked, and Joia nodded. "This is the circular room."

Joia looked up and saw that the circle went all the way to the top of the castle, open to the sky above, which was providing enough sunlight that she didn't need her candle. She looked around the room again, able to see for the first time that the entire room was circular, and in the middle of the floor was the pool of water.

"This is what you found last night?" he asked.

"Yes," she answered. "I couldn't see much, though."

"What is this place?" Hakon asked as he approached the water.

"Don't touch the water," she said. "Not yet anyway. Oh, Hakon, look." Joia pointed to a table in the room. It was beautifully made and decorated with intricate carvings in the wood. In the center was Athelstan's symbol and laid across one side of the table was the most exquisite cloth Joia had ever seen. She ran her hand along the cloth and felt how soft it was.

"It looks like something Sidonia would make," Hakon commented. "You've said that things made by the Patrons glow with your mystical Light. Are the things in here glowing?"

"Yes," she said, looking around and smiling. "Everything glows."

Hakon and Joia walked through the room, admiring every item that was in there. Gorgeous candles were sitting in elaborate wrought iron candelabras. A shiny silver goblet was on a table next to the cloth. A lute of the most beautiful golden wood that Joia had ever seen was lying next to a set of beautiful plates, cups, and bowls.

There was a pair of beautiful leather shoes sitting on top of a barrel with shiny copper rings. A loaf of bread was sitting on a small stool, next to a large spinning wheel with pure white thread in the spindle. The bread looked fresh and when Joia bent closer to it, she could smell the delicious flour and yeast. Her stomach growled and her mouth watered. She quickly moved away from the tempting food.

A curious wooden craft sat off to one side of the room. Joia approached it and looked inside. It was large enough for her to lie down in. "Hakon, what do you think this is?" Joia asked.

"I believe it is a boat," Hakon came over. "I have heard of such crafts. They float on the water and whoever is in the boat can travel from one side of water to the other side. Does it glow too?"

Joia nodded. "Yes, which means it was made by a Patron, but if this is a watercraft, how did the Patron learn such a craft? In these weeks of travel, we've never seen a body of water larger than a stream."

"Perhaps there is water close by, but we only travel by roads and so are not near the water," Hakon said. "It's a very curious object."

Joia nodded. "It is, and just like everything else in here, it is in perfect condition. There is not a single sign of age, nor even a speck of dirt."

Hakon went over to the wall that was opposite the door they walked in through and found a bundle of straw, perfectly bundled and shaped. "Do you think I can touch it? This was made by my Patron."

Joia nodded and Hakon laid his hand on the straw, feeling the tightness of the bundle, held together by a thin piece of wire. "This straw should not have survived the three hundred years. None of this should have."

"Hakon, listen," Joia said suddenly. They both stood still and listened. They could hear music, quiet and far away, beautiful but sad. "Do you hear it? The song?"

"Yes, it's like it's in the walls," Hakon pressed the palm of his hand to a wall. "The stone seems to vibrate with the music. It must be Edmund."

"It is," a deep and familiar voice said.

They turned in surprise to see Edmund and Seb in the doorway to the circular room.

"Edmund!" Joia cried. She ran to him and hugged him tightly. "You're all right!"

"Not quite, but mostly," Edmund grunted. He stumbled back a little on his wounded leg, but Seb caught him.

Joia let go when she realized something was wrong. She saw the red cut above his eye and on his lip. She gently reached out to the bandage but didn't touch it. "Edmund," she whispered, tears filling her eyes. They had done this to him. Scrios and the other Patrons had hurt her dear friend.

Edmund held a walking stick in his hand and hopped once. "I've got a bit of a bad leg right now," he said.

She looked and saw the large bandage on his leg and his torn, bloody pants. "Oh Edmund, I'm so sorry. I didn't mean to hurt you." She quickly apologized.

"You didn't hurt me, Joia." Now he reached out and touched her face, wiping at the tears that were falling. "I'm fine, Joia."

"I should have stayed with you," she said. "But I ran away."

He shook his head. "No. I wanted you to run. You did exactly what I asked you to do. If we had both been arrested, things would have been worse. You did what I asked you to do, which was run and get out of there."

"You saved my life," she said. "Scrios was trying to choke me."

Edmund looked at her neck, which was very nearly healed of its bruising. "My sweet, Joia. I cannot believe he did that to you. It is clear he sees you as a huge threat, which means you are very important to us."

He put his hand behind her head and gently pulled her closer to him. She put her arms around him, careful not to knock him over. His arms wrapped around her. "I am not so easily broken," he said. "We are all here now and that is the most important thing."

He let her go and she stepped back, nodding her head. He was right, of course. Against all hope, they were all together. Joia took a few steps back.

Edmund smiled one of his lovely smiles at her. He then looked up to see Hakon frowning at the Patron. "It's good to see you again and you too, Hakon! Glad you both made it here safely." Edmund hopped further into the room. Seb walked in after him.

Joia went to Seb and kissed him on the cheek. "I'm so happy to see you again," she said.

Seb was surprised by Joia's greeting. "Yes, well," he blustered, "it's good to see you too. I'm glad you made it here safely."

"Thanks to your map and the food you gave us," she said. "When I opened my map to try and find which way I needed to take, a golden light appeared. We always made sure we were moving toward the Light and it brought us right here."

He smiled. "You are more remarkable than I initially believed. I don't know what you mean to us as Patrons, yet, but you are learning to use the Light to your advantage."

Hakon walked closer to them, and Seb reached out his hand to clasp Hakon's. "It's good to see you too, Hakon."

"I must say that I'm surprised to see you," Hakon said.

"To be fair, I never thought that I would be here or see either of you again," Seb admitted. He stepped back and silently looked around the room.

"Edmund, what happened? How did you get here?" Joia asked.

"It's a long tale for another time, but the short of it is Seb rescued me from the dungeons," Edmund said.

"The dungeons?" Joia cried out. "You were thrown into the dungeons?"

He nodded and Joia hugged Seb again. He blushed and shrugged but returned the hug.

"Thank you, Seb."

"I'm sorry about the way we parted, but if you hadn't spoken to me the way you did, I don't know if I would have been brave enough to enter the castle."

"You are so brave," Joia smiled at him. She looked back at the items in the room. "Tell me, where is yours?"

"Over here," he walked to the table. Next to the silver cup was a scroll.

"May I look at it?" Joia asked. When Seb nodded, Joia picked up the scroll and carefully unrolled it. It was the layout of the castle. All its rooms and halls, the courtyards surrounding the castle, and the names of the plants that grew in the gardens were written in tiny intricate writing. The borders of the map were decorated with beautiful drawings. "This is beautiful," Joia said with reverence. Seb blushed again. She re-rolled the scroll and placed it back on the table.

Edmund was quiet for several long moments as he looked around the room. "This room looks exactly the same as it did on the day we were granted our Patronage by Athelstan," Edmund quietly said.

"What about this pool of water?" Joia asked.

Edmund shook his head. "No. That was not here."

Joia went to the water and touched it. The golden light appeared, and the ghostly form of Athelstan rose from the water. Hakon, Edmund, and Seb watched in amazement. Immediately, Seb knelt on one knee. Edmund tried, but couldn't with his injured leg, so he bowed at the glowing figure.

"Rise, my sons," Athelstan said after his figure took its shape. They did. Joia noticed Edmund was hopping about awkwardly, so she went to him and put her arm around his waist to help support him.

"Athelstan, it is an honor," Edmund said.

"It's good to see you both again." Athelstan turned to Hakon. Hakon bowed. "Hakon, welcome to the home of the trades, young thatcher. Your being here honors us."

"Thank you, sir," Hakon said.

"Edmund," Athelstan said, turning back to the entertainer, "you are injured? Take a seat." He gestured to a beautifully made chair.

"But sir, that is your chair," Edmund said.

"It is and I am offering it to you."

"Thank you," Edmund said. With Joia's help, he hopped over to the chair and sat down, his injured leg stretched out in front of him.

"Seb, Joia told me that you made her one of your Life Maps, sheltered them, and helped her and Hakon escape the city. Thank you for all you have done. It is good to have you back."

Seb bowed to Athelstan again, "Thank you, sir. I was not as kind as Joia might have led you to think, though."

He regarded Seb for several moments. "I know your heart," Athelstan said. "And the most important thing is that you followed it."

"And he rescued me," Edmund said. "If it weren't for him, I would be dead."

"It was nothing," Seb said, his face red.

"It means a lot to me," Edmund said.

Athelstan nodded his approval and turned to face Joia again. "Have you thought about what I said last night?" Athelstan asked her.

"A great deal, but I still feel unsure about what I am supposed to do. Well, I mean, I know what it is I have to do, but I don't know how to do it. How do I fight Scrios?"

"So, it's true, then," Seb said. "It is the Uncreator."

"Yes, I'm afraid so. He wishes to destroy you and your work. To undo all you have done," Athelstan answered.

"No surprise there," Edmund sighed.

"Why does he want this?" Hakon asked. "Is he looking to take over and rule?"

Athelstan was quiet for a moment, "No, I don't believe he wants to rule. Ruling takes work and requires rules that must be made and followed. He is an uncreator. He wants to destroy."

"But he is in a position of power right now. He is making rules," Joia said.

"Ah, but that is just it," Seb said, walking around the room in thought, "He has accepted this position of power, so he can destroy in a subtle way. An all-out attack on the trades wouldn't work. We would see that right away and be strong in our opposition. But, as Trade Minister, he is on the inside of the power and can pull us apart slowly and cunningly, hoping that by the time we realize what he is doing, it will be too late to amend."

"That snake," Edmund growled. "Long ago, he took my entire collection of instruments that I made over a year's time and threw them into a river. All my work was destroyed. All the money I had hoped to make at the summer fair was lost. So, you can see that I have no sympathy for this man, and I do not hesitate to call him names," Edmund said, leaning forward in his chair.

"Hold on there, Storyteller," Seb came over and steadied Edmund. "We've got more important things to worry about."

"Do we think we might already be too late?" Joia asked. "The smithies are against the other trades."

"Yes, that is true, to a point," Athelstan said, "but not entirely. You, Joia, have already begun bringing the trades back together."

"How do you mean? I haven't done anything."

Athelstan shook his head. He gave Joia a hard gaze and she felt for sure that he knew she had given up and was making plans to return home. "Joia, the Patrons have, over the years, grown apart, no longer having contact with each other or working together. When this happens, it affects their Guilds. Everything starts here, with them. Since beginning your journey, you have reunited many of the Patrons."

"Yes, don't you see, Joia?" Edmund turned to her. "Before you were born, I had not seen any other Patron in many, many years, but after seeing you, as a baby, I gathered together Seb, Sidonia, and Kloma, so we could discuss you. We were reunited in our curiosity for you. And now, since the beginning of our journey, we have seen Sidonia, Grian, and Seb. You helped Seb and I to see how foolish we had been for so long and we have forgiven each other. You caused Sidonia to think of when she and Kloma were close friends and neighbors."

"I see," Joia said. "You know, when I was at the smithy, with Scrios, Wodwin, Ciar, and Aren, I almost had the Patrons convinced that Scrios was no good. They might have united together."

"They still might," Athelstan said. "You, Joia, are bringing the Patrons back together. You are reminding them of their purpose as Patrons."

"Well, that is all very nice," Joia said, "but it isn't enough to overthrow Scrios."

"I sense more of my children are approaching," Athelstan said suddenly. "This is a great day for me. Hakon, Joia, and Seb go and meet them. Edmund, if you will stay a moment longer, I have something to discuss with you."

"I'll be back soon to help you up the stairs," Seb said to Edmund. He bowed at Athelstan and followed Joia and Hakon out of the room.

"I wonder who's arrived?" Joia asked as she went back up the stairs and out toward the courtyard.

"Careful, Joia," Seb called out to her.

She stepped out into the courtyard and could see three horses coming up the road. "Sidonia!" Joia called out. "It's Sidonia, Grian, and another woman. I don't know her, but she is glowing."

"Then it would be Kloma. She and Sidonia are the only women Patrons," Seb called back to her.

The three horses arrived at the gate and with smiles and waves, they dismounted. Joia went to them. She hugged Sidonia and bowed to Grian. Sidonia introduced Joia to Kloma, the Spinner.

"It's an honor to meet you," Joia said to the newly arrived Patron.

"The honor is mine. I've heard so much about you from Sidonia and Grian." Kloma took Joia's hand in hers. Kloma was very different from Sidonia. She was small, plump, and had the friendliest face Joia had ever seen. Her hair was a deep auburn and pulled up into a loose bun with an intricately woven lace cap on top of her head. Where Sidonia was dressed in beautiful fabrics, Kloma was dressed like the women in Joia's home village. Joia liked her immediately.

They all walked into the great hall. It was a joyful reunion for all of them. Grian had not seen Seb in close to three hundred years.

"It's good to see you again," Grian said. "You're looking very well."

Seb nodded his head. "Where did you end up settling? Last I heard you were out in Colne."

"I was until it was destroyed by an earthquake," Grian answered. "After that, I decided to return to my family's ancestral home."

"Where is Edmund?" Sidonia answered.

"In the castle. He was injured," Seb said.

"Oh dear," Kloma said. "Let's go in and say a proper hello to him, then."

Sidonia, Kloma, and Grian turned to go back to the castle, but Seb turned to Joia when she did not follow.

"Are you coming in with the rest?" he asked.

"I'm going to go see if Hakon needs any help with the horses," she said. "I'll be in soon."

"Be careful," he said and followed the others into the castle.

Joia ran to catch up with Hakon and took the lead for one of the horses.

"Can I help you?" she asked.

He shrugged. "If you want to. It looks like they have much to say and reminisce about. They don't need me around."

"That's not true," Joia said. "Seb and Grian enjoy your company." They walked around the side of the castle until they found the entrance to the back courtyard. The horses joined Bard and Seb's borrowed horse. The courtyard was getting very crowded.

"If anyone else comes, we are going to have to find another place for the horses," Hakon said. He turned to Joia. "How did you know to find Athelstan in that room?"

"I found it last night on my midnight exploration of the castle," she answered.

"Why didn't you tell me about it?" Hakon asked.

"Because I wanted time to think about what he had told me. I wanted to see the rest of the castle and I didn't want to return to Athelstan without any kind of plan in mind."

"And what did he tell you?"

"He told me his story. He told me how he became the Father of the Trades by teaching the Patrons their trades. He told me about Scrios." Joia could see Hakon was upset about her not telling him about the room, the pool, and Athelstan. "I just needed time to think."

"And you didn't think you can trust me?" Hakon asked. "You couldn't tell me about the room?"

"No, that's not it at all!" Joia turned to face Hakon, but he backed up one step. "I trust you Hakon. I do. With all my heart and my life. Please don't think otherwise." She went to him, and they sat down on the wall together. "It wasn't about trust or trying to keep secrets. Everything has just been so overwhelming. There has been so much to learn," she said, holding his hand. "He told me the history of the trades, the Patrons, and Scrios. He told me to think about what I might need to do. Athelstan is expecting me to come up with a solution to the problem with Scrios. I didn't want to go back to that room until I could show that I had thought up something."

"I see," Hakon quietly said.

"I've been so afraid of disappointing him, the Patrons, and especially you. They seem to expect me to do something great and defeat Scrios. And now that we've talked about returning home, I have disappointed them."

"No one but us knows that we had talked about that," Hakon whispered.

"Athelstan knows. I'm sure he does," Joia sighed. "I've failed him and you. You gave up so much by joining me on this journey. And it was all for nothing." Joia sighed. "I have this Light and so I'm supposed to be knowledgeable, brave, or clever. They have all doubted me," she waved her hand at the castle. "They've all asked, why you? What is so special about you that you have this light? And I don't know."

Joia was shaking with emotion. Her arms accentuated everything she said, and she felt so sick from hunger.

"Joia," Hakon started, but Joia couldn't stop.

"They think I'm going to help them, save them even, and I don't know how. Make them hug each other and say sorry? I'm not a tradesman. Hakon, I can't tell you the number of times since starting this journey I have thought that they have the wrong person. You would be a much better champion for the trades than I am. You are a tradesman. You are brave and clever. You know so many things. I know nothing besides cooking and sewing. And a lot of help that is right now. We don't even have anything to cook. I don't have a trade and I'm not clever at all."

"That's not true," he said, squeezing her hand again. "Joia, I'm sorry. This hasn't been easy for either of us. You say you are not brave or clever, but you're wrong. You are what the Patrons need right now."

"How, Hakon?" She stood and faced him. "How am I what they need? What have I done that is of any use to any of them?"

"You brought us together."

Joia and Hakon turned to see Seb in the doorway. "This reunion of the Patrons has happened because you both have been brave and clever. Never doubt your value."

"This gathering was none of my doing. It was all Edmund, who took me from place to place to meet you," Joia sighed. She was so worried she would never figure out what it was she was supposed to do. If they only knew that she was ready to walk away, they would be so disappointed in her.

"The others are waiting. Come in and join us," Seb said.

"We'll be right in, Seb. I just want to collect a few more herbs for tea. Won't be long," Joia said. Seb nodded and turned to go back in. Joia went to the overgrown garden. Using the motions of searching for herbs, she was able to wipe the tears from her face. She took several deep breaths and tried to collect herself. Her stomach clenched in pain.

She was startled when a hand came and rested on her shoulder. She leaned into Hakon for several moments.

"Joia, we already have a pile of herbs in the castle and no way to make or serve tea, remember?" he whispered.

"You and I know that, but Seb doesn't." She leaned forward, pressing her hands onto the stone wall. "Seb, Grian, and Sidonia were such good hosts. They fed us and gave us soft places to sleep. I've got nothing to offer. Not even tea. How do I admit to them that I cannot offer them anything."

"We aren't required to offer them anything. This isn't our home, Joia."

"It was for a little while," she said. "And I'm a terrible homemaker. My mother would be so ashamed of me."

"You washed my clothes using the root of a plant. I had no idea you could do that."

She reached her hand out to the mint plant and pulled up a section. The burst of the mint's scent made Joia take in a deep breath.

"Joia, what's the matter?" he whispered.

She turned to look at him, pointing her finger at the door. "Don't you realize there are five Patrons in there? They are hundreds of years old, and they are so wise, but they are expecting me to do something, and I don't know what to do," she whispered furiously. "They will laugh at me. They will demand I leave. Athelstan will be very angry with me and take away my Light."

Hakon pulled Joia tightly in his arms. "They won't laugh at you and if they do, they will have to deal with me."

"But I have disappointed you too. You can't deny how angry you've been with me since we left Yondalla," she said. "Well, more like since we left Erthenhorn."

"I am not disappointed in you. Being the only person who doesn't have the Light has been frustrating and I don't like when you keep secrets from me, but I'm not disappointed," he promised.

"I think we're both too hungry," Joia said. "I can tighten my overdress much more than before."

Hakon nodded. "I had to add a notch to my belt."

She cleared her throat. "Well, there is nothing else to be done. It's time to face the Patrons."

Everyone was waiting in the main hall. Joia tipped the herbs into the pot of hot water. They had all gathered and were sitting on the floor in a circle so they could face each other, except Edmund, who had the chair from Athelstan's room.

"There is no furniture," Joia apologized as she approached them. "Our bedrolls are at your service."

"We're fine," Seb said and scooted over so there was room for Joia and Hakon. Joia sat down, but Hakon stepped back.

"Hakon, join us," Grian invited.

"No. This looks like important Guild business. I won't bother you," Hakon said.

"Sit down, Hakon," Edmund ordered. "You are Thek's representative. We need you."

Hakon hesitated a moment before he sat down. Joia saw him smile a little, proud at being treated as an equal.

"I'm sorry I don't have anything to offer you, except for the pleasant aroma of mint and hot water," Joia said. "It's not a fine way to repay your hospitality and I apologize."

The five Patrons looked back and forth at each other, and Joia felt sick at their realization of how pathetic she truly was. She looked uncomfortably at the cauldron hanging over the fire.

Edmund cleared his throat. "It's fine Joia. Now then," he said, "are you aware that the king's trade minister is Scrios the Uncreator?" he asked Grian, Sidonia, and Kloma.

They nodded their heads.

"Kloma heard about him and what he is doing," Sidonia told them. "She traveled out to see me and tell me what she knew."

"Yes," Kloma said, "It was not the kind of news I could keep to myself, so I made the journey to see Sidonia. She and I felt this urge to return to the castle right away. We came, hoping to find answers. Imagine our surprise when we met Grian along the way, also coming to the castle."

"What made you journey here?" Edmund asked Grian.

"Well, after you three," he pointed to Edmund, Joia, and Hakon, "left my home, I got to thinking about Joia, her Light, and everything Edmund told me. I started thinking about the others and how I hadn't seen anyone in so long. Once the idea was in my mind, I couldn't shake it. The best thing to do was come here and seek inspiration. I was surprised to find Sidonia and Kloma coming here too."

Sidonia nodded. "Yes, after you left me, I knew I needed to see Kloma again. I started for her home around the same time she started for mine. We met, quite by accident, halfway. It was the sweetest reunion, and we knew we needed to come to the castle. It was just a feeling. We needed to be here. And now we know why."

"It was the Light that has guided all of us here," Edmund said.

"I wonder if the others will feel the draw to the castle?" Kloma asked. "Is everyone here feeling the unease that Scrios is creating?"

They all nodded.

"What can be done about him?" Grian asked.

As one, everyone turned to look at Joia. She felt very nervous under the gaze of five Patrons and Hakon while knowing that Athelstan was probably listening too. They expected her to do something, and she had no idea what to do. She opened her mouth, but no words came out.

Hakon came to her rescue. He reached out and took her hand. "There is strength in numbers," he said. "We are many now. There are more here to represent the trades than there is of him."

"But Scrios has power over our tradesmen," Kloma said.

"No," said Hakon, "he doesn't. He can influence them, but he has no true power over them."

Joia felt such pride in Hakon, but so much disappointment in herself. He was a true leader. Not her.

"Even so," Sidonia said, "How do we get rid of Scrios and his influence?"

"I'm not sure that we can," Joia said.

Once again everyone looked at her. She shrank back, just a bit, but an idea was starting to form in her head. She needed to think, and she couldn't with everyone staring at her. She stood up. "I need to be alone for a bit. Will you excuse me?"

Everyone watched in stunned silence as Joia walked out of the great hall.

"Now what?" Grian said. "Isn't she supposed to be helping us?"

Hakon was about to speak when Seb cut him off. "She will Grian. She will. This is new to her. We need to give her some time."

Hakon nodded. "I say we are better off today than we were yesterday or even this morning. We are many now, so we are stronger."

"Hakon's right," Seb said. "Perhaps we should find more Patrons and bring them here."

"Do you think we could?" Sidonia asked. "Who is nearest? How do we find the others?"

Everyone shrugged their shoulders. No one knew where anyone else was.

"Perhaps," Edmund said quietly, "that is our problem."

CHAPTER TWENTY-THREE

Plans

Joia hurried away from the gathering of Patrons and headed down the stairs to Athelstan's room. She did not intend to disturb him again right now. She just needed a place to think, and it made her nervous to have so many Patrons looking to her, of all people, for instruction. All the doubts that felt since starting this journey came back to her. Seb had been right when he had said that the Light meant nothing to her if she didn't know how to use it.

Joia sat on the floor near the pool and put her head into her hands. She had a headache and her stomach cramped in hunger again.

But she remembered what she had told Seb. She had the Light and she was going to figure out what her purpose was and what it was she was supposed to do. She was going to make good on that. Now was the time.

Athelstan and Edmund had told her that for many centuries the Patrons had been separated from each other. They had all set up their homes and workshops in permanent locations and hardly ever left or saw each other. They were all forgetting how much they needed each other.

It seemed to Joia that they needed to come together, regularly, to be reminded of just what it was their fellow Patrons did. She also knew that most of the tradesmen of the country did not believe their Patrons to be real people. After all, until meeting Edmund, she had always thought the Patrons to be mystical legends and not real people at all and she knew her family and friends had felt the same way. Even

Hakon had not been completely sure if they were real, although he was very dedicated to Thek.

This meant that if the tradesmen thought their Patrons were legends, it would be easy for someone, like Scrios, to persuade them to a new way of thinking. He was actively working against the Patrons and their trades, but none of the Patrons actively worked with their tradesmen. And Scrios, in the position of Trade Minister, had great influence directly on the people.

Seb had been right. An all-out attack on the Patrons would never have worked, but the subtle influences Scrios was working to pull the Patrons and their tradesmen further apart. Not to mention that the Patrons, by keeping themselves apart from their people and each other, were helping Scrios.

It was becoming more and more clear to Joia what the Patrons needed to do. They needed to go out and be among their people. Their tradesmen needed to know their Patrons as real people who heard their dedications and blessed them.

And secondly, as Joia thought, was that the Patrons needed to be together regularly to discuss their trades and be reminded just how important each of them was.

It was a good plan, Joia thought, and doable for the future, but they needed something more at this moment in time.

Scrios was called the Uncreator. He was the opposite of a Patron, who lived to create. Perhaps the opposite must always exist. You can't have bad without the good and you can't have good without the bad. Joia wondered if it was the same with the trades. Creation exists, so uncreation must exist. Therefore, Scrios really couldn't really be defeated.

Athelstan had not defeated Scrios so long ago. He had only banished him. Perhaps that was all that could be done. Joia's stomach cramped uneasily. She wasn't sure if it was from hunger or the uncertainty of what she needed to do, maybe both. She rubbed her aching stomach, stood up, and started to pace the room.

"I don't like the idea of not being able to defeat Scrios," she said out loud to herself. She wrung her hands around each other and suddenly wished she had a pair of knitting needles. She always did her best thinking while knitting.

Scrios needed to be stopped. That much was certain. He had quietly deceived some of the trades into thinking they were better than the others. He had demeaned the trades that he didn't consider worthy by publicly humiliating them, sending them out of the castle, and declaring them to be inferior. When Edmund had tried to defy him, Scrios the other Patrons beat Edmund when they should have been protecting him and helping him.

The memory of Edmund's arrest still troubled Joia's heart and mind. He, of all people, did not deserve to be treated like that. She recalled Edmund getting punched and held down. Now he carried those injuries. His stitched forehead, split lip, and all the blue and yellow bruises that covered his skin. He couldn't walk far or move well because of the pain in his leg.

She didn't even want to think what would have happened if Seb hadn't rescued him. What would have happened to the entertainers if they didn't have Edmund? What would she have done if she had lost Edmund?

Joia rubbed her head. "Athelstan," she spoke quietly out loud once again. "I just don't know what I am to do. They are all sitting up there, waiting for me to come up with a plan. I just don't understand why you chose me. I am inadequate to do this task." She looked at the pool of water. What had Athelstan been thinking? She couldn't do this. Anyone else sitting in the great hall right now would have been better to lead this campaign, so why her? She had no talents and no experience. What could she do?

"The Trades need to work together, which means the Patrons need to work together," she quietly spoke. "But to do that, they need to come together, and no one knows where anyone else is or how to even contact them, and that is the key, isn't it? They must keep in good communication. They need to gather each year and support each other."

Joia walked around the room, rubbing at her empty stomach. "I don't know if Scrios can be defeated, but if they work together, they would be able to keep him from having an even greater influence among the people or the Patrons." She turned to look deep into the pool.

She didn't understand why Athelstan picked her, but no matter if she was the right person for the job or not, the Patrons were waiting for her, and she needed to go back to them.

She returned to the great hall. All the Patrons and Hakon still sat there together. They looked like they had been deep in conversation, except there was a delicious smell coming from the fire. It made her stomach hurt with the need for food.

Sidonia saw her first. "Joia, would you like some tea?" She held out a cup to Joia.

"Thank you," Joia said, taking the cup. "Where did you get the cups?"

Sidonia laughed. "They were in the kitchen, tucked away. Brynmore the Potter made these. Not his finest work, but they have withstood the test of time. They don't leak, anyway."

"Thank you," she said and eagerly sipped the tea. It was good and she recognized the herbs that were used. It didn't do much for her hunger, but anything to help fill her stomach was appreciated. She looked up to see six sets of expectant eyes on her. Her stomach churned and she quickly drank her tea again.

"Everyone, may I speak with Joia, alone?" Edmund asked. "Just for a few minutes."

There was a bustle of movement as everyone stood up, except for Hakon.

"We will wait for you in the kitchen," Sidonia said as she, Kloma, Grian, and Seb walked out.

"Hakon?" Edmund started, but Hakon shook his head.

"I stay with Joia, just like I have through this entire journey," he answered.

"Very well," Edmund nodded, and they waited as the room cleared.

Joia felt some relief at everyone going away and back to just being her, Edmund, and Hakon. She missed their time around the campfire in the evenings.

Edmund closed his eyes and rubbed his leg for several moments. Joia moved to sit in front of him. His bandage looked like it needed to be changed and she wanted to do something to fix his pants leg. She would have to cut the pants at the knee and then replace them with a whole new piece of cloth, but if she had the materials, she could easily make the repair. She looked back into his face and saw he was watching her.

"Edmund, are you in great pain?"

He nodded. "I am quite sore from my, um, ordeal, but the pain is bearable." He looked around at the great room that they were in, and his eyes lingered on the colored glass window for several heartbeats before he turned back to look at her. "I'm happy to be here again. It's good to be at the castle and surrounded by friends."

"The Patrons that have gathered here with us are very kind," she nodded.

"My friends include you and Hakon," he reached out and took her hand, giving it a squeeze. "Thank you, Joia."

"For what?" she asked in surprise. "I haven't done anything, except cause a whole lot of confusion."

"That's not true. You brought me and my fellow Patrons here, and it's good to be home." He smiled at her, and she couldn't help but smile back. "Now, I wanted to talk to you about something serious. Hakon, please sit with Joia."

Hakon sat down next to Joia, and across from Edmund. Joia felt her nervousness growing. If he had sent all the Patrons away to talk to them, it had to be personal.

Edmund took a moment to look at them both and Joia had to force herself to not squirm under his intense gaze. "Athelstan told me you decided to go home."

Joia groaned and rubbed her face with her free hand before turning to look at Hakon. "I told you that he knew."

"Did you tell this to the others?" Hakon asked.

"Only Seb," Edmund admitted. "But why, Joia? After everything we've been through."

Joia rubbed at her stomach. "I'm hungry, Edmund. And I know that's a dumb reason, but before you and Seb arrived, I thought you were dead and as far as I knew, Seb had no intention of going after you. I wanted to go back for you myself, but Seb told me to leave. I ran away, like a coward, and came here. Seb gave us food for the journey, but that ran out as soon as we arrived here."

Hakon put his arm around Joia's shoulder. "We have no food and no money to buy more food."

"Hakon was going to get work in the village and if we could get enough, we would buy food, go home, get rested, buy provisions, and then come back," Joia explained. "But, without you or any of the Patrons here, I didn't know what it was I was supposed to do."

"How long have you been without food?" Edmund asked.

"Two and a half days," Hakon answered.

Joia couldn't read Edmund's blank expression, but she felt very ashamed and looked away from his piercing gaze. "I was going to come back, I promise," Joia quickly added, not wanting Edmund's anger to fall on her. It was bad enough that he was disappointed with her, but she couldn't take his disappointment and his anger.

Edmund let go of her hands and reached for a bundle by his side. He untied the knots in the cloth and opened it. Without a word, he held out the bundle, which was filled with biscuits and dried meats.

Joia's mouth watered and her stomach cramped at the sight of food.

"Take some," he said. "We'll send Sidonia and Grian to Tillmere to purchase more food right away but have a little something now. Not too much. I don't think your stomachs will like the dried foods, but please, eat something." He looked over his shoulder. "Grian!"

The golden-haired Patron jogged toward them from the kitchen. "What can I do for you, Edmund?"

"Could you and Sidonia go into the village and buy food? I have some money in my wagon. We need enough food to feed everyone a couple of meals," Edmund said.

Grian nodded. "We can do that. I brought some coins along too, so we'll have enough for a feast." He turned to leave, and Edmund's gaze came back to the bundle of food that he still held out for her. She had not dared to touch his food.

"Joia, have some."

She shook her head. "We can't take your food," Joia said, looking away from the buttery biscuits that were practically under her nose. "You've done so much for us already and I've only been a disappointment."

"Joia," Edmund's voice was quiet and pleading. "Haven't I told you over and over that it is the entertainer's way to share? Please, my dear." He took one of the biscuits from the bundle and gave it to her before giving another to Hakon, who was quick to take it and bite half of it off in one go.

Joia was so hungry her hand shook as she brought the food to her mouth. She took a bite and nearly cried in thanks. The little cookie was flaky, buttery, and slightly sweet. She had never had anything so good. She ate another bite and then another. It was quickly gone.

"Drink some more tea," Edmund said.

Joia obeyed, still feeling too hungry to argue. She drained the rest of her cup. It wasn't much, but she felt better.

"I'm sorry, my dear," Edmund said and when Joia looked at him again, she was surprised to see he had tears in his eyes. His leg had to be paining him more than he was letting on. She wanted to help him as he had just helped her by sharing his food.

"I should be the one to apologize to you," she whispered. "Because of me, you got arrested. You were beaten and badly hurt," she looked at his leg. "I am so grateful you are alive and here, but I feel so incredibly guilty for my part in this." She took one of the shreds of Edmund's pants leg and rubbed her fingers over the fabric.

"No, Joia, none of this was your fault. When I walked into Ciar's workshop and saw you there, backed into a corner with Scrios's hands around your neck, I was furious. You did nothing wrong by going and speaking to Ciar and the others. Nothing. I am proud of you that you were confident enough in yourself and your Light to go and speak with him on your own. But the way they treated you—" he clenched his fists and took a deep breath before continuing. "Seb told me what you told him about how they all came in and blocked you from leaving. I can't even tell you how angry that makes me. They shouldn't do that to a woman at all, much less disrespect someone who has the Light."

Joia touched her neck for several moments, remembering the feeling of Scrios' hands there. "Scrios dampens the Light," she said. "When he was there, their Light seemed dimmer and the room grew hot, although Scrios's hands felt cold, but they still burned. And at one point, I thought I had convinced the Patrons that what Scrios was doing was hurting their trade, but Scrios' influence was stronger."

Edmund sighed. "I know. But all of this is to say that what happened to me was not your fault. You have done nothing that you need to apologize for."

"Except for giving up," she whispered.

"No, you didn't give up." His voice was calm and gentle and put her heart at ease. "You lost hope, but you didn't give up. I want you to know that you and Hakon are no longer alone in this. We are here now and will give you hope and help. Will you continue, Joia? Will you help us?" Edmund stroked the back of her head.

She nodded. "Yes, Edmund."

He smiled at her and looked up to Hakon. "Will you stay Hakon? Will you help us?"

Hakon nodded. "Joia has always had my support and if the fates are with us, I will support her the rest of my life."

Edmund smiled. "I had hoped it would be that way." He kissed the top of Joia's head. "Let's call the others back. I will tell everyone a story while we wait for Grian and Sidonia to return."

She sat up and hugged Edmund. "Thank you."

He held her for several moments and when Joia sat back, he called to Seb and Kloma.

Grian and Sidonia returned to the castle and brought with them not just food, but bowls from the local potter, and a sharp knife. Joia and Sidonia worked together to chop vegetables and slice the meat into small chunks. All of this went into the cauldron of boiling water that hung over the fire. Joia added the herbs she had collected, and the room was filled with the most mouth-watering smells. Joia's stomach cramped again, but she was relieved to know she would soon be eating.

Edmund sang to them and played beautiful songs on his lute. Joia leaned against Hakon and listened while the food bubbled over the fire.

When it was ready, Sidonia and Kloma ladled out the stew into bowls, handing one first to Joia, then Hakon, and then the others received theirs. No one ate, but all looked to Joia. They were waiting for her to take the first bite of food.

She put the bowl to her lips and took a drink of the hot broth in the stew. As soon as she did, the others followed. Grian pulled out a loaf of bread and carefully broke it into seven parts, giving everyone a piece. Joia eagerly dipped hers into her stew and let it soak up the delicious broth. It had to be the most wonderful stew and Joia thought she would never get enough, but before she could even finish all her food, her stomach protested. She set her bowl down, hoping she would be able to finish it later.

Hakon's arm came around her. "Can't finish?" She shook her head. "Neither can I. We've gone for too long without."

She leaned in and rested her head on his shoulder, and they waited while the others ate. When the bowls of food were cleared away, they sat in a circle and everyone's eyes fell on her.

Seb, who was sitting across from her, leaned forward. "Well, Joia?"

Joia felt as if the weight of the castle were on her shoulders. She took a deep breath and looked at Edmund, who nodded encouragingly.

"Well," she began, "I've been thinking a lot since coming here. I've heard stories and seen amazing things. During my journey, I have been privileged enough to meet eight Patrons. I have enjoyed the hospitality and company of the five of you and it has been an honor."

Sidonia and Grian nodded happily at her, but Seb's face didn't change as he continued to watch her. She remembered that Edmund had told Seb that she and Hakon had given up hope and were going to leave the castle. His disappointment was hard to face.

Joia swallowed hard and continued. "Before setting out on this journey, I did not know that the Patrons existed as real people. The idea of a Patron was something mystical and long past. And I think this is our first folly. Your tradesmen don't know you, except for Edmund's entertainers. If your tradesmen are anything like the people in my village, they don't believe you exist. They dedicate their days to you out of tradition. Just think how easy it is for Scrios or anyone else to persuade them that you aren't real and that the trades should be divided into groups?"

Joia could see as the realization of her words struck each Patron.

Sidonia nodded her head sadly. "I believe that this is the heart of most of our troubles."

Grian nodded. "Joia's right. Going out and making ourselves known to our tradesmen will make us stronger and our tradesmen stronger. They will be less likely to fall to the prey of Scrios."

Joia was relieved that they weren't laughing at her because she had no idea what she was talking about. She didn't feel confident in herself, but she hoped that because she was not a part of the trades, she might have different ideas about what was going on than the rest of them.

"Go on, Joia," Edmund encouraged. "What you say makes great sense."

Joia took another deep breath, feeling more confident. "I've also thought a lot about Scrios these last few days. He should not have lived this long. He wasn't part of Athelstan's plan or sacrifice, but everything in this world has its opposites. You create. He destroys. When you were granted unlimited time to be creators, he somehow must have been granted unlimited time to uncreate."

"Do you think that is what happened?" Kloma asked.

"There is no way to know unless we ask Scrios," Joia said. "It is curious, though that he has sat in the shadows for so long without giving any sign that he was still alive."

"That doesn't matter anymore," Seb said. "What matters is that he is here now and is actively working against us."

"The thing is," Joia continued, "There will always be uncreators. If it is not Scrios, there will be someone else, because you cannot have a creator without an un-creator. There must always be an opposite, but the two sides should not be equal. Creation and the trades are stronger and more numerous and must always remain that way."

Joia paused in her plea and waited for the Patrons to think.

"Joia," Grian said, "you are wise beyond your years. You speak the truth. For too long we have been separated from one another and our tradesmen. Even though I know the name of each chandler and I hear all their dedications, I have never met any of them. And what is worse, I haven't met any of my chandlers in over a hundred years."

"Yes," Kloma said. She looked to Sidonia, "I was happier when I saw Sidonia each day and a spinner's workshop was never meant to be a solitary place. It's a place that is usually filled with women working together. I've been alone and I have felt my work suffer for it as of late."

"That is all very nice and touchy-feely," said Seb, "but we are only five Patrons."

"And a thatcher," Edmund pointed out.

"And Joia," Grian said. "We are seven. Scrios is one."

"Except he's got Ciar, Aren, and Wodwin," Seb pointed out.

"That's still only four," Hakon said.

Joia leaned forward. "When I met Ciar and the others, they started to realize that Scrios was oppressing them as well. I don't think it would take much to turn them back to us and against Scrios." Joia turned to Edmund. "Are there any other Patrons close by that we could call to our aid?"

"None that I am aware of," Edmund answered.

"Well, I guess there is nothing that can be done about that right now, but as soon as we are able, we need to locate all the Patrons," Joia said.

The others nodded.

"Hakon," Edmund said. "As we have traveled together for many weeks, I have come to recognize that you are keenly observant. Have you any thoughts?"

"What Joia has said is correct," he said. "Before all of this, I did not know if Thek truly lived, although I said my daily dedications to him. But, after meeting all of you, I can only assume he is as real as you. I cannot presume to speak for him, and I do not possess the Light of the Guild, but as a thatcher, I will support Thek and all the Patrons. I give to all of you, Thek, Athelstan, and Joia my complete support as a tradesman."

Joia squeezed Hakon's hand. "Thank you," she said.

CHAPTER TWENTY-FOUR

Creation and Uncreation

Before the sun set, Joia managed to eat a little more food and they all listened to Edmund tell a great story before they settled down for the night. Joia went with Edmund to his wagon, where he would be able to sleep more comfortably with his leg. Seb helped him to climb into the wagon, where some of Edmund's belongings had been set aside. She was surprised to see he actually had a bed in his wagon.

"You've had a bed all this time and you chose to sleep on the hard ground?" she asked.

He chuckled. "When I travel alone, I will often use my bed, but there wasn't room for you, Hakon, and I in here. The tent was easier for all of us. Sit with me a moment," he said in his deep voice.

Joia climbed into the wagon and sat on a trunk next to his bed. He took a few moments to adjust his leg and place a blanket under his knee.

"Is there anything I can do for you?" she asked, pointing at his leg.

He shook his head. "Tomorrow, I will need to unwrap it, wash it, and put the last of the salve on it. I have been lucky that no infection has set in."

"Do you have clean bandages? I can wash them for you. I can also fix your pants. It wouldn't take me too long to replace the leg with some new cloth." Joia said.

"You are unfailingly thoughtful," Edmund smiled. "I do need my bandages washed, but I would hate for you to touch them. They are disgusting, but perhaps you can help me with getting some water for me to do all my washing."

"Of course, anything you need," she said. She appreciated the way he was so forgiving and did his best to put her at ease when she still didn't feel that she deserved his forgiveness. She was horrified to know that Athelstan had known about her conversation with Hakon and then shared it with Edmund. She would never be able to say anything in confidence to anyone.

"I was very impressed with you this evening," he said, startling her from her thoughts. "You showed great cleverness and forethought. I also did not fail to notice the way you said that 'we' need to find all the Patrons."

"Well, I mean, the Patrons should find the others," Joia stammered.

"You are one of us," he said. "You might not be a Patron, but you have the Light. You are one of us."

"But what if the other Patrons don't want me to be a part of them," Joia whispered.

"They will respect you because of your Light and with Sidonia, Kloma, Grian, Seb, and my support, the others will accept you as one of us."

"I don't think Seb will," Joia looked behind her.

"Why do you whisper?" Edmund asked.

Joia sighed. "Athelstan hears everything I say." She covered her mouth. "I have already disappointed him. I don't want to make him angry."

"He is not angry with you," Edmund assured her. "And you have not disappointed him. He sought my help to assist you. He knew what you needed at that moment, and I did not, so he asked me to help you."

Joia placed her hands over her face. "And you told Seb. He already hates me as it is," she furiously whispered.

"He does not hate you. He admires you." Edmund gave her a gentle smile. "This demeanor you see is Seb. Even when he and I were the greatest of friends, this is how he is. If he didn't like you, you would know. Trust me. No, no. Seb admires you tremendously."

She wasn't entirely sure, but she wouldn't argue with Edmund about it. If he said that Seb supported her, she would just have to believe him.

"You need to have confidence in yourself. Stop doubting who you are. You have the Light and you have all our support," Edmund said.

For a moment, Joia focused on Edmund's Light. It was bright around him. If he had such a powerful Light and was telling her she had his support, she couldn't help but believe him. It made her feel stronger. No matter what happened, she was going to work to make Edmund and all the Patrons proud.

The following morning, everyone stretched and groaned about their sore bodies after a night on the stone floor.

"The first thing we do to restore this place is get some proper mattresses," Seb grumbled.

They ate the rest of the food that they had for breakfast, but it wasn't enough for anyone to feel satisfied, and Edmund's leg was paining him, so Joia boiled up the last of his tea that Seb had gotten from the apothecarist. She washed his leg carefully and slathered the salve on the wound before wrapping it again.

After eating the remainder of yesterday's stew, Grian and Seb decided to go into Tillmere for more food and provisions, while Hakon decided to explore some of the forest around the castle. Joia got out some extra blankets from the back of Edmund's wagon and tried to make Edmund comfortable in the castle's single chair. Once he was settled with his lute and wood polish in hand, Kloma and Sidonia took Joia on a tour of the castle.

Joia learned where all the sleeping quarters had once been, as well as all the various workrooms. From a window, Kloma explained where the smithies had worked and where the stables used to be. While the castle had not aged with the centuries, the forest around it had grown big and wild. Things that used to be seen through the castle windows were now hidden from sight by the dense forest. Joia tried to imagine what it must have been like living in the castle when Athelstan was teaching his apprentices their trades.

Seb and Grian soon returned at midday with food. The three women worked together, talking as they prepared the meal, and Joia was happier than she had been in a long time. She still missed her mother and sister very much but being with Sidonia and Kloma was just as much fun, even more, in some way. They treated Joia as an equal, not as a daughter or little sister. Hakon returned just as the meal was being served. He had found a pond with a small stream and had managed to catch some fish. These were cleaned and set in the coals to cook.

More food was ready to eat in the early afternoon and everyone ate their fill.

"What was it like, living here?" Joia asked as they ate.

The five Patrons all looked at each other and laughed, even Seb.

"It was a good life," Grian said. "We were like one big family with arguments and misunderstandings, but most of the time, it was a lot of fun. We worked on our trades during the day. Sometimes we worked with others, and sometimes we worked alone. Seb preferred to work alone. But there were many times when groups of us would set up in this very hall or out in the courtyard, in the summer. I would dip candles, Kloma would card wool, Edmund would sand down wood for an instrument, Brynmor would shape his clay, Algar would fletch arrows, and we would just talk, sing, or tell stories. It was a good life together."

"Who are some of the other Patrons?" Joia asked.

"Well, there's Piers, he's the stone mason," Grian said. "And of course, there's Thek, and Ferran, the Baker. Wealcan's the Cobbler. Who else?" he sat back, thinking.

"Meical, is a shipwright," Seb said. "We don't see much of him. Even when we were learning together. He would travel to the lands with the seas and come back to the castle occasionally. Zand is the stained-glass worker and Falk is the glassmaker."

"Don't forget Garrick the Cooper," Sidonia added.

"I didn't realize there were so many," Joia said.

"If there is a trade that has a trade guild, there is a Patron," Edmund said. "But there are some crafts that have developed into trades that don't have a Patron. Farmers, tanners, and wheelwrights, for example."

"What does that mean for them?" Joia asked.

"It means that they are working on their own without the blessings and help of Patrons," Edmund answered.

"Not that we've been much help to ours," Grian said sadly.

Kloma reached out to him. "But we're going to change that."

After eating, Joia took the dishes to the large bowl that she used for cleaning. She started to wash the dishes, humming happily to herself, when they heard the sounds of horses approaching.

"I wonder who that could be," Kloma said.

"Perhaps more Patrons have come to help," Joia said.

Everyone except Edmund and Sidonia went out to greet the newcomers, but Joia stopped short when she saw who it was.

"It's Scrios," Joia whispered in fear to Hakon.

"Who are the others?" he whispered back.

"Ciar, Aren, and Wodwin," she answered.

Seb stepped up beside Joia. "You are not welcome here, Uncreator," he announced as they came to a halt just in front of the castle's open doors.

"And yet, here I am," Scrios said. He remained on his horse and looked at the others.

Ciar, Wodwin, and Aren looked in surprise at the three Patrons who stood with Joia.

"What?" Scrios said in mock surprise, "The entertainer is not here? He somehow managed to escape. I was shocked to think that this girl had been intelligent enough to sneak in and break him out."

His insult stabbed at her, but she knew he was right. She wasn't clever enough to have gotten Edmund out of the dungeon. She swallowed hard, trying not to let the hurt or fear fill her voice.

"And yet, here *I* am," Edmund said from the castle door. Sidonia stood next to him, supporting him.

Scrios sneered at Edmund. "When I found you were missing, I guessed you would come here. I sent for these three loyal men to come with me and show me the way to Athelstan's castle."

"And do you still stand by Scrios?" Joia asked the three newly arrived Patrons.

"Of course, they do," Scrios answered for them. "They know what they stand to lose if they go against me."

"Ciar," Joia looked to the blacksmith, "do you really think Scrios has the smithies' best interest in mind?"

"He allows us to stay in the castle and work."

"You have more smithies than the few in the castle," she said. "And if I remember correctly, he ordered you to make your work plain, ordinary, and nothing more than functional."

"He did," Ciar said before quickly adding, "but there is nothing wrong with simplicity."

"I agree," Joia said. "Sometimes simplicity is beautiful, but what about those times you feel like making your work ornate and he has forbidden you? Who is he to tell you, Ciar, Patron of Blacksmiths, how to work your trade?"

"I am the Trade Minister to the King! All who work the trades must do as I bid them." Scrios slid off his horse.

"Why do you not let Ciar speak for himself?" Joia asked. "Are you afraid you do not have his complete support?" Joia could sense the Patrons gathering behind her. "Neither you nor the king has the right to tell the Patrons how to work their trade."

"How dare you speak against your King!" Scrios spat. "You should be arrested for treason!" Joia took a step back in surprise.

"There is no one here to do your bidding," Grian said.

"Ciar, Aren, take the girl!" Scrios yelled.

Joia braced herself, and she felt Seb and Hakon move closer to her, but neither Ciar, Wodwin, or Aren moved.

"Ciar, Aren, Wodwin," Joia pleaded, "You are Patrons. You are masters of your craft and creators of the finest work your trade can produce. You cannot let this man tell you what to do. You cannot let him dim your Light or control your creativity."

"Oh, and you can?" Ciar asked.

"I would never tell you how to work your trade," she said. "I would never hold you back from creating your heart's desire."

Scrios laughed. "Feeling important, aren't you? I'll fix that soon enough." He walked closer to Joia, and she could feel the cold radiating from him. He turned to look at Hakon. "I have the ability to see the Light of the Guild. I see it on everyone here, except for you, boy. Who are you to think yourself worthy of being among these Patrons?"

Hakon stood tall next to Joia. "I am Hakon, son of Arik. I am a thatcher."

"Oh, a thatcher, are you?" Scrios said. He looked around the courtyard. "I knew your Patron long ago. Thek started out decent enough. He showed me his trade. I learned it and followed it, but always, the work I did could not keep out water. When I next saw him, I told him that his ways were flawed. He just laughed and said he knew. He knew his ways didn't work, but he taught them to me anyway."

"He was still learning," Grian said. "It was before he came to Athelstan's to learn better ways."

"It does not hide the fact that he taught me incorrectly," Scrios said.

"Your problem," Grian said, "was that you weren't willing to learn from mistakes. You blamed everyone else for your failure. So rather than learn, you burned his supply of straw and the house he had just completed the roof for."

Joia gasped, but Scrios turned back to Hakon and pointed a pudgy finger at him. "You stand in the house of Athelstan and the presence of eight Patrons and what have they done for you?"

"Much. They have welcomed me into their homes and shared meals with me," Hakon said.

"Only because you are familiar with the girl. You are not worthy of them without her by your side." Scrios stood his full height in front of Hakon, and while Hakon was taller, Scrios's words made him seem so much bigger.

"I might just be a simple thatcher," Hakon said. "But I have been loyal to my Patron and by doing so I am loyal to Athelstan, which gives me every right to stand here in his castle."

Scrios's cruel laugh filled the courtyard. "And have you been blessed by your Patron? Have you received his gifts? Of course not. You are nothing."

"That is not true!" Hakon shouted at the same time as Seb yelled, "Enough Scrios!"

Hakon took a step closer to Scrios and spoke in a calm voice. "I have not yet had the honor of meeting my Patron. But I have seen the gifts of the weaver, the chandler, and the map maker."

"You have seen them? How touching," Scrios sneered.

"I have also received a gift from one of them. Even though I am not his tradesman, I have received a candle of everlasting light from Grian the Chandler." Hakon pulled out his candle from his pocket and held it out to show Scrios.

Scrios laughed, "A candle? A plain white candle? That is all you have received?" He snatched the candle from Hakon's grasp and tried to break it, but the candle did not break, so instead, Scrios tossed it into the woods. "Leave us now, boy! You should not be here! I will make sure that the thatchers are the first trade to be completely dissolved under my rule as minister. Go!"

Scrios advanced on Hakon. Hakon took a step back and squeezed Joia's hand. Then, he let go and went back into the castle.

"Hakon, no!" Joia shouted, but he did not turn around. What was he doing? He left her. He promised her that he wouldn't leave her. Joia's heart sank. She didn't care about the Patrons and the Light anymore. Not if it cost her Hakon.

Seb and Edmund came and stood on either side of Joia, and she felt their support.

"It's going to be all right, Joia," Edmund spoke quietly.

"He left," she said, her quiet voice betrayed her hurt.

"Don't give up on him," Edmund said. "He would never leave you."

Scrios came towards them a few steps. "Well, well, Edmund," Scrios laughed, "You're looking a little worse for the wear."

Edmund placed his hand on Joia's shoulder for support. "At least I stand on this side of the line."

Scrios looked hard at Edmund leaning on Joia's shoulder. A cruel smile spread across his face. "It doesn't look like you are standing too well at that, either," he laughed. "But, it doesn't matter where you stand. My defeat over you has nothing to do with your imprisonment. I know you, Edmund. You will always oppose me. I cannot directly strike you." He began to pace as he spoke. "But I believe you recently met up with a troop of your own tradesmen just outside the King's castle. Am I right?"

Edmund didn't move.

"I know I am. I gave the orders for them to leave. Were they upset with you, Edmund? Were they upset because they were not permitted into the castle boundaries? Tell me, Patron," Scrios snarled and stopped his pacing in front of Edmund, "have you felt their dedication to you since that day?"

Joia felt Edmund's grip on her shoulder tighten, but he remained silent.

"And you two," he moved to where Kloma and Sidonia stood, "Have you noticed a change in your tradesmen? I am sure that fewer are dedicating their days to you since I kicked them out of the king's castle." He stepped forward and it seemed as if the darkness around him was growing. "You have felt yourself growing weaker, haven't you? Your people no longer want their Patrons and why should they? You were not there for them when I kicked them out. They were forced to leave the castle. Did you think they left quietly and happily with the intention of simply moving to a new location to set up shop? No! They cursed you for not helping them. They have shared with others their troubles. They are just spreading the word that you don't look out for your tradesmen and those people will wonder if their Patrons even care. The stories will spread, and you will find yourselves weaker and weaker until you waste away. And when the Patron goes, so does their trade."

"No," Kloma softly said. "They still dedicate their days to me. I still bless them."

"Then they say their dedications out of habit, not because they believe in you anymore," Scrios sneered. "You weren't there to help them when they needed it most and they know it." Scrios turned to face Seb. "Map maker. What a stupid trade. Maps are not needed. Most of the people in this wretched kingdom do not know how to read, much less ever leave their own villages and if by some miracle they ever do go on a journey, they simply follow the road. They have no need of maps. Thankfully, I was there to help the kings learn centuries ago how useless your maps are. Your trade is almost gone. Don't you feel it?"

"You were the one who had me expelled from the castle all those years ago?" Seb asked.

Scrios laughed. "It was wonderful."

Seb gave Scrios a smug expression and Joia knew that Seb would not show any weakness in front of Scrios, but she knew it had to have hurt Seb to discover what had happened.

"Scrios, this is wrong!" Wodwin came up to him.

Scrios spun around to face the carpenter. "It's too late. Your tradesmen have watched you follow my bidding. If you were to try and go back on me now, what do you think would happen? All three of you," he pointed to Ciar, Aren, and Wodwin. "You have done what I have told you to do. To go back now would show your tradesmen that you are weak and fickle in your loyalty and in your own workmanship. Nothing can be done for you. If you wish to retain the respect you have from your tradesmen, you will continue to do your work as I tell you."

"You care nothing for our trades!" Aren shouted.

"Oh, no, Aren. I care a great deal about your trades." Scrios smiled, baring his teeth, "I am the Trade Minister and I care to see all your trades destroyed."

Ciar, Aren, and Wodwin turned to look at each other and then walked as one to Joia and stood beside her. The eight Patrons formed a line and faced Scrios.

"You do not intimidate me," Scrios laughed. "I have already won against you all. The map makers, the spinners, the weavers, the entertainers, the smithies, and the carpenters are already under my influence. They have lost the respect for their Patrons." He laughed cruelly. "This is quite fascinating. I am watching your Light growing dimmer as you realize how right I am. I will enjoy watching it dim to nothing."

He paced in front of the line of Patrons, watching them and smiling. Once again, Joia noticed the darkness that surrounded him shimmered. She looked at each of the Patrons, their faces stricken with pain.

His darkness was growing while their Light dimmed. It was paining them, and their pain hurt her. Her head felt fuzzy again, the way it had last time she had been so near to him. The air felt constricting, and it was hard to breathe.

Scrios grinned, baring his teeth. "This is really quite fascinating; watching your Light dim. And did you know, Joia, that as the Patron's Light dims, so does yours. You feel it too, don't you? The trades are failing, and you cannot stop it. Your Light will fade, and you will all cease to be!"

Joia felt herself growing weaker. Her knees began to shake. She felt Edmund's grip on her shoulder lessen. His face was white, and he seemed ready to collapse. She had to do something; anything to save Edmund. She felt the tightness around her throat, even though he was not choking her.

"No!" Joia gasped. "You speak only words! You have not reached every spinner, every weaver, or every entertainer. There are many who are still loyal to their Patrons!" She thought of the Earthenhorn weaver, Ellota, and her apprentice Sara. They were very loyal. She thought of her father and brother. They were still loyal to Farran. "The tradesmen in my village are still loyal to their Patrons."

"And where are they?" Scrios asked. "I see no one here to prove their loyalty. The only tradesman you had with you, the thatcher, has abandoned you."

More than anything else Scrios had said, this hit Joia the hardest. He had spoken her greatest fear out loud. At her side, she felt Edmund starting to fall, and she grabbed his arm, trying to soften his fall, but his weight pulled her down. She saw his leg was bleeding badly.

She looked back at Scrios, who was grinning with delight at Edmund's fall. The dark shimmering air around Scrios was growing larger and darker. The shimmer in the air he caused when he moved seemed to grow stronger, as if he was taking the very Light out of them and turning it into his darkness.

"Joia," Edmund gasped. "Don't give in."

"I won't, but what do I do?" she asked.

Scrios raised his hands over his head in triumph and he looked to the sky, "I win, Athelstan! Do you hear me? I win!"

Joia felt sick. How did she stop this? Everyone had been right all along. She was not clever or talented. She could think of nothing to do.

The air around Scrios shimmered and darkened in the light of the setting sun. The sky turned a bright orange that might have been beautiful if Scrios hadn't been there, bent on destroying the Patrons. But then Joia noticed that the shimmering air around Scrios was also turning a deep shade of dark orange. Joia watched it in horror and fascination for several moments and then realized that while it was darker than the rest of the light around him, the shimmering air was still orange. It still had color and light about it.

Scrios might be dampening them, but as she looked to the other Patrons, she recognized that they still had their Light, and so did she.

Joia stood up, feeling some strength return to her with the realization. He had not won, and he never could. Creation was stronger than uncreation. Light was stronger than dark.

"You're wrong, Scrios," Joia said, stepping forward. "You can never win. Dark cannot cancel out the Light. You can dim the light, but light is always stronger. Light always chases away the darkness, and we still have our Light."

"At the end of the day," Scrios growled pointing at the darkening sky overhead, "the sun sets, and darkness takes over. Your Light will set too, and I will take over."

"Even in the dark of night, the darkness can be pieced and driven away by the light of a candle. But when there is light, there is nothing dark that can chase away light," Joia cried out as more and more understanding of the Light grew within in her. "I am a Light that will never set, and you cannot take it away from me."

Scrios lunged forward and caught Joia's arm in a painful grip. Her arm burned at his touch and the darkness that surrounded him crept onto her, spreading down her arm to her fingers.

Joia cried out in surprise and then in pain. "No!" she cried out and tried to pull her arm from his grip.

Next to her, Seb grabbed at Scrios to pull him away from Joia, but Scrios grabbed at Seb with his other hand. Seb cried out in pain and Joia watched him fall, his Light growing weaker.

She could not let this take her or Seb. She closed her eyes and tried to recall Edmund's music. She thought of Hakon on Grian's roof, repairing the bundles of straw. She thought of all the weavers and spinners she had known and of Seb, drawing the map. She thought of Grian and his candle that never went out. It would always burn with light.

With her free hand, she reached into her apron's pocket and found her candle. She held it up and it burst into flame of its own accord. The sudden light surprised Scrios and he let go. Suddenly, Joia felt like she could breathe again. It was like when Edmund had burst into Ciar's workshop. He had brought with him fresh air and hope. Scrios spell had been broken and she felt that way again now.

"This light will never go out," Joia announced. Her hands were shaking, and her arm burned with pain. She thought of Seb. Show no weakness.

Edmund stood, hopping as he did. "You can do nothing to us. You speak only words."

"Words are powerful," Scrios sneered. "You know that better than anyone, Storyteller."

"Yes, they are," Edmund said. "And I have the words for my tradesmen. I have the words to bless them and comfort them."

"So why didn't you bless or comfort them when I kicked them out?" Scrios sneered.

"I did bless them," Edmund replied. "They were protected from you. They may not have gotten to perform in Yondalla, but they were kept safe. I directed them to another place to go and perform. They had more success than they ever had in the castle."

Joia turned to Edmund. He never talked about these things. All this time, traveling with him and she had never asked what it meant for him to bless his tradesmen when they dedicated their days to him."

"Impossible!" Scrios cried out. "I kicked them out of the castle."

"But I blessed them, and they found better success elsewhere. I have not given up on them and they do not give up on me," Edmund said.

For the first time, Scrios looked nervous. "What about you, Spinner!" He turned to Kloma and Sidonia, who were standing together, leaning against each other for support, but standing tall. Scrios advanced on them both. "Your people were kicked out of their homes."

Kloma nodded. "They were, and it grieved me to feel their dedications when you did that. But I blessed them because they still dedicated their work to me. Those who you kicked out found places to go and work to do."

Sidonia let out a mirthless chuckle. "You and your king will have a hard time finding a spinner, weaver, or tailor who will be willing to make clothes for the king."

Joia took a deep breath. This was the moment. Scrios's spell had been broken and the words of Edmund, Kloma, and Sidonia were cracking Scrios's confidence. It was now or never.

"Scrios!" she cried. He spun around to face her and for a moment, the burning pain in her arm and neck flared, even though he no longer touched her. "Your uncreation stops now. You are banished from this land!"

Scrios was momentarily stunned at Joia's order, but he did not move. He threw his head back and laughed maliciously. "It is only a matter of time, child. You put up a brave front, but I see the fear in you. The Light of Athelstan will be extinguished."

"No, it won't!"

Joia turned in amazement to see Hakon walking from inside the castle, followed by ten people, who looked like they might have come from the nearby village. Joia's heart jumped.

Hakon walked forward and stood next to Joia. In his hands, he held a silver goblet of water. "I have with me ten tradesmen," he said. The tradesmen walked forward and stood in between each of the Patrons. The line they formed in front of Scrios doubled in size. "Look on us. We tradesmen are loyal to our Patrons. We may only be eleven, but as long as we eleven are loyal, you cannot win. You will never win!" He turned and traded with Joia the candle for the silver cup. She took it but was confused about what it was or what Hakon wanted her to do with it.

The line that they formed, moved into a circle around Scrios, who seemed to shrink before them. He spun around, looking at those who circled around him.

"What is this?" she whispered to Hakon, looking at the silver goblet of water.

He smiled. "Touch the water."

Joia did and the water turned a golden color. From the goblet in her hand, the golden figure of Athelstan rose out of the water. His light cast a warm glow around the darkening courtyard.

Scrios looked at the ghostly Athelstan in fear. "Athelstan!" he cried.

Athelstan frowned. "Scrios. What are you doing here? You were banished from this land."

"You think that your ghost will scare me away?" Scrios said to Joia. "It does not." His voice was shaking in uncertainty. "You are not really here. You can do nothing to me!"

"Nothing?" he laughed, and it was like music, filling Joia's heart. "I am doing something. My Patrons and their tradesmen see me here. My descendant's Light glows pure and strong while your darkness decreases, so tell me again that I am doing nothing to you." Athelstan's voice was calm but powerful.

"Look at them, Scrios," Hakon said. He turned to look at Joia. "You're glowing," he gasped. "This is the Light of the Guild?"

"It is, Hakon," Edmund said in his deep, gentle voice.

"I see it too," spoke up several of the other tradesmen.

Joia turned in surprise to Hakon. He was staring at her and smiling. "Your Light is very beautiful."

Scrios spun around, "Impossible!"

Joia looked at the people who circled Scrios. The Light of the Patrons shown brighter than ever and the light from Athelstan was almost blinding.

"Scrios, the Uncreator, hear me. I am Joia, daughter of Thomas the Baker, Heir to Athelstan, and bearer of his Light. You are banished from all the lands where the trades are established. You will have no influence over us ever again."

Scrios shrunk down when Joia announced his banishment. He spun in the circle and saw all the Patrons and tradesmen closing in on him.

"Go Scrios, or you will find yourself in a worse position than a simple banishment," Seb said.

They were all within an arm's reach of Scrios, who let out a roar of anger. He broke through their circle and ran to his horse. "One day, you will pay for this!" He climbed up and rode off.

"I'm going to follow him and make sure he leaves," Aren said and went to his horse.

"I'll go with you," one of the tradesmen said. He took another horse and he and Aren left the castle.

Joia felt exhausted. She looked to Edmund. His face was white and contorted in pain. He was looking dangerously close to falling into unconsciousness. "Edmund! Someone, quickly, help Edmund back inside." Two tradesmen took Edmund by the arms and helped him to hobble into the castle. The others followed them in, except for Seb.

He came to Joia and knelt before her. "Thank you, Athelstan. Thank you, Joia."

Joia looked at the goblet she was holding. Athelstan's form still rose above it. He had watched Scrios leave. He smiled down at Seb and then Joia. "Well done," he said and then fell back into the silver goblet.

Joia heard Hakon let out a sigh of relief. "It's over," he said.

Seb stood. "I'm going to check on Edmund."

Joia and Hakon were left alone in the dark courtyard with her holding the goblet and Hakon still holding her EverBurn candle. Its small light was nothing compared to the bright light that had filled the courtyard just moments before, but it was still bright, warm, and comforting.

"I'm so sorry, Hakon," she said.

"Whatever for?"

She couldn't bear to look at him. "For doubting you. I thought you left me; abandoned me to Scrios."

Hakon reached out and stroked her hair. "Do you really think that after all we've been through, I would let one man insult me enough to want to leave you? Never, Joia. I knew that we needed more help, so I went to Tillmere. But I couldn't tell you my plan and risk Scrios hearing it." He put a hand to her face and cupped her cheek. "Joia, I could never leave you. I love you."

Joia cried tears of relief and joy. "I love you, too," she laughed and pulled him into a hug. "You saved us, Hakon. You saved us all. Thank you."

She leaned over the burning candle, still in Hakon's grasp, and blew it out. She took it from him and stuck it back into the pocket of her dress.

"I should be the one who is apologizing to you," he said quietly. "It's not that I doubted your Light, but you know how much I've struggled to understand and accept it. I've seen it now, and I can never question it again."

"You truly saw it?" she asked.

"I did. I wish I still could, but as soon as Scrios broke through the circle, my ability to see the Light was broken too. But I saw it and you were beautiful." Hakon leaned down and gave Joia a gentle kiss. "Come on," he said. "Let's go in and check on the others."

CHAPTER TWENTY-FIVE

Athelstan and the Patrons

Joia watched as Hakon turned to go back into the castle, but Joia didn't move. She felt disconnected from everything else going on. What had just happened? Scrios had come here and filled her and the others with such despair. Then Hakon had come, with the tradesmen and Athelstan. It had driven away the darkness. How had she known to pull out her candle? How had it lit on its own? How had she known the words to say to drive Scrios away? Was she truly a descendant of Athelstan?

It felt like a dream now, even though it had only been minutes before.

A hand on her shoulder made her jump.

"Sorry," Hakon said, reaching out to steady her hands, who still held the silver goblet. "Joia, come inside."

"What just happened?" she asked, turning to him.

"You won," he smiled.

"Just like that? It's over?" she asked.

Hakon laughed as one of the tradesmen came out from the castle and approached them. "Your man in there is badly hurt and they've asked me to go for a healer."

"Do you have one in Tillmere?" Hakon asked.

"Aye," the man nodded. "But getting him here after dark won't be easy."

"Please try," Joia said, knowing it was Edmund who needed the help. "Hakon, maybe you can go with him?"

Hakon nodded. "We'll bring him back." He kissed her cheek and the two went for their horses.

Joia watched them leave and then let out a long breath that she had been holding. She needed to get in and see Edmund. The burning pain in her arm finally released her from her disconnected confusion. She could see the burn on her arm where Scrios had grabbed her, even in the moonlight.

She finally turned to go back to the castle. Through the main door, she could see a blazing fire in the hearth and people gathered around someone on the floor.

Joia hurried to Edmund and knelt. Seb had unwrapped his leg and it was bleeding badly. Without thinking, Joia took the silver goblet, held it over Edmund's leg, and poured a few drops of the water onto the bleeding gash.

The bleeding stopped immediately, and Edmund gasped in relief. "Joia," he said, his breath harsh. "What did you do?"

"It wasn't me," she said. "It was Athelstan." She stood again and went down the halls until she came to the staircase that led down towards Athelstan's room. Inside, she poured the remaining water from the goblet back into the pool.

The water turned a golden color for several moments and then faded into black. She set the silver goblet back on the table and left the room, closing the heavy wooden door behind her.

As she entered the kitchen, Sidonia approached her and pulled her into a tight hug. "You are my sister in the Light and I am so proud of you," she said.

Joia was surprised by these words, especially coming from a woman that Joia respected so much. "I didn't do much, honestly," Joia whispered.

"Surely you must be joking with me," Sidonia pulled away. "You were everything tonight."

"It was Hakon and the tradesmen and Athelstan and everyone else," Joia said. "I spoke only words, but without everyone else there, those words would have meant nothing."

"No, my sweet friend," Sidonia smiled. "What you did was everything."

Kloma approached Joia and hugged her too. "You have saved us all."

Joia started to protest again, but Sidonia stopped her. "She certainly did."

Instead, all Joia could do was nod in thanks. She still did not feel like anything had truly been done on her part, but she was too tired to try and point this out to the women before her.

Kloma was grinning. "Sidonia and I have been invited to stay in the village tonight with the two women who are the Tillmere spinner and weaver."

"I'm sure that will be more comfortable for you than the stone floor of the castle," Joia acknowledged.

"Indeed it will," Kloma laughed. "Which means the blankets and bedrolls we were using are yours to use tonight."

Joia's hips were already aching at the mere thought of sleeping on the floor again, so knowing she would have another layer or two of soft things under her was welcome.

"We are also going to dish up the rest of the food for you," Sidonia said, "and make sure that you all have something to eat. We'll bring more food when we return from Tillmere in the morning."

Grian approached them from the great hall. "Joia, Edmund is asking for you."

Joia hurried to Edmund. He was sitting with his leg stretched out in front of him. She knelt before him. "Edmund, your poor leg."

"Is doing much better than earlier. What did you do?" he asked.

"I poured a few drops of Athelstan's water onto you," she said.

"What if you poured Athelstan on me?" he asked. "We might have lost him."

Joia shook her head. "We didn't. He's safely in the pool," she said. "When I poured the rest of the water back in, I could tell."

"Then I will trust you on that, but how did you know that the water would help me?" he asked, looking down at his wounded leg.

"I just did," she shrugged. "I didn't even think about it. It was just the right thing to do." She looked into his blue eyes, which were rimmed with red from his pain, but they were also gentle. "I'm just sorry that you are injured at all."

"It's not your fault, Joia. Besides, if you hadn't just defeated Scrios, we would all be in a lot worse shape right now and a cut on the leg," he said.

She shook her head. "But Edmund, I didn't—" she didn't get to finish when Hakon and another man walked into the castle. The man went right to Edmund and squatted down to look at his leg.

Joia moved to stand with Hakon. "Thank you for getting the healer," she said.

"He's not in such bad shape as I expected," Hakon said.

They moved away to give the healer the space he needed. Sidonia and Kloma approached with two other women and the rest of the tradesmen from the village.

"Joia," Sidonia said, "I would like you to meet Frida, the weaver of Tillmere, and Agatha, the spinner of Tillmere."

The three women curtsied to each other. "It's a pleasure to meet you both," Joia said. "Thank you for coming to our aid tonight."

Frida smiled. "When that young man came in saying the Patrons needed our help, I had to go. My Patron has always been good to me."

"And she has always been loyal to me," Sidonia said.

"It is the same with Agatha," Kloma said.

The two women smiled shyly at their Patrons. "Never would I have guessed I would get to meet my Patron," Agatha said. "She has promised to work with me tomorrow and I am very honored."

"I'm sure they will enjoy your company and working their craft with you," Joia said.

"We will return in the morning," Sidonia promised. The four women left with the rest of the villagers who were returning to their homes.

With all the villagers gone, except for the healer, the castle seemed empty. Ciar and Seb stayed with Edmund while the healer worked on him, and then they carried him to his wagon afterward so he could sleep somewhere more comfortable than the stone floor. Joia took him some stew.

He was sitting in his wagon, panting, and looking very pained, but his leg was freshly bound and showed no signs of bleeding.

"Are you comfortable?" she asked him.

"As much as I can be with this leg," he said. He yawned and rubbed at his side, wincing a bit as he did.

"What's wrong? Did you break some ribs when you were beaten?"

He shook his head. "Surprisingly, I don't think I broke anything. They are bruised a bit," he answered. "I'm going to be just fine." He sipped at the stew.

"Seb said he would stay close," Joia told him.

Edmund nodded. "He will be sleeping under the wagon in the tent, but between the healing water you put on my leg and the ministrations of the healer, I will heal."

"Did you get some willow bark tea?" she asked.

He nodded and drank more of the stew. "I did, and I'm feeling much better."

Joia tried to stifle the yawn that came out. She was tired and it felt so late.

"You should get some sleep," he said.

Joia thought of the stone floor bed that awaited her. Her joints ached, but she thought about how Edmund had endured much worse. She might be uncomfortable, but no one was trying to kill her in her sleep. She had nothing to complain about. "I will, as soon as I make sure everyone else is settled."

"Make sure you get rest, too. We all need you, Joia." He finished the stew and handed the bowl back to her. "I feel much better now," he sighed with a smile.

"Can I get you anything else?" she asked.

He smiled at her and yawned again. "I'm all right. Just tired. Tomorrow will be better."

"Then I will leave you and let you sleep," she said.

"Wait, Joia," Edmund took her by the hand. "You just defeated Scrios."

She shook her head. "People keep saying that, but it wasn't me. It was Hakon. He brought the patrons and Athelstan. When I tried to banish Scrios, he just laughed at me."

"None of this could have happened without you," Edmund said.

"It doesn't seem real. He was here and now he's not. It's like it never happened," she said.

"It was real, and it did happen, but I think we all need some sleep and some time to ponder what happened here tonight," Edmund said. "When the morning comes, we can talk about it more."

Joia could only nod. "Night Edmund." He called out goodnight to her as well and she left him to sleep. As she was walking back, she went to the courtyard and tried to recreate everything that had just happened in her mind. She had been here, and Scrios there. She pulled out her EverBurn candle. It had just burst into flame on its own. She held it out now, but it didn't relight. She recalled how Scrios had taken Hakon's candle and tried to break it, but he had been unable to do so. He had thrown it.

She turned to look in the direction of where the candle might have landed and she saw the gentle golden glow of an item made by a Patron, lying in the bracken along the courtyard wall. She went over and picked up the candle. Thank goodness it had the Light or they might never have found it. She put it into her apron pocket and as she headed to the castle, Seb approached her.

"Is Edmund in his wagon?" he asked.

"Yes. He said you'll be sleeping in the tent under the wagon in case he needs anything?" she asked.

"Yes." He looked over her shoulder toward the wagon, and then back to her. "You look exhausted. I had wanted to talk to you about everything that happened tonight, but I think that conversation would be better to have in the morning," he said.

They said goodnight and Seb left to go to his tent. In the great hall, Ciar, Wodwin, Grian, and Hakon were sitting together around the hearth. She went to Hakon and held out his candle.

"I was going to go searching for it in the morning," Hakon said. "How did you find it in the dark?" She shrugged and started to tell him, but Hakon held up his hand and stopped her. "No, wait," he said. "I already know the answer. You see its Light."

"Yes," she said, and sat down on the ground next to Hakon. "Grian, may I ask you a question?"

"Of course, you can," he said, sitting close to her.

She reached into her pocket and pulled out her Everburn candle. Other than the blackened wick, there was no evidence that her candle had ever been used. It was as perfect as the day Grian had given it to her.

"Well, earlier, when I was confronting Scrios, he grabbed my arm and it felt like it was burning. I grabbed my candle and it just lit. On its own. Was it because of something Scrios did?"

"I saw that happen," he said, taking the candle from her and looking closely at it before giving it back to her. "But I don't think it was Scrios's doing. It was very curious, though. I've never seen any candle just burst into flame like that."

"Why do you think it happened? How did it happen?"

Grian shrugged. "You have the Light, Joia."

"That's it?"

He chuckled. "I told you, I've never seen that happen before, so I don't know. But you have the Light, and at that moment, you needed a true physical light. Your own Light was probably all it took to set the candle aflame."

"So, I can light any candle now just by thinking about it?" she asked.

His laugh echoed in the hall, disturbing some night birds. They cried out as they flew away. "Maybe," he said, "but I doubt it. I think it only happened because you needed that Light at that instant in time, but I just don't know. You are the first to be born with this Light. You might have some power over it that the rest of us do not. I wouldn't give Scrios the credit for lighting your candle, though. You lit it, through the Light."

"And because the candle was made by a Patron," Wodwin added.

"Very possibly," Grian said. "I am proud of you, though. No one else could have done what you did tonight."

"What, tell Scrios to go away?" she asked, giving a self-deprecating laugh.

"Everything. For a while, he filled my heart with such despair that I never thought I could be happy again or make another candle. His darkness filled me, and I was scared, but then you stood up with your candle and banished him."

"It wasn't me," Joia nearly yelled. "I did nothing. Why doesn't anyone understand that? It was Hakon bringing me Athelstan and all those tradesmen. I didn't do anything," she said.

The others all started to protest at once. But Grian held up his hands.

"Do I need to go get Edmund to talk some sense into you?" Grian asked. He smiled kindly at her and leaned forward to her. "No one could have done what you did tonight. I am bound to one trade. So are Edmund, Sidonia, and the other Patrons. Hakon is bound to one trade and so are the other villagers that came here with him. But you are not. You are all of us together. You take everything that we are and focus it. You make the Light work to your will," Grian said, gently pressing his hands to the sides of her face. "No one else could have done that."

Suddenly, all the remaining Patrons surrounded her and wrapped their arms around her and each other. Joia felt the heat of their Light comforting her like a blanket. She still didn't feel worthy of all the attention, but she better understood the part she had played in their victory.

The next morning Joia felt a strange anxiousness. She couldn't figure out what was wrong, but she needed to be busy. She was surprised to see Aren had returned after following Scrios to make sure he was far from Athelstan's Castle.

"When did you get back?" she asked.

"During the night. Hakon greeted me and found me a place to sleep," Aren said.

Joia was surprised she had slept through this considering how poorly she had slept on the stone-hard ground, but she must have managed a few hours of deep sleep.

Aren bowed low to her. "I want to apologize to you for the way Ciar, Wodwin, and I treated you in Yondalla. It was not our finest moment, especially when we realized just what we had done. We scared you and hurt Edmund. We are not normally like that, and I hope you will allow me to try and make a better impression of myself on you."

Joia smiled. "I would like that."

"I am Aren, the Silversmith," he said, giving her a slight bow.

"Good to meet you, Aren. I'm Joia, daughter of Thomas the Baker. Thank you for all your help last night."

"From now on, I will serve you and Athelstan again."

Everyone shared what food was left from the night before, which wasn't much, but Joia was finding she didn't need much food. She supposed she had spent too much time with too little food in recent weeks. Edmund, Grian, and Seb were talking, Sidonia and Kloma had not yet returned from Tillmere, and Wodwin, Aren, Ciar, and Hakon had gone off into the forest to hunt for game. Joia hoped they could find some wild fowl and bring it back for supper.

Joia went to the stream in the back courtyard to do some washing. She had brought out the two largest bowls they had at the castle. One was filled with hot water and soaproot and she had Edmund's bandages soaking in there. The other bowl was half filled with hot water. She would do the washing in that bowl.

Her arm was still burning, and she sought to relieve some of the pain by dipping her arm into the cold stream. It stung horribly at first, but then the water felt good on her burn and the sting went away. The cold water made her shiver in the morning air, but she was thankful for the relief.

When her arm felt a little better, she sat on the ground in front of the washing bowl and started to scrub the clothes with soaproot and a rock. Her thoughts were deep in the previous day's events and no matter what she recalled, she didn't feel she deserved the praise she kept receiving.

When she finished washing each item, she rinsed them in the stream and then wrung them out as tightly as she could. She laid each clean item over the low stone wall to dry in the sunlight. She didn't notice Seb approaching until he stood next to her.

"Oh, Seb, you startled me," Joia said. She flicked water from her hands up at him.

"Sorry," he chuckled. "Are you feeling well? You've been quiet today." He sat down on the grass next to her.

"I'm well," she said. It was more or less true. "I just wanted to wash these things," Joia said. She scrubbed at the shirt and dunked it in the water.

"How's your arm?" Seb asked, pointing to the burn, which was shaped like a hand.

"Not as painful as yesterday," she said. "And the cool water of the stream is helping. What about you? I know he burned you as well."

Seb rolled up his sleeve to show her. It was only slightly red. "It's not bad. He didn't have a hold on me for very long." He stretched out his legs on the grass. "Now tell me what's wrong?"

"Nothing is wrong, really," Joia said. "It just feels strange that it is all over. For the past two months, I've been traveling with Edmund and Hakon. We've been on the road nearly daily, and I've spent all this time talking about and searching for the reason why I have the Light of the Guild and what I was supposed to do about it. Even yesterday morning, I still wasn't entirely sure what I was doing, but by last night, it was all over, and everyone keeps thanking me, which I don't deserve." She dunked the bandage she was washing back into the stream. "I'm having a hard time grasping that it's all over, I guess."

"You think that the only reason you have the Light was so you could ban Scrios?" Seb asked and Joia nodded. "No, Joia, I think you're wrong." He leaned forward and rested his elbows on his knees.

"What do you mean? There is nothing for me left to do. I did what was needed and it's over. Right?"

"Joia, as you reminded all of us yesterday, the trades were splintering. Yes, Scrios had a part to play in that, but it began years before Scrios stuck his big nose into the trade's business. The people don't know their Patrons, and the Patrons don't know their people, except for Edmund's entertainers and the blacksmiths of Yondalla. We have allowed ourselves to become isolated from everyone and everything. Being this way has not been beneficial to any of us or our work. But you, Joia, you have brought us together again. You have reminded us of our heritage as Patrons and the importance of friendship. That is your purpose, Joia."

"But it is still over," Joia said. "Scrios is gone."

Seb leaned forward, crossing his legs, and resting his elbow on his knees. "There are more than two dozen Patrons, but only eight of us were here last night. That means all the others don't know what has happened and they need to know. You need to find the others and help them to understand. Your job as the bearer of Athelstan's Light is not over. I believe it is just beginning."

"Really?" Joia asked.

"Really." Seb looked around for several quiet moments. "This forest has changed a lot since I was here last. I've forgotten how peaceful it is here. Quite a difference after a few centuries in Yondalla."

Joia smiled. "I don't know if I could live in a place like Yondalla. I like the villages, like Tillmere and where I grew up in Erthenhorn, but I don't think I could live in that great city."

"I hope you will visit me again there," Seb said, looking to her again.

"Of course," she smiled.

Seb rubbed his hands over his face for several moments. "I feel bad about the way I treated you. I was angry with Edmund, but I was angrier with myself. It was wrong of me to take my anger out on you."

Joia's heart swelled and her fondness for Seb grew more. "It's all forgiven, Seb. You've done so much to help me. You gave me my map, helped me to escape, and stood with me when I faced Scrios. I couldn't have done any of this without you."

He smiled and they sat together for a long time, enjoying the peace of the forest. Joia took up her washing again as she thought about what Seb had said.

It was a relief to be done with Scrios, but she was happy to think that her journey and purpose did not end yesterday.

"Do you think I should go out and find all the Patrons?"

"I believe so," he said. "They need to know about going out to work with their tradesmen. But I am not you and I am not Athelstan, so I cannot tell you what you are supposed to do."

"How do I go about finding every Patron? I don't even know their names," she asked.

"We can provide you with the names, but I believe you've got a map," he said, his face serious, but Joia saw the twinkle in his eyes.

She smiled at him. "Yes, but only shows me where I am. How do I find the others?"

Seb looked at her for several long moments. "When you left Yondalla to come here, how did you find the castle?"

"I used your map," she said.

"But did the map have the castle on it when you began your journey?" he asked.

She shook her head. "No. It had only Yondalla at first, and then as we left, it changed to the road, and I saw houses and inns as we came here."

"So, you just followed the road without consulting the map?" he asked.

"No. I referred to it continually. We stayed off the road most of the time, deeper in the woods so we wouldn't be spotted," she admitted. "I suppose it was silly to do that."

"Not at all," Seb said. "So how did you know where to go?"

"The Light," she smiled. "As long as we headed in the direction of the Light, I knew we would get there."

"Exactly," he grinned and thumped his fist in the grass. "The Light showed you."

Joia didn't understand. "But it only showed me how to get here. It didn't show me where any other Patrons are."

"Because at that time, you had no need to find the other Patrons, only find your way here. Joia, as a bearer of the Light, you do have some control of it. My map responds to your Light. If you want to find someone else with the Light, or you are going out on Athelstan's errand, the Light will work for you in the map and guide you."

"Grian said something similar when I asked him why my candle just burst into flame last night. He said it was because I have the Light and I needed it last night. Also, because it was Grian's special gift, like the map is yours," she said.

"He's probably right," Seb agreed.

"But, that's amazing. It is magical," she laughed.

"The Patrons and their gifts are magical to some degree. You bear the Light too, so you have that magic as well. But you're new to it. You'll learn more about it, as time goes on," Seb smiled. "Your journey with the Patrons and the Light is just beginning."

"This is," she stopped and thought about it. Everything that Seb was telling her was overwhelming. "It's a little scary, to be honest. Just a few months ago, I didn't even know that I had the Light, if the Patrons were real, or that I would ever have any kind of dealings with the Patrons. I just thought I would have a simple village life."

"Now that you've had a taste of life outside of your village, do you wish you had never experienced all that you have done?" Seb asked.

Joia shook her head. "No. I wouldn't trade it for the world. But am I to give up the life I grew up thinking I was going to live?"

Seb leaned back in the grass and looked up into the sky. "I don't know, but Hakon is a remarkable man. The two of you will work it out."

"I hope we will," she quietly sighed. Joia collected her washing and sewing. "I'm done here. I want to check on Edmund and see what can be done about a meal."

Seb picked up the bowls of used water and emptied them into the forest, then he carried the washing into the castle for her.

The healer had been there and gone by the time Joia came in. Edmund was looking better, much to Joia's relief, and the healer had left extra herbs and bandages as well as a salve for her burns.

"How did he know to bring it?" Joia asked when Edmund handed her the tin.

"When he was here last night, I told him about your burn," Edmund said and looked up to where Seb was still holding Joia's basket of washing. "You too, Seb."

Joia scooped some of the salve onto her fingers and gently rubbed it onto the burn. It stung and she inhaled sharply, but as soon as the initial sting was over, it felt cool and soothing. She sighed in relief. Edmund held out one of his clean bandages and gently wrapped it around her arm for her.

Sidonia and Kloma had also returned and were knitting together, talking happily as they did. Bundles of food were sitting near the hearth, and something was bubbling in the cauldron over the fire. The two Patrons told Joia about their morning with their tradesmen.

Joia listened with interest and wished she knew better how to spin or weave or do any kind of trade. She used some of the food items that the Patrons had brought back to the castle and started to mix a dough. She kneaded the dough and placed it into a corner of the hearth where a special hutch had been built into the hearth, for the purpose of baking bread.

Joia had never been good at baking bread. That had always been her father and brother's specialty, but she knew how to do it and so a small, lumpy loaf was produced for everyone to share with their meal. Hakon returned with two guinea fowls, much to Joia's delight. She plucked and prepared the meat, roasting it over the fire with the spit iron from the kitchen's hearth, until the skin was brown and perfectly crispy.

When all was ready, the Patrons were called to supper. The conversation was so different from the night before. Yesterday had been tense and full of uncertainty, but today, Scrios was gone, and the Patrons were happy. It was easy to imagine what dinners must have been like back when they had all lived here.

In the early twilight, and after supper was done, the eight Patrons, Hakon and Joia made their way down to Athelstan's room. The Patrons were silent as they entered and each went to the items they had made, touching them, and remembering. Edmund hobbled over to the lute he had left, leaning on his walking stick.

The last light of the day disappeared from the open roof, so Joia and Hakon lit the room's torches with their Everburn candles. Then, they all gathered, forming a circle around the pool of water and Joia ran her fingers lightly over its surface.

The water rippled and shimmered, and Athelstan's glowing form rose out of the water. The group bowed to him, and he smiled back at them all.

"My children, it is wonderful to see you all again. I wish it had not taken so long, but I am glad you have come back."

"We apologize, Athelstan," Wodwin said. "Our future visits will not be so long in between."

"I hope not. I want to thank you for the complete support you showed me in the face of the Uncreator." They smiled at him.

"I'm afraid I," Ciar started and stopped. He took a deep breath and Joia watched him struggle to find the words. Her heart went out to him. She had spent part of the day in his company and found him to be a very intelligent man. He shared stories with her about how he had first started learning about working hot metal to create things that were strong and useful. "I was a part of Scrios' uncreation. I was never against you or my purpose as a blacksmith, but I forgot what it truly meant to be a Patron. I allowed Scrios to lead me and cloud my judgment with his uncreation."

"Scrios was one of the least clever persons I ever knew," Athelstan said, "while being very clever at the same time. He knew how to talk to people and how to influence them, but he was not clever with his hands. He could not create in the way you can. And that inability to create made him bitter. He learned his talent was in his words and instead of using words for good, the way Edmund does, he used his words to hurt."

"I hope you will find it in your heart one day to forgive me," Ciar said. He turned to Edmund. "And I hope you will find it in your heart one day to forgive me for what I did to you."

Edmund bowed his head. "All is forgiven," Edmund said. "We are friends of old and I know you. But the tradesmen that you wronged do not understand your heart. You will need to show them your true, kind nature."

Ciar nodded. "I will do everything I can."

"Tell me," Athelstan said, looking around the room at the eight Patrons. "Did you learn anything from this experience?"

They were all quiet for a moment before Aren spoke up. "We're not enough by ourselves. We need our tradesmen and each other."

"That's right," Athelstan smiled. "You must return to your people. I didn't make you Patrons so you could hide away. Your tradesmen need you. Visit them, teach them, encourage them, and learn from them. They will make you strong and you will make them better."

They nodded in acceptance. Joia looked at each of them and her love for the Patrons grew. She looked forward to getting to know the smiths and Wodwin better. She wanted to know Kloma, Sidonia, and Grian better. She was fond of the grumpy Seb and adored Edmund. They were all dear to her because, in the end, they had all stood beside her.

Athelstan's clear voice rang through the room. "You are also better when you work with each other. Just because you are Patrons and masters of your trades, does not mean that you know everything there is to know. Work together and learn from each other."

"Yes, Athelstan," many of them said.

He turned to Hakon. "Young thatcher," he said, "you have shown me great loyalty and strength of character. It was very wise of you to go and get help from the village and it only proves the point that we are not enough alone. We need our tradesmen. We could not have been rid of Scrios without your actions. I also found it very clever and if I may say, surprising, the way you brought me to Joia out in the courtyard. The silver goblet you carried my water in was made by none other than Aren. It is a perfect piece of workmanship and nothing other than a creation from a Patron could have taken me away from this pool. Yes, indeed, Hakon, you are very clever, and I will, at this time, bestow upon you the trade status of Master Thatcher."

"Thank you, sir," Hakon bowed.

Joia's heart swelled with pride on Hakon's behalf. He deserved Athelstan's praise. He had been nothing but loyal and honorable in his trade. She took him by the hand, squeezing it.

Athelstan then turned to Joia. "Now Joia, we come to you. You realized last night who you are. You announced it to Scrios and all who stood with you."

"That I am your descendant?" Joia asked.

"Correct," Athelstan smiled. "In my youth, before I met the men and women who would become my tradesmen, I had a wife and a son. My son was talented in the ways of working with wood. He met a young woman from another village and saw the need that the village had for his talents. He stayed there. Our limited correspondence let me know he had several children, but after I started working with the trades, we lost track of each other. You are the descendant of my son, and so my heir. This castle is yours."

Joia gasped. Had she just heard him correctly? "Mine?"

"Yes, and I have a request of you."

"Yes sir?" Joia said, still shocked. This castle was hers?

"I want you to restore this castle and once again make it the home of the trades."

"I will sir, but that is…" she began.

"A huge task," Athelstan finished for her. "Yes, it will be. But you need not do it alone."

"Of course not," Wodwin said. "We will all help. And the first thing I'm going to do is build chairs and beds so that we have somewhere comfortable to sit and sleep."

Joia laughed and Grian groaned in agreement, rubbing at his back.

Athelstan nodded. "Good. That is what I wanted to hear. You are all to visit regularly. Joia will always welcome you. Continue to dedicate your work to me, Patrons, as you always have, but now I ask you to journey here, see Joia, and renew yourselves as Patrons."

"We will do as you ask, Athelstan," Edmund said.

"Good. Help spread the word to the others. I expect this from all the Patrons, not just the group assembled here."

"We will find the others and tell them," Grian promised.

"Excuse me, Athelstan?" Joia asked. He turned to her with a kind smile. "You have been most generous, giving me this castle and I thank you for it. But I was wondering, and please don't think of me as being ungrateful, but must I remain here always?" Joia asked. She wanted to go home and see her family.

"Of course not. You are not a prisoner in this castle. You are free to leave and free to live where you wish, but I want this castle to be restored; to be the home of the trades. A place the Patrons and indeed, any tradesman, may visit for rejuvenation and instruction."

"I understand, Athelstan. Thank you," Joia said, although she still felt daunted by everything that had just been told to her.

When Athelstan finished his instructions, he bid them all goodbye and returned to the pool. The ten people went back to the great hall and made ready their bed rolls. Joia and Hakon helped Edmund out to his wagon.

"May we sit and talk to you for a while?" Joia asked.

Edmund smiled and lit the lantern in his wagon. "I would like that. After all our time on the road, I've missed our evening conversations."

"So have I," Joia said and Hakon nodded.

They climbed onto the wagon to sit on the trunk, next to the bed. Hakon put an arm lovingly around Joia's shoulders, and she leaned into him. So many things were swirling about in her mind. She needed to talk it out and she valued the wisdom of Edmund.

"I can't believe everything that has happened in the last few days," Joia said, after several quiet moments.

"You've inherited a castle," Edmund chuckled. "Lady Joia of Athelstan's Castle."

"I know." She said, shaking her head in disbelief. "Athelstan said that I am his descendant through his son, which means that my father or mother is also of his line and my siblings as well. I have an older brother and sister. Wouldn't my brother David inherit the castle before me?"

"They don't have the Light," Edmund said. "You do."

"But I am the youngest, why did it skip my siblings and come to me?" Joia asked.

"Why did it skip your mother or father?" Edmund shrugged. "There's no telling. But your brother has his trade and the bakery he will inherit. And I don't know your sister well enough to say one way or another about her, but from what you have told me, do you think she would have come on this journey? Do you think she would have left her home and done everything that you have endured?" Edmund shook his head before Joia could answer. "The Light and Athelstan chose you and I believe it chose Hakon as well. Don't you remember that first morning, you were called by an unknown voice to follow Joia."

Hakon nodded. "I remember."

"There is no doubt in my mind that the Light was calling to you. Like Grian said when he made you your candle, this was as much your journey as it was Joia's."

"And I don't know that I could have supported Joia if she had returned from the journey without having experienced it all myself," Hakon said. "I would not have believed it if she had just told me she did all these things."

Joia nodded. "It has all been quite amazing. I still have a hard time believing everything that we've seen and done." Joia smiled and took Hakon's hand in hers. "But, Edmund, there's one other thing that I've been wondering about," Joia said.

He smiled. "And what is that?"

"You just spent many weeks of your time taking me up and down the countryside to collect three gifts from the Patrons. And while Sidonia's Life Tapestry has helped to guide me, Grian's candle has provided light in dark castle hallways, and Seb's map led me to Athelstan's castle when Hakon and I were alone, when it came down to it, I only had my candle with me when I confronted Scrios, and it was more an effect rather than a use of purpose. If we had just come to Athelstan's castle immediately instead of going to the Patrons, I might have accomplished the same thing. It was finding Athelstan in the pool that told me what I needed to do, not collect the gifts."

Edmund smiled gently but shook his head. "It wasn't Athelstan that told you what you needed to do. His power doesn't extend beyond these walls, and he doesn't know what is going on in the rest of the world. And you're right, it wasn't the gifts of the Patrons that you wielded in your confrontation with Scrios. It was what you learned about the trades and about yourself while collecting those gifts."

Joia thought back to everything she had done and all the people she had met. "I learned more about the Patrons and their gifts, and I learned about Scrios as the Trade Minister," she answered.

Hakon nodded. "You learned much more than that. We all did. I mean, you and I didn't think that Patrons were real and through our travels, we met eight of them. We learned that the separation of all the Patrons from each other wasn't good for them and that their separation from their tradesmen was worse. If you hadn't gone out and met all those Patrons before coming here, you never would have known any of those things."

"Yes, I guess that's true," Joia said, thinking back.

"Hakon is correct. I didn't see it at the time either, but looking back, I see how important our full journey was. Do you really think that the Joia who left Erthenhorn could have come right to Athelstan's castle and done everything you did? Could that Joia have accepted a room full of magical items? Could she have summoned Athelstan and not been scared? Could she have understood the troubles that the Patrons were going through?"

Joia shook her head. "No. I couldn't have done that."

Edmund smiled. "Exactly. It wasn't collecting the gifts of the Patrons that you needed to do but to go out and meet the Patrons. Because you did this, you were able to see and understand what the trouble was."

Hakon put an arm around her shoulder. "I'm very proud of you."

She shook her head. "I couldn't have done any of this without your help. And everything that Edmund says about me, is true of you. Do you think the Hakon that left Erthenhorn could have ridden into Tillmere and called tradesmen to our aide?"

"No," he answered. "You're right."

Joia held Hakon's hand in one of her hands and she reached out to Edmund with the other. She held tightly to the both of them.

After three more days together, the Patrons started to head home. Ciar, Aren, and Wodwin were the first to go, leaving just as the sky started to turn gray with the first morning light. They planned on stopping at villages along the way back to Yondalla to meet with their tradesmen. Before leaving, they apologized once more to Edmund and Joia for their treatment towards them in the king's castle and they apologized to Sidonia and Kloma for having supported kicking out their trades from the king's castle and promised to have the decree revoked upon their return. Wodwin also promised to personally help the spinner and weaver return to their homes.

While Grian didn't live far from Tillmere and Athelstan's Castle, he wanted to escort Sidonia and Kloma back to their homes to make sure they got there safely. Joia was sad to say goodbye to them. She would miss the smiling, joyful Chandler and the gentle spinner and weaver. They had become dear friends of hers.

Once the others had left, only Seb, Edmund, Hakon, and Joia remained at the castle. Edmund's leg still needed some more time to recover before he would be able to travel, so they decided to stay a few days longer.

Hakon and Seb set about clearing the great hall of its debris while Edmund played music on the various instruments he owned, lamenting how he felt very out of practice. He showed Joia his panpipes and let her try to play them, but she only ended up making lots of airy whistling sounds, making Edmund laugh.

"Edmund, what are your plans now?" Joia asked while applying a new poultice of herbs to his leg.

"That depends on several things," he said. "I desire to return to one of my traveling groups of entertainers. I miss not being with them and performing. But I will not do that until you have decided as to what you are going to do next. I will not abandon you."

"I want to go home and see my family again, but I understand I have a duty here at Athelstan's Castle."

"I believe you may call it Joia's Castle now," Edmund smiled.

"Oh no, I don't think so," Joia laughed. "Perhaps it should be named Trade Castle."

"I like that." Edmund stretched his leg, shuddering a bit at the pain. "It's feeling better," he promised after seeing her concern. "I believe by the end of the week I will be able to travel on it."

Joia smiled in relief. She was so very fond of him. He had been with her through almost all her journey. He had guided her, taught her, provided for her, and protected her. She loved and respected him. Saying goodbye to him, whether it be at the end of the week or in a year, would be very hard. She didn't want to ever say goodbye to Edmund.

"Are you all right Joia?" Edmund asked.

She nodded. "Mostly."

"What's wrong, dear one?" he asked.

"I don't want to say goodbye to you."

"Oh, my dear, I don't want to say goodbye to you either," he said, taking her hand in his. "But Joia, listen to me. When we part, it won't be forever. You are a part of the trades now. You are a part of me. We'll see each other again."

"Promise?" she asked.

He nodded. "I promise. But, for now, go home and be with your family. Perhaps you can marry Hakon," he watched Joia blush.

"He has already asked me," she said, her cheeks glowing. "But I suppose we still need my father's approval."

"I am happy for you," Edmund said. "Hakon will make you a wonderful husband. And when the time is right, you will return to Trade Castle and do what Athelstan has asked you."

"I will miss our journeying together," Joia said.

Edmund smiled. "We have one final journey before we say goodbye. Seb and I are going to accompany you and Hakon back to Erthenhorn.

Then, I will go and find one of my traveling groups to rejoin and Seb will return to his home in Yondalla. We are going to try and locate more of the Patrons. If we can find anyone, we will tell them they need to return here, to Trade Castle, in one year. We will all return for that day."

"Thank you." Joia reached out to hug Edmund. "I'm going to miss you," she said.

"I'm going to miss you too," he said, returning the hug. "But, knowing that we will see each other in a year will help the time to pass."

CHAPTER TWENTY-SIX

Going home

They set out a week later. Edmund's leg was doing much better, and he was able to walk about without much pain. Joia and Hakon rode with Edmund in the wagon, pulled by Bard, while Seb rode his borrowed horse, which he had named Quill.

Autumn had arrived and the morning they set out had a chill to it. Joia wore the cloak Seb had given her, grateful for its extra layer of warmth.

Joia was excited to be returning home and was surprised when she realized that they weren't as far away from Erthenhorn as she thought. "It's a two-day journey from Tillmere to Erthenhorn," Edmund answered when Joia asked how long the trip home was going to take.

"Only two days?" Joia asked. "It took us weeks of traveling to get from Erthenhorn to Trade Castle."

"Yes," Edmund answered. "We took the long, scenic road to get there. We went to Sidonia's, then Grian's, and then to Yondalla before we made it to Trade Castle."

Only two days. Joia was so excited. In two days, she would be with her mother and sister again. She would be back in her familiar home and comfortable bed. No more bedrolls. No more sleeping on the hard ground. No more hours upon hours in the wagon. No more of Edmund's music. No more sitting next to Hakon, holding hands, and talking about everything.

She sighed as she realized there would be many things from this journey that she would miss, most especially, the wonderful company of her three companions.

The two days on the road went quickly as Edmund entertained them with some new stories he had thought up over the past few weeks. Joia found them to be wonderful, exciting stories, but Edmund was not entirely pleased with them and declared they needed some work.

On the afternoon of the second day, the woods became more familiar to Joia, and she squealed with delight when she saw the first homes on Erthenhorn's borders. They rode straight to Joia's home. Once the bakery came into view, she jumped out of the wagon and ran down the street to her home.

Joia burst into the bakery, much to the surprise of her father, brother, and Derry.

"Joia!" they all cried out and her father came running from behind the worktable. "Oh, Joia," Thomas cried, pulling her into his arms.

"Father," she hugged him tightly. Then her brother David's arms were around her.

"Where did you go?"

"Are you injured?"

"What happened to you?"

Before Joia could answer, the door that led to the stairs opened and Joia's mother and sister came through the door. Joia was passed into her mother's arms.

"You're home!" Liadan cried out, taking Joia's face in between her hands, and looking at her. "I can't believe it. You're home."

"Where have you been?" Ebba asked as they hugged.

Joia couldn't answer. Tears fell as she hugged each family member. She was so happy to see them all. It didn't feel real, being back in the bakery with her family. After everything she had experienced, home was exactly the same, and Joia was very thankful for that.

The door to the bakery opened again and Edmund, Seb, and Hakon came in. Thomas scowled to see Edmund, but Liadan went to him and hugged him. "You brought her back."

Edmund chuckled and patted her back. "Yes, dear lady."

Liadan moved to Hakon and pulled him into a hug, much to Hakon's surprise. "And Hakon, you did go with Joia, didn't you?"

"Yes, I did," he answered.

"I knew it. When you disappeared, everyone wondered what had happened to you, but I guessed you had gone with Joia. I'm so glad you did, but you need to go back to your father. He has missed you so much," Liadan told him.

Hakon looked nervous and Joia knew he had been fretting for the last two days about how he would explain his disappearance to his father. "I guess I'd better go then. Don't leave town until I can say goodbye," he said to Edmund and Seb.

"Do you want me to go with you?" Seb asked Hakon.

Joia was amused at Seb's attempt to leave the bakery. He wasn't comfortable around a group of people most days, even when it was a group of Patrons. To be around a group of strangers was probably more than he could bear.

Hakon shook his head. "No, I think I should face my father on my own and accept my fate."

Hakon and Joia's eyes met at the same time, sharing a look of confused farewell. They had hardly been apart since leaving on their journey. Now they were home. She was at her home, and he needed to go back to his. It was odd and melancholy to just walk away like this after such an exciting adventure, but he had to go find his father.

She watched as Hakon turned, opened the door, and with one last glance at her, he left. Joia felt as if part of her left too.

Liadan invited Edmund and Seb into the house and introductions were made all around. Ebba immediately produced tea and cakes and offered them to the guests while Liadan made sure that Joia was sitting between her parents with Seb and Edmund opposite her.

"I can't believe you're home," she said to Joia before turning to Edmund. "I wondered if you would ever bring her back or if she left home forever like I did when I married Thomas."

"This is nothing like when you left your home to marry me. That was a respectable reason to leave home, but this?" Thomas gestured to Edmund and Seb, which surprised them both. "Tell us what happened," Thomas said, turning to Joia. "Where did you go?"

Joia looked over to where the two Patrons sat. Neither of them had any expression on their face, but their eyes were all Joia needed to see to know their current feelings. Seb was angry and Edmund was frustrated. "Well, I left with Edmund to go—" Joia started.

"Did you run away with him and marry him?" her brother, David asked, nodding his head toward Edmund.

"What? No," Joia said. "It wasn't anything like that."

"Did you and Hakon run off with the entertainers so you could marry him?" David asked.

"No," Joia said. "Hakon came—"

"Well, what happened, then? You didn't just disappear with this entertainer and Hakon for two months for no reason," David said. "And who is this guy?" he pointed at Seb.

"David, let me talk," Joia said and took a deep breath. "When Edmund came that day to speak with us and told me about my Light and that I needed to travel with him, I—" she was interrupted again by the sound of knocking at the door.

Thomas pounded his fists on the table. "Go away! The bakery is closed!"

"Thomas," Liadan scolded. She got up to answer the door.

Joia gave Edmund and Seb an apologetic look. Edmund chuckled, but Seb was scowling.

"Hakon, Arik, come in," Liadan said, opening the door wider.

Joia grinned to see Hakon coming in. She was surprised at how much she had missed him when they had only been apart for maybe half an hour. Hakon gave her a smile, but his father, Arik, was frowning. He was clearly not happy about being at the baker's home with the girl his son had run away with.

Joia stood to greet him, but her father grabbed her wrist and pulled her back to her chair, keeping her from getting too close to Hakon. Instead, Ebba offered her chair, and Airk sat in it. Hakon stood next to his father while Ebba moved to stand with Derry. The house was full with Joia's family, the two Patrons, a cobbler, and two thatchers.

Two months ago, Joia would have been nervous about speaking in front of so many, but after meeting eight Patrons and confronting Scrios, this wasn't so hard. But in some ways, it was harder. This was her family. She just wished they were more patient with her and more friendly towards her guests.

"I thought it would be best to bring my father here so he can hear the story of our journey," Hakon explained. "I wanted him to meet Edmund and Seb so they can back me up."

The two Patrons stood up and took turns grasping Arik by the hand. "I'm Edmund the Entertainer and this is Seb, the Map Maker," he introduced.

"Arik the Thatcher," Hakon's father returned. "And I demand to know what has been going on. Hakon disappeared unexpectedly and reappeared just as unexpectedly. Where did my son go?"

"We were just about to hear the story ourselves," Thomas said. "And this had better be good."

"Everyone please," Joia said. "We'll explain everything. Edmund? Would you please begin the story? There are so many things to tell."

Edmund nodded and cleared his throat. Joia smiled to see his Light glowing a little brighter as he was about to practice his trade. Edmund was in his element, and it showed. She quickly glanced at Seb, who looked at her with a wink.

Edmund started at the beginning, for Hakon, Arik, and Derry's sakes about seeing Joia as a baby, blessed with the Light. He went on to talk about how he, Joia, and Hakon had traveled from place to place, meeting with the Patrons, the excitement of the king's castle in Yondalla, and the encounter with Scrios the Uncreator at Athelstan's Castle. The story took Edmund a good hour to get through. Joia and Hakon filled in the few places when they had been separated from Edmund and even Seb chimed in a few times.

Hakon sat on one side of the room, in between his father and Seb while Joia sat on the other side of the room, between her father and mother. They kept watching each other, keenly feeling the separation after two months of constantly being together.

When Edmund finished, there was silence for many long moments.

"Wait, wait, wait!" David said. "Are you telling me that my baby sister is some special person with this weird mystical light?"

Seb's fists clenched, but Hakon quickly stood up. "I know it's hard to understand," he said, looking at Joia for several long moments. "I was there and it's still hard for me to understand, but Joia has a special Light that normally, only Patrons can see, but I've seen her Light. It's golden and bright and beautiful. It is real and everything Edmund has said is real. I was there. Seb was there. A dozen people from the village of Tillmere were there. We all saw Joia's Light. It was only for a few moments, but I can never deny what I saw."

"Thank you, Hakon," Joia said, her voice choked with emotion.

"This is too fantastical," Airk said. "Even for a storyteller."

Edmund intensely stared at Airk for several long moments before he quietly spoke again. "Sometimes, truth is more fantastical than a made-up story. What we have said this evening is all truth."

"I find all of this extremely difficult to believe," David said. "If Joia is truly this ancient ghost's descendant and heir, why am I not? I am older and I am the son."

"The Light chose Joia," Edmund said. "She is Athelstan's heir."

"Does this mean that Ferran is a real person?" Thomas asked quietly, looking at Edmund. "Is my Patron as real as you?"

Edmund and Seb both nodded. "He is," Edmund answered.

Seb turned to Arik. "And so is Thek."

"You have met our Patron?" Arik asked his son.

"No," Hakon answered. "I have not. Not yet, anyway, but I plan on it."

"He would be happy to meet you both," Seb said.

"And so will Ferran," Edmund added. "We will find them both and tell them they need to come to Erthenhorn."

Thomas's lips twitched into a smile, only for a moment, but Joia didn't miss it. She would do everything she could to make sure her father, brother, and Airk met their Patrons.

Several more moments of silence followed before Ebba asked, "What now?"

Edmund gave her a kind laugh. "Now we celebrate being all together."

There were many more questions from the family and Edmund and Joia patiently answered them all. The afternoon passed and Liadan invited Derry, Arik, Hakon, Edmund, and Seb to stay for supper. They accepted. Thomas and David had to get back to their bakery to clean and close for the day, but the other five men sat together at the table, talking to each other while Joia, Ebba, and their mother started to prepare the evening meal.

"I can't keep silent any longer," Ebba finally said as they were cooking some strips of meat in a skillet.

"What?" Joia asked, smiling at the way Ebba was practically bouncing with excitement.

"I'm getting married in two days!" Ebba cried out.

Joia threw her arms around Ebba and the men at the table stopped their talking. They all started to congratulate Ebba and give her their best wishes on her upcoming nuptials. Joia went to where Derry was sitting and kissed his cheek. "You are to be my new brother."

He grinned and nodded at her. "I am and I could not be happier."

"I am so happy for you both," Joia said, hugging her sister again.

"I'm so glad you made it back in time," Ebba said.

"So am I," Joia laughed.

"Girls, please," Liadan said with a grin. "I'll never get supper fixed with you two."

"Sorry, Mother," they said and laughed again before going back to their cooking. Ebba told Joia all about her courtship and the upcoming ceremony.

There was never an opportunity for Joia to be with Hakon again that evening. It was obvious to Joia that their families were doing everything they could do to keep them apart. Whenever Joia started to move toward him, Arik, Liadan, or Thomas would intervene, asking them questions about the journey or pulling them aside to talk about something else.

Liadan invited Edmund and Seb to stay in their home for the night.

"You are kind to invite us," Edmund said, smiling gently, "but I have my wagon with my bed."

She turned to Seb. "Will you be staying?"

"No, thank you," he said. "Edmund has a tent, and I'll be quite comfortable there. Thank you for having us over tonight. It has been very nice to meet Joia's family."

They shook hands with Derry, Arik, and Hakon and Joia waved to them from where her sister was keeping her on the other side of the room.

"Goodnight!" she called out as they waved back and left.

Joia barely had a chance to say good night to Hakon as he was ushered out the door by his father not long after Edmund left and then Derry left a few minutes later. After all those weeks together, on the road with Edmund and Hakon, Joia couldn't believe they were just gone. There was no campfire or listening to Edmund singing while leaning against Hakon, holding his hand. They were gone with a wave and Joia felt disoriented.

"Joia, come and help me wash," Liadan called out to her daughter as Joia stood, staring at the door. The house had grown quiet without the five extra guests. "Have you forgotten how to behave? You help clean after supper."

"Yes, Mother," Joia said, going back to where the dishes were stacked, waiting to be washed. She poured hot water into the bucket of dishes and started to clean them. All these weeks of wanting to go home and now that she was home, Joia felt out of place and wished she was back on the road with Edmund, sitting around a fire as he sang.

She tried to listen to Ebba as she went on and on about her upcoming wedding to Derry and Liadan caught Joia up on everything going on in the town, but it was hard for Joia to focus when all she wanted was to be with Hakon and Edmund again.

With the dishes done, they sat down to their sewing baskets. Joia had a ball of yarn and two knitting needles, but she didn't feel like knitting. Instead, she opened her bundle and took out the extra clothes she had taken with her. Her smaller bundle which contained her Life Tapestry, Life Map, and Everburn candle, was tied up and tucked away in a safe place. She wasn't ready to share these precious gifts with her family yet.

Joia's dress was badly frayed at the hem, and she wanted to mend it, but just as Joia started to pick apart the hem, Liadan called Joia to join her in their back garden.

Joia recalled that the last time she was in the back garden was the morning she had left to join Edmund on the adventure. Now, all these months later, she was back.

It felt so odd to be home. The house was the same and her family was the same, but Joia was not the same, and everything felt wrong.

The two women sat across each other in the garden with Liadan holding Joia's hand, afraid that if she let go, Joia would disappear again.

"Joia, it's so wonderful to have you back," Liadan said.

"It's good to be home. I've dreamt of this day for so long," Joia looked around at the garden. She couldn't see much in the dark, but the air was still fragrant and the stream still sang its constant burbling song. It was cooler than it had been the last time she was here, and Joia found herself wishing she was wearing the green cloak that Seb had given her.

"You have seemed far away this evening, though. You are back with us, but you aren't all here," Liadan said.

Joia smiled at her mother. "I am very happy to be with you again, but after months on the road with just a few people, it is a shock to come back to a house filled with ten people."

"You are thinner," Liadan said, looking at Joia's face.

"Food was not plentiful these last two weeks," Joia admitted. "But I'm fine." Her mother didn't need to know how Joia nearly passed out from hunger more than once.

"We'll make sure to feed you properly," Liadan said.

The door to the house opened and Joia's father stepped out into the garden. He sat down with his wife and daughter. "What are we discussing? The last time you two came out here, alone, to talk, Joia left home the next morning. I am still upset with you for leaving the way you did after I forbad it," he said.

Joia looked down to the ground. She had known her father was going to be upset, but hearing his disappointment made her feel terrible. This reaction was exactly what she had expected from him, but it was still hard to bear. She never wanted to disappoint her parents. She had always tried to do right and be obedient. She did not regret her decision at all and given the choice, she would do it again, but Joia had hoped that her father would be proud of her after hearing about everything she had done. She wanted him to forgive her for running off, but it seemed that no matter what she did, she could not make him proud.

"No decisions like that will be made again without me." His voice was stern and Joia felt properly chastened.

"I'm sorry, Father." Joia's voice was hardly more than a whisper.

"Joia, tell us truly what happened," her mother said, looking very concerned.

Joia looked at her mother with confusion. "It is just as Edmund said. If you think that Edmund lied to you, I can assure you he did not."

"No, Joia, it's not that. But I want to know, what about you and Hakon? Why did he leave his home and father?"

"It is exactly as Edmund said," Joia repeated. "Hakon came with me and protected me. There is no way I could have done what I needed to do without Hakon."

"But did anything happen between the two of you?" her mother pressed.

"Did anything happen that would make it absolutely necessary that you marry Hakon right away?" her father asked.

"No, of course not!" Joia cried out at the understanding of her parents' line of questioning. "I would never. You taught me better than that. I can't believe you even asked." She paused, thinking. She was not the same person who left Erthenhorn and her relationship with Hakon was not quite the same either. She thought of the kisses they had shared and the burning she felt when he kissed her. "Well, I suppose yes, something did happen."

Liadan and Thomas exchanged looks. They waited for their daughter's confession.

"Father, Mother, I have always hoped you would consider Hakon as a husband for me. We have always been friends and I thought it was such a romantic idea to be married to Hakon, but now, after everything we've been through together, I couldn't imagine marrying anyone else. I love him. I love Hakon. He was never anything but a gentleman to me. He watched out for me, helped me, protected me, made me laugh, and I loved being in his company." Joia sighed, "I love him, and he has asked me to marry him," she confessed.

Her father let out of sigh of relief. "Personally, I have no problem with the union. I would be very happy to see you married to Hakon. But Joia, Ebba is marrying in two days. We have nothing to offer as dowry for you at this time," Thomas said.

"I have," Joia looked at her parents. "Remember when Edmund told you about Athelstan's Castle?" Her parents nodded. "Athelstan bequeathed the castle to me. It and all its lands are mine. I can return to live there at any time, although right now, it has no furnishings."

"An entire castle?" Thomas asked in surprise.

"A small one, but yes. It is located outside the village of Tillmere, just a two-day journey from here." Joia watched her parents as they looked at her and each other in disbelief. "But whether Hakon and I marry or not, I will be returning to live there. My duties with the Trade Guild are not over."

"You will leave us again?" Liadan asked.

Joia nodded. "Just as you left your home for another, so must I."

"And what about Hakon? He is in training with his father," Thomas asked.

"Hakon has been declared a master thatcher by Athelstan, himself. The village of Tillmere will gain a new thatcher if Hakon returns with me to Trade Castle." Joia wasn't sure of her father's thoughts and feelings on the matter, but she hoped with all her heart that her father would agree to the union.

"I will speak with Arik tomorrow," Thomas said quietly. "Come inside. The night is growing cold and it's time we were all asleep."

Joia hugged her mother and father, and they went back into the house. She was very grateful that her father agreed to her marriage to Hakon and could only hope that Hakon's father would bless the marriage as well.

But it hurt Joia's heart to know that her parents were still disappointed in her. After everything she did, the only thing they really cared about was knowing if Joia had disgraced herself by having inappropriate relations with Hakon. Their disappointment in her was more painful than she had expected.

She was equally disappointed in her family. Their small world and mindset couldn't understand everything Joia had just been through.

Joia climbed into her own bed, feeling its softness. Such a wonderful difference after months of sleeping on a bedroll on the ground. This was luxurious.

Ebba rolled to face her in bed. "Will you help me gather flowers for the wedding tomorrow?"

"Of course," Joia yawned. She wanted to think about her journey, about the joy and sorrow of coming home and being with her family, but the bed was so comfortable, and she was so tired, that she fell asleep almost immediately.

Joia couldn't decide what to do with herself the following day. She was so happy to be home and with her family, but she also wanted to go see Edmund and be with Hakon. Ebba was acting especially difficult. She was so excited to be marring the following day, but at the same time, she was anxious and feeling utterly overwhelmed. In the late morning, after chores were done, Joia and Ebba went out to find flowers to weave into a crown for Ebba to wear. They stopped at Edmund's camp on their way and Joia was happy to see her friends again.

She ran to Edmund, "Good afternoon," she said.

"Good afternoon. I was wondering if we would see you today," Edmund said.

"I've wanted nothing more than to be here with you since I woke up, but Mother reminded me of all the chores I have each morning. I'm out of the habit of working."

"I'm sure it won't take you long to readjust to your old life," Edmund quietly said, sitting down on a log near the fire.

Joia chewed on the inside of her cheek for several moments. "It's just, I don't know if I want to return to my old life."

He smiled, leaned forward, and patted her hand. "A journey such as yours changes you more than you might realize. Nothing is ever quite the same. You see the world with a whole new set of eyes."

Seb came over with an armful of logs for the fire. He dropped them in a pile near the campfire. "I don't know what you were like when you left home, but you've changed since I met you. I'm sure returning to the old ways is not easy."

"My parents questioned me again about our travels. They don't believe me and the only thing that they cared about was if I had any relations with Hakon," she blushed.

"There is no way they can understand," Edmund sighed.

"I know," Joia said. "I just hate their disappointment in me."

Seb was about to say something when Ebba came into the campsite with a couple of flowers already in hand. "Joia, we need to get working on this. The day is quickly passing."

"Coming, Ebba," Joia said. She looked back at the two Patrons and their glowing Light. Yesterday, after they had left, Joia had been plunged back into a darker world. There were no glowing things in her home, except for the three Patron gifts in her hidden bundle. For months, she had spent time around Patrons and their items, all of which glowed with the soft, golden Light of the Guilds. It was nice to be with the Patrons again. These were her people now.

"Mother wanted me to invite the two of you to supper at sundown," Joia told them.

Edmund nodded. "Thank your mother for the invitation. We accept and will see you again this evening."

Joia had to say goodbye to them and follow Ebba out to the meadow where the last of the summer flowers and the first of the fall flowers were growing together. They started running, and Joia felt like a child again. She and Ebba laughed as they ran through the fields. They started picking flowers and after having gathered enough, they sat in the shade of a tree and began weaving the flowers into a crown.

"I haven't run around like that in years," Ebba said after they had caught their breaths again.

"Neither have I," Joia laughed and passed a flower to Ebba, who carefully wove it into the headdress. They were silent for a few moments as they worked, each of them lost in their own thoughts.

Joia reached down and plucked a blade of grass. She started to pull it apart, fiber by fiber. It reminded her of how she had spun flowers and grass into thread in Sidonia's garden. It all seemed so long ago, like a dream now.

"Have you had much of an opportunity to get to know Derry?" Joia asked.

"We've had him over for supper several times," Ebba answered. "And he calls for me at the house at least once a day."

"And what do you think?" Joia asked, smiling slyly at her sister.

"He is very nice, and always a gentleman." Ebba wove another flower into the crown. "We've never had much time to talk together. Mother or David have seen to that."

"Do you think you will like living with him and being around him every day?"

Ebba gave her sister a quizzical look. "I suppose," she stammered. "I hadn't really thought about it like that, but, yes, I think I will like living with him. He works in his shop all day, so it will only be evenings we will be together. Much the way mother and father live, I guess."

"What about children? Do you want to have a baby right away?" Joia asked.

Ebba blushed slightly. "Yes, I think so. It's a lovely idea, isn't it?" Ebba had a faraway look in her eyes. "Derry, going to his shop every day to work and me, caring for our home and our baby. It will be perfect."

"Do you love him?"

"Yes," Ebba answered immediately. "Well, I mean, yes. I don't know him that well, but he is very nice. I'm sure he will be a good husband."

Ebba wove several more flowers into the crown. A cool wind blew and caused several leaves to fall from the tree they were sitting under.

Joia thought about her own feelings for Hakon. There was no doubt in her mind that she loved him. She thought about how he had fought off an attacker, just to keep her safe. He had accompanied her to Athelstan's castle and put his trust in a map that only she could truly read. He had ridden into an unfamiliar village to round up a group of strangers to go to the castle to support her while she faced off with Scrios. They had held each other when their prospects were uncertain and almost starved together. They had laughed together and worked together. She loved him and knew that he loved her too. And his kisses. Oh, how she missed those kisses.

She felt a little sorry for her sister who was going to enter a marriage with a partner she barely knew. Derry was a kind and thoughtful man, but Joia knew she would be nervous about marrying someone she didn't know as well as she knew Hakon. It had to be scary for her sister.

After several minutes, Ebba set the crown of flowers down in the grass in front of her. "Joia?" she said, "Do you think I'll be a good wife?"

Joia looked at her elder sister and saw the look of worry in her eyes. Ebba had been so excited and had talked about marriage for so long, Joia was surprised to realize that Ebba was nervous. "You'll be the best wife, Ebba. Derry is the luckiest man in Erthenhorn."

"Besides Hakon, you mean," Ebba teased.

Joia shook her head and handed Ebba another flower. "I don't have your sweet temperament. Derry is probably the luckier of the two men."

"You've changed, Joia."

Joia was surprised. "Have I truly?"

"You seem surer of yourself and you're more, well, mature. Did you really do all those things Edmund said you did?" Ebba asked.

"Yes."

"That's amazing. I never could have done all of that."

"Well," Joia said, "I couldn't have done it without Hakon and Edmund's help."

"Hakon's changed too. He is confident and when I look at you two, I see something very different. You have this look of understanding between the two of you. Love."

Joia smiled. "Yes. I love him."

"Do you think I'll ever love Derry the way you love Hakon?" Ebba whispered.

"I'm sure of it," Joia said.

CHAPTER TWENTY-SEVEN

Party Surprise

Edmund and Seb arrived at Joia's home just as the sun set. Liadan had fixed her best food and Thomas had brought his finest breads and pastries from the bakery. It was a feast and a celebration for Ebba. Joia was delighted when Hakon, his father, and Derry arrived to join in the festivities. The house was packed again and very noisy, but everyone was happy. Only Seb looked uncomfortable. Joia watched him slip out, down the stairs, and into the back garden. She made her way across the room and followed him out.

"Is everything all right Seb?" she asked as she closed the door behind her.

"Yes," he answered, "I just needed some fresh air." He took a deep breath of the cool fall air.

"It is rather loud and crowded in there, isn't it?" Joia chuckled.

"And hot." He turned to her, "Joia, I am very honored at being so accepted by your family, but after years and years of living alone, all these people, well, it's a bit much for me."

"It's all right. I kind of understand." Joia stood next to Seb. She looked up at the night sky. It was clear and full of stars. "You know, during most of my journey, I just wanted to come home. But now that I'm home, I keep thinking of how nice it was when it was just three or four of us on the road." She saw Seb smile at her. "I guess we always want what we don't have. I'm silly, I know."

"You're not silly at all," Seb said. "You lived a different life for a while. To have seen the things you've seen and do the things you've done; those kinds of experiences change a person. You just need to find a balance between your old life and the new."

"Do you think I have changed?"

"Yes, I do. I have only known you for a short while, but you are not the same girl as the one I made the Life Map for."

Joia had grown very fond of Seb. She remembered when they first met how unfriendly he was. She had tried to run from her destiny because of Seb. She had been so mad at him when she thought he wasn't even going to try and save Edmund from the king's dungeons. But Seb turned out to be very different. He had searched for Joia and found her at the spinner's house. He had rescued her from the castle and helped her escape Yondalla. He did save Edmund. He had taken such an important role in the defeat of Scrios. He had been a voice of calm reason when Joia had needed it the most.

"I think you've changed, too," Joia smiled.

Seb nodded and took another deep breath. "I don't know if I've changed, but ending my feud with Edmund has lifted a heavy weight off my shoulders. That kind of forgiveness is life-altering."

"For the better," she said.

"Yes," he looked into her eyes. "For the better."

The back door opened. Joia and Seb turned to see Hakon walking out to them. "I thought I saw you escaping out here," Hakon said. He came up to Joia and slipped his hand into hers. She felt her whole arm tingle at his warm touch. "I've missed you today."

"I've missed you too," Joia said. "Both of you." She took Seb's hand in her other one and held it for several moments.

Hakon gave her hand a squeeze. "You and Seb need to come in now. I believe your father is wanting to make a toast." Hakon pulled Joia to the door.

She pulled at Seb's hand. "Come on, Seb, you too."

They all returned to the hot, noisy room, but Joia cracked open a window to let the cooler night air into the hot house. Thomas began hitting the iron kettle in the fireplace with a spoon. Soon the room had quieted down. Liadan passed the cups of ale around.

"Thank you everyone for coming tonight," Thomas began. "It is an honor to have our guests, Edmund the Entertainer and Seb the Map Maker, here with us." Cups were raised to the guests. "We are also very happy to have Joia and Hakon back among us after their long disappearance." There were some quiet chuckles and Joia's face blushed with embarrassment. "But tonight is for Ebba and Derry. We are all so very happy for you both and we wish you, with all our hearts, the very best!"

"To Derry and Ebba!" everyone cheered. They raised their cups and drank to the couple.

Derry held up his hand to everyone in the room and once again the group became quiet. "I want to thank you all. I'm a very happy, lucky man." He looked lovingly at Ebba, who smiled and nodded at him. "Today, however, has been a day of secrets. Words have been spoken in whispers and plans have been formed. I have been lucky enough to have been in on some of these plans and I want everyone to know that Ebba and I fully support these schemes." They gave each other sly smiles.

Half of the heads in the room turned to look at each other in wonder and confusion. The other half of the group smiled knowingly. Joia was part of the confused group and she looked at Hakon, who was smiling, and then she looked at Edmund, who was grinning at her.

"What do you know?" she asked Hakon.

Hakon turned to her and held her hands in his. "Joia, daughter of Thomas the Baker and Liadan, Heir of Athelstan, Friend of all Guild Patrons, bearer of the great Light, and my dear, beautiful friend," he watched Joia blush. "I know that several weeks ago, I asked you to marry me, but tonight I would like to ask again, in front of our family and friends, if I may have your hand in marriage. Will you marry me, Joia?"

Joia looked into Hakon's bright eyes. "Hakon, you have been my dearest friend for many years. You followed me to the end of the world and back, and during that time, I came to realize just how much I love you. So, yes, I will happily marry you."

The room broke into cheers again. Hakon pulled Joia into a hug. She laughed as she realized what had just happened. She would get to marry Hakon. She had wanted this for so long and now it would be.

"To Hakon and Joia, everyone!" Derry called out.

"Hakon and Joia!" came the cheers.

Ebba ran to Joia and hugged her. "Oh Joia, I'm so happy for you. It is the greatest thing in the world for me to share my wedding day with you!"

"What?" Joia said and pulled away from Ebba.

"Share your wedding day with me?"

"Well, yes, of course, that is, if you want to. You and Hakon can be married tomorrow with Derry and me."

Joia looked to Hakon. He smiled. "It's true, Joia. If you wish to be married tomorrow, all the arrangements have been made. We can have a double wedding."

"It works well for us," Thomas said. "We are already throwing a wedding and have all the food, wine, and celebrations in place. A double wedding! Both of my daughters. It is hard to believe you have both grown so much. You aren't little girls, playing at your mother's feet anymore. You are grown women who are ready to make your own homes now."

"So, Joia," Hakon asked, "is it going to be a double wedding tomorrow?"

Everything was happening so quickly. Joia's mind was spinning. She looked at Seb. He was nodding at her. She looked at her mother, who was smiling and crying at the same time. She looked at Edmund. His eyes were bright and moist. He smiled and nodded at her.

"I think tomorrow would be wonderful," Joia said. She turned to look at Edmund, "But I have a request," she paused and squeezed Hakon's hand, "that Edmund sing a song at the wedding."

"Nothing would please me more," he said.

Joia ran to him and hugged him. "Thank you," she whispered in his ear.

"Congratulations," he whispered back.

Joia was then passed around the room, hugging everyone there. She had never felt happier.

EPILOGUE

One year to the day of Scrios's banishment, Joia and Hakon led fourteen Patrons and one other special guest to Athelstan's room. The sky above them in the circular room was clear and blue. They formed a circle around Athelstan's pool and watched as Joia stepped forward and touched the water.

Athelstan's golden form rose from the water and the seventeen people who surrounded the pool bowed low.

"Rise children," Athelstan said. "Rise and let me look at all of your faces."

They all stood straight and looked at Athelstan. His form, hovering over the water, spun in a slow circle, and smiled at each person in turn. He stopped in front of Joia, who stood next to her husband, holding his hand.

"Joia, Hakon, I wish to thank you for bringing everyone here today. It is an important day and you have done well by welcoming everyone into your home."

Joia blushed, "It is your home, Athelstan, and home to all the trades. We are privileged to be its caretakers."

Athelstan nodded and turned to face the young man who was standing between Sidonia and Kloma. "I see we have someone new among us. Tell me, young man, who are you and why do you stand here tonight?" Athelstan smiled at the young man.

"Sir," he bowed, "I am Radstan, son of Wystan, and great-grandson to Sidonia the Weaver and Kloma the Spinner. For many years, my father was a messenger between Sidonia and Kloma, but since they were reunited last year, at the banishment of the Uncreator, they have had no need of me or my father as a messenger." He looked up at Athelstan, seemingly resolved to ask what he came here for. He took a deep breath. "I would like, with your permission, sir, to be the messenger to all the Patrons. I will carry messages from you or the Lady Joia to all the Patrons and from any Patron to Trade Castle. Please, sir, may I be your official Messenger?"

Athelstan smiled at the young man who stood in between his two great-grandmothers. "I think having an official messenger is a fine idea, but I will leave the decision to Joia. She is the one who now bears the great Light of the Guild and is Lady of Trade Castle. She speaks for me in all decisions regarding the trades, now."

Joia looked in surprise at Athelstan. This was his castle, and he was the father of the trades, but everyone turned to look at her. Athelstan nodded his head, and she knew that whatever choice she made in this matter would be honored by him and all the Patrons. She turned to Radstan, who looked as white as a ghost.

"Radstan, I agree with Athelstan that it's a good idea for the Patrons to have a messenger, but how will you travel the land to take the messages between Patrons and myself?" Joia asked the youth.

"I will take whatever mode of travel that is necessary to get the messages conveyed in a timely manner. Mostly I will go on horseback. I have a horse, his name is Swifan, and he is as fast a horse as can be," Radstan said.

Joia smiled. "Radstan, I see that you are true in your desire." She went to Radstan and took him by the hands and closed her eyes. She inhaled deeply, thinking of the words she wanted to say, and opened her eyes. "Radstan, son of Wynstan and great-grandson of Sidonia the Weaver and Kloma the Spinner. You come from a great heritage, and we are happy to call you friend. You are now to be known as Radstan, Messenger of the Trade Guild Patrons."

The group of people gathered around the pool began to cheer. Radstan was hugged by his great-grandmothers, who were also wiping tears of joy from their eyes. Radstan bowed to Joia before turning to Athelstan.

"Thank you," he bowed to the Father of the Trades.

"This is a good day, my children. Remember it. Seb," Athelstan turned to Seb, who stood next to Edmund, "I expect you to help our young messenger, here, by providing him with a map of the kingdom and the known location of every Patron. As more are found, you will add them to the map."

Seb bowed, "It will be done, Athelstan. I will make the map this week."

"Thank you, Seb. I wish to welcome back, Edmund, Seb, Kloma, Sidonia, Grian, Aren, Ciar, and Wodwin. Thank you for returning this day. I am also very happy to see several of you who were not here with us one year ago. Welcome Ferran the Baker. Welcome Brynmor the Potter. Welcome Algar the Fletcher and Falk the Glassblower. Welcome back Thek the Thatcher and Wealcan the Cobbler. Do not let this be the last time you visit Trade Castle."

"It won't be Athelstan," Thek said. "We promise."

"Very good." Athelstan's body slowly turned in place again and he addressed the assembled group. "My children, a year ago, our trades were almost lost to the world. You forgot that part of being a Patron meant you were to go out and teach others the trade. You became legends to your own people and became a divided and lost group. But when our trades were threatened last year, some of you came together and stood up to the force that would destroy you. In standing up to the Uncreator, you learned you were not strong enough on your own."

"Athelstan," Kloma stepped forward. "Forgive my question, but for Joia to banish Scrios, it took her, the eight Patrons that were here, Hakon, and a dozen tradesmen from the village. There were many against one. Is uncreation that much stronger?" she asked.

"No, dear one," Athelstan said. "It is not stronger, but it is an easier path, so you must be careful. The best way to make sure that it doesn't happen again is by getting to know your tradesmen. If they know you, they will not easily be swayed by uncreation."

"Thank you," Kloma said.

Athelstan spoke with each Patron, asking them about what they had been doing the last year and he seemed very pleased as he listened to them all. Most of them had gone out into the land and made sure that they met all their tradesmen in those areas. They taught them, set up new workshops, and helped them with repairs and improvements. All of them reported that they had enjoyed getting out and working with others.

Joia was impressed with all of them, and it was clear to see that Athelstan was pleased too as he smiled down at them all. Joia could see the love he had for each of these Patrons.

Finally, he turned to Joia and Hakon. "I wish to congratulate you on your marriage. I am very happy you have chosen to make this your home."

"We are very thankful for the castle, and thanks to the Patrons, we have nice furniture. It is a comfortable place to live. We are getting the bedrooms of the Patrons refurnished so that when they come to visit you, they will have a place to stay. And we invite all of you to visit as often as you like. And bring your tradesmen if you wish. There are so many rooms that sit empty that could be used for instruction. That is, if Athelstan approves."

Athelstan nodded. "Joia, the castle is yours and Hakon's. The responsibility of directing the trades is yours. Whatever decisions you and Hakon make about the castle and whatever decisions you make about the trades, if they are in the best interest of the Guild, is agreeable with me."

"Thank you, sir," Hakon said. "We hoped you would agree."

The golden figure nodded. "Now that you have taken your place as Lord and Lady of Trade Castle, the power and influence I have had over this castle will begin to diminish. I will always be here, but the protection of the castle and the trades will now be yours entirely. I am proud of all of you. Gather again in a year and bring more of you. Wake me at that time and report to me how your efforts have been going. Remember your purpose. Remember what you stand to lose if you let yourself return to your old ways. Until next year, my children."

Athelstan's form fell back into the pool. The bright glow of his light went out and the room plunged into near darkness. Joia heard several people sniff in the silence. They gathered their candles and turned to go back out the door and through the hall.

Joia felt the responsibility Athelstan placed on her shoulders growing heavier. Managing the Trade Guild was not going to be an easy job. But Athelstan had included Hakon in the responsibility. He had called them Lord and Lady of Trade Castle. It wasn't her burden alone.

They would work together in all things.

They slowly made their way back up the stairs to the great hall. Joia picked up a tray from the kitchen and brought it out. She served tea or wine to everyone there. For a long time, the Patrons were quiet as they sipped their drinks, each lost in their thoughts.

Edmund retrieved his lute from where he had placed it in a corner and began to play. He sang the old song of Athelstan and the birth of the trades. Joia had heard him sing the song before, but it was even more beautiful now that she understood its history so much better. What surprised her was when the song should have ended, Edmund kept singing with several new verses, telling the tale of the banishment of Scrios and the placement of Joia and Hakon as the Masters of Trade Castle. When he finished, the group applauded, exclaiming their delight in the song and the pleasure of his music and voice.

Dinner was served and there was much joyful chatter as the Patrons recounted stories of their days living here in the castle and Joia loved each story. The evening was filled with music and dance with Edmund playing instruments and others taking turns dancing. Thek, it turned out, was quite the dancer, and Grian had a very nice singing voice, joining in with Edmund whenever he knew the song.

Joia danced a few of the dances but preferred to play hostess to her distinguished guests. As night came on, she bid each Patron a fond goodnight, made sure everyone had everything they needed and accepted their thanks for hosting them.

Joia returned to the kitchen to clean the last of the dishes while Hakon went out to the stables to check that all the horses were safe and well. Joia's hands worked at washing dishes in the bucket of warm water, but her mind returned to the meeting with Athelstan and what he had said to her. The castle was hers and Hakon's and the responsibilities of the trades were hers. It seemed like too much to bear.

How would she do it?

After their wedding, they returned to Grian's house, where Hakon spent several weeks replacing the entire roof of Grian's cottage. He wanted to get it done before winter set in and he finished just in time. An early snow came a week later and Grian said he had never been so cozy in his house that didn't let snow in or heat out.

They spent the winter in Erthenhorn in Hakon's father's house. Joia was happy to live there and take care of the two thatchers and their home. When spring came, they made their way back to Trade Castle. Hakon quickly became known in Tillmere for his trade status and his excellent work. He was regularly employed, thatching roofs from Tillmere to Erthenhorn and everywhere in between.

While Hakon worked, Joia spent her days cleaning and fixing up the rooms of the castle.

She planted a garden and tended it, singing the songs Edmund had taught her as she worked. She sewed clothes for Hakon and herself and started doing all she could to prepare them and the castle for the Gathering and the upcoming winter. If there was anything Joia felt completely confident it, it was how to be a good hostess.

But how was she supposed to care for the trades? What did that mean? With Scrios gone, what was there for her to do? These questions plagued her in the quiet hours she spent working and after six months of being here, she still wasn't sure. All she knew was that the castle needed to be a welcoming place for the Patrons and so that was what she would do.

Her thoughts were interrupted by the sounds of footsteps coming across the stone floor.

"Is all well at the stables, Hakon?" she asked.

"I wouldn't know," Edmund's deep voice answered, "but if you would like, I can go to the stables and find your husband."

"Oh, Edmund, I'm sorry. I thought you had gone to your room for the night." Joia dried her hands on her apron and turned to Edmund. "Can I get you anything?"

"No, thank you." Edmund sat down in one of the kitchen chairs. He leaned back and crossed his arms across his chest. "Look at you. Just a little over a year ago, you were a young girl who had never left home, and now, here you are, Lady of Trade Castle and caretaker of the Trade Guild."

Joia chuckled. "When you say it like that, it sounds pretty impressive, but I'm not that special." She sat down across the worktable from her old friend. "I'm so glad you came back, Edmund."

"How could I not? I've been looking forward to seeing you again for a long time. How are you?"

"I'm well, thank you. And what about you? How have you been?"

"Busy as ever," Edmund chuckled. "You remember the troop of entertainers I was traveling with when you first joined me on our trip?"

"Yes, of course. I think of them often. I especially liked Elin," Joia said thinking back to the girl who had reminded her so much of her sister and helped her through those first few days away from home.

Edmund laughed, "Elin is very well. She just had a baby six weeks ago and her little son has his father's bright red hair."

"Oh, I am glad!" Joia said. "And how are the rest?"

"We have had a good year together. I said my goodbyes to them when I left to come here, and I will be joining up with another one of my companies after I leave. I saw them in Yondalla a year ago. They are led by a man named Jack, a talented musician, who can play any instrument he picks up. I'm looking forward to being in their company again."

"I will miss you, but I wish you all the best," Joia said.

"Thank you." They sat together in a comfortable silence for several moments. "You know something, Joia, when I returned to my company of entertainers, they joked with me about how different I was from when I had left. I didn't think I had changed at all. I knew you and Hakon had. I watched as you left behind the scared girl from the little village to become a confident woman. Hakon went from a quiet man, unsure of himself into a master tradesman and self-assured man. You both changed so much. What I didn't realize was how much I had changed, but my company noticed it right away."

Joia laughed. "I didn't realize it since I was with you every day, but thinking back, you did. When we first met, you were solemn and mysterious, even a little cold. But then, do you remember that night we stayed at the inn near Yondalla?"

"You mean the inn with the bread that could be used as building material?" Edmund laughed. "Yes, I remember."

She laughed at the memory and nodded. "It was the first time I heard you laugh and be happy. I was surprised. Then, if you think about what happened over the two days that followed, we went to Yondalla, and you and Seb were on terrible terms with each other. I saw you get arrested, and I ran for my life. The next time I saw you, you and Seb were like brothers again and you were much happier, despite your leg being injured and the trouble with Scrios that we were dealing with. When Hakon and I married, you sang all through the celebration after the wedding. I don't think the Edmund I first met at the beginning of the journey would have behaved quite so carefree and happy."

"I guess you're right, Joia," Edmund said as he rubbed his chin in thought. She had seen him do this many times. "You were a breath of fresh air that I didn't know I needed. It was good for me to have a quest that took me away from my station as the Patron of Entertainers. It was also good for me to spend time with some of the other Patrons and to finally have made amends with Seb."

"That kind of forgiveness can heal the heart and make you joyful," she said. "You know," she leaned forward on the table, "I remember sitting in the spinner's home with the other ladies while I was growing up. The spinner is a wonderful lady, and I enjoyed her company. She would tell stories and give out advice, that the other women took as the absolute truth, but I don't think she ever left Erthenhorn and rarely left her home except to go to the market. She never changed. Her life never changed. I cannot imagine living a life like that anymore." Joia said.

Edmund nodded. "I suppose if you never leave your village and you don't know what you are missing, then you can be content. But for those of us who have traveled," he chuckled to himself. "Well, we cannot be content with accepting that the ways of one village are the only ways that exist."

"I hope to go to the great mountains one day," Joia said, leaning forward. "Have you been to the mountains?"

"I have and they are beautiful. They are also huge. You cannot imagine their size. You must go there one day. Perhaps I will take you and Hakon and we will travel to the mountain towns."

Joia sighed happily. "Yes, I would love that." She leaned forward and rested her arms on the table. "By the way, how is your leg? You seem to be moving on it very well."

"Oh yes," Edmund chuckled. "It healed up very nicely and except for the lovely scar that it left, I wouldn't even remember it happened at all."

"It's so good to be with you again," Joia said. "I've missed you."

"It makes me very happy to be with you too," Edmund smiled.

They let several moments pass before Joia looked up to Edmund again. He held her in his intense gaze. "What troubles you?" he asked.

Joia had not been able to get the meeting with Athelstan out of her mind. "I knew you could read my mind with those blue eyes of yours," she said, and he chuckled but shook his head.

"I cannot read your mind, but I see in your eyes that something is troubling you. Tell me what it is."

She took a deep breath. "Well, Athelstan placed a rather large task on me. I feel as unsure of myself as I did the day I first left Erthenhorn. How can I do justice to Athelstan and the trades?"

"It's good to feel unsure of ourselves once in a while, Joia," Edmund said.

"What? Why would you say that?" Joia frowned.

Edmund smiled kindly and reached across the table and took one of her hands in his. "If we were confident in everything we did, we would never learn. That was the problem with the Patrons, don't you remember? We became settled and sure of our knowledge, never being able to grow or learn. Just like your spinner in Erthenhorn. If you ever reach the point in your life when you feel like you know everything, then you have stopped learning and you need to go on another journey." He kissed her knuckles. "It's all right to be unsure, as long as you try your best."

Joia leaned over to Edmund and kissed his cheek. "Thank you. Edmund, please don't be another year before you visit me again."

"I will bring my company to see you at mid-winter and we will have a jolly celebration." Edmund smiled at Joia.

She had missed him so much and knew in her heart that if she didn't have Hakon, she would fall very much in love with the entertainer. "I look forward to it." Joia stood up and went to the fire to get the kettle off the iron arm. "I was going to fix some tea. Are you sure I can't get you anything?"

"Nothing, thank you." He spoke quietly. She turned to him, and they stared at each other for several moments.

She took a deep breath; she had something very important to tell him. "Edmund,—" she started but the back door to the kitchen opened and Hakon walked in.

"Ah, Hakon, how are things at the stables?" Edmund asked. He winked at Joia. She blushed and smiled.

"Fine. What have you two been up to? Not plotting to take Joia away on some grand adventure, are you?" Hakon asked.

"And what would you say if I was?" Edmund asked.

"I would say wait for me," Hakon answered in his most serious tone.

Joia laughed. "I wouldn't dream of going anywhere without you, Hakon." She put the kettle back over the fire and went to her husband. "We weren't plotting any adventures. Not yet anyway. Although Edmund suggested that we all go visit the mountain villages one day."

Hakon nodded. "Sounds like that will be an exciting trip."

"And," Joia went on, "Edmund has promised to return at mid-winter with his company."

"We will have the castle ready for your arrival," Hakon said.

"Thank you," Edmund gave a quick bow of his head.

"There's one more thing I need to tell you," Joia said. "As much as I look forward to our trip together to the mountains, I think it will have to wait for a while. See, I, um…"

Hakon put his arm around her, and Edmund took her hand. "What's wrong?" they asked together.

"It's not that anything is wrong, it's just, well, I am with child." Her hand rested on her belly and the small swell there.

Hakon and Edmund both stepped away from her and stared at her. Hakon's eyes were wide. "You're going to have a baby?"

Joia nodded and Edmund let out a big, hearty laugh. He slapped Hakon on the back and gently pulled Joia into his arms. He hugged her. "I am so happy for you. Congratulations."

"A baby?" Hakon asked again.

"Yes. I asked one of the local midwives. She told me the symptoms and felt my stomach, and she confirmed that I am probably three months along, although she said I seemed a little big, so I might be in my fourth month."

"I am very happy for you. When will the baby come?" Edmund asked.

"We figure it will be in the spring," Joia said.

Edmund took her hand in his. "Dearest Lady of the Light, I am so very happy for you." He took her hand and kissed it.

Joia blushed. "Thank you."

Hakon still stood with a silly smile on his face.

Edmund laughed again and patted Hakon on the back. "It is late and I'm sure you are both tired from hosting so many guests. And it seems you have much to talk about. Joia, take care of this husband of yours. He seems to be in a bit of shock." Edmund walked to Joia and Hakon. "I'll see you both in the morning." He shook Hakon's hand and kissed Joia's forehead.

"Good night."

"Night," Joia said as she watched Edmund walk out the kitchen doors and back to his wagon in the courtyard. She handed Hakon the bucket of dirty dish water and he took it outside to dump it. Joia blew out all the candles except her own Ever Burn candle Grian had made for her. It still looked the same as the day he had made it. No matter how many times Joia used the candle, it never grew smaller, and it never went out until she was ready for it to go out. She waited for Hakon to return, and they went to their bed chamber together.

When Joia and Hakon had returned to Trade Castle, six months ago, they had brought very little furniture with them, deciding it would be easier to employ the Tillmere carpenter once they arrived. So, they had only the very basics, a straw mattress, a table, and four chairs. To their surprise, upon their arrival back at the castle, they found one bedroom completely furnished with a large, elegantly carved bed, two small tables, and a wardrobe, all glowing with the Light and bearing the mark of the ornate 'W', which was Wodwin's signature in the corner of each piece of furniture he made. On the tables, two single candle holders made of shining silver sat with carved yellow candles sitting in their bases, having been left for them by Aren and Grian. And, a soft and warm bedspread of deep blue covered the bed, made for them by Sidonia and Kloma. Never in all of Joia's life had she seen such a fine room. She was sure that the king himself couldn't have such a beautiful room.

Joia had hung her Life Tapestry over the bed and the map that had been made for her by Seb was rolled up and tucked safely away in the pocket of the traveling cloak he had given her, which hung in the wardrobe.

Hakon closed the door to their room and changed out of his clothes. Joia had a small basin with water in the corner, where she washed her face and neck before changing into her sleeping clothes. The nights were growing cooler with the onset of autumn and Joia was grateful for the soft bed and warm blanket. She climbed into bed and pulled the blue blanket up to her chin. She and Hakon lay on their sides, facing each other and holding hands.

"It's been quite the day, hasn't it?" he asked her.

"Yes, quite the day," Joia answered.

"Are you truly going to have a baby?" Hakon asked.

Joia chuckled and nodded. "I am. Here, you can feel." She took his hand and placed it over her stomach. "Feel the swell?"

"Why didn't you tell me?"

"I only confirmed it yesterday with the midwife. I didn't feel good for a few months, and I thought it was just the excitement of moving here, settling in, and getting ready to host the Patrons here. But when my belly started to swell, I started to think back to the last few months, and I realized that all the signs were there. But I've never been expecting before and so I didn't know to recognize the signs."

"This is the most wonderful news I have ever heard. Surely you are not still planning on going to Erthenhorn in a few weeks," he said, pressing his hand a little more firmly against her belly.

"Of course, I am," she smiled. Joia's sister, Ebba was expecting her first baby in a month and Joia had promised to go be with her. She was very excited to see her family again and to become an aunt. "I want to be there for her birth, so I know what to expect come this spring. And I can't wait to tell Ebba and my mother about our baby."

He chuckled. "I love you, my sweet Joia."

She leaned forward in the dark and found his lips with hers. "I love you, too."

They were quiet for a long time, although Joia knew Hakon wasn't asleep yet. He was still rubbing gently at her stomach.

"Hakon, I've been thinking about what Athelstan said. The castle and its care are ours. The overseeing of all the trades is mine, which means it's ours. It's a huge task and I don't know if I'm the right person for it."

"It is a huge task that you've been given," Hakon agreed. "But if anyone can do it, you can, Joia."

"But we're going to have a baby now. How will I do both?"

"I'll be by your side every day of my life. We will do this together," he promised.

Joia kissed him again. "Thank you, Master Thatcher and Lord of Trade Castle."

He chuckled. "I love you, Lady of Trade Castle and the Light of the Guild."

The End

"I Have a Yong Suster" anonymous, Medieval English Riddle-Poem, circa 1430, *Sloane Manuscript* 2593

Other books available from Molly McGinty:

<u>The Pineridge Series</u>
Fun Run
Social Hour
Hazel Summer
A Merry Little Christmas

Crimson Mist

The Light of the Guild
Healing the Guild *(coming soon)*